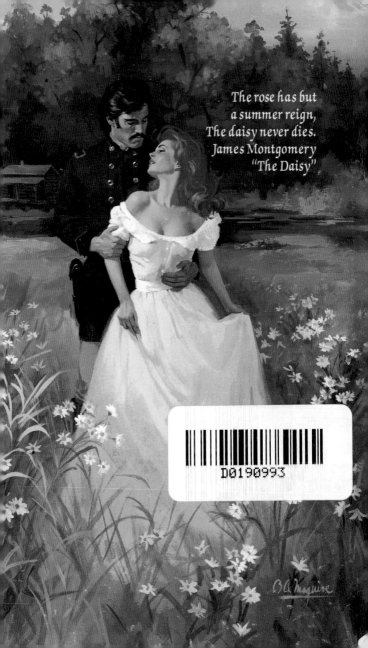

The rose has but
a summer reign,
The daisy never dies.
James Montgomery
"The Daisy"

Dear Reader:

I'm delighted to present to you the first books in the HarperMonogram imprint. This is a new imprint dedicated to publishing quality women's fiction and we believe it has all the makings of a surefire hit. From contemporary fiction to historical tales, to page-turning suspense thrillers, our goal at HarperMonogram is to publish romantic stories that will have you coming back for more.

Each month HarperMonogram will feature some of your favorite bestselling authors and introduce you to the most talented new writers around. We hope you enjoy this Monogram and all the HarperMonograms to come.

We'd love to know what you think. If you have any comments or suggestions please write to me at the address below:

HarperMonogram
10 East 53rd Street
New York, NY 10022

Karen Solem
Editor-in-chief

THROWING CAUTION TO THE WIND

Dancy gazed up into his scorching brown eyes. Clint was rugged, he was rough. In some ways he was savage. She could feel the danger smoldering in him when he held her. She did not care what tomorrow held or whether their union was a sin. Nothing concerned Dancy except the magic of the moment, the splendor of this glorious hour.

Clint's desire raged until he felt he would surely explode. "I want you," he whispered huskily, "but only if you want me, Dancy. Tell me, show me."

And she did so.

Also by Patricia Hagan

Midnight Rose
Heaven in a Wildflower

Available from
HarperPaperbacks

Harper Monogram

PATRICIA HAGAN

A FOREVER KIND OF LOVE

HarperPaperbacks

A Division of HarperCollinsPublishers

This is a work of fiction. The characters, incidents, and
dialogues are products of the author's imagination and are not
to be construed as real. Any resemblance to actual events or
persons, living or dead, is entirely coincidental.

HarperPaperbacks *A Division of* HarperCollins*Publishers*
10 East 53rd Street, New York, N.Y. 10022

Copyright © 1992 by Patricia Hagan
All rights reserved. No part of this book may be used or
reproduced in any manner whatsoever without written
permission of the publisher, except in the case of brief
quotations embodied in critical articles and reviews. For
information address HarperCollins*Publishers*,
10 East 53rd Street, New York, N.Y. 10022.

Cover illustration by R.A. Maguire

First printing: December 1992

Printed in the United States of America

HarperPaperbacks, HarperMonogram, and colophon are
trademarks of HarperCollins*Publishers*

❖ 10 9 8 7 6 5 4 3 2 1

A FOREVER KIND OF LOVE

1

Spring 1854
Middle Tennessee

The women circled about Edana O'Neal. Speaking in low, almost reverent tones, they offered words of encouragement as she groaned in the throes of her labor.

Edana sat on two chairs that had been put together to provide support for her legs. Feeling the beginnings of yet another wrenching pain, she began to swing her head wildly from side to side, damp hair flying about her face as she whimpered, "I can't breathe. Get away from me. . . ."

Standing behind Edana and holding her shoulders firmly against the back of the chair, Lucille Byrnes urged, "Forget about yourself and let's get this child born before the cord wraps around its neck and chokes it. Now brace your feet against the floor and push hard."

Clara O'Toole frowned as she sat on her midwife's stool positioned between Edana's knees. She never liked having a mother in labor reminded of any possible complications. They needed support and comfort, not fears and doubts. "You'll be just fine, Edana," she reassured with a scathing glance at Lucille. "And so will your baby. Now don't you fret. I've delivered lots that weren't in a hurry to get here, and they were fit as a fiddle."

But they were not conceived in sin like this one, Edana cried silently as the hot, seeking fingers of pain twisted and wrenched inside her belly. Only Clara did not know that, nor did anyone else suspect, but—and dear God forgive her—Edana knew better, knew with absolute certainty whose baby now fought to keep from leaving the life-giving cocoon her body provided . . . and it was not her husband's.

The agony bore down like an unseen fist, squeezing her breathless. Edana gasped, felt herself swaying, and, finding solace in the comforting cloak of oblivion, yielded to its clutching embrace.

"She's fainted," Clara all but shouted with relief. "I was hoping she would. Now I can turn it."

The women exchanged incredulous looks, and

it was Lucille who dared question the midwife's supreme authority. "Seems to me a woman's got to hurt a certain amount, and—"

"And I've delivered enough babies to know when it's time to turn one. Now hand me that lard bucket," Clara said to no one in particular, "and let's get this baby here before its mother's heart gives out."

Outside the log cabin, Carlin O'Neal sat on the front porch steps and waited for his wife to give birth. He stared out at his land, most of it lush with lofty pines stretching to the ridge tops and beyond, like tall, green sentries. His hands, resting upon his knees, opened and closed in rhythmic anxiety. Clouds gathering to the southeast meant rain was on the way, probably by nightfall, and he was wasting precious time. He had planned to get his corn crop in this day, not sit around waiting for the baby to be born, but he had awakened that morning to find the straw mattress soaked with birth water and Edana huddled in a ball next to him, bawling like a baby herself. So he'd pulled on his overalls and headed out to fetch Clara, the midwife, and gather the other women, as was the custom of the hills.

And here he sat, and it was near midafternoon. He shook his head, disgruntled to think how

Edana just wasn't hearty enough stock to be a farmer's wife. And what really annoyed him was the thought of all the trouble he had gone to in order to get her. Sent all the way to Dublin, he had, wanting good, strong Irish blood like his own. He'd paid a good price for her, too. Oh, she had been pretty enough. No doubt about that. But from the minute he'd laid eyes on her, he'd known she was puny. Way too skinny, she was. And it had taken nearly five years for her to get in the family way, and then she'd had a girl child, which was a big disappointment. After all, he had plans for his hundred acres of land, and those plans included lots of sons, as many as the good Lord would give him to help farm it. Daughters, Carlin felt, were mostly useless, not to mention the trouble of trying to get them married off early, so's somebody else could feed and look after them.

To make things worse, once the girl child was born, Edana had become obsessed with her. And Carlin strongly suspected, though she denied it, that she was deliberately trying to keep from getting in the family way again. He knew how it was believed that tea made from juniper berries kept a woman from conceiving, and when he'd found some jars in the root cellar, he'd thrown them out, just in case it was so.

Then, finally, after nearly seven years this

time, she had suddenly started acting as if she wanted another baby and come to his bed every night. So now he had his heart set on a boy, and if it was another girl . . . well, he just didn't want to think about that awful possibility.

The truth was, he wasn't sure if he could go on keeping her as his wife if she didn't bear him a son. Besides, he felt nothing for her romantically, anyway. He was too busy trying to build his farm, by God, to think about such foolishness. Working and living by the Good Book and having sons to help out and carry on the family name. That was all Carlin O'Neal felt was important in life, and that was all he cared about.

But, he supposed he did not have any real complaints. Edana was obedient, didn't sass him or nag. Actually she mostly stayed out of his way, though she did see to it he had clean clothes, mended when needed, and he had to admit she was a good cook. In bed she was dutiful but most of the time found an excuse to stay up late, not turning in till after he fell asleep. So, it really wouldn't cause him any distress if he got rid of her and took another wife and got on with his dreams before it was too late.

Right now, though, he just wished this agonizing time would end, so he could get to the fields.

*   *   *

Dooley O'Neal knew his brother was upset and wondered if he should attempt conversation as they sat together on the steps. Carlin kept things inside and didn't like it when people—"do-gooders," as he derisively called them—interfered. But the fact was, Dooley was having a hard time keeping his own nerves from showing. Every time he heard Edana scream, it was like a knife to his heart.

Unable to keep still any longer, Dooley forced a smile he did not feel, trying to make his voice light as he leaned over to whisper, "I think we could both use a taste of corn squeezin's. Want me to fetch the jug from the barn?"

For an instant Carlin's expression flashed with interest, but, seeing a horse and buggy approaching, he declined. "Sounds good, but I better not. If Addie McCabe smells whiskey on me breath this day, I'll never hear the end of it."

Following Carlin's gaze, Dooley was barely able to hold back a groan as he also recognized the McCabe buggy. "What is she doing here? You didn't send for her, did you?"

Carlin hooted. "Are you crazy? Nobody ever sends for Addie. She just shows up, 'cause that's the way she is. A busybody wanting to keep her nose in everybody else's business."

A moment later Addie McCabe was reining in her horse. Despite their displeasure over her appearance, the men could not resist warmly greeting her twelve-year-old stepson, Clint, as he scrambled out of the buggy and waved before disappearing around the side of the cabin, heading for the creek.

Dooley stared after him, thinking how Addie called him a mischievous rascal, but Dooley reckoned he was just all boy. Addie's own son, ten-year-old Jordan, was the one he had uneasy feelings about. Folks said he was quiet and shy, a real little gentleman. Dooley thought he was just plain sneaky. One thing for sure, Addie spoiled him rotten, at the same time mostly ignoring Clint. Dooley supposed Clint was a living reminder that she hadn't been first in Angus's life, and maybe that was more than she could bear after he himself had let her down; but Lord, that seemed a lifetime ago.

Addie stared coolly at Carlin and Dooley in turn before demanding, "Well, is it here yet?"

Carlin shook his head.

Dooley would not look at her, instead glancing away to watch Jordan following in the direction Clint had gone.

In her characteristic way of speaking her mind, Addie remarked with a sneer, "Probably another girl. No doubt she'll be puny like her sister. Looks like Edana wasn't meant to have all those boys you bragged you were going to have when you brought her over here, Carlin. Maybe you should've just married yourself a mountain girl."

Dooley was barely able to resist firing back that she didn't have anything to boast about herself when it came to producing a large family. After eleven years of marriage to Angus, she had only the one child. But he kept silent. Addie had a tongue as sharp as a serpent's tooth, and since she made no bones about the fact she loathed and despised him, he'd learned through the years it was best just to stay out of her way.

"Awful quiet in there," Addie said, cocking her head to listen for any sound. "Either the pains aren't coming close together, which means she's nowhere near birthing, or else she's fainted.

"I suspect that's the case, her being so frail," she added with a mocking sneer.

Carlin lost himself once more in his brooding over not being able to get on with his planting, and Dooley was gritting his teeth to keep from asking Addie why she had bothered to come if all she intended to do was criticize Edana. Neither offered to help her down from the buggy and knew she would decline if they did. Addie rarely accepted assistance from anyone for anything.

She got down by herself and breezed right by them with a swish of her skirts.

The women were gathered in a far corner, near the fireplace, where a kettle of water was boiling over the flames. The room was sweltering.

Seeing Edana slumped in her position between two chairs, Addie thought how old-fashioned Clara's birthing methods were. When Jordan had been born, she had given birth in a real bed. But, of course, she'd insisted Angus have a real doctor attend her, like the upper-class women of Philadelphia and New York. Clara, like most midwives, contended babies came easier in a sitting position, and Addie had asked her more than once why she didn't just have her laboring mothers go out in the fields and squat like an Indian squaw and be done with it.

Ignoring hostile glances, Addie began to remove her gloves, plucking one finger at a time as she regarded Edana with narrowed, thoughtful eyes. "Well, what's taking so long?" she asked of no one in particular. "I hear her time came before daybreak. It should have been born by now, it not being her first."

Clara knew the others expected her to respond. "It was turned wrong. I turned it right. It shouldn't be much longer."

Addie nodded but did not offer to help, instead continuing to observe while brooding over how much better off everyone would be if Carlin hadn't been so stubborn. She had done her best to convince him her cousin Olive was the right wife for him, but no, he'd insisted on Irish stock, and Olive's family had come from

England, like her own. Olive's heart had been broken when Carlin spurned her, and she was now a lonely spinster.

And the same thing could have happened to me, Addie thought angrily, her lips twisting as her own malignant memories needled.

It had been understood that Edana and Dooley O'Neal would marry, and they were just about to set their wedding date when Carlin asked Dooley to go to Philadelphia to meet his bride and bring her back to Tennessee. And, sadly, after he returned, nothing was ever the same between them.

Oh, to be sure, Dooley denied it had anything to do with Edana, but Addie knew. Dooley wasn't himself. He moped around, always changing the subject whenever she said something about marriage. Finally, when she kept pushing, he told her he'd decided he didn't want a wife, not ever, that he just preferred to live alone.

Addie had been heartbroken and humiliated, convinced she would spend the rest of her life as an old maid. Then Angus McCabe started calling on her. He was a widower, having lost his wife in childbirth the previous year.

At first Addie was reluctant to encourage him. She was, after all, still very much in love with Dooley. Also, she did not like the idea of being thrust into the position of mother to a one-year-old child who was not her own.

Eventually she'd decided she had to get on with her life and hoped being the wife of a rich man would help her forget Dooley—but it hadn't worked out that way.

Staring at the woman responsible for tearing up so many lives made the anguished memories cut deeper.

Sometimes Addie felt that if she could prove it, she might be doing Carlin a favor to make him see how his wife and brother coveted each other. Yet she had to admit she had never seen them actually do anything wrong. The fact was, it was what they *didn't* do that convinced her they were crazy about each other. Like in church, or at the socials, they stayed as far apart as they could get, never looking at one another, as if they were scared of what might show in their eyes, their faces, if they did. And if that wasn't proof positive, Addie didn't know what was. Why, they didn't even have a normal family relationship like a body would expect between brother-in-law and sister-in-law, and—

Suddenly, Edana's eyes flashed open, and her body went stiff, rigid, as she threw her head back and screamed long and loud.

Addie backed farther away.

The women moved quickly to hold Edana in position, while Clara crouched, ready with a towel as she cried in triumph, "It's coming. I see the head. Get ready . . ."

The baby slipped easily into Clara's waiting arms.

"A boy," someone shouted.

No one noticed Addie's disappointed scowl. She had hoped spitefully for another girl, so Carlin might wonder whether he would have had the sons he wanted with Olive as his wife.

Outside, Carlin heard and broke into a rare grin that spread all across his sun-lined face. With a joyful slap to his brother's shoulder, he exulted, "Did you hear that, Dooley? I've got me a son at last!"

Dooley heard all right and only hoped Carlin did not notice the way he was clenching his fists and how the muscles in his jaw had to be tightening, because he felt as if he had gone all stiff inside. A son! Yes, Edana had given birth to a son, but the question burning him from the very core of his guts was—just whose son was it?

When he had heard from Carlin, right after the first of the year, that Edana was in the family way, Dooley had dared get her off to herself and ask if there was a chance it might be his. She swore not, then warned him they could not see each other again.

But Dooley could not stop loving her. After all, he had adored her from the first instant he'd set eyes on her. And, somehow, he had known she felt the same way about him.

They had tried, God knew they had, to fight the feelings surging. For over ten years they had mustered the strength to resist. Then it had happened, in a weak moment, and like a mountain river run wild, they had yielded to the demons of their lust and consummated the love that would not be denied.

Both were all too painfully aware that sin was all they would ever have. Neither wanted to hurt Carlin, for none of it was his fault.

And there was also Dancy to be considered.

Dooley smiled from his heart to think about the niece he adored, with her blazing red hair and emerald-green eyes. With a sprinkling of freckles across her upturned nose, she reminded him of a wood sprite prancing in the morning mists.

Never would Dooley forget the day she was born. He had waited with Carlin then, too, but when word came Edana had given birth to a daughter, Carlin was so disappointed he just got up and wandered off without a word. It had fallen to Dooley to go in and share the joy with Edana, as she cradled her newborn daughter in her arms.

"Carlin doesn't care what I name her," she said in a voice thick with hurt. "Have you any suggestions, Dooley?"

He did not have to think long. "Dancy!" he declared firmly, happily. "Because the angels had to have danced the day such a beauty was born."

"Dancy . . . " Edana had whispered the name in wonder, then laughed, delighted to agree, "Dancy O'Neal she will be."

Carlin disappeared inside the cabin, oblivious of Dooley's suddenly pensive mood.

Just then Dancy came running around the side of the house, shrieking at the top of her lungs, with Clint right behind her. The dress she was wearing was wet and muddied, and the rag doll she carried in her arms was a sopping mess.

"Here, here, what's going on?" Dooley moved from the steps, then dropped to one knee and opened his arms to his niece, who flung herself against him.

Whipping about, secure in her uncle's embrace, Dancy promptly stuck out her tongue at Clint.

"I'll get you sooner or later, Dancy O'Neal," Clint warned, shaking his fist.

Dooley noticed that Clint had the beginnings of a black eye. "I think," he said, lips twitching as he fought to keep from smiling, "you might ought to tell me why you're chasing my niece, Clint."

With eyes locked furiously with Dancy's, Clint

explained how they had been playing down by the creek and Dancy had lost her temper. "Like she always does," he accused. "And then she hauled off and hit me."

"You drowned my dolly." Dancy tried to kick out at him, but Dooley held her tight.

"I was playing," he said defensively. "But you got mad. You're no fun. I should've known better than to play with you, anyway, 'cause you're always getting mad."

"It's your fault. You're always mean to me. I hate you, *Clinton* McCabe." She grinned to see his anger flash, knowing he hated being called by his full name.

Just then Jordan came running up to excitedly confirm Dancy's story. "He was teasing her, saying he was killing her doll. He took it away from her and held it under the water, and we begged him not to, but he kept on."

"Aw, it was just a game," Clint said, digging his toe in the dirt before turning away, hands stuffed in the pockets of his overalls. "Girls are just no fun, anyway."

Dooley bit back a laugh, then scolded him for playing so roughly. "Have mercy on these boys, Dancy. They aren't used to little girls who fight back."

With a stubborn pout, Dancy said, "Then they shouldn't play so rough with me, Uncle Dooley."

"What's going on here?" Addie bellowed as she came out on the porch. Eyes narrowing, she turned on Dancy. "Have you been acting like a little hellion again, child? Did you hit my Jordan? I'm going to ask your father to give you a good thrashing if you did."

Dancy, eyes growing wide, pressed further into her uncle's protective embrace.

Dooley knew it was best to let Addie have her say. Otherwise she would linger, determined to have the last word.

"Well?" Addie turned to Jordan expectantly. "Did she hit you, son? Or was Clinton provoking her again? I'll tan his hide if he started it."

Dancy, not about to tattle and figuring Clint had been punished enough with the shiner he was going to have, spoke then to smooth things over. "We were just playing. That's all. And Clint fell down and bumped his face."

"Good," Addie snapped, motioning Jordan toward the buggy. "That will teach him not to be so rowdy. And he can walk home, too."

"As for you, young lady"—she wagged her finger under Dancy's nose—"don't you be keeping a fuss. Your mother just had her baby, and she needs her rest."

"She had it?" Dancy clapped her hands together and began to bounce up and down on her toes. "Do I have a little sister like I wanted?"

"No. You've got a little brother. Scrawny thing, too. Like your mother. Wouldn't be at all surprised if the Lord decides to call him home."

Dancy watched her go, tears stinging her eyes. "She doesn't sound like she even cares, Uncle Dooley," she murmured, lips trembling. "I think I hate Miss Addie as much as I hate Clint."

"You aren't supposed to hate anybody, little sprite." Dooley hoisted her up into his strong arms, brushing dirt from her dress. "Especially Miss Addie. She's not as mean as she pretends to be."

"Why would anybody pretend to be mean?" Dancy asked innocently.

"Sometimes," he began hesitantly, "people suffer disappointments in their lives, and they take it out on other folks. What you have to do is look inside them for their goodness and not pay any attention to how they act on the outside."

Dancy pondered that a moment, then decided it was just something else she'd have to wait till she was older to figure out. But for now, it really didn't seem important.

"Now, Miss Dancy O'Neal, let's go meet your new brother."

And with a hug, Dooley carried her on up the steps.

2

It had been two days since Edana had given birth, and she knew, like everyone else, that something was terribly wrong with the baby boy lying quietly at her side.

Dancy, she recalled, had been all pink and peachy when she was born, not pale and ashen like this child.

Dancy had squirmed and kicked and cried and done all the things healthy babies do. But this infant, this child of sin, Edana was ever tortured to remember, did none of those things.

He did not want to suckle at her breast. All he did was lie quiet and still, his breathing shallow and uneven, his eyes closed.

From the bedroom door, Carlin fumed, "I just don't understand it. Look at the lad. He's big and husky, and he ought to be drinkin' his fill. Even Doc Howard said so."

Edana remained silent. She knew Carlin was extremely upset or he would never have sent for a doctor. Carlin did not believe in doctors, but in this instance he was willing to try anything to save his son. But what could anyone do? she fretted with heavy heart. It was as though the baby just didn't want to live and refused to try.

"It's you, isn't it?" Carlin accused suddenly, glaring at her with cold, hooded eyes. "You're so puny your milk is no good."

Edana drew her baby closer. "No. That's not true. He just won't try to nurse. Clara even made him a sugar teat and put it in his mouth, and he wouldn't even suck on that. And I had good milk for Dancy, you know that." Her voice rose shrilly, and she felt as though she were teetering on the brink of hysteria.

But what was the use in arguing, she asked herself silently, miserably. She knew why God was going to call her baby home, to heaven, but no one else could ever know, because if the truth about his conception was discovered, he would be considered a bastard, and they would not allow him to be buried in the churchyard. He'd be placed outside the fence, in an unconsecrated grave, and she could not bear the thought of that.

Turning her face into the pillow, still clutching her baby tight in her arms, Edana yielded once more to the tears.

Carlin gave a disgusted snort. Inside, his heart was breaking, but, masking sorrow with anger, he lashed out cruelly. "You cost me a lot of money, but what have I got in return? Broken dreams, that's what. Buying you was like buying a cow that don't give milk, or a mare that can't foal, or a hen that don't lay." He struck at the air with his fist for furious emphasis as he roared, "I wish, by God, I could send you back, that your papa would return my money, and then I could start over while there's still time.

"I wish"—he paused, red-faced, to gasp before continuing his tirade—"that I'd listened to Addie and married her cousin instead. I'd have saved myself some misery, for sure."

Edana longed to confide how, so many, many times through the years, she had also wished for a different life. Far better t'would have been for everyone had she never come to America to meet and wrongfully fall in love with Dooley O'Neal. Their secret but undeniable attraction to each other had brought them only pain and misery.

And now, an innocent baby was suffering as well.

"And I promise you one thing," Carlin raged on, slamming his beefy hand against the door frame for emphasis. "If my son dies, you'll have one more chance to give me another and only a year to do it in.

"Or so help me"—he spoke through clenched teeth—"I'll send you back where you came from."

Despite her anguish, Edana was driven to remind him, "You've a daughter, Carlin O'Neal. A fine, healthy daughter you should be thankful for."

"Daughters won't help me make a living off this land," he muttered bitterly, turning away.

With a soul-wrenching sigh, she pulled her son to her breast once again, urging him to take of her body's life-giving milk.

And all the while she prayed—to be forgiven for her sin of adultery, for her baby to live.

Carlin stalked out and headed straight to the barn and his stash of corn whiskey. He had hung around the cabin all morning, while the ladies came and went with their kettles of soup and pies and cakes. Now he reckoned he could go and have a nip without anyone nosing about.

From the ridge, Dooley watched his brother disappear inside the barn, then quickly made his way to the cabin.

He had been waiting to catch Edana alone, because when he'd taken Dancy in to see the new baby, all the women were gathered around. And, as always, Edana was very polite but avoided looking at him.

He had some private things he wanted to talk to her about, and even though she might try to lie, he felt if it was just the two of them, alone, he could get the truth out of her. This time she couldn't run off as she had the day he'd cornered her to ask if the baby she was carrying was actually his. And if he was still there when Carlin returned, Carlin would not think a thing in the world about his brother stopping by to visit his new nephew.

Dancy was playing contentedly down by the creek and never noticed her uncle quietly going in the back door of the cabin. She did not want to go anywhere near her parents, not after the scolding she had received yesterday from Miss Addie.

Clinton's eye was terribly swollen and bruised, and Miss Addie had called her an unladylike heathen and said she deserved to have her backsides tanned, which Dancy knew would probably have happened if her daddy and mommy weren't so worried about the baby. All her mommy did was cry.

Well, Dancy decided she would just stay out of their way. Maybe Uncle Dooley would come get her later, anyway, and take her out to his place. She loved it there. He would let her sit in front of him while he rode his horse, and he'd show her wonderful, secret places, like caves where little girls could hide from goblins if they ever came, though Uncle Dooley swore all the goblins were in Ireland, not America. And he would take her fishing, too, and show her how to catch wily trout right in her hands in special pools of the rushing streams that ran through his land. It was a magical place of wonder and beauty, and though Dancy would never hurt her mother by telling her so, she would much rather live there than here.

The truth was, Dancy just didn't like her daddy very much. He hardly ever spoke to her, and when he did it was just to fuss at her about something. And she could not remember a time in her whole life when he had touched her except to spank her. There had never been a hug or a kiss. He never even held her hand.

But Uncle Dooley did. He called her a sprite, and sometimes, if she'd been mischievous, he'd call her a leprechaun. And he was always hugging her and telling her how much he loved her.

She was sitting on the creek bank, holding her dolly. It made her so mad to see how awful the doll's yarn hair looked since Clint McCabe had put her in the water. Oh, she hated that awful boy. He'd only done it to get revenge because she'd beaten him skipping rocks. She'd sent her stone singing all the way across the creek, while his had fallen short.

Of course, Dancy recalled with a wicked little smile, it had made matters worse when she had laughed out loud and Jordan had chimed in. Clint couldn't stand it then, and that's when he'd got mean. Poor Jordan. He'd wanted to do something but hadn't dared. But *she* had, and that's why Clint had a black eye, and she was glad.

Dancy was also glad Jordan wasn't like his brother, because she liked Jordan, a lot. In fact, though it was her biggest secret, and she'd never tell anyone, not even Uncle Dooley, she liked to pretend that Jordan was her dolly's daddy, and when she played house, it was always Jordan she thought of as her husband.

And maybe, Dancy pondered dreamily, as only little girls could, one day when they were both grown up, she and Jordan would get married and live happily ever after. And like the dragon stories Uncle Dooley told her about, on those wonderful, lazy, storytelling afternoons, Jordan, like a brave, ancient warrior, would slay Clinton McCabe. They would never, ever, have to worry about him drowning all the beautiful babies they were going to have.

A tiny frown creased her brow.

That was the part she didn't understand—what would make the babies.

She had asked her mommy, but all she'd said was that Dancy shouldn't worry about it, because babies were a gift from God, and it was up to Him to give them to folks, if He wanted to. So Dancy told herself not to think about that part and just be happy instead.

Suddenly her lips turned up in a saucy smile.

She liked these special times so much, when she could just dream about the future . . . and how wonderful it was going to be.

And in that special moment, in the early spring of 1854, Dancy O'Neal could think of no reason why her life, her dreams, would ever change.

Dooley let himself in quietly. He could smell the food he had watched the women bringing from time to time. He saw, however, that none of it appeared to have been touched. No doubt Edana was worried about the baby, and he could understand that, but she needed to keep up her strength. She was going to need it to care for the little tyke, being as it looked as if he were going to be a sickly thing.

He crossed to the cabinet and took down a bowl, then ladled out some of Lucille Byrnes's squirrel stew. Taking a few of Dorothy Peacock's thick lard biscuits, slathered with fresh churned butter, he headed to the back room.

Edana's eyes were closed but flashed open at the sound of footsteps.

Dooley entered, feeling his heart warm, as always, at the sight of her lovely face. Only this day, he noted with a jolt, she was a wretched sight to behold. Her eyes were dull, lackluster, her skin pale, her face gaunt. She looked as though the very essence of life had been nipped away and only the shell of what was remained.

He couldn't see the baby very well, as he was lying on the other side of her.

"Edana, me darling. . . ." He set the food aside and tumbled to his knees beside the bed. Swept by his love for her, he reached to tenderly caress her cheek. "Saints preserve and bless, are you this sick? Maybe the doctor should be fetched again—"

"No." Her voice was thin, barely audible. "The doctor can do nothing. Neither can you. Please go. I don't want Carlin to find you here."

"And why not?" His bluster was as forced as his smile. "I've a perfect right to visit my nephew, now don't I? And if me sister-in-law be ailing, I should offer to help, shouldn't I?"

Her lips trembled. She wanted to cry, but there were no tears left. "Just go. Please. I beg you."

Dooley continued to stroke her face lovingly with his fingertips. "I'll not be bowing to your wishes this day, love. I've waited for this moment for months, to find you alone, so I could beg for the truth. I think you lied to me before, and I've got a right to know." He drew a deep breath, let it out slowly as he mustered all his courage to ask the question that burned in his blood. "Am I this baby's father?"

She turned her face toward the wall. With heavy heart, she lied. "No."

He cupped her chin, forcing her to meet his commanding gaze. "I don't believe you. I think you're lying, because you feel guilty about what we did, but you shouldn't, me darlin'. We never meant for it to, but it did, and we can't go back and undo it. It's there, between us, the bonding of our love, and it always will be."

That much was true, Edana conceded silently, painfully, thinking back to last harvest season, when the world was shaded in gold-and-crimson hues of autumn.

They had found themselves alone one evening, when Carlin had taken some of his tobacco to market in Nashville, and Dooley, as always, had come to help tend the curing barn fires. She had taken him his supper, and somehow, though they never meant for it to happen, it had. And for a time there was no turning back. She had allowed herself to be swept along in a river of passion from which she was helpless to escape. Only the realization that she was carrying Dooley's child made her aware of what a horrible sin they had committed.

She squeezed her eyes closed, feeling tears coursing down her cheeks once more. "No, you mustn't say such things. We have to forget. We have to pretend it never happened. I'm married to your brother, and that makes it even worse. It can't happen again. Not ever.

"Please," she repeated lamely, "go now. And pray to God to forgive us, and then forget me, Dooley."

"Forget you?" he echoed incredulously, rocking back on his heels, hands clutching the edge of the mattress as he stared at her in wonder. "I'd sooner forget how to breathe, Edana. Sweet Jesus, no. I could never forget the angel who holds my heart in her hand."

He glanced nervously over his shoulder. Through the open door he could see across the main room of the cabin and the windows beyond for a clear view of the barn. Carlin was still inside, but he knew this tension had to end, lest he return and feel the tension and wonder why.

Neither spoke for long, heavy moments, and then Dooley begged, "Tell me the truth, Edana. Tell me he's my son."

In a strange, thin whisper that seemed to emerge from somewhere deep within her very soul, Edana declared shakily, "He's God's. He belongs to Him now."

For some reason he did not understand, fear

began to creep over Dooley. Nervously he asked, "What are you talking about?"

"The baby . . . " She paused to press her lips against the cold flesh of her son's forehead. "He belongs to God now."

Edana, dressed in a plain black muslin dress and matching bonnet, stared at the tiny wooden box beside the open grave. With fists clasped tightly against her bosom, she made no effort to shake the hands of those who filed by, offering condolences. They touched her, however, some embracing her slumped shoulders or pressing their lips against her cold, pale cheeks. Still, she did not move or speak but stood as passionless as the monuments in the church cemetery. "You'll have another," someone said.

Clara, the midwife, admitted, "I knew something won't right when I saw him, Edana. You have to think of it as a blessing God called him home. He'd have been a sickly child, to be sure, a real burden."

Addie McCabe, priding herself in always dressing properly for any occasion, felt quite regal in her outfit of gray bombazine. She'd bought it during a visit to Nashville a few months earlier, but there'd been no funeral to wear it to till now.

As she approached Edana to pay her respects,

she was aware of the glances of the other women milling about and knew once again she had reinforced her position of social matriarch of Pinetops, Tennessee, wretched little town though it was, she thought with a sniff of disdain.

"Edana, bless you," she said piously, touching gloved fingertips to the grieving mother's cheeks. "Remember God, in His infinite wisdom, knows best."

Addie moved on, purposely toward Dooley. Let him see her exquisite costume, she thought with a bitter flash. Let him see her expensive carriage, her finely dressed husband who reeked with the air of money. Let him witness, damn him, how well she had fared without him.

But Dooley paid her no mind, even though she brushed right by him. Neither was he listening to Parson Brooker, who was droning on about how glad he was he'd insisted on establishing a church cemetery for his flock when he'd come to Pinetops six years earlier. No need to bury folks in backyard and fields, he was saying, when they could lie in God's own garden.

Dooley was lost in his own misery, waiting for the right moment to approach Edana.

Edana, however, was not washed with sorrow as everyone thought. Oh, no, she had dutifully accepted God's will and punishment. Now all she wanted was to go forth with her life, regarding the future as a kind of purgatory, where, if she toed the straight and narrow and committed no sin, she would be forgiven past transgressions, and when her time on earth was over, she would go to heaven, where she would surely see her son again. So she was not listening to anything anyone said, merely hoping it would all be over soon, so she could go home and secretly begin atonement to her husband for her betrayal.

She thought back to the night before, when Carlin had come to her and gruffly told her he expected her to try and make another baby just as soon as she was able. He said he reckoned he'd married her for keeps and would just have to make the best of things, but he expected her to do her part. There would be no more excuses for her not coming to his bed, he had warned. He intended to take her each and every night, planting his seed over and over. Edana had nodded mutely and obediently.

Edana glanced around and realized she was, at last, alone. Carlin was standing at the bottom of the cemetery hill, talking to some men next to his wagon. With a last glance at her son's casket, she began to walk down the path to join him. Then, with a gasp, she jumped, startled, as Dooley seemed to appear from nowhere.

"Please." Her hand flew to her throat. "Leave me alone."

"I wish I could," he said miserably as he twisted his hat in his hands, "but I can't. I love you, and I always will. And you love me, too, Edana. You can't deny that, any more than you can deny that's our baby in that coffin. We'll always love each other, and somehow we've got to find a way to be together. You think about that."

Parson Brooker was approaching, and Dooley moved on.

She stared after him to see that he was going back to where Dancy was wandering about at the edge of the woods bordering the cemetery.

Suddenly all of Edana's thoughts and fears crystallized, and she knew in that moment, beyond all doubt, there was only one thing she could do to escape certain damnation into hellfire eternal.

She had to go away.

To stay would mean forever trying to resist that which would not, could not, be denied. The temptation, because of her deep, abiding love for Dooley O'Neal, was too great, and the price for yielding was her very soul.

If Carlin should ever find out, either he or Dooley would die. Of this she was certain. Carlin was a proud man, and though given neither to love nor affection, being a cold-hearted man bent only on survival and the perpetuation of his family, he would never stand to lose his wife to his own brother.

She and Dooley were actually risking their lives.

Frantically, the plan came to her. She would return to Ireland. She would take the money Carlin kept hidden in a jar under the porch step and run away with Dancy. Her father would be furious, but her mother, bless her, would welcome them with open arms.

It was the way it had to be, and she was now desperate to be on her way.

Gently, lovingly, Dooley asked the child he adored, "What are you doing over here by yourself, Dancy? Your mommy and daddy are waiting for you."

"I'm looking for something, Uncle Dooley," she said solemnly.

He knelt beside her. "And what might that be, sprite?"

She looked up at him with wide, innocent eyes. "Do you remember what you told me about the leprechauns in Ireland? How when they died, if they haven't been too mischievous, God will take them into heaven, and as proof they went to heaven, a bright yellow daffodil grows on top of their grave?"

Dooley nodded, brows knit together as he wondered what she was leading up to.

"Well, I'm looking for a big yellow daffodil to put on my little brother's grave, because I'm sure he went to heaven, and I want everyone to know it. I don't want to wait for God to make one grow. I want it there now. . . ." Her lower lip began to tremble. "But I can't find one, Uncle Dooley. I've looked everywhere, but I can't find one."

Almost fiercely he drew her into his arms and hugged her tight against him. "Oh, sprite, listen to me. Daffodils only bloom in early spring, and here 'tis, nearly June."

She began to cry. "But we have to find one. He has to have a daffodil on his grave to show everyone he's in heaven, with Jesus and all the angels."

Dooley continued to hold her against him as he looked at the woods beyond. And then he saw what he would later believe could only have been a miracle. "Come with me, sprite." He smiled down at her as he straightened and took her hand. "Come see what we've found."

Together they went to a patch of daisies blooming beneath a leafy oak tree.

Dooley bent and plucked one. Holding it out to her, he said, "You see, daisies can almost always be found, Dancy, because, like love, they're forever. And you know what I think?"

She looked up at him expectantly and shook her head, red curls whipping about her face.

"I think if we put some daisies on your little brother's grave, everybody will know God loves him and he's in heaven for sure."

Eagerly, Dancy joined him, and as they picked the daisies, she wondered why, when he should be so happy to have found the forever kind of flowers, her uncle Dooley was crying.

3

Ireland
Spring 1866

John Houlihan, sexton of the St. Joan of Arc Catholic Church, just outside Dublin, was pruning hedges when he saw Dancy walking through the cemetery. He paused to slip his watch from his pocket, noting she was right on time. She'd not missed a day since her mother's burial nearly three weeks ago, always bringing a bouquet of daffodils just before sunset.

He frowned to think how she was on her way to work at her grandfather's tavern. A pitiful job for a lass so lovely. Everyone in the parish shared his opinion, too, except of course, for the godless heathens who frequented Faolan Curry's place. Instead of the decent pubs, the rowdies gathered at Faolan's.

And John had no doubt Curry's customers enjoyed having a beauty like Dancy serve them their ale. With hair as fiery red as sunrise on a clear day, eyes as green as shamrocks, he felt she was truly one of God's finest works of art.

He knew she was a good girl, too. Never a breath of scandal, though Father Toole had confided that her spirit was a might peppery sometimes, and she was bent to mischief. But she and her mother, Edana, God rest her soul, John mused as he crossed himself, had been good and faithful in their church attendance since they had come from America. That was many years ago, though he couldn't remember exactly.

They'd had the sympathies of the parish, too, the way Faolan Curry made them toil. It was said he was terribly angry when Edana had returned with a child, and she'd been forced to endure untold misery ever since.

Father Toole had confided to John more than once how he dreaded the day he'd be called to give last rites to Faolan, for he'd be grievously tempted to refuse. But he'd be called all right, for dying folk suddenly got very concerned about their souls when death was hovering. And even though Faolan had turned a deaf ear when Father Toole condemned him for selling Edana to a trader buying up wives to take to homesteading Irishmen in America, he'd be falling on his knees begging forgiveness when it came time to meet his Maker. Neither John nor Father Toole had any doubts about that.

Now, as John watched Dancy place the yellow flowers on the mound of raw dirt that was Edana Curry O'Neal's grave, he worried about what was going to happen now that her mother wasn't around to look out for her anymore. Folks had also said that while Edana slaved for her father and put up with his cursing and sometimes beatings, she was like a mother wolf fiercely defending a cub when it came to Dancy.

He shook his head in pity and returned to his task, making a mental note to offer a special rosary for the lass.

Dancy knelt to place the daffodils on the grave, then tenderly patted the fresh mound of earth as she whispered, "I miss you so much, Momma, so very, very much."

Rocking back on her heels, she stared out at the rolling Irish Sea beyond. A cooling breeze sent her long hair whipping about her face, as she was carried back in time to another place, another grave. It seemed so long ago, that day Uncle Dooley had shared her childhood grief for the death of her infant brother, but she would always remember it.

She looked toward the hill gently sloping down to the water. A bittersweet smile touched her lips at the sight of the butter yellow flowers swaying in the wind. The scene always evoked memories of Uncle Dooley's tale of the leprechauns buried below. "If you believe it in your heart, it's so," he'd assured.

Thus Dancy allowed herself the childish innocence of fantasy, along with the comfort of believing her mother knew, somehow, about the daffodils placed daily on her grave, a symbol of eternal love.

She did not want to think about the miserable evening ahead working at the tavern. It had been bad enough when her mother was alive, but at least then she'd had someone who cared about her and would dare speak up to the ruffians when they went too far in their crude banter. But now she was on her own, because Grampa didn't like it when she rebuked the drunken men. He said they were all there for a purpose—the men to have a good time, he to make money, and she to do as she was told.

Her mother had likewise suffered, and the one comfort Dancy had in her sorrow was knowing she was now at peace.

The future, Dancy knew, looked no better than the present, so it was comforting to turn to ancient memories of yesterday, those she could still remember. Her mother, however, had refused to discuss the past and would not answer her questions.

Dancy supposed she should feel guilty about not missing her father, but she remembered him as a cold, uncaring man. It was different with Uncle Dooley, however. Thinking of him always filled her with sadness, for she missed him terribly and knew she would never forget the happiness he'd brought her as a child. Several times, after she'd learned to read and write, she'd asked her mother for an address so she could write to him, but always her mother refused, urging her to forget him, forget everything about her past life in America.

Then Dancy heard of the terrible war raging over there. The Civil War, they were calling it. North against South. Father against son. Brother against brother. It had to do with slavery, Dancy learned, and something called state's rights. But she could not understand, or comprehend, why people were killing each other. Why didn't the owners just free the slaves and be done with it? her child's mind rationalized. It was not right to hold people in bondage.

Worried about her uncle Dooley and whether he might be involved, and pushing down feelings that it was wrong not likewise to be concerned about her father, Dancy began to read everything she could find on the conflict. When she discovered middle Tennessee had fallen to the federal army, she shared what she considered grievous news with her mother and was shocked by her reaction.

"I don't care about the war," Edana had declared coldly, "and I don't care about Tennessee. It's all I can do to get through each day of my life here, and I certainly don't have time to waste thinking about people who don't care about me. I've told you time and again, forget all of them."

Timorously Dancy had pointed out, "But I don't want to forget Uncle Dooley. I care about him."

"Well, *he* certainly forgot *you*," Edana had responded bitterly, "and he never cared about either one of us. Neither did your father. So stop bothering me with talk of that silly war," she had finished, "because I'm not interested."

Dancy knew something terrible had to have happened to make her mother so angry, and the only time she mentioned the conflict again was when it ended. Even then her mother expressed no remorse over the surrender of the South, neither did she care to discuss what impact the North's victory would have on the place they had once called home.

Not once in the years since they had arrived in

Ireland had they heard directly from her father. The only correspondence had been the letter from a lawyer, soon after their return, informing them that Carlin O'Neal had been granted a divorce.

Dancy remembered how her grandmother had held her tight, both of them crying in terror as her grandfather, furious over the divorce, had beaten her mother with his leather razor strap.

Her mother had not made a sound, nor had she attempted to ward off the blows. But when it was over she had struggled to her feet and, clinging to the back of a chair for support, told him with eyes blazing that it was finally over. "God has punished me. You have punished me. Never strike me again, I warn you."

She had fainted then, and Dancy recalled how her grandfather had sneered and said he wasn't afraid of her threats; but the fact was he had never hit her again. And the only time he'd hit Dancy was when her mother wasn't around.

And so the years had passed. For a time Faolan hoped a man would come along and marry his daughter and take her, and his granddaughter, off his hands. But Edana's beauty was masked by her malignant temperament, and suitors passed her by.

Dancy recalled another time when her mother

and her grandfather had had a terrible fight. It was the occasion of Dancy's fifteenth birthday, and he'd suddenly declared it was time he found a husband for her. He'd said he knew of some rich men who would love to have a young and pretty wife like her, men who would be willing to pay a good price.

They had been sitting at the little kitchen table, quietly enjoying the birthday cake Gramma Muira had baked. It was one of the rare festive occasions in their drab, hardworking lives, but when her grandfather had spoken up to say it was time to find a husband for Dancy, Edana had gone to pieces.

After snatching up the knife used to cut the cake, Edana had waved it menacingly before Faolan Curry's face and screamed, "You'll not do to her what you did to me, do you hear me? I'll see you dead before I let you ruin her life like you ruined mine."

Dancy had watched, wide-eyed with fear and wonder, as her grandfather had first sat there, equally as stunned, not saying a word. But then, at the same time he'd recovered with rage erupting, she had witnessed her mother, apparently realizing what she had done, crumpling into a mass of hysteria as she'd fallen to her chair, sobbing wildly.

Faolan Curry had bolted across the kitchen and

grabbed his leather shaving strap from where it hung on a peg by the back door.

Edana had dared stand her ground. "I mean it, Poppa," she'd whispered raggedly, "I don't care how much you beat me, I swear I will kill you if you sell my daughter."

Gramma Muira, head bowed and trembling hands clasped to her bosom, had run out the back door to hide in the root cellar, where she'd not have to hear the screams. She'd beckoned to Dancy to go with her.

But Dancy was not running. Not this day. Instead she'd thrown herself across her mother and begged her grandfather for mercy. Furiously he'd tried to wrestle her away, but Dancy had held fast, not about to be torn from protecting her mother. Finally, with an oath and a warning that he'd beat Edana to death if she ever did such a thing again, he'd stormed from the room after ordering them both to get to the tavern and get to work right away.

Nothing was ever again said about the incident, but Dancy knew, like her grandparents, that Edana had meant what she had said.

There were suitors, however, young men in their late teens and early twenties, but none of them came from wealthy families and Faolan Curry chased them all away. Dancy did not protest, for she had no interest in marriage anyway. All she had to do was look to her mother's obvious misery, as well as her grandmother's, and feel she would be better off a spinster.

Dancy could not remember her mother ever being sick a day in her life, and that was why she was so frightened the morning she'd awakened in the tiny basement room they shared to find her moaning and delirious with fever. Reluctantly Grampa had summoned a doctor, who'd admitted he didn't really know what was wrong with her. He'd left medicine, which did not help, and Dancy had kept a constant vigil at her mother's bedside for two days and nights till she'd finally died.

It was during those last days that Dancy was shocked and bewildered to witness her mother's raving. "Why," she'd asked her grandmother, "is she calling for Uncle Dooley? She's always acted as though she hated him, and now she's crying out for him."

Her grandmother's eyes had widened. "It doesn't mean anything, it doesn't," she had nervously assured Dancy. "Pay no attention. She's burning with fever. She doesn't know what she's saying. And when she gets well, don't ask her any questions. Leave it be, child. Leave it be."

But she had not gotten well, Dancy felt like screaming to the heavens above. Her mother had taken a turn for the worse, and the doctor had said it was as if she just didn't want to live and her heart was giving out. It was as though she'd been waiting for Father Toole to minister the last rites, for when he was done she'd breathed her last.

After her mother had died, Dancy had intentionally worked harder than ever before, wanting to stay busy so there would be little time to dwell on her grief. What did life hold for her now, anyway? she miserably reflected. With her mother gone, she had no one. Her grandmother was just a shadow of a life, meek and frightened to death of her grandfather.

There was no one she could turn to, except Seann Durham. She knew him from church, and they had become good friends. Dancy was aware he wanted more but had not dared attempt to court, for he came from a poor family and knew how her grandfather felt about that. Actually she was content with friendship, aware she could never feel more for him, and, after her mother's death, she cherished his company.

The days were long, the nights even worse. She was up at dawn to scrub the tavern floors, always sticky with spilled ale and whiskey. Then she would hurry the short distance home to help her grandmother with her chores. There was the cow to be milked, and chickens to be fed, not to mention hoeing and weeding the garden. Barely was there time for the trip to the cemetery before reporting back to the tavern for the grueling evening hours of catering to the boisterous customers.

There was one man in particular whom Dancy found especially offensive—Brice Quigley—and her aversion was not motivated by his appearance, for he was not unattractive. The problem was his foul mouth, as well as the way he bullied everyone. But he was also quite rich, which meant her grandfather treated him like royalty, catering to his every whim. Brice always got the biggest slice of kidney pie or slab of cheese, and his mug was refilled with ale before he had consumed even half. And whenever he started a fight, which was often, her grandfather always sided with him.

Dancy despised him, because each time she went to his table she had to dodge his wandering hands. One night, when she was emptying trash in the barrels in the alley behind the tavern, she'd run into him as he was returning from relieving himself in the privy station. He had grabbed her and slung her up against the side of the building to maul at her breasts with his big hands, while his wet, sloppy lips tried to devour her mouth. She had fought and kicked and screamed, which had brought her grandfather running, but he had just laughed when he'd seen it was Brice.

Her mother, however, was right behind him, and she'd gone at Brice with nails arched, only Faolan had grabbed her and slung her to the ground with a warning that he'd take his belt to her then and there if she didn't calm herself. Brice was just having some fun, he'd said. But she'd given Brice a good tongue-lashing all the same, warning him to leave Dancy alone. And he had, for a time.

Now, however, with Edana no longer around, Brice Quigley was starting to get very bold once more, and Dancy knew she had to be constantly on guard, lest he catch her alone.

She had heard his wife had died the year before, leaving him with nine children. Some of them had grown and moved away, but several were still quite small. There was some gossip in the parish about his hiring a young and pretty nanny, and it was being said that Father Toole was furious over what he considered an ungodly situation in the Quigley household.

Dancy did not care about any of the gossip. All she wanted was for Brice to leave her alone, and everyone else, while she tried to figure out what she was going to do with the rest of her life.

All was still and quiet as Dancy straightened and turned to leave the burial grounds. The ancient stone church dominated the setting, framed in a golden-green hue as the bleeding sunset cast hallowed shadows among the canopy of trees. She felt at peace there and wished she could linger.

She started toward the village, then hesitated. Her grandfather would not be too angry as long as she showed up before dark. Confident there was time to take the long way down by the seashore, which was always lovely, she turned in that direction.

Soon she was lost in deep reflection, thinking how her mother had feverishly called Dooley's name in her final hours. What did it mean? Dancy knew her mother had liked him before they'd come to Ireland, but not long after, she'd seemed to loathe him.

Could it be possible, Dancy wondered, that her mother had actually been in love with Dooley? If so, perhaps the forbidden romance was the true reason for her having left America, and perhaps her mother's feelings for him had eventually turned to hate.

With a dismal flash, she knew it made no difference, anyway. Her life was not going to change. Time and again her mother had angrily said Uncle Dooley had never really cared about them, so Dancy could not go to him. How could she go anywhere anyway, with no money? She received no wages for her work. Her grandfather said she had to earn her keep. Thus, she was hopelessly, helplessly, trapped.

Realizing darkness was falling more rapidly than she'd first thought, Dancy quickened her step.

Her grandfather was always talking about how, if he had the money, he would buy the land next door to the tavern and build a bigger place, a tavern, where he could serve food. She hoped he never got the funds necessary, because it was also his dream to build a place upstairs for their living quarters. He didn't like residing so far from his business, but Dancy knew it was her only respite. If he ever moved her and Gramma onto the tavern premises, she'd never know a moment's peace.

Suddenly Dancy jumped at the sound of someone rapidly coming up behind her, and she whirled about in fright. She breathed an instant sigh of relief to recognize Seann Durham's boyishly handsome face.

"I'm sorry, Dancy. I didn't mean to scare you. I went by your house, and your grandmother said you'd left for work early so's you'd have time to go by and visit your mother's grave. I thought I'd catch up to walk with you, but the sexton said I missed you and pointed you'd come this way."

"It's all right." She laughed to put him at ease,

and reached for his hand to pull him in step beside her. "I'm glad you came, really. You've been such a wonderful friend to me these past weeks."

Boldly, gravely, he reminded her, "You know if you'd let me, I'd like to be more."

Dancy knew all right, and the last thing she wanted was to hurt him or give him false hope. "It has to be friendship, Seann. Besides," she added with a wink, and squeezed his hand, "my grandfather would skin us both alive if he knew we were out alone like this. Isn't proper, you know." She wrinkled her nose to tease.

Seann felt his pulse quicken. He thought Dancy O'Neal was the prettiest girl he'd ever known. He loved the way her mouth curved as though she were smiling, or about to, all the time, and the way her nose kind of tilted up, saucy and sassy. She was fun to be with, too, always trying to joke and laugh, but he knew it was an act. He knew that deep down, despite her reputation for rascality and mischief, Dancy was a very lonely and unhappy girl, even more so since her mother's death.

"I'm just making sure you get to the tavern safely," he said with forced gaiety. "Surely no one can find fault with that."

Dancy shot him a discouraging look. "You don't know my grandfather, Seann. He believes the worst of everybody and everything. He wouldn't like it a bit if he knew we were out here alone, especially about to walk through that stretch of woods ahead." She pointed to the thicket, a known trysting place for young lovers wishing to escape chaperones and prying eyes. "It'd be best if you left me here."

He shook his head stubbornly. "I'll see you through. The tavern is a short ways beyond. If you're afraid it will cause trouble for you if I go the whole way, then I'll turn back, but I'll not be seeing you go in there with it nearly dark."

Dancy wasn't afraid but knew his mind was set. "All right, but I will want you to turn back, Seann. No need for trouble if we can avoid it."

"And when will you let me call on you proper?" he asked hopefully as they stepped into the darkness of the thick trees and shrubs, straining to see the path and make their way without stumbling.

Dancy didn't say anything for a few moments, wanting to frame her response carefully. The way was narrow, and it was necessary for them to walk single file. Seann went first, reaching behind him to keep hold of her hand. She waited till they could see the lights of the village beyond, so they'd be nearly through with no time for him to argue, then told him gently, "I don't think you should come to see me with serious thoughts in mind. I'd like your friendship. I've told you that many times, but for now, and maybe for always, that's all I can offer you."

Seann ground his teeth together with irritation. He admitted guilt to pressuring her about such a sensitive matter as courtship so soon after her mother's death but feared there was not time to tread softly and properly. There was talk among the menfolk, and he'd not meant to tell her, but because of her candid rejection of him, he could not hold back. "Maybe you shouldn't be so quick to turn up your nose at me, Dancy O'Neal." He tried, but did not succeed, to keep the anger and resentment from his tone. "There's talk your grandfather will be arranging for you to wed Brice Quigley. I can't see you taking a fancy to a crude bloke like him, but maybe for his wealth you could overlook his failings."

Dancy jerked her hand from his.

He turned about to see, despite the scant light, the rage shining in her emerald eyes. "I didn't mean to make you mad. I just wanted you to see maybe I wouldn't be such a bad choice for a husband after all."

"I don't want a husband," she said tightly. "And if I did, I wouldn't be choosing a man who'd accuse me of letting money turn my head. I don't appreciate—"

Suddenly overcome with the need to show her how much he cared for her, wanted her, he pulled her into his arms and silenced her with his lips.

Stunned, Dancy could only stand there, but within seconds she came alive to struggle against him.

But she had not moved fast enough for Faolan Curry to think she was actually resisting. And how glad he was old Paddy Noonan had seen the two of them heading into the thicket and come to tell him about it.

"Harlot! Just like your mother," Faolan roared as he grabbed Seann by his shoulders and jerked him away.

Dancy screamed as Faolan's fist met Seann's nose in a crunch of bone and a spurt of blood. "I ought to kill you," he raged, "for luring her into the woods. And if you sully her good name by telling anybody about this, I'll rip out your tongue. Now get out of here, before I wring your worthless neck."

Scrambling on his hands and knees, Seann wasted no time disappearing into the shadowy forest.

Swept with anger and humiliation, Dancy faced her grandfather. "He was only kissing me. We weren't doing anything wrong. How could you—"

Faolan's slap sent her reeling backward.

"You've got your mother's blood, but you aren't going to disgrace me like she did. Now get to the tavern and get to work and keep your mouth shut. It cost me plenty to get Paddy to swear he wouldn't say anything about this, so don't you be letting on anything is wrong. I don't want Mr. Quigley asking questions."

With a trembling hand pressed against her stinging face, Dancy moved away from him, out of his reach. No longer caring how angry he got, she unleashed her own wrath to cry, "I don't give a damn about Brice Quigley. I don't give a damn what he or any of your besotted customers think of me. You had no right to treat Seann that way. We weren't doing anything wrong.

"And so help me," she raged on, continuing to keep her distance, "if you ever hit me again, I'll run away. I don't know where I'll go, or how I'll live, but I'll not have you beating on me, Grampa. I swear it."

"I won't be caring what you do much longer, lass," he said with a chuckle, "though I ought to tan your hide for your sass. Now get along with you."

Bewildered, Dancy paused. Washed with sudden dread, she called after him, "What do you mean—you won't be caring what I do?"

His reply made her blood run cold.

"Brice Quigley wants to marry you."

"I won't!" Dancy cried, feeling the first knot of hysteria work its way from the pit of her stomach. "I won't do it."

He whipped about fiercely to decree, "Yes, you will. And you'll make him a good and obedient wife, because if you don't, I'll beat you to within an inch of your life. I'll make you wish you'd never been born, by God. He's paying a good price for you," he raged on as he walked toward her.

Retreating, she found herself trapped, pressed against a tree, too terrified and heartsick to speak.

"Now I can fix the place up like I've always wanted. Best of all, I won't have to worry about you turning into a harlot like your mother.

"You *will* marry Brice Quigley, just as soon as the arrangements can be made. And there's not a thing you can do about it."

Numb, stricken, in that miserable moment Dancy could only wish to be lying in the ground next to her mother.

4

"I don't like it," Quigley said, slamming down his mug. He and Faolan were sitting together at a table off to one side in the tavern, watching as Dancy served up mugs of ale to three rowdies at the bar.

"It's not fittin'." He downed the rest of his drink and brushed bits of foam from his mustache, neglecting the froth clinging to his beard. "I don't like seein' the woman who'll be my wife this time tomorrow servin' whiskey tonight."

Faolan was unconcerned by Brice's griping. After all, he had his money, a tidy sum, too, hidden behind a loose brick in the chimney at home. "I told you," he remarked nonchalantly, "the girl I hired to replace her can't start till Monday, and Saturday night is always my busiest time. What do you expect me to do?" he went on to ask with a sarcastic sneer. "Close down tonight because you're marrying my help tomorrow?"

"Your *help*," Brice sneered. "She's your grand-daughter, and it's her wedding eve, but all you care about is money."

"That's right." Faolan smiled. "Nobody is going to look after me except me, and I try to do that very well."

"Aye, and you do a good job, too, as bloody much as you got out of me. Four times the price Torry O'Leary wanted for his Nelda."

Faolan laughed. "He cuts his price every year. By the time the ugly wench turns twenty, you can either get her for free, or he'll pay you to take her off his hands. Dancy is the prettiest girl in the village, and you know it. Well worth the price."

With a solemn nod, Brice agreed, at the same time feeling a warm rush as he stared at his betrothed. She was a beauty, to be sure, and he would be the envy of every man around when he took her for his wife on the morrow. His tone thick with desire, he murmured, "Better spend your money wisely, Faolan. You'll not be getting my business for a long time. I'll have more impor-tant things to do."

Faolan joined him in a nasty chuckle but could not resist bragging, "I'll not be missing your busi-ness, being as I'm sure to have more than I know what to do with once I finish fixing this place up—rooms upstairs for travelers passing through or those wanting some time alone with one of the new girls I'll be hiring." He dug his elbow into Brice's side and winked. "This is something I've wanted to do for a long, long time."

"But, of course, you couldn't," Brice goaded darkly,"not till you sold your granddaughter, and you couldn't do that as long as your daughter was alive. Didn't wait till she was cold in the ground to do it, either, did you? Well, you better hope I get me money's worth, you old goat, or I'll be getting it back. Now you go tell Dancy I'll be taking her home in a few minutes, and you can serve these plug-uglies yourself. She needs her rest," he added with a leer, "'cause she'll sure be busy this time tomorrow."

Faolan was not about to let Brice Quigley see how his warning had unnerved him, but the truth was, he knew how mean Brice could be when he was riled, and if Dancy did displease him, he'd want his money back for sure. However, it wouldn't be there for long, because he intended to have every bit of it spent before Brice and Dancy's honeymoon even got started good. Come Monday morning, he'd be paying in advance for everything he wanted done to the place, and if Brice thought he could take his tavern away from him just because Dancy didn't perform her wifely duties in bed, he had another thought coming.

As Faolan walked toward her, Dancy looked at him with loathing. It had been nearly a week since the bargain had been struck for her to wed, and she had not spoken a word to him since. He didn't care. In fact, he didn't care if he never saw her again once she was Mrs. Brice Quigley. She was trouble, just like her mother, only more so, because Dancy still had spirit. When she'd returned from America, Edana was like a flower wilted in the sun, and what times she did sass him, he put her in her place.

With Dancy out of the way, Faolan could look forward to having peace in the house again. Muira never gave him any trouble, because she had learned to keep her mouth shut from the day they married, nearly forty years ago. Since Edana's death, however, she had been a little too quiet, acting very strange, and he was starting to worry that maybe she was getting tetched. She never talked, even when he railed at her for the way she was acting. She had practically stopped eating altogether. All she did was sit and stare out the window. Even Dancy couldn't get through to her. So he had made up his mind that next week he was taking her to a doctor and maybe think about having her locked away with the crazy folk.

"Finish up what orders you got," he told

Dancy, "your husband-to-be is taking you home. He wants you rested proper for the wedding."

The men around started laughing, and Dancy felt her cheeks burning with humiliation as she rushed to finish serving them. She wasn't about to allow Mr. Quigley to take her home, wanting to prolong the time when she'd have to be alone with him. And keeping watch lest he realize what she was up to, she carefully worked her way toward the door leading to the alley. She would leave all right, she vowed fiercely, but *alone*.

Dear Lord, she prayed as she hurried through the night, desperation hammering with every beat of her heart, if only there was a way out of the nightmare. The thoughts of being married, enslaved, to a man like Brice Quigley for the rest of her life was unbearable.

Sadly, Dancy knew that when her mother had died, so had their dream of one day running away to make a new life somewhere else. They had talked about how they would go together, maybe north to Belfast or, if they had the money, all the way to London. Praying for a miracle was how they faced each day, but it had not happened. Now Dancy could only look to the future and see reflections of the miserable past.

Her grandmother was no comfort, for she was no more than a shadow in life, drifting in and out, elusive and fading, never quite present.

She left the tavern and hurried along in the shadows. It was not too late, only nine o'clock, but the cobblestone streets were deserted. Folks were either gathered at home with their families or had sequestered themselves for the evening at their favorite pub. Dancy was all alone as she left the alley and rounded the building, and the echo of her footsteps, ringing in the foggy night, was the only sound.

Suddenly Brice Quigley leaped out of a doorway to block her path. "I said I'd be taking you home, Dancy."

Defiantly she reminded him, "It isn't proper yet for us to be alone, and you know it, Mister Quigley, so—"

"So you'd best learn your place and keep your mouth shut, and I don't give a bloody damn what's proper and what isn't." He grabbed her arm and began to jerk her along to where he'd left his buggy. "I paid for you like I paid for these horses, and if you get me riled enough, I'll just claim what's mine this very night. Now get in." He lifted her and gave her a rough shove.

Dancy fell across the seat, bristling with fury as she righted herself and turned on him with a vengeance. "You'll be doing nothing of the kind, Brice Quigley. I don't care what kind of deal you have with my grandfather, if you—" She fell back against the seat as he popped the reins sharply to send the horses into a jolting trot.

"Ah, stop your wailing." He laughed down at her. "I'll follow the rules and wait till we're proper married before I see what it is I've purchased with my hard-earned money, but it better be worth it, I'm warning you."

Crossing her arms across her chest, Dancy moved as far away from him as possible. Waves of revulsion rippled through her as she contemplated the horror of having such a brute defile her at will.

They rode in silence, but when Brice came to a stop in front of the Curry cottage, he seemed to sense what she was thinking. Placing a possessive hand on her thigh, he assured her, "I doubt you'll ever love me, but that doesn't matter, because I don't intend to love you, either. But I know ways of pleasuring a woman, ways that will make you beg for more. You'll be kicking and screaming in my bed, night after night, I promise—"

"Stop it!" Dancy pushed his big hand away. "I don't want to listen to your filthy talk."

At that he threw back his head and laughed raucously. "Ah, you think a wife's duty to her husband is dirty, do you? Oh, you've a lot to learn, me girlie. A lot. And I can see your first lesson will be in obedience. Never interrupt me when I'm talking, and never, ever talk back to me, or so help me, I'll lace that pretty little bottom of yours with strap marks."

Dancy was undaunted, and with the spirit that had gotten her in trouble so many times in the past, she fired back, "If you ever take a belt to me, Brice Quigley, you'd better not close your eyes around me or you might not open them again. I'll not be having any man beat on me, even my husband. This, I swear on my mother's grave."

"You'll be in it with her." He grabbed her wrists, and twisted them behind her as he pressed her down on the seat and began to squeeze her breasts roughly. "Faolan warned me your mother spoiled you, and you'd have to be broke, but break you I will, and I'll get started right now."

Dancy attempted to scream, but he silenced her with his lips, which she bit. With a howl of rage he released her, spitting blood as he cursed and swung at her, but she moved swiftly. She leaped from the buggy on the opposite side, lifted her skirts above her ankles and ran up the walkway toward the house. Frantically, she called out to her grandmother to open the door.

Muira, brooding over the misery of her life, came alive as she heard her granddaughter's shrieks. She bolted to her feet, concern mounting as she saw Brice Quigley, a man she hated, stumbling out of his buggy right behind her granddaughter.

Later Muira would wonder why she paused to

pick up a stone bookend on her way to the door. She had never lifted a finger to defend herself or anyone else in her life.

Dancy tumbled into her arms, crying, "I don't care what Grampa does to me, Gramma, I won't marry him, I won't—"

"Oh, yes, you will, you arrogant little bitch!"

Brice grabbed her and slung her to the floor. He unbuckled his belt and began to remove it. Noticing Faolan Curry's timid wife, he yelled, "Get out of here. I'm going to give her the thrashing she deserves, and then a sample of what she's gonna learn to love, and I don't think you want to watch."

Dismissing her, he turned on Dancy and raised his belt, ready to strike.

"I think not, Brice Quigley." Without a twinge of fear over the possible consequences of her action, Muira Curry brought the bookend crashing down on the back of his head.

With a grunt of pain and surprise, he went to his knees, then toppled forward onto his face, unconscious.

"Oh, Gramma, he'll kill us both when he wakes up," Dancy wailed, scrambling to her feet, "but only God knows how much I love you for what you did."

"I know, dear, I know." Muira nodded solemnly, surprised by her calm in the wake of what she'd done. There would be the devil to pay, for sure, but there was no time to worry about it.

"I've always despised him," she went on to say after a ragged sigh. "I knew his wife, God rest her soul, knew how she suffered, and I've not known a moment's peace since I heard that your grandfather bargained for you to marry him. It was bad enough losing your mother, without losing you, too. I guess that's why I just withdrew inside myself and didn't care if I died. But something happened tonight. The Lord spoke to me, telling me I had to try and stop it, like I should've done all those years ago when your grandfather sold your mother.

"But we haven't much time," she said, then quickly, brightly, asked, "Can you pack a small bag from the things you had ready to move over to the Quigley cottage tomorrow? You can travel a lot faster if you don't have a lot of things to carry."

Dancy was bewildered. Never had she witnessed such behavior from her grandmother, but she was not about to abandon her to face either Brice Quigley or Grampa alone. "I'm not going anywhere. God knows I'd like nothing better than to run from this nightmare, but I won't leave you, and we've nowhere to go, anyway."

Muira pursed her lips. Things were happening fast, but somehow she knew what had to be done. Taking up a lantern, she motioned Dancy to follow. "I've got something to show you. Maybe it will provide some answers as to how to get you out of this dilemma. I always figured some things were better left alone, but something tells me the time has come for you to see them."

Burning with curiosity, and with a wary glance at Brice, who was still not moving, Dancy followed her grandmother as she hurried down the narrow hallway that led to the tiny kitchen at the rear of the house.

"In here." Muira pushed open the pantry door and stepped inside. "Now don't be angry at me for not showing these to you sooner, but I didn't dare, Dancy, I just didn't dare."

Seeing her tears, the way she was trembling, Dancy knew that despite the strange show of spirit, her grandmother was terribly frightened. She slipped an arm about her frail shoulders and promised, "I could never be angry with you about anything, Gramma. Now tell me, quickly, what this is all about, because I think we should probably call a doctor for Mr. Quigley. We'll say he stumbled and fell. He didn't see you hit him, so—"

"Hush and listen," Muira protested, pale and tight-lipped. "We don't have much time. You've got to get your things and be on your way before he wakes up."

Dancy watched, silent and baffled, as her grandmother stood on tiptoe to reach an upper shelf. Pushing aside dust-covered jars, she groped about, then gave a soft gasp of relief as she found what she was looking for. Triumphantly she held out two envelopes. One, Dancy noticed, was old and yellowed and even had scorch marks, as though it had been burned.

"I pulled it from the grate," Muira explained, nervously wringing her hands as she watched Dancy for her reaction. "Your grandfather got hold of it when it arrived. It was right after you two came home. You know I can't read, but I did recognize Edana's name, and I knew it was for her. But your grandfather, he opened it and read it and got real mad and said he was going to burn it, and if I ever told your mother, he'd beat me till I couldn't walk. He would've, too, but something told me I shouldn't let that letter be destroyed, so as soon as he turned his back, I snatched it up and hid it here, with that other one, that came for her over a year ago. He didn't see that one," she declared proudly.

With a jolt, Dancy saw the return address and realized the letters were from Uncle Dooley. "Why didn't you show these to Mother? Why did you keep them from her?"

"Oh, I wanted to, Dancy. Believe me. But I was scared. I didn't know what they said, and I was afraid of what your grandfather would do if he found out I kept them.

"I knew something bad had happened over there to make her come back like she did," she rushed on. "She'd never tell me what, but after that first letter came, and your grandfather got mad like he did, I started thinking it all had something to do with him, your uncle Dooley, and I knew whatever it was, it was wrong. But I still couldn't bring myself to throw those letters away."

Dancy took out the first letter, saw it was dated the summer of 1854, and began to read the barely legible lines.

> *My darling, darling Edana,*
>
> *When I read your letter, I fell on my knees and gave thanks to God. I do love you, and I always will.*
>
> *I grieve to hear of your father's mistreatment and how miserable you are. If only I had known you were planning to run away, I swear I would have found a way to stop you. When you left, you took my heart with you.*
>
> *I will do anything to be with you and my precious Dancy. If you have not changed your mind, just tell me what you want me to do. I will either come over there and get you, or I will send you the money to return to me. We will go anywhere you want to go, live anywhere you want to live. I will sell my land. I will do anything. My*

*brother does not matter. The only thing that does
is that we be together.*

*I wait to hear from you. My life is yours to
command, dear, dear Edana.*

> Forever my love,
> Dooley

Dancy was unaware that tears were spilling from her eyes till her grandmother handed her a handkerchief and urged, "We have to hurry, dear. He could wake up any time."

"My God, Gramma, do you know what this means?" Dancy exploded. "Mother and Uncle Dooley loved each other. She ran away from my father, because she was so unhappy with him, and then when she got over here, she realized she had to be with Uncle Dooley, so she wrote him and told him so, and he wrote her back and assured her he loved her, too. Only she never got it, because you kept it from her, and all these years . . .

"All these years," she went on after choking back a pitying sob, "she thought he didn't care after all. And now I see why she turned on him the way she did, why she refused to talk about him and became so bitter. Did he ever write to her again?"

Muira nodded guiltily. "I seem to remember a few other letters. Your grandfather burned those completely, though. I couldn't save them. Your mother tried to write another letter, too, but he got hold of it without letting her know it and destroyed it."

"Damn him," Dancy cursed, opening the second letter with shaking fingers. She began to read anxiously,

Dearest Edana,

> *Twelve years ago, you decided you did not love me, after all, but I have never stopped loving you. I suppose you met another, and as I want only happiness for you, I pray your life has been filled with the joy you deserve.*

> *The reason I am writing you now is because I am in the midst of a war and could be killed any time. If I am, I want Dancy to have all my possessions. This letter, signed and witnessed by a preacher, will serve as her claim. Dancy will love my land as I do. Tell her it is like daisies. It is forever. Like my love for you both. She will understand.*

> *So please see she gets this letter, as I want her to know how much she means to me. Truly, the angels danced the day she was born.*

> *You broke my heart, Edana, but I hold only good thoughts for you.*

Forever my love,
Dooley O'Neal

For a moment Dancy could not speak, and it was only when her grandmother urged her again to make ready to leave that she realized just what it all meant. If Uncle Dooley had made it safely through the war, and she prayed he had, then he would welcome her with open arms. And if he had been killed, his home was hers.

Slowly, almost reverently, she folded the letter and returned it to the envelope. Calmly she announced, "I have somewhere to go after all, Gramma. I'm going to Uncle Dooley. I don't know how I'll get there, but I'll find a way somehow. And you are coming with me."

Muira's eyes widened as she swung her head sharply from side to side in protest. "Oh, no, I'll not be leaving here, Dancy. I'm too old to be starting over, but not you. You've got your whole life before you. Now I want you to go Father Toole. Tell him I sent you and asked that he give you shelter for the night. He won't ask any questions. He knows of the misery in this house. He's prayed with me over it so many times through the years.

"And tomorrow morning," she rushed on excitedly, feeling spirit for the first time in too long to remember, "you'll go to Dublin and make arrangements to go on the first ship leaving. You'll need to hide out till it sails, though, because for sure your grandfather and that heathen Quigley will be looking for you."

Dancy's laugh was bitter. "And what will I be

using for money? And don't go suggesting I steal Mr. Quigley's purse. He'd have the law after me then, and I'd be caught and sent to jail. Besides, I doubt there'd be enough to get me all the way to America and Tennessee, anyway."

Muira's eyes, uncommonly vibrant and alive, gleamed mysteriously in the lantern's glow. "I've something else to show you, me darling. Come along."

They returned to the parlor. It did not look as though Brice had moved. Dancy carefully leaned over him to listen for his breathing and then, satisfied she would not be leaving her grandmother to face murder charges, followed her to the fireplace, where she was pulling frantically at a brick to one side of the chimney.

"He thought I was asleep in my chair," she was saying gleefully, "but I was watching, and I saw him put the money in here. The way I see it, it's fitting you should have it. Mr. Quigley can afford to lose it, and I'll have the satisfaction of watching Faolan Curry squirm for the first time.

"Maybe," she added with a giggle as she handed over the bundle to Dancy, "he'll even be so scared he'll run away, too, and I can live out my old age in peace. Wouldn't that be a special blessing?"

Dancy blinked away the tears as she gathered her grandmother close. "The blessing would be if you could go with me. I can't bear the thoughts of never seeing you again."

"I've not been to you what I should've been." Muira pulled away to say, "I've been weak and cowardly, and you know it. I've never been able to stand up to Faolan Curry and doubt I ever will, but at least I've done this much, and I can go to my grave knowing I saved you from the same wretched fate as your mother, God rest her soul." Her own tears began to trail down her cheeks.

"Now go." She gave Dancy a firm pat on her back and stepped from her embrace. "He could be waking any time now, and I want you safely at the church when he does."

Dancy hurried to gather what she could stuff into one small bag, then, with a final embrace and a promise to write in care of Father Toole, she said good-bye.

At last she walked out of the house, closing the door to her past and taking the first step toward her destiny.

5

When Dancy left Ireland, she promised herself not to look back. She knew she would probably never see her grandmother again, nor visit her mother's grave, but the future would be a challenge, requiring all her thoughts and energy.

She smiled each time she thought of the money hidden away inside the lining of her bag. Mr. Quigley must have thought she was worth a great deal, for there was still a small fortune left, which she would change into United States currency upon arrival in New York. When she reached Tennessee, it was her intention to turn it all over to Uncle Dooley, assuring her support for many years to come. The last thing she wanted was to be a burden.

Dancy had always been an avid reader, but with no newspapers available on the Atlantic crossing, she decided she could learn much by eavesdropping on the conversations of the men. So, being careful not to appear obvious, she lurked about wherever they gathered on deck. The really interesting talks were held in the smoking parlors, of course, and she did not dare intrude. Still, she was able to hear enough to fill her with worry and dread over the world of which she was about to become a part.

The South, she learned, though struggling to rebuild, had a long way to go to overcome the utter desolation that prevailed. Cities lay in ruins yet were crowded with freed slaves, now homeless, and widows with children and nowhere to go. Everywhere there were burned-out shells of houses, weed-choked gardens, grass-grown streets.

Some states were worse than others, such as South Carolina, which for hundreds of miles lay like a broad black streak of devastation in the wake of General Sherman's infamous march to the sea.

In rural areas all over, plantation and farm lands lay abandoned or uncultivated. Fences had been ripped out by the invaders for firewood. Factories had been destroyed. Roads and bridges were either in disrepair or completely destroyed. Some crops, she was pleased to hear, had been harvested last year, but those farmers who attempted to recover were faced, of course, with the difficulty of securing labor.

At first, Dancy heard, they had tried to work their lands by hiring workers, most of whom were freed slaves, but that did not succeed because there was not enough cash to sustain a wage system. It was said a sharecropping and crop-lien system was taking the place of money. Dancy soaked up every word the men spoke, wondering all the while which system Uncle Dooley was using for his large farm.

Hearing how many railroad tracks and rails in the South had been destroyed, she realized she might find it extremely difficult traveling on to Tennessee once the ship reached New York, for she'd thought of no other transportation than by train. Again, she was washed with frustration to think just how helpless she was. If Uncle Dooley had been around, he'd have taught her to ride a horse and shoot a gun, because she still remembered how he'd promised to do so when she was old enough to learn. As it was, she felt vulnerable and defenseless.

At last they arrived in New York, and Dancy found the city to be a nightmare of noise and long lines as she made her way through immigration.

A Roman Catholic priest was offering assistance to arriving Irish passengers. When she told him she was traveling alone, going to Tennessee, he immediately registered concern and displeasure and advised her to remain in New York. "Most of our Irish Roman Catholics are making new lives right here in the city," he said. "A young girl like you belongs here. I'll find a job for you as a nanny with a family in my own parish, and you'll have a room right in their house. The South is no place for a young girl, especially one traveling alone with no definite home to go to.

"People are homeless and starving," he warned. "They roam the roads and countryside robbing and killing. It's not safe. You belong here."

Dancy was not about to be dissuaded, so all the priest could do was bless her and send her on her way. He did, however, assist by directing her to go by train from New York to Baltimore, Maryland. The Orange & Alexandria Railroad was operating down into Virginia. How far, he was not sure, but he felt if she could manage to connect with the Virginia & Tennessee line, she could surely get coach transportation the rest of the way.

There were no private accommodations on the train, and fearing she might be robbed while dozing on her chair, Dancy tried to keep her arms locked about her bag. In addition she divided some of the money and hid part inside her underwear. If her bag were stolen, she'd at least have some of the money left.

When she arrived in Baltimore, Dancy was delighted to find the Virginia & Tennessee train running, but the stationmaster could give her no hope of being able to make it all the way into Tennessee. "The tracks from Glade Spring into Knoxville are completely destroyed. What you'll have to do," he advised as he scanned a crude map spread out on his counter, "is go by coach to Bristol, then take a flatboat down the river to Chattanooga. You won't find the tracks repaired there, either, but you could probably get another coach up to Nashville."

Dancy stood on tiptoe to poke her head through the opening in the wire cage that divided the counter. Scanning the map, she could not see Pinetops marked, but then she remembered that it was a very small town, probably not worthy of a map maker's noting. She knew it was due south of Nashville and felt confident that once she got farther along, someone would be able to provide directions.

Leaving Maryland, Dancy found herself alone until the train stopped in a town just across the Virginia line. There dozens and dozens of men boarded, some with their wives and children, heading farther south to labor on the rails, crowding in till every seat was filled.

Dancy could not help noticing how bedraggled they were. They wore tattered clothes, some almost in rags, and desperation was etched in their faces. She felt out of place in her fine traveling clothes, which she'd taken time to buy in New York, wanting to look nice for Uncle Dooley. The glances of some of the workers' wives made her uncomfortable, and she turned her attention to stare out the window at the passing countryside. Everywhere there were signs of the ravages of war.

Despite the heat and noise, Dancy began to nod and was almost asleep when a woman across the aisle began to carp, "Well, well, seems like we got *female* carpetbaggers headin' south now. I tell you, I got more respect for a whore."

Dancy glanced about to see all eyes upon her and said nervously, "I'm afraid I don't know what you're talking about."

"Carpetbag." The woman nodded, lips curved in a sneer of disgust. "That's what we call you leeches that carry them bags made out of rugs. You come down here to make whatever you can off us, like buzzards pick the dead. Disgusting, that's what you are."

Dancy swung her head in protest, "No, you don't understand—"

A man across the aisle cut her off angrily, "We

know your kind. No need to lie. Look at you—all dressed up, travelin' like a princess in your finery. I'll just bet you're on your way to meet your carpetbagger husband."

"No, I'm not married. I . . ." her voice trailed off, as she silently admonished herself even for arguing with them.

The rest of the way to Glade Spring, Dancy dared not sleep for fear of what might happen. She could feel menacing eyes upon her constantly, though she sat with her own closed or riveted out the window. She shuddered to think someone might become angry enough over the bag to grab it and toss it out.

Trembling with relief to at last reach her momentary destination, Dancy hurried from the train. The first thing she did before seeking out transportation by coach to Bristol was find a store and purchase a leather valise. It was bigger and bulkier, but she was not about to endure the stigma of being a despicable carpetbagger.

After an uncomfortable wagon ride and a flatboat cruise down the Tennessee River, Dancy found her spirits once again dashed in Chattanooga to be told there would be no transportation to Nashville for nearly three weeks. Rails were completely impassable, and all available wagons and carriages had already been hired out.

"Thing for you to do, little lady," advised the kindly station master, "is get you a room over at Miz Leland's boardinghouse and settle down for a while."

Dancy was not about to dally around Chattanooga a day longer than necessary. The city, for the most part still in ruins, was overrun with the dreaded carpetbaggers, freed slaves, Union soldiers, homeless dispirited Confederates, and desperate widows.

After one night at the boardinghouse, she knew she had to keep going. She hadn't been able to sleep for the sounds of screams and occasional gunfire and the acrid odor of charred ruins wafting through the open windows.

Early the next morning, dragging her bulky leather bag with her, Dancy found a livery stable willing to sell a wagon and two horses for a price she knew was outrageous, but at that point she was desperate. The owner did, however, redeem himself by drawing her a crude map of the direction she needed to travel.

"You got a gun, miss?" he wanted to know as she prepared to depart.

With a self-conscious grimace, Dancy shook her head and admitted, "I wouldn't know how to use it if I did."

"Well, if I was you, I'd get me one just the same. At least if you get stopped by bandits, you could point it and make 'em think you do."

Dancy thanked him for his interest, snapped the reins over the horses' backs, and left. She saw no need to worry since she intended to travel only during the day. If she came across someone to hire on as driver and guard, she intended to do so.

She had left near noon and within an hour realized she had taken on a formidable task. The horses were spirited and seemed to know an unfamiliar hand held the reins. Periodically they broke into a jarring gait, and she found herself being bounced painfully up and down on the buckboard seat. The sun bore down mercilessly, and she was forced to remove her jacket and roll up her sleeves. Soon her carefully braided red hair was streaming about her sweaty face. It was, she realized with dismay, going to be a miserable trip. Already she could feel blisters beneath her thin cotton gloves.

Yet with every turn of the wheels Dancy felt exhilarated to think she was getting closer to her true home. The past had been but an interval shared with her mother, who had fled the callings of her heart. But she would never run. Not now. Uncle Dooley would take her in, and they'd be a family. And it was thinking, dreaming, of the happiness awaiting her that gave her the strength to continue in the smothering heat and the misery of attempting to keep the horses under control.

As soon as she was settled in, she planned to ask Uncle Dooley to give her riding lessons. Next she wanted to learn to use a gun. She felt it was important to be able to take care of herself, because Uncle Dooley would not always be around, and by God, she didn't want to have to depend on a man anyway. Doing so had brought her mother nothing but anguish, and had it not been for her grandmother coming to her rescue, Dancy knew she'd have lived no better than the former slaves as the wife of Brice Quigley. She'd fend for herself and never be relegated to servant or chattel for any man.

Just before sundown she came upon a dilapidated cabin set back from the road in the woods and decided to camp there for the night. It took nearly half an hour to wrestle the harnesses from the horses, and she only hoped she could remember how to put them back on in the morning. After giving them water from a still functioning well, she tied them to a tree and carried her bag inside.

The one-room structure was bare, but she had thought to add a blanket to her supplies. After a quick supper of hardtack washed down with water from her canteen, she curled up on the floor and, at once, fell into an exhausted sleep.

Dancy did not hear the three men as they crept into the cabin sometime during the night. She was unaware that anyone was about until a loud, guttural voice pierced the stillness.

"Shit, I don't believe this. If our luck had been this good at Gettysburg, maybe we'd have won the danged war."

She sat straight up, every nerve raw and terrified as she struggled to see in the garish light of the lantern held before her face.

"Pretty, too, ain't she? Gawd, look at that hair. All red and gold."

Dancy shrank back in horror as thick, stubby fingers reached for her.

"Aw, no need to be scared. We just want to share your cabin. Ain't that right, boys?"

A lusty round of guffaws wrapped her heart in terror. "Please," she managed to say around the knot of fear bubbling in her throat, "leave me alone. I'm on me way home, to Pinetops, and—"

"Oh, listen to the Irish brogue," someone in the shadows hooted.

Despite the crashing horror, Dancy cursed herself. She had tried so hard to lose her accent, for one of the things she'd managed to overhear during the Atlantic crossing was how southerners resented the Irish for coming in to take work from them.

One of the others snickered, "Where the shit is Pinetops?"

Another chimed in to cry, "Who gives a damn? Let's have a look inside that bag she's hidin' behind her back."

At that Dancy sprang to her feet, pulling the bag with her, but she was helpless against them. The bag was yanked away, and she was pushed back to the floor.

They laughed among themselves, and the bag disappeared from view, but with a wave of horror Dancy realized she had much more to worry about than that. Hands were snatching at her, tearing at her clothes.

"We'll take the bag and something else, too . . ."

She could smell the sour odor of whiskey as she fought, scratching and kicking, but she did not have a chance against them. They laughed and taunted as they ripped at her, and then one of them cried, "Look. Money. She had it hid in her clothes."

They gathered it quickly, while Dancy screamed and cried, and then they turned on her once more, chuckling with delight. A burly hand clamped across her mouth to stifle her shrieks of protest as another held her arms.

"Now we're gonna have us some fun."

"You go first, Hawkins. You spotted her wagon and found her."

"Then I'm next."

"Hey, there's plenty for everybody. It's a long time till daybreak, and ain't nobody dumb enough to be on this road after dark, 'ceptin' her."

In that moment of frozen horror, Dancy began to feel panic yield to anger that she could be so damnably helpless. What a fool she had been to strike out on her own, with no weapon, so gullible as to think no harm could come. How stupid could she be? her brain taunted. She had been so proud, traveling all the way across the Atlantic Ocean to make a new life for herself, independent and free, determined to fend for herself, and now she lay powerless beneath a band of drunken bandits, about to be raped, perhaps even murdered.

One of the men, goaded by his comrades, was unbuckling his trousers. The faces above her were like glowing demon heads in the eerie glow of the lantern someone held high. She saw lips curled back in macabre grins, heated eyes devouring her. She looked at each in turn, desperately seeking one among them who might have mercy.

Then she saw something else—the gleam of a pistol tucked in the belt of the man crouched directly above her head. He was the one holding her wrists.

Suddenly she knew she had but one chance, and she took it.

Dancy opened her mouth wide to allow the fingers across her lips to slip inside. Viciously she clamped down. With an oath the man tore his hand away, and with everyone caught momentarily off guard, she lunged upward to throw off the man holding her wrists. Quickly she grabbed the pistol, felt her fingers tighten about it, and jerked it free.

"She's got Gurley's gun," yelped the one called Hawkins. "Get the hell out of here!"

"Douse the lantern!"

The cabin, plunged into darkness, echoed with the sounds of boots stampeding across the floor as the hoodlums rushed outside. Sobbing brokenly, Dancy held the gun with shaking fingers, completely ignorant of what to do with it. There was a trigger to be pulled, she knew that much, but in the darkness she feared she'd wind up shooting herself.

"Damn it!" She felt stupid, helpless, as she struggled to stand on wobbly knees. By the time she got to the door, framed in the light of a half-moon, she had managed to hook her finger around the trigger. But was too late: they were well on their way. And with a jolt she realized they had taken not only the bag containing all her clothes and the rest of the money, but the horses and wagon as well.

Sick at heart, she sank to the floor, still clutching the gun with both hands. The clothes she was wearing were ruined. Stranded miles from nowhere, she had nothing left. Yet it was not the desperate predicament she found herself in that needled so painfully—it was knowing none of it would have happened if she'd been smarter and able to take care of herself. Still, there was consolation in knowing she'd managed to fight back and keep them from raping her.

With a fierce shake of her head, Dancy blinked away the tears, determined not to wallow in self-pity. She crept back to where she'd been sleeping, still clutching the gun. If they came back, she would be ready for them.

Throughout the rest of the night she was wide awake with worry, but as dawn began to streak the eastern sky, Dancy's head began to nod. Weary and exhausted, she told herself they wouldn't come back in daylight. She could dare to close her eyes for a little while and rest before having to strike out on foot.

Moments turned into several hours, but Dancy had no idea how long she had been sleeping when she was finally awakened by the sounds of a horse approaching. Instantly alert, fingers once more tightened around the trigger of the gun she still held, she swiftly got to her feet and backed away from the doorway and into the shadows.

Watching with pounding heart, she saw the man's hulking shadow as he picked his way across the rotting boards of the porch, then seemed to fill the doorway as he hesitated before entering.

"Stop right there, you hooligan, or I'll put a hole right between your eyes."

Even as she spoke, Dancy was amazed to realize the strong, unwavering voice was actually hers.

"Eh, who's there?" The intruder strained to see as he cajoled, "No need to be scared, little lady. I mean you no harm."

He took a step forward, and Dancy pulled the trigger. The unexpected recoil knocked her backward, and she landed on her bottom, hard. The bullet never even went near its target, instead thudding into the cabin wall nearly six feet to the left of the door.

But the stranger was taking no chances. In a flash he lunged to jerk the gun from her hands, shouting, "Are you crazy, girl? I told you I mean you no harm. And you don't know what you're doing, anyway. Are you all right?"

He tucked the gun in his belt and held out a hand to her, which she promptly slapped away as she stood. "Just back on out of here, mister, and leave me be, and I'd like my gun back."

"Your gun?" He chuckled. "And what would you be doing with a Remington Army revolver? You obviously ain't never shot it before, or you'd know it's got a kick like a danged mule. . . ."

His voice trailed away as he saw how she was holding the bodice of her torn dress together with one hand. Warily he asked, "What happened? Did somebody attack you, girl?"

"What do you care?" Dancy fired back testily. "It's none of your business. Now give me back my gun and get on out of here, like I said."

"I'm not going anywhere till I find out who you are and what you're doing here. So you might as well start talking, and I promise I'm not going to hurt you."

Dancy fell silent for a moment, unnerved by his steady, speculative gaze. She couldn't tell much about his face, for most of it was covered with a beard. His eyes, however, were a friendly shade of blue. He wore a felt hat, a plaid shirt, but the trousers, she noted, were gray, with a red stripe. Frowning, she remembered that her attackers, too, had been wearing gray.

He saw her expression, could sense her revulsion. "So, they were ex-soldiers, too. Well, all of us old Rebels aren't devils, but I reckon there's a few bad apples in every barrel.

"Now I'd really like to help you, little lady, if you'll let me," he assured her. "My name is Ben Caudell, and I live back yonder in the woods about a mile or so. I've been hunting, and while I didn't have much luck, me and my wife will be glad to share what I did get, if you want to come along home with me."

"Your wife?"

"Adele. That's her name. You'll like her. And she'll be glad for the company, especially if you'll give her a hand with little Ben. That's our new son," he informed her proudly, thrusting his chest out a bit. "Born two weeks ago, and already he's a handful. Now why don't you just come along home with me?" he went on. "We'll get you cleaned up and fed."

Still wary, Dancy asked, "Will you give me back my gun?"

He laughed softly. "You got grit, I'll hand you that. But you got no business totin' a gun when you don't know how to use it."

Masking her panic with anger, she cried, "Then you're stealing it."

"I'm no thief. And I'll be glad to give it back—*after* I teach you to shoot it."

Dancy stared up at him in frowning disbelief. "You'd do that?"

"Sure, but it'll take some time. And maybe we can help each other. Tell you what. You come home with me and help Adele, and in exchange, I'll teach you how to use this gun. And don't worry," he assured her warmly, "I promise you'll be safe as a rabbit in a briar patch. You've nothing to fear. I just want to help you, like you was my own daughter."

They had moved outside as they talked, picking their way across the precarious porch floor to stand in the warm summer day. Something about him just made her want to trust him, and after all, she really had no choice.

"All right," she said finally, firmly. "We got a deal, but there's one other thing I'd like to ask you to do."

He waited.

"Will you teach me to ride a horse, too?"

"Little lady," he said, bowing humorously, "you're speaking to a former rider of the Confederate Cavalry, and everybody knows we rode circles around them Yankees. I can even teach you trick riding, if you want."

"I want!" Dancy cried, exhilarated at the thought of becoming an expert rider as well as marksman.

"Suppose you could tell me your name now?"

She did so, and placing a fatherly arm about her shoulders, he led her toward his horse. "Then let's be heading home and getting started, Miss Dancy O'Neal, 'cause I've got an idea

I got my work cut out for me."

"That you do, Mr. Ben Caudell." Dancy grinned up at him impishly. "But I can promise you've never seen a more eager student."

6

Lila Coley stretched languorously, then snuggled closer to Clint. He was lying on his side, his back to her. With her hands slipped beneath his arms, she walked her fingers through the thick mat of dark hair that covered his broad chest. Smiling, she thought maybe this was the way a cat felt when it was all curled up, purring and satisfied, because Clint McCabe was one hell of a man, and wonderful hours of wild passion in his arms always left her fulfilled and just plain glad to be a woman.

Lila had known plenty of men intimately, but Clint was the first she'd allowed herself to care about. The others were meaningless encounters, only for money, a way to survive amid the turmoil of war. Clint, however, was different in many ways. Not only was he tender and kind, he also treated her like a person rather than an object to be used, then carelessly tossed aside. They enjoyed each other's company, in bed and out, and as a result had become good friends. But then, Lila had to remind herself, neither one of them were held in favor by the locals. She was a prostitute, and he was considered a traitor. No matter that the North had won the war. Clint McCabe had gone off to fight for the Confederacy but then had switched loyalties, and everybody in Pinetops hated him for it.

But none of that mattered to Lila. She knew only that she cared for him more than she should, yet she had no illusions as to anything permanent. He had never led her to believe he might fall in love. She accepted that, having learned long ago not to expect much out of life and then she wouldn't get disappointed.

Clint stirred in his sleep and shrugged off her embrace.

Lila's laugh was deep and husky as she hoisted herself up and over him, landing playfully in his arms.

He smiled lazily. "You never get enough, do you?"

"Not with you." Boldly she slid her hand downward.

Clint knew he should push her away and go. He had already started cutting trees for more pasture and needed to finish up. If he wanted to get a small herd of cattle going before fall, fences had to be repaired or completely replaced. But last night he had celebrated becoming legal owner of Dooley O'Neal's land and had had too much to drink downstairs in Buck Sweeney's saloon. As a result, it hadn't taken much persuasion to get him to stay till morning.

"I really should get out of here." He took note of the bright sun streaming through the window and guessed it had to be after ten. With supplies yet to buy, a half hour's ride to the farm, he'd be lucky to get to his work by noon.

"You can stay a little longer," Lila urged, caressing him. "And don't tell me you don't want to. I've got the proof right here in my hand. And afterward, I'll even ride with you out to that dirty old cabin and help you clean it up. I'll pick up some food, make lunch for us. We'll have a wonderful time."

She had lowered her head, her tongue tracing a hot, wet trail down his chest. Giving a deep moan, he decided the damn fence could wait.

The heated embrace did not last long. Within seconds the sound of loud, angry pounding on the door caused them to spring apart. "What the hell—" Clint leaped out of bed and reached for his trousers with one hand, his revolver with the other.

"Clinton McCabe, I know you're in there. Probably naked as the day you were born, too, rutting with that whore like a dog in heat. You get your clothes on and open this door, or so help me I'll find somebody to break it down."

"She will, too," Clint muttered as he laid aside the gun to jerk on his clothes.

Lila had scooted up against the iron poster headboard. Pulling the covers up to her nose, she nervously asked, "For God's sake, who is she?"

"Guess," he said dully. "Who else around here would have nerve enough to march right upstairs and bang on the door?"

Lila gasped, "Your mother?"

"*Step*mother," he corrected wearily.

"What's she doing here? And how did she know where you were?"

"It's no secret I stay here sometimes, Lila. Besides, my horse is tied up outside, and she probably told Sweeney if he didn't tell her where I was, she'd beat on every door till she found me herself."

"But why? What does she want?"

"There's no telling," he hedged. Actually he knew why Addie was looking for him, madder than a wet hen. She had found out what he had done over at the courthouse yesterday, and now he wished he had gone home instead of staying the night. At least way out there nobody would be around to witness her ravings.

Banging the handle of her parasol against the

door, Addie warned, "I'm giving you one minute, Clinton. Open this door or—"

Clint yanked it open so fast that she lost her balance and tumbled into his arms.

After righting herself and jerking down her short-waisted jacket, Addie reached to tug at her big feathered hat. Then she took a deep breath and unleashed all the wrath that had been choking her since she'd left the courthouse. "Not only are you a traitor to your people, but you're a lying sneak as well. You knew I was planning to pay off Dooley's taxes. You knew I had plans for all that timber, and—"

"Wait a minute," he interrupted. "You had the same chance I did, Addie. You knew yesterday was the first day the courthouse would be open for business, that the records had been found and put back in place, but I didn't see you standing in line. You also knew I'd been living out at Dooley's since you slammed the door to my father's home in my face."

"How dare you even speak his name? Why, he's probably turned over in his grave so many times since you swapped gray uniform for blue that the ground over him has ripples. He'd have thrown you out, too."

"You're probably right," Clint could not resist firing back sarcastically. "He would have agreed with you, like always."

Addie glared up at him. "I didn't come here to argue. I came to tell you that if you know what's good for you, you'll get yourself over to the courthouse and tell them it was all a mistake. You didn't want to pay Dooley O'Neal's taxes. I've got the money right here in my bag to do it myself. I'll go with you, and we'll get this whole mess straightened out. I'll even pay you a fair amount, actually buy the land back from you if you'd rather do it that way, and then you'll have money to start over somewhere else."

Solemnly Clint shook his head. "No, ma'am. I'm not going to do any such thing. Dooley would have wanted me to have that land, not you."

"Do you have proof of that? Did he leave something in writing?"

"He didn't have to. Anybody that pays the taxes can claim the land. It's the law. And I would've done it long before now, but we both know that when the Confederates managed to invade right before the war was over, every county court south of Nashville was thrown into turmoil and shut down again. It was bad enough back when Nashville was captured in the first place, and all the magistrates and clerks took off, and the whole court system fell apart. Taxes haven't been collectible, and records have been missing, and it was only recently they turned up and business could get going again. I was waiting for that."

Addie stuck at the air with her closed parasol. "But I didn't know you wanted Dooley's land."

"I didn't intend for you to."

They faced each other in angry challenge.

Unfortunately, at that precise moment, Lila could not hold back a giggle. The sight of Addie McCabe standing there, face red with anger and trembling from head to toe, was a joy to behold. Addie wasn't used to being bested by anybody, and Lila had just witnessed Clint taking the starch right out of her petticoats, to be sure.

But Lila's grin promptly faded as Addie withered her with a scathing look.

"Whore. Harlot. How dare you laugh at me?" Addie pointed the parasol. "And you—" She turned back to Clint, catching him unawares and whacking the side of his head with the parasol. "Even if I don't consider you a member of my family any longer, you could show some respect for your late father's good name by not acting like the whoremonger you are."

Clint was fast losing patience. He grabbed the irritating weapon away from her and hurled it out the open window. "I want you to get out of here, Addie. Now. We've nothing to say to each other."

"We'll see. This isn't over." She backed toward

the door, shaking her gloved fists at him. "If poor Jordan were able, he'd thrash you to within an inch of your life for daring talk to me this way. And you aren't getting away with stealing that land, either."

"Hell, Addie, you talked your cousin Olive into selling you Carlin's land when he got killed at Bull Run right after the war started. Isn't that enough for you?"

"My reason for wanting to own all the O'Neal land is my business, not yours."

"Well, you can forget about Dooley's. It's mine now."

"We'll just see about that. This isn't over. That land was meant to be mine, Clinton, and—"

He slammed the door in her face.

"Oh, my God, I don't believe any of this!" Lila shrieked, throwing her arms up in the air. "The nerve of that old biddy. What do you think she'll do next?"

"Go screaming to my half brother, I suppose."

"I feel so sorry for you. I mean, to have your whole family turn against you—"

"Forget it." Clint grinned down at her as he began to remove his clothes. "I believe we were in the middle of something."

Eagerly Lila opened her arms to him.

*   *   *

Addie stormed down the steps and out of the saloon, and anyone who saw her coming leaped out of her way. She retrieved her parasol, went to her buggy, and wasted no time in covering the short distance back to Pinetops.

When she walked into the bank, Matilda Warren, the one and only employee, dared not speak. She knew Addie McCabe well enough to know when it was best just to blend into the woodwork and not be noticed.

Addie flung open the door to Jordan's office without knocking and declared, "Something has to got to be done about Clinton."

Jordan took a deep breath of resignation and leaned back in his chair. He knew he would not like what he was about to hear. She had come to the bank earlier, right after leaving the courthouse in a frenzy. He had tried to talk her out of going to look for Clint, but she hadn't listened and gone storming out.

She threw herself onto a chair. "I found him upstairs over that bawdy house just outside town, with Ned Coley's girl, the one who turned out to be a whore. Disgraceful, absolutely disgraceful."

"About the land, Mother," Jordan prodded.

"He swears he's going to keep it. I offered him more than the taxes he paid, but he refused."

Jordan grimaced with annoyance. "I told you to let me handle it."

She waved away his protest. "I don't understand why he even wants it, why he wants to settle here. He knows people hate him for the traitor he is."

"I told you. He wants to get back at you for disinheriting him and kicking him out, but sooner or later he'll get bored and want to leave town. We can pick up the land then for a fair price. Till then, leave him alone. The more he knows he's agitating you, the longer he'll dig his heels in and stay."

Addie sprang to her feet and slapped her palms on the desk. "I don't want to wait. I want that land, I want it now, and I want him out of here."

"I know you do, Mother," Jordan said with forced patience. "And so do I. Dooley's place has one of the largest timber stands around, and people are desperate for lumber now, and I never thought we'd have any problem taking it over, but then I never thought Clint would be after it, too."

"I don't want to wait. I can't afford to wait. It will take a while to get cotton going again, and it's costing plenty to pay those Negroes to work the fields in the meantime, and you know it. And I've still got to give them food and a roof over their heads. Take care of them just like when they were slaves, only now they get paid ever' week.

"Damn it!" She straightened to turn away in agitation. "Why didn't the damn Yankees leave us alone? They've turned our world upside down, that's what they've done. And nothing is ever going to be the same. I'm going to have to work my fingers to the bone to keep what I've got and struggle to get more. I was never mean to my slaves. They lived good. I even took care of them during the war. It isn't fair that I still have to support them and pay them, too, and—"

"You could do like a lot of other plantation owners that have managed to hang on to their land. Let them sharecrop."

"I'll do no such thing. I'll never rent out my land. Not one inch, do you hear me? And that's not the issue here, anyway. It's Clinton, wanting revenge, and I want him to turn over Dooley's land, because that timber is worth a fortune."

"You made it through the war by having patience, Mother. You'll do it again."

"Patience, hell," she said with a snort. "I was smart, that's what I was. Do I have to remind you how I got my crop sold before the Yankees threw up a blockade, and how I made sure I got paid in gold and then hid it and pretended to be dirt poor? Just like I pretended loyalty to the Union? They believed me, the idiots, and even let me start up this bank, and that's why I'm rich today, when everybody around me is barely surviving. But I won't *be* rich," she cautioned with a final rap of her fists before straightening, "if I don't get my hands on more timber. I can make just so much money on cotton, and you know it.

"Maybe," she went on, musing aloud, "if we gave that little strumpet he's taken up with some money to get out of town, he'd go after her. From what I hear, he's spending most of his time with her. Maybe he fancies himself in love with her."

"I doubt that."

"Well, why wouldn't he? What girl from a decent family would want to get involved with a traitor?"

"I doubt he's really smitten with her, Mother."

Irritably she countered, "Unless you've got a better idea, I don't see why it wouldn't hurt to try."

He laughed. "And what happens if she takes the money I offer and leaves town, and Clint doesn't care and stays right here? We're out the money, and we still don't have the land."

Addie's eyes narrowed thoughtfully. "There are other ways. Maybe if someone talked to her, like—"

"No, just let me think about it," he urged. "Maybe I can come up with something."

"Well, while you're *thinking* about it, I'm going to *do* something about it."

"Mother, don't—"

But Addie McCabe had already left the office with a swish of her petticoats.

* * *

Dancy pointed the gun at the bottle sitting on the tree stump.

"Remember," Ben called, "squeeze the trigger. Don't pull it. You don't want a sudden movement to throw your aim off—"

His voice disappeared as Dancy fired off a round, methodically clipping the bottle a piece at a time as she aimed the bullets with precision.

"Got to show off, don't you?" Ben pretended to scold. "Can't do like I tell you to do."

She whirled about to give his cheek a loving pat. "But I do what you tell me, and that's why I am a good shot, Ben, and you know it."

"For a fact." He grinned, pleased with himself. "I've taught you all I know, and then some, I reckon, 'cause you're a damn sight better than I was in the cavalry. Wish we'd had you riding with us in the war. No telling how many Yankees you'd have picked off."

Dancy made no comment. The truth was, she doubted she would have sided with the South, for she did not hold to slavery. Dear Lord, it pained her to remember how close she felt to having been in bondage herself, the way her grandfather had so brutally dominated her. She could easily imagine how terrible it must have been for the slaves. And she had decided the best thing to do, since she was going to be living in the South, was to keep her opinions to herself as much as possible.

"I've learned a lot from you, Ben," she said finally. "And I'll always be grateful."

Ben knew she was dodging, as she always did, and he suspected she wasn't altogether Southern in her loyalty. Well, it didn't matter to him, but it still mattered to lots of folks. No matter that the war was over and the North had won; there was still plenty of hatred and bitterness all around. He only hoped she wasn't called on to say which way she would have leaned if she'd been around back then.

"Hope you know me and Adele appreciate your helping us out like you did." He checked the cinch strap and made ready to mount.

She hated to see him go. "Are you sure you don't want to ride on into Pinetops with me? I'd love for you to meet my uncle Dooley."

"Another time. I need to get on back. You can make it the rest of the way on your own. It's just over that ridge yonder, maybe an hour's ride. Heaven help anybody that gets in your way now, anyhow," he added with a chuckle and a wink, "the way you've learned to ride and shoot . . . . Though you look like a real fine lady in them duds Adele fixed you up with."

Dancy smoothed the skirt of the traveling outfit Adele had insisted she take. It was a bit warm, with a high neck, sleeves puffed at the shoulder and tapering to her wrists, but the color was lovely—a sky blue that went well with her hair, which she had braided beneath the bonnet she wore. She smiled to think how she presented a picture of true femininity—but rode with a loaded gun tucked in the folds of her skirt. Never again, she had vowed fiercely, would she be so helpless and vulnerable as the night those hoodlums robbed her.

"You got enough money?" Ben asked again. "Wish it could be more, but—"

"It's enough, and I thank you," she was quick to say, hurrying to throw her arms about his neck for a parting hug. "I can buy my lunch, and if for some reason I can't get up with Uncle Dooley today, I can stay the night at the hotel . . . if it's still standing," she added with a touch of worry.

"Probably will be. Folks in this section, I hear tell, bellied up pretty much to the Yankees, so they didn't get burned out."

"Uncle Dooley will see you get your money back and that you get paid for your horse, too."

"You don't worry about that. Just remember what Adele told you. Help somebody else. Pass kindness along instead of sending it back where it came from. Spreads farther that way and makes people treat each other a little nicer."

Dancy watched till he disappeared over a ridge, out of sight before swinging up on her horse.

Then, with a deep, excited breath, she headed, at long last, for home.

7

Jordan rolled his chair to the window. Thunder rumbled ominously beyond the ridges nestling the town, and the thick clouds overhead promised eventual downpour. He could see people scurrying about, anxious to finish their errands before rain turned the street into a muddy bog. Besides the bank, thanks to his mother's conniving, they also owned the only dry goods store in town. Then there was a small hotel with a restaurant, and Jordan grinned to think that if old Harold Hubert missed another payment on his note, the McCabe family would own that establishment as well.

It was a small town, and Jordan was proud of how it had survived the war unscathed. He supposed the Yankees hadn't found it worth bothering with. Young men like himself, had ridden off to war, while the older folks, including the banker, whose office he now occupied, had fled. Those who'd remained, like his mother, pretended to surrender. But not a one had been as cleverly deceiving as his mother.

Not only had she hidden her gold, but all the family valuables as well. After stashing everything away in secret caves in the ridges, when the Yankees had invaded to plunder she'd tearfully blamed foraging Rebel deserters for stripping the place.

For the remainder of the war she had become a recluse, never leaving the plantation, unobtrusive and humble. The occupying forces had left her alone, not even questioning why so many of her slaves declined to desert her. Of course, the Yankees did not know Addie had promised the Negroes she'd take care of them, as always, and since she'd never mistreated them, they'd stayed. So, through and by her scheming, she had not suffered as terribly as her neighbors.

But there had been lean times, Jordan recalled. At the end of the war, the immediate concern for white and black southerners alike had been survival. Because conflict and hostilities carried on into the spring of 1865, the beginning of planting season, there had been a dangerous shortage of food. Poor people of both races were starving all over, and only now, over a year later, were conditions starting to improve.

Jordan snorted with disgust at the sight of the dandyishly dressed men standing around outside the hotel. Carpetbaggers. No better than vultures. They moved in and either bought up land cheap for taxes owed or leased it, then hired freed slaves and began planting. If it weren't for them, the Negroes would take whatever the southern planters were willing to pay them to keep from starving, instead of demanding outrageous wages.

He shook his head as he thought of all the years of misery and carnage.

When the conflict first began, his mother had been determined to keep him out of it. She had paid someone to take his place and gotten hysterically angry when he'd marched off to fight anyway. He'd wanted to defend the South from the invading Yankees, by God. Besides, he couldn't bear the taunts of those who called him a coward.

As it turned out, he wasn't involved very long. A fall from a horse had sent him home in a wheelchair, and the army doctors had said it was doubtful he would ever walk again.

Drawn from his brooding, Jordan noticed how the carpetbaggers were intently watching a young woman heading toward the marshal's office. Even from a distance he could see she was quite lovely, and he wondered who she was. He knew everyone in town.

She disappeared inside the office, but he knew

she wouldn't be in there long. Frank Cox, the marshal, would already be out at Sweeney's saloon, drinking.

Sure enough, she reappeared promptly. Jordan sat up straight in his wheelchair, interested and alert.

Pausing to speak to the carpetbaggers, she then started walking toward the bank. Excited, he rolled himself to the door, maneuvered it open, and called to his clerk, "Matilda, there's a young lady on her way here. Send her in to me at once."

"Of course," Matilda Warren responded with a compassionate smile. So sad, she thought, how Mr. McCabe was interested in the ladies, despite being in a wheelchair. Seemed a waste of time to her.

The bell above the door jingled.

"Good morning," Dancy said brightly, unable to contain her excitement over her first day home. "I was told to come here to find out what I need to know. I went to the marshal's office, but there was nobody there."

Curiosity piqued, Matilda forgot all about Mr. McCabe's request. "Well, what is it you need?"

"I'm looking for my uncle." Dancy was almost shaking, she was so happy. "You see, I used to live here a long time ago, when I was just a little girl, and I can't remember the way out to his place."

Matilda prodded impatiently, "Well, what's his name?"

Jordan had rolled himself back behind his desk in anticipation of greeting a lovely new customer and was annoyed to hear the conversation outside. Matilda could be so nosy, damn it. He started for the door again.

Dancy announced, "Dooley O'Neal."

Matilda's eyes widened, and she sucked in her breath sharply. "Why, he was a—" was all she had time to say before Jordan appeared in the doorway to drown her out with his angry reminder.

"I told you to send her in here, Matilda . . ." And then his own voice faded, for the name he'd just heard struck a nerve at the same instant memories surfaced. Could it actually be, he wondered, and dared to hope, could the beauty standing there actually be she? "Dancy O'Neal," he whispered raggedly.

Dancy stared at the man in the wheelchair, wondering who he was. "Yes, that's me," she acknowledged, then ventured, "Do I know you?"

"Of course you do." He burst into delighted laughter and held out his hands to her. "Surely you remember me—Jordan McCabe. We played together when we were children."

It was Dancy's turn to be delighted, and she rushed to take his hands, then hugged him impulsively. "Of course I remember you. Oh, this is wonderful. I didn't think anyone would remember *me*."

He motioned her to follow him into his office. "I'm not surprised you didn't know me. I believe I was standing up the last time you saw me."

Dancy, sitting down, was washed with sympathy. "Jordan, I'm truly sorry."

He waved away her pity. "I get by very well, believe me. But let's not talk about me. I want to hear about you, where you've been all these years." He drank in the sight of her, unable to believe she had turned into such a radiant beauty.

Dancy was likewise struck. Skinny, scrawny Jordan McCabe had grown up to be quite handsome, but boyishly so. Immaculately dressed, manicured and polished, and a gentleman as well, she sensed, but then he had always been charming and polite.

"Well, I'm looking for my uncle Dooley," she began, then, seeing Jordan's reaction, asked sharply, "Is something wrong? First that woman outside practically faints at the name, and now you—"

"That will happen everywhere you mention him, I'm afraid," he informed her regretfully. "Dooley sided with the North. Fought as a Union soldier. People around here can't forgive that."

Dancy stiffened. She had not been involved in

the war and would not debate loyalties now. "I don't care about any of that, Jordan. All I want to know is where I can find him. I'm afraid I can't remember the way out to his place."

He knew of no easy way to tell her. "Dooley's dead. He was killed toward the end of the war."

"Dear God," she breathed, clutching her throat. She'd accepted the possibility, but to have it confirmed was a shock all the same.

"Clint brought his body back," Jordan went on, all the while devouring her with admiring eyes. "Folks didn't like it. They didn't want him buried in the graveyard with Confederate soldiers, but—"

"Clint," Dancy interrupted. "Your half brother. I remember him. He was always bedeviling me."

Jordan scowled. "Don't call him my brother. He's a turncoat. A traitor. He went off in gray and came back in blue, and my mother disowned him."

Dancy was too caught up in her own predicament to be interested in his family problems. With Dooley dead, she might have his land, but no family, unless . . . "My father," she dared venture. "Is he still alive?"

"I'm sorry," Jordan said. "He died early in the war. His widow moved away."

"His widow? I didn't know he'd remarried, but

then we never heard from him, anyway."

"He married my mother's cousin. Mother bought his land, and they opened a store. When she left, Mother bought that, too." Seeing the indecision on her face, he was prompted to inquire, "What will you do now, Dancy? With no family around, no place to go, you're all alone, and that's unfortunate.

"Let me help," he eagerly offered. "Stay with my mother and me till you decide what to do."

Incredulous, she told him, "But I don't have to decide anything. I know what I'm going to do. I'm going home."

Jordan felt hope slipping away. Now that she had come back into his life, he didn't want to let her go. Disappointed, he argued, "Oh, surely you can't go back to Ireland so soon, Dancy. Stay with us a while, and let's get to know each other all over again. If you only knew how I've thought about you all these years. I was terribly in love with you, you know," he added with a whimsical grin.

Ignoring personal banter, she informed him, "But I'm not talking about Ireland, Jordan. I'm talking about home. *My* home. Here."

He was jubilant. "Then you will stay with us."

"No. I'm trying to tell you, I have a home, and—"

He was confused. "I just told you, your father sold everything to my mother."

"But Uncle Dooley left all he had to me."

Jordan felt a glimmer of hope. If what she said was true, there might be a chance to recover the land from Clint. He could not be sure till he spoke with a lawyer, but he knew he would bear any expense to pursue the matter for her.

Dancy went on to explain, "He wrote a letter to my mother and told her if anything happened to him, he wanted me to have his land."

Trying to keep his hand from shaking, he held out his hand. "May I see the letter?" Then, seeing her instant look of dismay, he felt the first stabs of apprehension. "You *do* have it, don't you?"

"I'm sorry," she said, kneading her fingers together nervously, then told him how she had been robbed, losing the letter, her money, everything.

"But it doesn't matter," she added with finality, determination glowing in her eyes. "The land is mine. Uncle Dooley intended for me to have it. There are no other heirs. The courts will have to give me title."

Jordan was inclined to agree with her but not about to tell her what Clint had done. That would be his revenge on his traitorous half brother, to let him face the wrath of Dancy O'Neal when she learned someone else had laid claim to what she considered hers. "You're probably right," he said, swallowing his amusement to think of what a scene that would be. "But suppose you accept my invitation anyway, and come home and rest up a day or so."

"No. I'd like to ride out there now," she said stubbornly. "I've come a long way, Jordan, and I won't rest till I'm on my own land. Only then will I feel like I'm truly home."

He nodded as though he understood and sympathized, all the while thinking wistfully how nice it would be to settle her cozily into his house. That would be very convenient since he had just made up his mind he was going to marry her.

"Very well," he conceded gently. "What can I do to help?"

"I need directions."

"Of course you do." He opened a drawer, took out a sheet of paper, reached for a pen, and quickly drew a crude map. "It shouldn't be over a half hour's ride. At least let me take you by carriage. I can send for my driver, have him here in no time. I'd take you myself, but"—he gestured to the wheelchair—"fighting for what I believed in left its mark, I'm afraid."

Dancy felt pity but knew he would not wish her to express it, so she let it pass. Instead she thanked him but declined, explaining, "I have a horse tied outside, and I'd like to get started right away since it looks like it's going to pour down rain any minute."

"Do be careful, Dancy," he cautioned. "Poachers sometimes take over deserted cabins. I really don't feel good about you going out there by yourself, the way things are around here."

"I'll be fine." She took the map and slipped it into her purse. "I have a little money left, and I suppose I should stop by the dry goods store and buy a few supplies. I don't know what I'll find out there. Maybe the cabin isn't even standing," she added with a wry smile.

"Oh, it's there," he assured her, amused to think of what else she would find. It had been over a week since his mother's confrontation with Clint, and he had not been seen around town since. But Jordan had men who kept an eye on things and reported back to him, and he knew Clint was still living out there. Lila came and went at will, sometimes staying the night, and he'd started thinking perhaps his mother was right, that Clint just might be seriously involved with her, even if she was a prostitute.

Dancy rose, held out a gloved hand. "Thanks for offering your friendship, Jordan. When I get settled in, I'll have you out for supper, and you can fill me in on all the years I've been gone."

"And you can tell me what it was like living in Ireland all this time."

Dancy managed not to grimace. She had no intention of talking about the yesterdays in her life. All she cared about were the todays, and she was real anxious to get started on the one at hand.

She was about to open the door when he said, "Wait. You said you had a little money. If you won't accept my hospitality to stay at my house, I insist you let me help out in another way." He raised his voice to call out, "Matilda, will you come in here, please?"

When she appeared he instructed her to send word to Emmett Peabody that Dancy was to be given credit at the dry goods store. "And you can also open an account here with a hundred dollars to start. We'll draw loan papers later."

Matilda's brows shot up. Never had she known Mr. McCabe to be so benevolent. His mother was going to go right through the roof when she found out about it, and find out she would, because not much slipped by her.

"Miss Warren," Jordan prodded, annoyed at her hesitation. "I gave you orders."

Matilda rushed to obey.

Dancy was quick to protest, "Jordan, that's awfully nice of you, but I may not be able to repay you right away. I have to admit I'd thought of the possibility that Uncle Dooley might not be here when I arrived, so I made a few plans of my own for the land, but it will take some time to work them out."

"I have all the time in the world. Besides, I think you'll see when you ride out there that your uncle has one of the largest and finest stands of pine trees in middle Tennessee, and you'll get top price. Thanks to the Yankees, lumber is in desperate demand. You have a gold mine in those woods, believe me."

Dancy thanked him again and left. She had plans for the pines all right, but they did not include cutting them down.

Thanks to what Ben had told her, she now knew those trees could actually be worth more standing.

But for now, that was her secret.

Miss Warren returned with the money, then hurried to complete her assignment at the dry goods store. And by the time Dancy arrived, word had spread that Carlin O'Neal's daughter, and Dooley O'Neal's niece, had arrived in town, and dozens of people had gathered to stare.

Dancy, aware she was the center of attention, smiled to convey her friendliness but was met with suspicious glares. Surely, she argued with her pounding heart, they did not hold her accountable for her uncle having sided with their enemies. After all, if her father had been killed in battle, that made him something of a hero, didn't it?

No one offered to start a conversation, and Dancy was relieved. There would be time later for making acquaintances and renewing old ones. At the moment, she was anxious to get home.

Securing saddlebags, she mounted the horse and swiftly kicked him into a fast trot, for the skies were becoming more threatening with each passing moment. The map was easy to follow, for it was nearly a straight shot to Dooley's land, but there were a couple of near hidden turnoffs to be alert for.

Amazingly, even after so many years, Dancy began to recognize landmarks along the way. Passing the white clapboard church, with its cemetery to the side, she recalled that it was the last place she'd seen her uncle, the day of her baby brother's funeral. It was a strange feeling to think how, when there was time later to visit, she would find him there again.

As she crossed the wide, rushing stream and remembered the times she and Dooley had fished there, catching the wily trout right in their hands to toss up on the bank, her heart was pounding excitedly. She could almost hear his laughter in the wind as she recalled his hearty voice, laughing eyes, and how wonderful it felt to have his strong arms about her in a big, warm hug.

Tears of joy mingled with the raindrops splattering upon her face, as she turned at last into the path leading back into the deep woods and the little cabin concealed there. The air was sweetly pungent with the smell of the moist pine needles that carpeted the ground.

It was, she realized happily, exactly as she remembered it—a porch across the front, with a slanted roof over the one large room, a stone chimney at one end.

Just then, a fork of lightning split the sky. The horse froze, then reared up on its hind legs to paw the air in terror. If not for Ben's instructions, Dancy would have slid right off his rump, but, squeezing her knees tight and digging in her heels, she managed to stay in the saddle. "It's all right, boy." She patted him, dismounting quickly. "I know you don't want to be out in this storm any more than I do."

Holding tight to his reins, she ran to the barn, grateful it, too, was still standing. She unsaddled the horse, promised a rubdown later, then took the saddlebags and ran all the way back to the cabin. She made it to the porch just as the skies erupted and rain came down in torrents.

Out of breath, she opened the door and all but tumbled inside. Glancing about, she felt apprehension creeping to see it was not as she had expected—stripped bare and layered in dust and cobwebs. Not only were there furnishings—a bed and table and chairs—but everything looked clean. Wood was even stacked neatly in the fireplace, and staples were lined up neatly on the shelves in the cooking area. Obviously Jordan had been right about the problem of poachers. Well, she had a gun and knew how to use it, and if they returned, they'd have a surprise waiting.

Wearily, she put the bags on the table, then stripped out of her clothes. It was hot and humid, and she was exhausted. She padded across the wooden floor, slipped her gun under the pillow, then stretched out across the straw-filled mattress to rest a few moments before unpacking and settling in.

It was so good to be home at last, and for the first time in her whole life, Dancy felt free, both in body and in spirit.

She closed her eyes and fell instantly into an exhausted sleep.

Clint's stallion wasted no time in bolting through the barn doors the moment they were opened, anxious to escape the raging storm. Clint likewise did not tarry, did not see the strange horse inside as lightning flashed.

He ran all the way to the cabin, already soaked to the skin. Hunting up on the north ridge, he'd been on the trail of a large buck and dared hope he might beat the storm. But he'd lost on both gambles. The buck got away, and the rains came pelting down. With streams swollen, he'd had to take the long way home, and he figured it must be near to midnight.

Wearily he went into the cabin and peeled out of his wet clothes. He did not bother lighting a lantern; all he wanted was to climb into bed.

He groped for a towel, rubbed his bare skin dry, gave his long hair a few swipes, then, naked, headed for the bed. He was almost there when another white flash momentarily blew away the shadows.

And that was when he saw her.

She was lying on her stomach, sideways across the mattress, and he had but one glimpse of high, rounded buttocks, smooth and bare, before darkness descended once more. Lovemaking was not what he had in mind, weary as he was, but if Lila had come all the way out to surprise him, he sure as hell would not disappoint her. Evidently she had fallen asleep while waiting, but he didn't think she'd mind being awakened.

Smiling, he placed one hand on each side of her shoulders, then slowly lowered himself onto her naked body.

8

At the same instant Clint slipped his hands under her breasts and knew with a jolt that it wasn't Lila, Dancy awoke in panic to feel the weight of a body, *a man's body*, pressing down. She was further horrified to realize the body was very naked and something unfamiliar and hard was pressing against her buttocks.

Clint immediately started to lift himself up, and when Dancy felt him move, she twisted furiously and rolled out from under him.

Just then a flash of lightning lit up the cabin, and that was when Clint saw the glint of steel as Dancy lunged for the gun. Quickly he fell on top of her again, grabbing her wrists and squeezing tightly as he commanded, "Hold it, little lady. I don't mean you any harm."

Dancy struggled wildly, but futilely, as he held her in a viselike grip. "Then why are you attacking me, you bastard?" she demanded.

Despite the seriousness of the situation, Clint could not help laughing as he said, "Actually, I'm not. I'm just trying to keep you from shooting me."

"Which I will do," she assured him, "as soon as I get my hands on my gun."

Clint had no doubt she meant it and wasn't about to let her go till she calmed down. Maneuvering to hold her with one hand, he reached with his other to knock the weapon from the table to the floor and out of reach. Then, before she knew what was happening, he slung her up and over and onto her back, then stretched her arms above her head and held tightly as he attempted to reason with her. "Listen to me. I don't know who you are or what you're doing here, but I made a mistake. I thought you were someone else. Now start with telling me your name."

"I'll ask the questions, if you don't mind," she fired back at him. "Being as you're the poacher here, not me."

"Poacher?" he echoed, bemused. The storm was unleashing its full fury, and now the light was flashing almost constantly. He was afforded brief glimpses of her and liked what he saw, for despite her fury, he could see she was quite beautiful. And he could not resist quick glances of her body, as well, which was also a lovely sight to behold. It was no wonder he'd realized right away she wasn't Lila, for Lila's breasts were not so large, or firm, the nipples not quite so tipped and delectable.

Dancy saw how he was staring so boldly and struggled even harder to free herself. "Are you going to let me go? I swear, if you rape me, I'll kill you."

"Rape you? Not me." He laughed out loud, then wickedly decided to goad her further. "Actually, I'm the one who usually gets raped. I guess I just have that effect on women."

Her loathing increased with his arrogance. "Damn you to hell, if you don't let me go, I *will* kill you!"

"Not till you tell me what you're doing in my bed."

Dancy bristled. "You're forgetting one thing, mister. It's not *your* bed. It's *mine.*"

With an exasperated sigh he asked, "Woman, what are you talking about?"

She could hear the plea in his voice, how he sounded genuinely perplexed, and she ceased her struggles to stare up at him in the brief bursts of light. He certainly did not look like a hoodlum. In fact, from what she could tell, he was not unattractive. So, she thought, handsome or not, he was still a poacher, and probably an outlaw, and she wanted him out of there, because for the moment she was at his mercy. "Tell you what," she said finally, calmly, despite ire still boiling, "you just get your clothes on and back on out of here, and I won't reach for my gun till I hear that door close behind you. I know you're the one who's been poaching here, but I'll forget everything if you'll leave and not come back."

Clint admired her for her bravado, to be sure. He would never make it to the door before she shot him, and they both knew it. "Tell *you* what," he countered. "*I'll* keep the gun, and *you* get *your* clothes on and *you* leave . . .

"But I'm afraid *I* won't forget anything." He again raked her with insolent eyes as a flash of light lit the room.

"Damn you!" Dancy caught him off guard, managed to free one hand, and almost succeeded in slapping him, but he was quicker.

"This could go on all night," he pointed out, again restraining her. And, well aware of his erection, he murmured huskily, "And it's already getting a bit embarrassing."

Dancy felt her face flame and turned her head to the side, chest heaving with humiliation. "Damn you, you're torturing me and enjoying it."

"Actually, I'm torturing myself." After all, she was every bit a woman, and he'd never in his life felt so much like a man. With flesh touching flesh, it was all he could do to keep from taking her then and there. "Please . . ." He spoke the unfamiliar word, not used to begging anybody for anything. "Just tell me what this is all about."

Hoping to end the madness, speaking with feigned patience, as though endeavoring to communicate with a simpleton, she began, "My name is Dancy O'Neal, and this is my property. Left to me by my uncle Dooley, and—"

"Dancy," he said slowly, incredulously. "Well, I'll be damned."

Stunned, he relaxed his hold, and Dancy took advantage to bound off the bed in a flash. Dropping to the floor, she groped for the gun and brought it up swiftly to point it at him. "Now it's your turn to talk, mister."

"McCabe. Clint McCabe," he said in wonder as he sat up. "I remember you. You're Dooley's niece all right. We used to play together."

Though awareness dawned, she kept the weapon trained. "And I remember you, if you're who you say you are, but you're wrong. We didn't play together. You bedeviled me, and I hated you. And I'm not surprised you grew up to be a hooligan."

"And you were skinny and ugly, and you gave me my first black eye."

A faint smile teased the corners of her lips. "You deserved it, as I recall. You said you were going to drown my doll."

"You were stupid enough to believe I could."

Dancy fought to keep from laughing, not only at his jesting, but with relief that the terror had subsided. Apparently he was telling the truth and had mistaken her for someone else, but, with a jolt, Dancy suddenly remembered she was standing there naked. After laying the gun aside, she snatched up a blanket folded across the bottom of the bed and wrapped it about her. She could feel her face flaming.

Clint, likewise chagrined, also covered himself before suggesting, "Now maybe we can find out what this is all about and what you're doing here."

Sitting down on one of the chairs, getting as far from him as possible in the small cabin, she saw no reason not to tell him everything, leaving out the part about running away to keep from being forced to marry a man she loathed. That, she decided, was none of his business.

He listened in silence. Only when she got to the part about talking with Jordan did he feel the first waves of suspicion. "Did he send you out here after you told him you intended to claim the land?"

"Yes, he did. He even drew me a map, because I wasn't sure I could remember the way. He was very nice. He even loaned me money and arranged credit for me at the store."

"And what did he tell you about this place?"

"Nothing really. He sure didn't tell me you were staying here looking after things," she hastened to point out, "or I'd never have moved in without letting you know."

Clint was getting angrier by the minute, because it was obvious Jordan had deliberately not informed her *he* had paid the taxes and was now the owner. Jordan wanted her to feel like a fool, so she'd turn to him afterward, vulnerable and helpless, with nowhere to go. And according to what Lila confided hearing from some of the other girls, Jordan's inability to walk did not affect his capability to function as a man in bed, and from what Clint had seen of Dancy so far, any man in his right mind would want her.

As he thought about what he should do, he got up and found his trousers and put them on, then lit a lantern and turned to get a really good look at her. He was right: she had grown into an extremely lovely young woman, and, remembering how it had felt to lie close to her, he felt a rush of desire. Irritably he suggested, "How about if I turn my head and you get some clothes on? We need to talk about what to do with you, but it's distracting as hell knowing you don't have a damn thing on under that blanket."

Dancy didn't like the situation any more than he did. She went to pick up one of the saddlebags and fumbled inside for a muslin dress she'd rolled into a tiny ball, then hurriedly put it on. It was wrinkled, but at least, she told herself, she was covered.

Meanwhile Clint had kept his back turned, busying himself getting a small fire going in the grate, as well as a pot of coffee. When at last they were seated opposite each other at the tiny table, he began by suggesting she let him see she got back to town safely.

"Oh, no," she declined firmly. "I'm here to stay, Clint. I appreciate your looking after things, but—"

"Dancy, you don't understand," he cut her off as he ran agitated fingers through his hair. "You can't stay here."

"And why not? All of this is mine now."

Damn it, he cursed silently, he wasn't sure exactly what to tell her. She was a stubborn little filly. He'd seen that already. And if he told her he was now the legal owner, she'd never accept it. She would challenge, and Jordan would foot the bill. But he could not imagine the court being sympathetic to a woman wanting to take title to land away from a man, especially in a federal court and the owner in question a former Union officer. She didn't stand a chance, but he knew it would be a big mess. And, of course, Jordan would be waiting to console her when it was all over.

No, he told himself firmly, he would tell her nothing. Maybe when she got a taste of hard work, he could figure out a way to make her believe he was actually buying her out, give her enough money to start over somewhere else. It was the least he could do, he felt, out of respect for Dooley. And it wasn't likely Jordan would ride out to see what was going on, because he knew Clint would be waiting to chew him out for pulling such a trick.

Clint gingerly presented his hastily concocted plan. "You're going to need help, and frankly, Dancy, you should be well aware after what you've already been through that it isn't safe for a woman to be alone, especially way out here.

"Your uncle and I were close," he confided, "and I know he'd want me to look after you. How about letting me be your hired hand? There's plenty of work to be done, as you'll soon find out. I can stay in the barn."

Dancy found his offer inviting and also silently acknowledged that maybe she did owe him something. After all, if he hadn't been taking care of things, real poachers might have moved in and, God forbid, started cutting down the trees. "I can't pay you," she pointed out.

He shrugged, as though it were of no consequence. "I'll work for my keep. I've nowhere else to go. And I can get started cutting trees, and you'll have quick money."

"No. Absolutely not. Uncle Dooley loved those trees, and they won't be cut."

"But he wouldn't want you to starve. He'd tell you to sell off the trees, and you know it."

"Not if there's a way to make money without cutting them down."

"Like what?" he asked dubiously.

Dancy downed the last of her coffee. "We'll talk about it later."

"Then you'll let me stay on?"

Dancy hesitated. His offer was enticing, for she was well aware there was much work to be done, and a lot of it would have to be done by a man. Still, she felt strangely uneasy after what had transpired between them earlier. "I'm not sure," she said finally. "It might cause talk."

He scoffed at her fears. "I think folks are too busy trying to survive these days without worrying about what goes on way out here. Besides, it's only natural you'd have a hired hand.

"And again," he added, eyes twinkling, "I didn't mean to scare you. Like I said, it was a mistake."

Dancy saw how his mustache twitched, knew he was having a hard time keeping from bursting out laughing. "You haven't changed a bit, have you, Clint McCabe? You still enjoy bedeviling me, but if I do allow you to stay on, you'd best remember who's in charge here.

"And another thing," she hastened to add, "it's obvious the woman you were expecting didn't show up, and I suggest you get a message to her that she's no longer welcome."

"The barn will do nicely," he said with a wink.

Dancy's eyes narrowed. "I'm not having you entertain your women on my property. Do it somewhere else."

Clint doubted he would be thinking about Lila or any other female when Dancy O'Neal was around. "All right," he conceded, then decided to change the subject. "I know it's late, and we're both tired, but I'd really like to hear how you plan to get by without selling off any timber."

Proudly, confidently, she declared, "I'm going to produce turpentine."

"What do you know about turpentine?"

"Enough to know it's a good way to make a lot of money and not have to cut down the trees Uncle Dooley loved so much. The man who helped me after I was robbed told me all about it, how it's desperately needed for paint and medicinal purposes. They're discovering new uses for it every day. And with as many trees as there are here, I can make a real good living."

Clint was impressed. Turpentine production was something he hadn't thought about. He'd planned a small herd of cattle and maybe a few acres of tobacco. The rest of the vast acreage, thick with pines, would bring a good price for timber. But to be able to make decent money and still keep the trees, well, he had to admit Dooley would've liked to have it that way.

"Well, it just might work. Sure can't hurt to try."

Dancy absently made little circles on the table with the empty mug. Though exhausted, she realized she did not want the time with him to end just yet. Suddenly she blurted out, "All I've done is talk about my problems. I hear you've had some of your own."

"I did what I had to," he said easily. "Folks around here hate me for it."

"So why did you come back? Why didn't you settle up north?"

He laughed. "Just because I fought for the North doesn't mean I want to live up there. This is home. My home. And I don't intend for anybody to run me off."

"But your family . . ." she began, then realized she was meddling. "I'm sorry. I have no right—"

"Oh, that's all right." He was quick to put her at ease, then shared his gratitude for friendly conversation. "I might as well have been walking around with the pox all this time. There aren't many folks who will have anything to do with me. Not that I was surprised at my stepmother's reaction. She's always wanted an excuse to kick me out."

Dancy had not forgotten Addie McCabe. "I used to be terribly afraid of her, but she's obviously a very smart woman. Jordan says they made it through the war without losing everything they had."

"Addie was shrewd," he said blandly.

Dancy felt sorry for him. "Well, it must be terrible for you to come home to nothing."

"I came home alive, in one piece. Some didn't." Clint did not meet her sympathetic gaze, feeling just a trifle guilty to think she was actually the one who was destitute. But he would see to it, by God, that she would have the funds necessary, even if it meant hard times for himself in order to do so. The truth was, he felt sorry for her, and in further honesty, he found himself wondering how things might have developed between them under different circumstances, for he was undeniably drawn.

"Tell me about it," Dancy urged, hungry to know as much as possible. "Tell me everything. All about you and Uncle Dooley and the war."

He poured them both fresh mugs of coffee, then turned his chair around to straddle, arms resting on the back as he talked. He told her everything, the hows and whys of the terrible war as he understood it and why both he and Dooley had taken sides with the North.

He told her, too, of Dooley's death, and how, with his last, labored breaths he'd confessed to loving her mother all these years.

"And my grandfather kept them apart," Dancy said in mingled anger and bitterness. "Otherwise I think they'd have found a way to be together."

"Probably, but maybe it was best they didn't. If your father had ever found out his brother and his wife were in love with each other, somebody would have got hurt. Maybe killed. I think your mother knew that and wanted to avoid it."

"But what was his purpose in admitting everything to you as he died?" Dancy wanted to know. "Did he mention sending the last letter?"

Clint hated telling her he hadn't. "He just said he loved her, whispered her name a few times, and died."

"It happened the same way with my mother. She died with Dooley's name on her lips. Oh, dear Lord . . ." She blinked furiously against the tears filling her eyes. "So many lives ruined by deceit."

"It's late." Clint rose. He could tell Dancy was physically and emotionally drained. "The storm is over, and I'm going out to try to get a little sleep before starting work. You take it easy today."

Dancy walked with him to the door and assured him she'd be up bright and early, eager to start her new life.

Clint turned, and for an endless moment their gazes locked as they assessed one another. Finally, to break the uncomfortable silence, he gave a careless grin and said, "Well, thanks for not shooting me, Dancy. I'd hate to think I got through four years of war only to wind up getting killed by a woman."

"Well, thanks for backing off," she stated flatly, "or I'd have had to do just that."

With his shirt thrown casually over his shoulder, Clint laughed, turned on his heel, and disappeared into the early morning mist.

Dancy watched him go, feeling yet another warm rush at the sight of his broad, bare shoulders, the way the muscles rippled across his back. He was, she acknowledged, a very appealing man. She liked the way his smoldering brown eyes crinkled at the corners so mysteriously. And her first impression had been correct—he was handsome, in a rugged but appealing way.

Unlike Jordan, with his polished good looks, there was something almost feral about Clint McCabe, but deliciously so. Yet she had to remember there was obviously someone else in his life—the woman he'd mistaken her for—so she could not allow herself even to think of him in a romantic way. Yet even as she argued with herself, there was no denying that she actually felt a little stab of jealousy.

"Enough of this nonsense," she chided herself out loud, going back inside and closing the door. "The last thing I need is a man, especially one who used to be a bratty little boy I couldn't stand."

Yet as she curled up on the bed and felt herself drifting away, Dancy could not help but recall, wickedly and deliciously, how good it had felt when he had held her captive, if only for a little while. . . .

9

Dancy sat up and looked about the cabin wildly, trying to remember where she was. Then, with a smile, she remembered everything. Lying back against the pillows, she stared up at the rough crossbeams and reveled in being somewhere familiar. It was almost as if the hands of time had turned backward, and she was once more a child, about to spend a wonderful day with her beloved uncle Dooley.

But she was *not* a child, she reminded herself as thoughts of Clint McCabe and last night's incident came to mind, and she was wasting precious time. There was work to be done and lots of it, and most of all, this was the first day of her whole new life.

She bounded out of bed, filled with enthusiasm. There was a wash bucket next to the fireplace, and after freshening herself, Dancy brushed back her hair and tied it in a knot at the nape of her neck. The dress she'd slept in was even more mussed than when she'd put it on, but she had nothing else to wear except her traveling clothes, which were also in a sorry state.

Seeing a trunk, Dancy hurried to open it. Inside she found some of Dooley's old clothes. Big and baggy, they would still be more comfortable than the dress she was wearing.

After rolling up the sleeves and the legs of the trousers, she plopped an old straw hat on her head and hurried out, intending to go to the barn and wake up Clint. The sun was high in the sky, and she figured it was near noon, but she was starving. She had bought some fatback and eggs and would make them both a big, hearty breakfast before starting work, and— She stopped short. Blinking in surprise, she realized Clint was already up and working. She could see him out beyond the barn, where he was chopping away at a stump.

As she drew closer she could see that a lot of clearing had been done, trees cut down, other stumps removed. Before she had a chance to ask him what he thought he was doing, he glanced up, saw her, and waved cheerfully.

"About time you got up, sleepyhead," he called, swinging the ax mightily. "There's work to be done."

Trying not to look at his broad shoulders, the huge muscles in his arms, the way his trousers stretched across taut thighs, Dancy asked, "Why on earth have you been clearing out here? You haven't been selling off for timber, have you?"

"Not yet," he replied, continuing rhythmic blows with the ax. Wood chips were flying, striking his bare chest, flying through the air about his face, but he paid no mind. "What trees I've taken down, I've been stacking for wood this winter, but we've got enough now, and we can start selling."

"But I told you," she said, frustration mounting, "I don't intend to clear any of my land."

Clint felt the nerve in his jaw tighten. *Her* land. Damn Jordan, he swore silently, giving the ax another vicious swing. Why did it have to fall on him to be the one to tell her?

Managing to keep his tone even, he explained, "I want to get a small herd of cattle going, and they need grazing land. Once this is done, we can think about your turpentine idea."

"Cattle," Dancy said slowly, thinking it might be nice to have a few, for beef and for sale. "All right," she decided, "but we don't want many, so there's no need to clear out any more space than you already have."

Clint brought the ax down even harder as anger grew. He wanted three times more cleared than already was and knew he was going to have to speed things up and get rid of her if he was going to be ready for late grass planting before winter set in.

"Besides," she was saying, "we need to get started on the turpentine as soon as possible. But first let's eat breakfast. I'm starved. Didn't have any supper last night—"

"No time," he ground out between tightly clenched teeth. "I've been up for hours, and I could use a hand, so if you don't mind, let's work a while and then stop to eat."

Dancy's stomach gave a rolling groan of protest, and she started to tell him she'd run back to the cabin and grab a bite before joining him. But just then he stopped swinging the ax. Giving her a heavy-lidded glance of amusement, he taunted, "How do you expect to run a farm if you aren't willing to work, Dancy?"

"I do," she assured, "but—"

"But you're hungry, I know." He laughed softly. "Well, you go ahead. I guess it is too much to expect a woman to work on an empty stomach."

He started swinging again. Dancy stared at him for an instant before calling haughtily in challenge, "Just tell me what you want me to do."

He paused again, this time to gesture at the

cluttered field. "There are lots of branches out there that need to be dragged into a big pile for burning. Think you can manage while I work on breaking up the stumps?"

Dancy wrinkled her nose, thinking the battle-fields of war couldn't be a much bigger mess. She had seen none of it in the darkness last night, and if she had, she wouldn't have liked it. "I've got just one question," she said stiffly. "What made you think you had the right to just take over Dooley's land? I don't think we got around to discussing that last night."

"He would have wanted me to," Clint retorted a bit defensively. "And how did he know you'd ever get that letter, or, if you did, would even want it? Now are you going to work or not?"

Dancy began dragging the limbs. It was hard working in the sun, and she was soon drenched with perspiration and miserably swatting away pesky gnats and mosquitoes. But she knew Clint was watching and was determined to prove she had the necessary grit to work beside him.

An hour or more passed in silence, then, as Dancy passed by him dragging a particularly cumbersome limb, he was moved to remark, "Rough work. I'm sorry. I don't guess you've ever done anything like this. What do women do in Ireland, anyway? Cook and mend? The same things they do over here?" He was trying very hard to appear genuinely sympathetic and interested, instead of goading, which he was, of course, secretly doing.

"I don't know about other women," Dancy answered irritably. "All I ever did was scrub and clean my grandfather's house during the day and serve foul-mouthed drunkards in his tavern at night. Frankly, I'd rather be doing this."

He was struck to hear such bitterness in the voice of a woman so young. Still, he could not allow himself to feel sorry for her. The sooner she got fed up and wanted to move on, the better. "You'd probably like it farther north," he suggested carefully. "I spent a little time in Washington after the war. It's a nice place. You could probably have a nice little business running a boardinghouse, or maybe a little tea room."

She was almost to the rapidly growing pile of debris but suddenly let go of the limb to whip about and face him, hands on her hips. "Now where would I get the money to start up a boardinghouse or a tea room? And why would I want to when I've got all this?" She gestured wildly.

As she raised her hand, Clint saw the blood and quickly tossed aside the ax and hurried over. She tried to snatch her hands from his grasp, but his strong fingers wrapped around her wrists, forcing her palms to turn up. He winced at the scratches and blisters and cried, "Damn it, Dancy, why didn't you say something? You should've had on gloves. I didn't think—"

"Neither did I," she admitted. "I guess I was just being stubborn, trying to prove I can work as good as any man. Silly, wasn't it?" She looked up at him in chagrin.

"Come on, let's get you cleaned up." Clutching her elbow, he steered her from the field and back to the cabin, where he set her down on the porch and went inside for the water bucket and clean rags. All the while, he was fiercely reminding himself that this was what he wanted—to wear her down, make her miserable, make her suffer, so she'd leap at the offer he intended to make when the time was ripe and hightail it out of here. No matter that she was a fine-looking woman, and he liked to think how things might have worked out under different circumstances. Facts were facts. Middle Tennessee was no place for a female alone, especially with all the trouble brewing between vengeful southerners and freed blacks, not to mention the carpetbaggers and scalawags. Dancy could well be in danger if she stayed, because he had reason to believe things were only going to get worse. So he had no business feeling sorry for her. If this was what it took to get her out of here, so be it.

She watched in silence, wincing now and then but holding back cries of pain, as he gently bathed her wounds. Intent on proving her worth, Dancy had not noticed how bad her hands were getting. When he began to smear on a salve, she felt relief at once and asked Clint what it was.

"Pokeberry leaves boiled in flour, sweet oil, honey, and eggs. One of my father's slaves used to make it and taught me. I keep a batch around."

She was impressed and thanked him. When he had finished bandaging her hands with the rags, she held them up for inspection and said, "Well, I guess they'll be all right in a few days, and next time I'll know to wear gloves. Meanwhile, I'll just putter around the cabin, and—"

"Putter around the cabin?" Clint echoed incredulously. "Dancy, you can't make an invalid of yourself because of a few blisters. Those bandages are nice and thick. You should be able to finish clearing that field." He went to the door and turned expectantly. "Well, are you ready? Looks like another storm might be brewing, and we need to get as much done as we can."

Dancy knew he was right, but she was so weary,

and miserable. "Shouldn't we eat something first?" she suggested. "I'm terribly hungry—"

"Do what you want," he said, forcing impatience into his voice as he walked out, slamming the door behind him.

He did not have to glance back, for he knew she'd be on his heels.

The afternoon wore on. Clint kept telling himself he was doing the only thing he could do—wear her down and make her want to leave. Still, he did not feel good about it, because the more they were together, the more he was drawn to her. Not only was she pretty, she was also enjoyable company. They talked of anything and everything while toiling close together.

She told him about Ireland, how even though it was a beautiful country, green and fresh with an air of eternal spring, she'd never stopped longing to return to America.

And he shared with her more tales of the war, how it was something that had to happen to end man's inhumanity to man, but how glad he was it was over.

Eventually they began to speak of Dooley and his dying admission of love for Edana.

"You look just like her, you know," Clint remarked, "as best I can recall. Red hair. Green eyes. I remember my stepmother having a fit once when my father said something about how pretty she was. After that, he never dared even look in her direction if they passed on the street."

"I remember we used to call your stepmother a witch." Dancy giggled. She was having a wonderful time, despite the grueling work. "I can imagine you were happy to grow up and get away from her."

"I don't know," he said thoughtfully. "Somehow, no matter how mean she was to me, I managed to feel sorry for her. Never knew why. Still don't. There was just something about her that made me think maybe it wasn't all her fault she's like she is."

Dancy nodded, recalling Uncle Dooley had once said practically the same thing. "But why would you want to stay here after she turned you out of your own home? You speak of me going somewhere else to make a life. I ask you the same thing."

Clint felt himself tense. Damn it, none of this would have happened if Jordan just had told her the truth. Clint had paid the taxes, all nice and legal, and the land was his, and here he was, involved in a hoax that would only get more cruel if he didn't hurry up and get her out of there.

"I'm a man," he said bluntly, "and I belong here. You don't. If Dooley did want you to have his land, it was because he thought you'd bring your mother with you. He sure didn't expect you to come trailing all the way over here by yourself to be robbed and ravished. If he was alive, he'd be the first to tell you to hightail it out of here and go where it's safe."

They had taken a break for water and were standing in the cooling shade of the barn. Now they faced each other warily, anger fueled by exhaustion.

"You know what I think?" Dancy could hold back no longer. "I don't think you really had any intentions of farming this land. I think you were poaching, chopping down the trees a few at the time to sell."

Clint swallowed an angry retort. Arguing was not the way to get her to move on. Obviously he had succeeded in wearing her out, but not to the point that she was ready to give up. "Look," he began, "you're wrong, and—"

He fell silent, eyes widening as he stared beyond her.

Turning, Dancy discovered the reason for his shock—a young woman was standing next to the barn, watching them. Even from a distance, Dancy could see she was quite pretty—in a rather garish way. Flaxen hair trailed from beneath a feathery green bonnet, and the bodice of her bright gold satin gown dipped low, revealing deep cleavage.

Her cheeks were splotched with orange and her lips painted a bright cherry color.

Dancy knew, in that frozen moment, that she was staring at the woman Clint had anticipated finding in his bed. This provoked her to sudden and impatient anger. "I think the guest you were expecting last night has finally arrived. A bit late, don't you think?"

The woman, with a soft gasp and a mildly stricken look on her face, turned and pattered back toward her carriage.

Without a word, Clint headed in her direction.

Dancy watched and waited, knowing Clint would inform his visitor that she was no longer welcome to come and wait for him in bed. Their trysts would have to take place elsewhere.

Dancy told herself it was none of her business. Clint was a hired hand, nothing more. He could sleep with whomever he wanted to.

Yet even as she lectured herself, Dancy could not deny the searing waves of jealousy washing over her as she watched the two of them disappear inside the cabin.

They were not inside long, only a few moments. Then the woman left without even a glance in Dancy's direction.

Clint hurried back. "Sorry about that," he said almost flippantly.

Dancy made no comment, for all of a sudden she was afraid to speak for fear what she was feeling inside would be evident. Instead she shrugged as though it didn't matter at all and headed for the cabin.

Clint watched her thoughtfully as she walked away.

He'd had a devil of a time getting Lila to leave without explanation. She'd gone with him inside without a fuss but once there had blown sky high, demanding to know just who the hell Dancy was and what she was doing there. Clint wasn't about to explain right then; Lila knew the land was now his and just might get riled up enough to storm out and tell all. He couldn't risk it.

Besides, he hadn't realized just how serious things had got on Lila's part till he had a taste of her fury over finding him with another woman. No matter that the circumstances were anything but romantic. All Lila cared about was finding them together, and she didn't like it. They needed to talk, she had insisted, about a lot of things.

He'd promised to come into town later to talk about it, and he'd persuaded her to leave, but she was still mad.

* * *

Dancy could not remember ever being so tired. Work at the tavern had been hard but could not compare to hours in the broiling sun. All she wanted was to crawl into bed and sleep, but she knew Clint was probably as hungry as she was. Supper had to be made.

Potatoes and onions for a soup, she decided wearily, as she splashed water from the basin on her face. Maybe a few strips of fried bacon. Anything to fill them up. Later, when she became more used to toiling in the heat, she would cook more delectable dishes.

Remembering that she had seen bags of vegetables stored under the front steps, where it was cooler, Dancy went outside.

And that was when she saw Clint leaving.

She had turned toward the clip-clopping sound of a horse trotting down the road, picking up speed, and recognized the stallion she'd tussled with all day in the field.

She knew he could only be going into town to see that woman—and cursed herself for even caring.

Addie slammed her parasol across Jordan's desk so hard the inkwell turned over, spilling dark, thick liquid across the papers he'd been working on.

"Mother, please!" he yelped, wheeling himself backward, lest the mess trickle down on his trousers. "There's no need for you to act like this."

Addie was livid. "You knew the little brat was back, and you deliberately didn't tell me. I had to hear it from Emmett, and oh, how he enjoyed being the one to tell me Edana O'Neal's daughter had arrived. I felt like such a fool, with everyone watching and laughing behind my back.

"You already knew," she raged on, "but when I got back from Nashville last night, you deliberately didn't tell me!"

Jordan bit back the impulse to confide that if he'd had his way, she still wouldn't know, because when she had left town two days before Dancy showed up, she had planned to be away a week, visiting a cousin. He figured there would be plenty of time for Dancy to have a big fight with Clint and come running to him for help. Even when his mother had returned unexpectedly last night, he'd dared to hope Dancy would be storming into his office first thing this morning, giving him a chance to get things started with her before his mother found out.

She slammed down the parasol again, and Jordan yelled, "Mother, will you stop it, please? I was going to tell you, but it slipped my mind."

"You're lying. Something like that couldn't *slip* your *mind*," she mimicked, making a face, "and you know it. Now where is she? I intend to find out what she's doing back here, because she needn't think she's going to claim my store or anything else her father once owned. And where's her mother? Edana would never have let her come alone."

"She's dead." He went on to reveal all he knew, knowing there was no reason to hold anything back any longer.

Addie sank onto the nearest chair to listen, and when he'd finished, she demanded, "Well, why didn't you tell her Clint has claimed the land by paying the taxes? Why did you send her out there? Why didn't you just give her the money to go back where she came from? She has no business being here."

He spread his hands in a helpless gesture. "She's stubborn. She believes the land is hers, and nothing I could have said would have made any difference. I figured the best thing to do was let her find out for herself, and after Clint got through making her look like a fool, she'd realize she has no choice but to leave."

Addie stood and drew a sharp breath of resolution as she glared at him with eyes narrowed, pointing the parasol menacingly. "Well, that was yesterday, and your stupid plan obviously hasn't worked, so I'll just ride out first thing tomorrow morning and find out what's going on and then see to it she realizes she's wasting her time trying to claim anything an O'Neal ever owned in this county."

Desperately he called after her, "Mother, wait—"

But Addie was already through the door, slamming it behind her in finality.

10

When Dancy went to the barn to awaken Clint and found he wasn't there, she thought perhaps he'd risen earlier, as he had the day before, and was already up and about. But when there was no sign of him anywhere, she decided he'd stayed out all night and told herself the only reason she was angry was that they had made a bargain. If he was going to be her hired hand, she expected him to be at work every single morning, regardless of his personal life, and when he showed up she intended to tell him so in no uncertain terms.

Irritable and lost in thought, Dancy did not see the carriage until she was almost back to the cabin. Preoccupied, she hadn't heard anyone coming up the road. Deciding it could only be Jordan, she quickened her pace, happy that he had, no doubt, had someone bring him out to see how she was getting along. She knew she was going to have to ask for a substantial loan to get her plans for turpentine production under way, and she intended to accept his generous offer of help. When she had been in his office, she'd been too overwhelmed at all she was hearing to explain her financial plight.

But as Dancy drew closer and realized that no one was in the carriage and that the cabin door was standing open, she knew that her visitor was not Jordan. Jordan was crippled and would not have been able to get down by himself. With apprehension creeping, she approached the cabin steps, glad she'd got in the habit of strapping on her holster whenever she ventured out. Slowly she drew her gun.

Addie McCabe stepped onto the porch to find herself looking down the barrel of a gun. Glancing from it to Dancy, she snapped, "Oh, put that thing away before you hurt somebody, girl." Cocking her head to one side, she sneered, "I might have known you'd grow up to be the sort to tote a gun like a man."

Dancy thought the woman looked like a bantam rooster, with the bright yellow and white feathers of her bonnet swishing to one side of her face. There was something vaguely familiar about her, and as Dancy returned the gun to its holster, recognition dawned. "Addie McCabe," she said in wonder. "You have to be Addie McCabe. I remember you."

"Little ruffian. All grown up to be a big ruffian. How dare you come here and besmirch the good name of my late cousin-in-law?"

"Cousin-in-law?" Dancy had no idea what she was talking about.

"After your mother ran off like she did, your father came to his senses and married the woman he should have married in the first place—my cousin Olive. That made him my cousin by marriage, and I'll not have you come into this community and bring shame on my kin."

"Shame? Ma'am, I don't understand."

Addie's eyes narrowed. "Don't pretend with me, you little hussy. I know you've moved in here with my stepson, and you're living in sin, and I tell you one thing"—she shook her fist for emphasis—"the good Christian folk of Pinetops won't tolerate such wanton misbehavior.

"Now where is Clinton?" Addie looked around wildly, as though expecting to see him lurking about somewhere. "I'm going to tell him a thing or two. It's bad enough he had the nerve to even come back here, without flaunting blatant sin in my face and everyone else's in this Christian community."

Dancy nervously attempted to pacify the woman. "You don't understand. You've got it all wrong. Clint agreed to stay on and work for me because he's got no place else to go. He sleeps in the barn, and I sleep here. We aren't doing anything wrong, I promise you."

"*Works* for you?" Addie said contemptuously. "As much as he wanted this land there is no way he'd give in to you without a fight in court, much less agree to work for you. That's the most ridiculous thing I've ever heard."

Dancy had to laugh. "Now why on earth would Clint want to fight me in court? He was only staying here because you kicked him out of his own home, and he had nowhere else to go, and he knew Uncle Dooley would want him looking out for things till I could get here. So, he was glad to stay on as my hired hand," she added with a confident lift of her chin. "Now when he comes back, I'm sure he'll tell you the same thing. But I'm not sure where he is at the moment, because when I went out to the barn to wake him up this morning, he wasn't there. I promise you when I do see him, I'll send him into town so he can tell you the same thing I have, that he's working for me now, and there is absolutely nothing improper going on between us. And there will be other workers moving onto the land as soon as I'm able to provide some kind of housing for them."

"Other workers?" Addie asked, "What kind of workers?"

Dancy wished with all her heart this confrontation had never happened. She did not want hostility and hard feelings with Jordan's mother, because she might just convince him not to grant a loan. Attempting to smooth things over, she offered, "I've got some plans, Miss Addie. Perhaps I could stop by your house and talk to you about them sometime—"

"I'll not be entertaining the likes of you," Addie interrupted coldly, "and you needn't be sending Clinton to call, either. I've nothing to say to him, nothing at all. You can relay my message that I think it's a disgrace that he's allowed you to move in with him, and he's only making things worse on himself with such reckless behavior."

"I told you"—Dancy tried wearily once more to make her understand—"Clint sleeps in the barn."

Addie stomped down the steps and hoisted herself up into the carriage before turning to say frostily, "You insult my intelligence, Dancy O'Neal, if you think for one minute I don't have sense enough to know what's going on out here. There is no way Clinton would just hand this land over to you because you happened to show up and claim it was left to you by Dooley McCabe. He connived and schemed to make sure he got the taxes paid only hours before he knew I intended to, because he knew I wanted this land. It was his way of getting back at me for refusing to welcome him home with open arms after he betrayed his people."

Addie was about to leave, but Dancy stopped her by grabbing the harness of the horse closest to her. "What are you talking about?"

"How dare you grab my horse!" Addie snatched up her parasol and started swinging, but she couldn't reach Dancy. "I'm warning you, you little hellion. Get out of my way. You're only making more trouble for yourself."

"Not till you tell me what you're talking about when you say Clint took this land away from you."

"I didn't say he took it away from me. I said he stole it from under my nose, and he did. Ask Jordan. He knows how Clinton was ready the minute the collector's doors opened the day the records were all back in place and folks could start paying their taxes. He rushed in and paid up to keep me from getting it."

Somehow Dancy knew Addie had not come so far out of the way to make up such a lie. It was also starting to dawn on her why Clint had taken it on himself to start clearing land and making plans for the future.

"Let me get this straight," Dancy said slowly, evenly. "Clint owns this property? Free and clear?"

"He certainly does."

"Jordan didn't tell me any of this."

"He probably thought it wasn't his place to," Addie snapped.

Dancy reasoned that perhaps Jordan remembered her for the stubborn little girl she'd been and realized it was best she ride out and discover the situation herself. But by loaning her money, he had made sure she would know that he was waiting and ready to help her. It was also his way of letting her know he was her friend.

"Give me those reins," Addie said tightly, holding out one hand while still waving the parasol in threat.

Dancy handed them over and stepped back.

"You little fool," Addie cried just before sending the horses into a fast trot. "Clinton was using you like he used that strumpet, Lila Coley. When he got tired of you, he'd have run you off like he did her. I hear the marshal had to go over to that bawdy house where she works yesterday evening, because she was all riled up and throwing whiskey bottles at him.

"You'd best pack up and go back where you came from," Addie called. "Just like your mother, you don't belong here."

As Dancy watched the horses galloping away, white hot fury was spreading from head to toe.

Damn Clint McCabe, she fumed with fists

clenching at her sides. He had made a fool out of her, and the whole county knew it.

But no more, she vowed, breaking into a run toward the barn. Clint would learn quick enough she'd fight him tooth and nail for possession of what was rightfully hers. And once he found that out, she was going to see Jordan and enlist his help. Surely Jordan would loan her the money to pay off Clint and get him out of the way. Later she'd go see Addie McCabe and, somehow, find a way to make peace.

But first she had to saddle her horse and find Clint, and then, by God, he'd see who got the last laugh.

Clint loaded the last of the fallen pines onto the wagon. The night of the big storm, the night he'd mistaken Dancy for Lila, he'd heard lightning strike on the ridge. Sure enough, he'd been right; a big tree had gone down, taking a few smaller ones with it, perfect sizes for fence railings. All he had to do was chop off the branches and skin off the bark.

Pulling his hat lower in an attempt to shield his face from the merciless sun, he reflected that the job wouldn't have been quite so rough if he'd had a decent night's sleep. But after the scene with Lila, he couldn't relax. Not wanting to drown his misery in drink, he'd got into a poker game at Sweeney's, once the law cleared out, and wound up playing till dawn. So here he was, bleary-eyed and exhausted, with nearly a day's work ahead.

He touched a fingertip to his forehead, beneath the shock of dark hair tumbling down, and winced slightly with pain. The cut wasn't deep, but it was sore as hell. Lila had really bashed him a good one when she'd caught him off guard with that first bottle she'd thrown.

He supposed he'd been a pretty big fool to think she wouldn't be rip-roaring mad to ride out and find another woman around, and an even bigger idiot to think he could explain it all and she would understand. It was later, after the marshal had come and gotten her calmed down by threatening to put her in jail, that Clint discovered it was more than just jealousy. Lila had thrown herself in his arms, collapsing in tears as she confessed to falling in love.

Clint felt bad about that, because the last thing he wanted was to hurt her. He'd told her all that again, and she said she understood, assuring him he'd made it clear from the beginning that he thought a lot of her but love was not on his mind. She apologized and told Sweeney she'd pay for the damages, but Clint had said hell, no, the least he could do was take care of it for her. So Lila had finally gone about her business, or pretended to, and the last Clint saw of her, she was getting back to work, leading somebody up the back steps to her room.

She would be all right, Clint had finally decided, and it was all probably for the best. For the time being he had only one thing on his mind, and that was getting rid of Dancy.

According to all he'd heard, hell was going to bust wide open real soon. Rumors were flying about a secret organization being started up by former Confederate officers and soldiers, in an effort to maintain white supremacy. The Union officer telling him about it had confided the federal government was concerned over the recent attacks and raids, fearing they weren't merely a continuation of the guerrilla groups that had managed to wreak so much havoc since the war ended but were, instead, planned acts to frighten and intimidate.

Clint recalled an incident in another county two weeks earlier, when a former slave had been found badly beaten. Terrified, he had claimed the ghosts of dead Confederate soldiers were responsible. They had warned him, he said, to abandon the little farm he'd managed to buy for delinquent taxes, or they would return and kill him. The Union officer who'd related the story to Clint had laughed about the ex-slave claiming to see ghosts bearing down on him, but Clint didn't find it amusing at all. He knew most of the Negroes were superstitious, and he suspected that some very alive ex-soldiers were donning ghostly costumes to stimulate those fears.

So he had decided to go ahead and tell Dancy the truth. Perhaps he would be able to make her understand that while Dooley might have intended for her to have the land, it just hadn't worked out that way.

He turned the wagon around and started for home. Once it was over with, he planned to pay a visit to his half brother and let him know what he thought of his cruel prank. They had never gotten along, and the situation had worsened since the war—and Clint was not entirely convinced it was caused by his switching uniforms. Jordan had changed. True, he could not walk, and Clint allowed as to how that had to be an awful way to have to live. But after Addie had set Jordan up to run the bank, he'd turned into a real tyrant. According to the gossip Clint picked up at Sweeney's, the only place any of the locals would talk to him, and then only because they'd had a few drinks and forgot to hate him for the moment, it was said Jordan seemed to delight in the misery and desperation of people he'd known all his life.

Clint figured Jordan and Addie made a good pair, because they were sure two of a kind. Both wanted money and power and would stop at nothing to get it.

But, Clint was proud to know, he had managed to best them for once in his life.

He had just topped the ridge when he saw Dancy coming, riding hard. Absently he wondered where she'd learned to handle a horse like that, riding astraddle and bareback, in total control as she leaped over a ditch with ease. She reminded him of cavalrymen in the war, charging hard and fearless.

Then, as she drew closer, he could see the furious look on her face. He brought the cart to a stop.

"Dancy, what—"

It was all he had time to say before she came to such an abrupt halt that her horse reared up on his hind legs, pawing the air furiously in protest before dropping to stamp and snort, restless to run again.

"How much, you conniving bastard?" she asked through gritted teeth.

"How much what?" He had an idea what she was getting at but dared hope he was wrong.

"How much did you pay for the delinquent taxes? And don't pretend you don't know what I'm talking about. Your stepmother was just here, mad as thunder and accusing me of moving in with you to live in sin. She was only too happy to tell me what a fool I've been.

"I don't know what your motive was, and I don't care," she continued hotly, "and if you won't tell me how much I owe you, then I'll go to the tax collector and ask him, and I'll see you get paid."

"I don't want your money, Dancy," he told her. "Now if you'll listen, I'll try to explain everything—"

"What is there to explain? It's quite obvious you enjoyed making a fool of me, trying to work me to death in hopes I'd give up and go away. You didn't plan to tell me, did you? You were hoping to steal this place from me."

He mustered every grain of patience he possessed. "It's not yours, Dancy. It's mine. But it could have been anybody's who came along to pay the taxes. Addie. Jordan. A carpetbagger.

"As for trying to make you give up and go away, yes," he admitted, "I'd hoped it would work out that way to keep from having to hurt you with the truth after Jordan sent you out here without telling you how it was. But I had decided I'd have to level with you and was on my way right now to do just that."

Dancy hooted. "You expect me to believe that?"

"You don't have the proof anymore, but you expect *me* to believe Dooley left everything to you."

"That's right." She gave a curt nod. "And right now I believe I'd like for you to clear off my land."

Clint could see by the determined gleam in her eyes that there was no way he could convince her she didn't belong here. But he had to try. "First, you're going to listen to something you've got to know, Dancy," and he proceeded to tell her of all the dangers abounding, reminding her that even though the war was officially over, there were still those who would carry it on in other ways, and she could find herself in the middle of it all.

"I'll help you get settled somewhere else," he finished. "I don't have a lot of money, but what I've got is yours."

"Oh, you're so generous, Clint McCabe. How could I think for even one minute you'd changed? You're still a hooligan, and you always will be.

"And now it's *my* turn to tell *you* something." She poked his chest with her finger for emphasis. "I didn't come all the way over here from the other side of the ocean to claim my inheritance only to have you steal it away from me. I intend to fight for what's mine, if need be."

"You can't do it alone. You've got to have help."

"Jordan will help me."

"Sure he will." Clint laughed. "He'll help you all right, straight into his bed, but that's all. Addie owns the bank, just like she owns Jordan. And she also wants this land as much as you do."

Dancy swung her head from side to side, hands on her hips, feet apart in a stance of defiance and determination. "I'm not going to listen to any more of your lies, Clint. Just get your things and get out of here, and I'll see to it you get your money."

"I already told you, I don't want the money. What I want is for you to let me help you make a life somewhere else."

"I'm not going anywhere."

Their eyes met and held in challenge, and in that prolonged moment of silence, Clint knew Dancy O'Neal had to be the most bullheaded woman he'd met in his whole life. "All right," he said finally, "I reckon the only thing to do is let you find out how things are for yourself. But the land stays in my name, because I'll be waiting for you to hightail it out of here."

"Hell will freeze over," she was quick to say.

"We'll see. And for Dooley's sake, I'll try to keep you from getting in too much trouble."

"You just stay out of my way," she warned. "Maybe," she added, preparing to mount her horse, "Lila will let you move in with her."

So, he thought, smiling to himself, Addie had said something to her about Lila, because he sure hadn't mentioned her name. "Oh, you don't have to worry about her," he said. "She got so mad when she found out about you, you'd have thought I tried to drown her dolly."

Furious, Dancy whirled and cried, "Clint, you—"

He silenced her with his mouth, reaching out to grab and crush her against him in a searing kiss.

For one frozen instant, Dancy was caught off guard and helplessly lost in the whirling, swirling madness of delicious passion ignited as he held her tight. So dazed was she by the wonder of it all that she could only yield to his seeking tongue, melding against her own. Slowly his lips moved, as though gently devouring her.

It was only when his hands began to move over her back, sliding down to cup her buttocks and press against his warning hardness that Dancy came out of her stupor. Placing her palms against his chest, she pushed hard, struggling to free herself. "Damn you, let me go."

With a soft chuckle, he released her. "No black eye this time?"

Dancy did not respond immediately, but hoisted herself up on the horse. Despite everything, there was no denying Clint was indeed the legal owner of the land and had every right to send her away. And even though he was magnanimously leaving himself, she knew he was confident she'd soon give up and accept his offer. But underneath it all, she also had to admit she was shaken by his kiss, shaken by him. Even though she dared not let him know it, Dancy felt inexplicably drawn to him—but she would fight it with everything she had.

Finally, suppressing the nervous flutter still coursing through her body, Dancy faced him. "No black eye," she said evenly. "Just stay out of my way, Clint."

"Sure you don't want me to work for you?"

"I'll find someone else, and"—she pointed to the wagon—"you can just unhitch your horse and ride on. I'll take care of those."

"No, I'll finish what I started," he said, then looked her straight in the eye. "Believe me, Dancy, I always do."

11

Sleep eluded Dancy as she tossed and turned, plagued with uneasiness.

When she'd first arrived in Pinetops, she had been far too buoyed by happiness over being home to worry about anything else. Now, however, it seemed she'd been hit with both barrels of a misery-loaded shotgun.

And to add to her problems, she had to admit she'd never felt so alone in her whole life. Still, she was not sorry she had come back, and fervently, angrily, she vowed nothing would drive her away. It would be difficult, but she was not afraid of hard work. It was all she'd ever known.

Her thoughts drifted to her mother and those rare and precious moments when she would take Dancy by her hand and slip away to stand at the edge of the sea. "It's dreaming time, Dancy," she would say, and stare out toward the horizon where water meets sky in a blending to infinity. And while she would appear about to cry, Dancy knew it was not the glimmer of unshed tears she saw in her mother's eyes, but the mist of memories—sad memories.

But what struck Dancy so perversely there, in the middle of that still and lonesome night, was the awareness that she had seen the same look that morning in Addie McCabe's eyes. Despite the anger, there had definitely been the mist of unhappy memories. And, as she'd done as a child, Dancy found herself wondering just why Miss Addie seemed to despise both her mother and Uncle Dooley. Could be that Addie had been in love with Dooley long ago, and he'd hurt her terribly? But if that were so, Dancy figured it was time Addie quit carrying a grudge. Maybe she would just help her realize that fact.

As for Mr. Clinton McCabe, Dancy brooded, he had made her feel ridiculous in more ways than one. Oh, how could she have been so gullible as to think he could ever change? Truly, it was best she had chased him away, and now it was time to pay Jordan a visit and ask for that loan he had promised. Maybe he could even think of a way to get rid of Clint legally.

Finally she drifted away, and the next thing she knew someone was pounding on her door.

Groggily she sat up and realized it was morning, at the same instant she recognized Clint's voice.

"Dancy, don't make me come in there and drag you out of that bed. There's work to be done."

She got up and opened the door with an irritable yank. "What are you doing here?"

He was leaning against a post, dark eyes merrily crinkled so they looked almost closed as he grinned down at her. "I thought maybe after a good night's sleep you'd see it's best for both of us if we make peace."

"I'll not make peace with a traitor and a liar."

He shrugged. "I guess being called a traitor is something I've got to get used to around here, but you can't call me a liar. What did I lie about? You didn't ask me if I owned the place."

"You don't," she was quick to decry, "and you've got no business being here."

"Yes, I do." He sat down on the top step, facing away from her.

Dazed by his boldness and not wanting to talk to him with his back turned, Dancy hurried down the steps to face him with arms folded across her chest. She was wearing one of Dooley's old nightshirts, and it was way too big and made of some scratchy kind of material that was terribly uncomfortable, but it was all she had till she could get into town and buy something else. At the moment she didn't care what she looked like anyway. "Now wait a minute. I want you out of here—"

"Why?" He turned and looked her straight in the eye. "You need my help, and I need a job."

With a sweep of her arm, she reminded him coldly, "But you think all this belongs to you. I'm surprised you aren't wanting *me* to go to work for *you*."

Clint took a deep breath of resolve. He'd been up most of the night trying to figure out a way to ease the tension between them so he could be around to keep an eye on her till she did move on. "Well," he began, "I've thought about it and decided maybe you're right. Maybe you should have the place. After all, Dooley knew he didn't have long, and he used up his last breath to admit how he'd always been in love with your mother. He never got around to telling me about that letter. But, thinking back to what all he said about her, I've decided it stands to reason he'd want her daughter to have everything.

"I'm willing to go along with that," he conceded, "but the deed stays in my name till you prove yourself."

Emerald eyes flashed with ruby flames of resentment. "That's not fair."

"You don't have any choice," he pointed out bluntly. "That way, if you borrow from Jordan, he won't have a mortgage to foreclose on if you can't pay him back."

Dancy said coolly, "I don't intend to fail, Clint."

"Then what are you worried about? If you succeed, I give you my word I'll sign over title and ride out of your life. If you fail, you admit it and ride out of mine."

"You sure you won't be trying your best to make sure I do?" she asked warily.

He looked at her for a moment, framing his answer carefully. He wasn't about to let her know what he was starting to feel for her, how he didn't like to think of her riding out of his life. With a lazy grin he said, "Of course not, because I intend to hang around and help all I can. You see, part of the deal is, you've got to let me work for you. Agreed?"

He held out his hand.

After a moment, Dancy shook it, all the while chiding herself for the thrilling rush of relief she felt over his return. But it had to be strictly business, she told her once again pounding heart. Clint McCabe was not the sort she could allow herself to fall in love with.

"One more thing," she said tightly. "No more of what happened yesterday."

Dancy found his smile beguiling as he murmured, "Well, to tell the truth, I wanted to do that when we were kids, but I was afraid you'd blacken both my eyes."

"I still might," she snapped. "We've got a business arrangement. Nothing more."

He got to his feet. "Well, if you'll get your work clothes on, Miss Dancy, I could use some help clearing that pasture. We might be able to finish today."

A short while later Dancy was beside him, and the morning sped by as tension eased and they were able to enjoy talking about their childhood days and everything in between. Dancy was eager to hear anything about her uncle and felt the familiar twinge of guilt to have only mild interest in her father.

Clint also confided some of his reasons for changing sides in the war, explaining how when he'd been working as a guard at the infamous Libby Prison in Richmond, Dooley was one of the prisoners. It had been time spent with Dooley that had really changed his way of thinking, and finally he'd helped Dooley escape and the two of them had ridden north, inseparable till the day Dooley was killed.

While they ate lunch at midday, Dancy brought up the subject of gathering sap for turpentine. "Ben told me it runs high mostly in the spring, but since we're late getting started this year, we'll have to depend on hot weather to bring it out. All we do is make a diagonal slit down through the bark and then hang a bucket beneath it for the sap to run into till it clots. Then we boil it and let the impurities settle, and what's left on the top is turpentine.

"There's going to be a big demand for it," she went on enthusiastically, "but I'm going to have to hire a lot of workers to help out."

Clint told her she might have a problem. "You can't pay the kind of wages the railroad can, and you may have trouble finding workers."

"Not among the freedmen. Ben says they're desperate for work and willing to do just about anything. All I need is a stake to get me going and put up a few cabins for my workers, and in no time at all, I'll have my operation going."

Hesitantly Clint pointed out, "There are folks who won't take kindly to your hiring Negroes, Dancy, not when there are whites who need work."

She looked at him in surprise. "You just got through saying I'd have trouble finding white workers because I can't compete with railroad wages."

With a frown he agreed with the irony of the situation. "You'll have to come up with the money to hire whites."

Tightly she informed him, "I'll pay a fair wage, and it doesn't matter to me what color the skin of the man willing to work for it."

Clint knew there was no point in arguing and said they'd best be getting back to the field if they wanted to finish before sundown.

"I'll ride into town tomorrow and talk to Jordan," she said as they walked along together. "I also want to pay a visit to your stepmother and convince her she's wrong in her thinking about us."

Clint laughed. "Nobody has ever been able to convince Addie of anything. It's usually the other way around, because folks would rather agree with her than argue."

"We'll see. I intend to make lots of folks around here see they're wrong about me."

Clint picked up the ax and began swinging, his strokes almost vicious.

Sometime later, Dancy, a mischievous twinkle in her eyes, probed, "What about your lady friend, Clint? Won't she have something to say about your working for me, especially since she got so mad to find me out here?"

"She won't say anything," he assured her quietly, then changed the subject. He didn't want to talk about Lila.

Dancy thought it strange that he got so moody after she mentioned Lila Coley but told herself she had no business bringing her up anyway. Wanting to end the sudden tension, she remarked, "Well, it's nice you could come here when you got home. A ready-made cabin, and all."

His laugh was bitter. "I didn't go straight to Addie's expecting a clean bed and a home-cooked meal, Dancy. Fact is, before the war, I'd just about moved out. I'd either stay with Dooley or camp out at Honey Mountain. That's where I spent last night, as a matter of fact."

"Then you know about the secret place?"

"Oh, yes, Dooley showed me."

Dancy mused aloud, "I wonder if that's where he and my mother had their rendezvous. It would be the perfect spot, because nobody realizes there's a cave running all the way through the mountain. It looks as though the creek just disappears under it, but if you know where the hidden opening is, you can walk right through to the other side."

"Could be," he agreed, then watched her face for reaction as he probed, "Do you condemn them?"

She thought a moment, then answered in all honesty, "No, I don't. I remember my father as a cold man with a nasty disposition, and I can understand why my mother wouldn't love him. I can also see why she loved Uncle Dooley. He was everything my father wasn't—warm and kind, always smiling. It's hard to believe they were brothers.

"No," she repeated, almost reverently, "I don't condemn them at all."

It was late afternoon, and they were almost finished when they heard the sound of a carriage approaching. With a groan Dancy predicted, "It's probably Miss Addie, coming back to raise hell all over again."

"Afraid not," Clint said, recognizing the horses. "It's Jordan. Probably he got tired of waiting for you to go screaming into his office to ask for help in getting rid of me and came out to see what was going on."

Dancy left the field and started down the path to the cabin, waving. She wanted Jordan in a good mood, so she could explain the situation and let him know she would be needing his help, and something told her if the two stepbrothers got together, the atmosphere would be anything but pleasant.

Jordan, however, had seen Dancy coming toward him and instructed Gabriel, his driver, to continue on, then had him rein to a stop when they were alongside her. "I was worried about you," he said anxiously. "I understand my mother paid you a visit yesterday, and I doubt it was very pleasant. I'm sorry."

"She's mistaken about some things, but why

don't we go inside to talk? It's terribly hot out here."

"In a minute. Is Clint around? I need to speak with him."

Dancy seized the opportunity to say quietly, "You should have told me the situation here, Jordan, how he had claimed the place."

"Yes, you're probably right, but you were so happy I didn't want to spoil your first day home, and to be perfectly honest, I thought he'd be gentleman enough to bow to the wishes of Dooley and step aside. But when has Clint ever been a gentleman?

"But don't worry about him," he continued airily. "We'll fight him in court if we have to, but right now I have another matter to discuss with him. Would you get him, please?"

She noticed that he seemed upset, so she nodded and went to call Clint, who threw down the ax reluctantly and came.

Dancy stood back as he walked up to the carriage to greet his half brother coolly. "Thanks for letting me be the one to tell Dancy the news, Jordan. Mighty nice of you to send her out here thinking she owned the place."

"Forget that." With a sweep of contempt, Jordan denounced curtly, "You succeeded in running off the Coley girl, and you sure chose a cowardly way of doing it."

Clint's face darkened. "What the hell are you talking about?"

"Don't pretend you don't know what I'm talking about. The marshal himself told me how she carried on over finding Dancy out here. No doubt you decided it'd be best to get rid of her, so she wouldn't get in the way of you trying to impress Dancy."

Clint's fist clenched at his sides. "I'm losing patience real fast, Jordan."

"When one of them dragged that coffin around behind his horse, she couldn't get out of town fast enough, and—"

Clint snapped then, reaching out to grab Jordan by his collar. "Are you telling me the Klan scared Lila into running away?"

Gabriel glanced about uneasily. He didn't want to get involved with white folks' business but knew Miss Addie would be terribly mad if he sat by and let Master Clint beat up on Master Jordan. He had known the two all their lives and had witnessed some pretty bad fights between them, with Master Clint always the winner. He said gently, "Mastah Clint, you know you can't hit on Mastah Jordan like you used to, him being crippled and all, and, yassah, he is tryin' to tell you the Klan run that woman off."

Clint released him, then stood back a moment to stare reproachfully before stalking away.

"Jordan, what's going on?" Dancy asked uneasily, staring after him.

"It's not pleasant. Let's go back to the cabin. Gabriel will help me inside and we can talk."

Dancy nodded, opting to walk alongside the carriage. A few moments later, Clint went thundering by on his horse. He didn't even glance in their direction.

Once inside, with Jordan seated at the table, Dancy poured glasses of apple cider from the jug she found under a cabinet. "Now tell me, please. What's this all about?"

Jordan took a long sip of the cider before speaking, and when he did so, his reluctance was obvious. "They call themselves the Ku Klux Klan. Everything about them is a secret, especially the identities of the members. They wear disguises when they ride."

"Ride where?" Dancy pressed. "What is it they do, and what was it they did to Lila Coley to make her so afraid that she'd run away?"

"They're vigilantes, trying to restore white supremacy by scaring the freed slaves, as well as anybody else they consider misbehaving—like Lila Coley. They dragged a baby's casket around on the end of a rope, for God's sake. Someone who saw it said they specifically called out her name and told her to get out of town, that they didn't want her kind living here.

"It worked," he said sadly, helplessly. "I heard she was running out the back door with all her belongings in one bag, while they were still outside the front. I don't condone the kind of woman she is, mind you, but I certainly can't defend what those monsters did. And the tales about them are atrocious—beatings, lynchings. They terrorize anyone they choose, and the law is helpless because they're so clandestine. It's impossible to know who's a member."

Dancy folded her arms across her bosom and shuddered to think of such a horror. "I don't even know this Coley woman, but I feel sorry for her."

"Haven't you wondered why she was the one singled out?"

She shook her head. "What are you getting at?"

"Sweeney has lots of prostitutes working at his place. Seven or eight, I hear. Yet Lila was the one the Ku Klux called to and told to get out of town. Don't you wonder about that?"

Dancy shrugged. "Maybe one of them had it in for her."

"Right." He nodded grimly. "Clint."

Dancy, who had leaned back in her chair, suddenly bolted upright, stunned. "You don't mean Clint is a member, do you?"

"It all adds up. Think about it. Lila rode out, found you here, and raised so much hell with Clint later that somebody sent for the marshal, because she was tearing up Sweeney's saloon." He leaned forward, locking his eyes with hers. "Clint was, no doubt, shocked to his boots when you showed up, but he's got sense enough to know I have the money and influential friends to help you beat him in court if it comes to that. So, he figures the easiest way for him to get rid of you is pretend to be your friend and hope you give up and leave, but he can't do that if Lila is coming around raising hell about you being here.

"So what does he do?" He slapped his palms on the table for emphasis. "He gets his friends in the Klan together, and they scare poor Lila into leaving town."

Dancy was skeptical and said so. "Frankly, Jordan, I find it hard to believe a bunch of diehard Rebels would take someone into their group who fought for the North. I can't believe Clint is involved."

A shadow crossed Jordan's face, and he felt himself tensing. Dancy was not as gullible as he thought, and the seed of doubt would not be easily planted. "Well, he could have paid somebody to talk the Klan into doing it," he offered as logic. "Folks are desperate. Besides, the Klan might be forgiving if Clint was willing to take an oath of loyalty to them."

"I don't know," Dancy said, more to herself

than to him. "I just don't think Clint is a part of this. And you saw how upset he was."

"That was for your benefit," he remarked with a sneer. "Believe me, Clint cannot be trusted. Surely you remember how he was when we were children."

"But that was a long time ago. . . ." Her voice trailed off as she wondered why she was so bent on defending Clint, not wanting to admit she was feeling more and more drawn to him. "I just don't believe it. There has to be another reason the Klan wanted Lila to get out of town."

Jordan warned, "Don't turn your back on him. Frankly, it would please me if the Ku Klux drove *him* out of town. But now let's talk about you and your plans."

"I'm going to stay here," she told him firmly.

"Then you'll need my help."

Dancy felt a happy rush to realize he wasn't going to be like Clint and his mother and try to convince her to make a life somewhere else. Impulsively she reached across the table to squeeze his hands in gratitude. "If it weren't for you, I don't know what I'd do, and I promise I'll pay it all back as soon as I've got my business going."

She proceeded excitedly to tell him of her ideas for the production of turpentine. He listened quietly, eyes transfixed upon her, mesmerized not by the words she spoke, but by her intoxicating beauty. He could remember when he was a little boy how he'd fantasized about marrying her when they grew up, and from the time his body and mind changed from childhood to manhood, he could envision making love only to Dancy. Every woman he'd ever bedded had become Dancy when he closed his eyes.

"Jordan, are you even listening?" Dancy asked, noting his strange expression.

He snapped back to the present. "Yes, yes, of course I'm listening. It all sounds fine to me, except for the part about Clint staying around to work for you. I don't like that at all, and I'm sure my mother won't, either, but then I don't intend to let her know I'm making you loans."

"I thought"—Dancy was hesitant—"that your mother owned the bank."

"She does, but she doesn't own me, and I've got a few enterprises of my own she doesn't know about, some money of my own, and I'll do what I want to with it."

She nodded, satisfied that it might be best if Addie was unaware of what was going on. Then, addressing his concern about Clint, she assured him, "It will all work out. We have an agreement."

Jordan swallowed any farther protest. He knew either he or his mother would take care of Clint in time. For the present, he had other things on his mind, and when Dancy tried to withdraw her caressing fingers, he held tightly with his own, once more embracing her with his eyes as he whispered, "Dancy, I want you to know I've got other reasons for wanting to help you."

His smile was warm, intimate. "Surely you know how I've always loved you. Don't you remember when we were children, how we played house? I was the daddy, and you were the mommy, and that dolly"—he paused to force a laugh—"that Clint was always tormenting you by drowning, was our baby. Yours and mine."

Gently she maneuvered her hands from his, uncomfortable over the intimate turn the conversation had suddenly taken. Maybe long ago she had childishly daydreamed about one day growing up to marry Jordan, but even though she still found him charming, and certainly handsome, she could not feel anything romantically now. It had nothing to do with his being confined to a wheelchair. She simply could not regard him in any way other than a friend, and now she endeavored to make him understand that.

He listened calmly, but he was raging inside and not about to give up. If he could make her beholden to him, wrap her up financially in his debt, he was confident of manipulating her into marriage.

"All I am asking," he said finally, pretending to be quite cheery despite her rebuke, "is that you allow me to properly court you. I was wrong to present myself this way just now anyway. You've hardly settled in, but once you have, once we get to know each other all over again, who knows?" He flashed a wide, optimistic grin. "Maybe you'll want to play house . . . for real."

Again she said, "I'd like to be your friend, Jordan. More than that, I won't promise.

"And I'd like to be friends with your mother, too," she added impulsively.

He frowned slightly. "Well, let's take it all a step at a time, shall we? Now suppose I get back to town, and as soon as you can, come in to the bank, and we'll arrange for you to borrow whatever you need. In a week or so, I'll have Mother invite you to supper."

Dancy doubted that would happen but made no comment, because she was ready for the visit to end. Jordan's statement of intent to court her was unnerving, especially when all she could think of for the moment was Clint, wondering when he'd be back so she could ask him for the details of what had happened to Lila Coley. She had some questions for him about the Ku Klux Klan as well.

She went to the door and called Gabriel, who was obediently waiting on the steps. Then, when

Jordan was safely back in the carriage, she said good-bye.

"I'll change your mind," Jordan insisted, taking her hand and pressing it to his lips. "You're going to be my wife for real, I promise you that."

She managed a nervous smile and turned away, wondering why all of a sudden all she could think of was Clint—and how wonderful it had felt when he'd kissed her.

On the other side of Honey Mountain, on land that once belonged to Carlin O'Neal, there was a dilapidated shack that had been nearly destroyed by a cyclone the previous winter. Next to the ruins was a grove of barren, storm-whipped trees, lending a haunted and desolate atmosphere. It was here that the local Ku Klux Klan held most of its meetings and initiated new members. But on this night they had not gathered to discuss their future. Instead they were busy hiding the white robes and high conical hats they'd worn on their earlier raid, placing them beneath what was left of the cabin flooring.

One among them wore a garish red costume, and he stood back from the others without removing the mask with holes for his eyes and nose. He was the leader, known as the Grand Cyclops.

"A good night, eh?" One of his appointed Night

Hawks stepped to his side and pulled off his own disguising hood. "When that old slave is able to walk again, he probably won't stop till he gets all the way to Canada. Hell, he deserved it. Stupid bastard. Thinking he could take over Leon's farm. Leon didn't die at Gettysburg so one of his own slaves could take it over."

Slade Hawkins nodded to Buck Sweeney. "That's right. And sooner or later the Negroes and the carpetbaggers and the scalawags will all realize we ain't gonna let 'em take over. Just because we lost the war, and the slaves ain't slaves no more, don't mean they're going to run things."

Buck snickered. "Well, I don't blame 'em for takin' off like a scalded dog when they see us ringing around, dressed like ghosts, carrying torches. It's eerie. I can tell you that, 'cause when I looked out of my place the other night, it almost scared *me*."

"Well, you sure couldn't be with us. Folks might have wondered why you weren't around when we rode on your place."

"Oh, I understand that," Buck agreed, "but what I still can't figure out is why anybody would want to run Lila out of town. I never had no trouble with her a'tall, 'cept for the other night when she was raising hell with McCabe. He ain't by any chance the one who wanted her done away with, was he?"

Slade exploded, "Don't be stupid. I'd never take orders from that goddamn traitor."

"Well, I'd just love to know who it is you do take orders from. Sometimes I think it's Miss Addie, and then I'll get to thinking maybe it's Jordan, and then I even start figuring it's both of 'em together."

"Well, maybe you'd be better off not worrying about it, just like you're better off not knowing." Slade's grin in the scant moonlight was taunting. "You might live longer that way."

Buck stared after him as he walked away and with a cold shudder, knew he wasn't joking.

12

Addie stormed into the bank, as usual breezing right by Matilda without so much as a glance, walking straight into Jordan's private office without bothering to knock.

"Mother, please!" he cried. "What if I'd had a customer? You've just got to stop barging in here like this."

"If you weren't having Gabriel spirit you in and out of the house at odd hours so you can avoid me, I wouldn't have to come here to talk to you, so it's your own fault. Now then." She sat down. "Suppose you tell me what you were doing visiting that little carpetbagger earlier this afternoon?"

Jordan sighed, leaned back in his leather chair, templed his fingers, and closed his eyes momentarily before responding, "So who told you? I know it wasn't Gabriel."

"Oh, no, you've got him well trained, the old

goat!" She slammed her fist on the desk. "How could you do such a thing? Annabelle Prine saw you pass by the church. She was visiting her son's grave and said you went right across the bridge and into Dooley's woods. And of course she couldn't wait to spread the word, because it's all over town that the little trollop is back, and now Felicia is all upset, because Annabelle said to her mother, right in front of Felicia, that she hoped you weren't still sweet on Dancy O'Neal like you were when you were youngsters.

"And that better not be so!" Addie hit the desk again, wishing she hadn't forgot her parasol because her hand was already hurting.

Jordan wanted to wring Annabelle Prine's neck, but he told himself it was ridiculous to think he could have ridden out of town without somebody seeing him. "I paid a social call to make up for your rude visit yesterday. You had no business going out there accusing Dancy of immoral behavior, Mother. Clint is working as her hired hand, as she told you. I believe they're trying to work something out between them for her to have the land like Dooley wanted."

"That can't happen! And I thought with his whore gone, Clint would just ride on. No doubt he's going to hang around sniffing after a bitch in heat."

"Mother!" As always, he was shocked by the

vulgar speech she used when she got riled. "What if someone heard you talk this way?"

"Have you forgotten you're betrothed, and it isn't proper for you to be calling on other women, especially without a chaperone around?"

"And have you forgotten it's not official? That's something you and her mother decided without consulting me."

Addie countered sharply, "You've been courting her. You've had Gabriel take you over there in the evenings I don't know how many times. And you sit together in church. It's just understood that the two of you are going to get married, and that's as it should be. Felicia is deeply in love with you, and you know it."

Jordan knew that much was true. The fact was, he had been seriously thinking about asking her to marry him. She was pretty, came from a good family, although they were presently dirt poor like so many others, but she would make him a good wife. But since Dancy had come back into his life, he had not given Felicia Peabody a thought.

"I want to know why you went out there," Addie was demanding.

"I told you—to make up for your rudeness."

Addie bit out each word sharply: "Don't you dare ever apologize for me, Jordan. And don't you dare even think about loaning that girl any money. She can starve to death for all I care. All I want is for her to get out of here, and Clinton to do likewise, so I can get what's rightfully mine— the richest piece of land in this county."

It was not the first time he had asked her, "Just what makes you think you've got a right to it, Mother?"

Addie was not about to tell him that if it hadn't been for Edana's bewitchment, Dooley would have married her, and the land would have been hers by rights, and since a piece of her heart had been buried with him, Addie figured she had something coming to her to make up for all the misery and heartache she'd endured through the years. "Just don't you worry about it. And you'd best remember this is my bank, and I'll not have any of my money going out to that girl. You stay away from her."

Jordan watched her go, then broke into a big grin the instant the door slammed behind her. His mother, for all her pretense and bluster, was not as smart as she thought. It was her bank all right, but he'd been juggling the books from the very first day the doors opened. And how good it felt to know he was fast approaching the time when he could be financially free of her. All his life she'd dominated and domineered, forcing him to endure taunts of "Mamma's boy" from his peers.

But one day, one day soon, he vowed fiercely,

he'd show everybody that he, Jordan McCabe, was his own man, by God. And no one would ever ridicule him again.

Outside, Addie walked briskly down the boardwalk. Stylishly and richly dressed, she was well aware of the envious and, yes, occasionally malevolent stares from the women she passed. On the surface they respected her, and not a one of them would dare cross her, but underneath the tight, polite smiles, Addie knew they loathed her. Fine. She didn't care if everybody in the state of Tennessee hated her.

She didn't need them.

She didn't need anybody.

The only person Addie had ever needed had let her down, broke her heart, and nobody else mattered, and if they knew what was good for them, they'd stay out of her way.

The war might have ended, but Addie intended to win every single battle that came along, because for her, the South was going to stay the same—one way or the other.

The day was magnificent, a soft breeze blowing as silver-tipped clouds drifted across a tranquil blueberry sky.

Clint sat on the bluff overlooking the waterfall that cascaded down the side of the mountain and into the glistening pool below and thought how it was the most peaceful place he'd ever known. During the war, in the times when he wondered if he'd actually got caught up in hell and if there'd ever be a way out, he'd think of this spot and experience a glimpse of heaven, a glimmer of hope.

He knew it was one of his reasons for coming back. With his father long dead, and Dooley also gone, there was nobody else in Pinetops he cared about.

It had seemed only natural to return and claim Dooley's place—till Dancy appeared. Oh, he had no doubt she was telling the truth about the letter from Dooley leaving it all to her, and he could accept that, no matter his disappointment. And maybe, after all was said and done, he should've just ridden off like most folks wanted. But it was too late now. Questioning the other girls at Sweeney's, he'd listened to their hysterical account of the Klan's visit. Men in pointed hoods and robes, carrying torches and guns, firing into the air and screaming out profanities and threats against Lila Coley, warning her to get out of town.

Clint had become angrier with each word they spoke, and they'd all finished by asking him the same question: Why was Lila singled out?

Clint had his suspicions but nothing to back them up, so he'd kept silent. Still, it galled when

Marshal Cox had showed up and started asking him about his whereabouts that night. Clint had fired back a question of his own, as to why he would have anything to do with Lila leaving town when he was one of her steady customers. Cox had pointed out they'd had a fight, and Clint had told him to go to hell and leave him alone.

He didn't like Lila taking off instead of coming to him for help. Maybe he hadn't been able to love her, but he sure as hell considered her a friend and would've moved heaven and earth to help her out. Now, however, he was worried about Dancy maybe getting in trouble with the Klan. He had seen right off she was every bit as hotheaded and stubborn as she'd been as a child. If she started giving freed slaves work, instead of whites, there could be big trouble.

He had another concern, too, and there was no getting around it. He was drawn to Dancy. And the last thing he needed in his life right now was to get tied up serious with a woman. These were dangerous times, *lean* times, and if he ever did get a marrying notion, he knew he would be a fool to take a wife raised in a city somewhere.

Sure, Dancy had worked alongside him in the field and probably had blisters on those dainty little hands of hers to prove it, but she'd been trying to prove herself. When it came right down to it, she was probably living for the day when she could hire everything done so she could sit back in the cool of the shade and give orders.

Bossy. Domineering. Feisty. A temper as volatile as gunpowder. Pity the man, Clint resolved, who took Dancy O'Neal as his wife. Trying to tame her would be like reaching in the nest of a setting hen and—

His breath caught in his throat, and instinctively he drew back from the edge of the bluff, retreating behind a jutting rock. He would not be noticed, but he had a clear view below, and he liked what he was seeing.

Dancy had stepped from a clump of plum bushes, stark naked, and was walking slowly toward the sky-hued water.

Clint swept her with a quick, hungry gaze. She was exquisite, and he felt a warm rush as he watched how her large and perfectly sculptured breasts, tipped ever so slightly upward, bounced enticingly as she walked. Her waist was tiny, and her buttocks cupped and round, swinging from side to side, innocently provocative.

Wading out, she began to scoop up handfuls of water to splash herself, then lunged and dove into the crystal depths, surfacing in the middle. Lifting her face to the warmth of the sun, she rolled to float upon the rippling surface.

Clint watched, mesmerized, for long, tormented moments; finally he could stand it no longer.

He began his descent.

Dancy gave herself over to the jouncing waves, spawned by the cascading falls.

She had spent another restless night as she listened for Clint to return, cursing herself for caring that he hadn't. Then, in the morning, she had decided to ride into town to arrange the loan with Jordan. But first she wanted a bath and a swim. So with soap and towel she had set out to try to remember the trail from her childhood.

The way was overgrown with weeds, but, happily, Dancy was able to spot a few landmarks Uncle Dooley had pointed out so very long ago. The weeping willow tree was much, much larger than she remembered it, but fortunately it was still there to mark where she was to turn and follow the curving creek that flowed down from the falls.

In a short while she could hear the inviting sound of the cascading waters. Quickening her pace as she climbed upward among the rocks, heading for the plateau and the waiting pool, she was heady with anticipation.

Life here was going to be wonderful, she promised herself as she undressed. She did not need to be entertaining romantic notions about Clint McCabe or any other man. There was far too much work to be done in order to make her dream a reality.

She thought about calling on Addie, because for reasons she could not understand, she wanted to make peace. Perhaps it was merely a challenge, because the cantankerous lady was, no doubt, considered indomitable, but Dancy remembered something else, too, and that was how tolerant her uncle had been where Addie was concerned. Even as a child Dancy puzzled as to why he seemed so compassionate toward a woman who obviously despised him, and her mother had been likewise charitable in her regard for Miss Addie and refused to allow Dancy to speak ill of her. A perplexity, to be sure, Dancy deduced, and one she felt compelled to solve.

Lost in thought, Dancy was unaware when Clint entered the water, making hardly a ripple or sound. It was only when she felt someone watching that her eyes flashed open and she saw him. Gasping with surprise, she sank, swallowed water, and came up gasping and coughing.

"How dare you sneak up on me?" she sputtered, making sure only her head was exposed.

He was grinning, which served only to infuriate her all the more. "I figured you were just hoping I might swim by."

Slapping the water with her palms, she sent a spray of water into his face. "You have no right—"

He reached for her and with a throaty growl whispered, "Shut up and kiss me, Dancy."

He cupped his hands beneath her breasts to hold her buoyant for an instant as his mouth claimed hers, then slid downward to cup her buttocks and press her against his hardness.

Effortlessly they sank downward. Dancy was powerless to do anything except yield to the overwhelming passion that surged and held her as captive as the enclosing waters.

The pond was not terribly deep, and their toes touched the bottom, lightly propelling them upward.

Dancy did not realize when her hands went to his shoulders to press closer against him, for she was enraptured by the delicious feeling of his tongue against hers and how her loins burned with the feel of his swollen shaft tucked snugly between her thighs.

They came apart to gasp for air, their gazes locked first in question, then assumed consent. With arms and legs entwined about each other, they melded together in yet another searing kiss.

Breathless, Clint drew her out of the water and onto the grassy bank, pulling her down to lie alongside him. For long, heated moments they lay in silence, neither moving, assessing each other in crystallized gazes of misty contemplation. Slowly he began to trail his fingertips across her shoulder and down her arm, finally reaching the swell of her hip and onward to gently cup and squeeze her buttocks as he pressed her close against him.

Dancy felt as though a million butterflies were shimmering in her veins. With a will of their own, her hands began to explore his rock-hard chest, fingers twining amid the thick mat covering. She gave a soft moan as he lowered his mouth to her neck, devouring her with gentle, nibbling kisses, pausing now and then to lick and savor the delicious taste of her warm flesh.

Her fingers moved to clutch his shoulders, reveling in the awesome sensations coursing within. She could feel his hardness pulsating against her belly, and easily he maneuvered her hips so that it was sliding once more, to and fro, between her legs. Unfamiliar yet ecstatic emotions ignited to send liquid fire up into her belly, and she pressed herself yet closer as desire burned hot and wild.

Like frost in the sun, Dancy's earlier resolve melted away. She wanted him, pure and simple and without rhyme or reason. It was as though she had been born to give herself up to the raging, all-consuming passion that was hypnotic in its intensity. Everything within her screamed for fulfillment, commanding only total surrender.

Clint rolled her easily onto her back, lifting his mouth from her kiss-bruised neck to suckle each nipple in turn as he straddled her, imprisoning her in soft shackles of desire. Suddenly he lifted his head to gaze down at her and whispered, "I can only promise you the glory of the moment, Dancy. Nothing more. . . ."

Her response was to clutch him even tighter against her, for she could no more have turned the tide of passion consuming her than will the waterfall to flow backward.

Easily he spread her legs, pressing her knees back against her chest. Knowing instinctively it was her first time and would cause her momentary discomfort, he maneuvered to enter her slowly, careful not to thrust hard lest he cause even more pain.

Dancy held her breath, wondering how her body could accept something so large, for she had seen him, marveled at his size, and, yes, been frightened at the thought, despite her hunger.

High above, a hawk circled to view the lovers curiously, then continued on his way as a gentle breeze swept to offer coolness to their hot, fevered bodies.

At last he was inside her, and she quivered as he began to thrust to and fro. Hooking her feet at the small of his back, she dug her nails into rock-hard flesh and clung to him, every nerve in her body deliciously raw and screaming for the moment never to end.

The tremor began, slowly at first, then catapulting along to clutch the very core of her being and explode in a feeling unlike anything Dancy had ever experienced before. It was awesome in its intensity, nearly frightening in its delectable scope, and she could not hold back the wild scream of rapture that seemed to erupt from her very soul.

Only then did Clint take himself to release, forgetting to be gentle as he ground his hips against her in a savage kind of fury. As his pleasure exploded, he gripped her yet tighter, and they locked together and soared together . . . as one.

For long, silent moments he held her, riveted with wonder that never, ever before had it been like this with any woman.

Finally, when he realized she had to be uncomfortable, he rolled to his side, taking her with him to cradle her head against his shoulder as he kept his arms tightly about her.

Herself shaken by sweeping emotions that confused her, Dancy tried to ease the awkwardness by saying, "If this is the way you want to earn your pay, Mr. McCabe, it'll be all right with me, but I'm afraid we won't be getting much work done."

"Sure we will." He gave her bottom a playful slap, knowing he had to end the tension hovering between them. By God, what he was feeling was only going to lead to trouble if he didn't back off fast. Pushing her gently away, he got to his feet. "Let's take a swim and then get started."

She watched him go into the water and felt a thrill at the sight of his naked, perfect body. She supposed she should feel shame, but she could not, for how could anything so wonderful be wrong? Now it seemed that from her first night home destiny had led them to the consummation of passion that would not, could not, be denied.

She raced to join him, and they swam and frolicked in the water, intoxicated by the pleasure of the blue-and-golden day as well as by their newly discovered, and affirmed, awareness for each other.

After they had dried and were dressed, Dancy could not resist asking about Lila.

"She's gone," he told her, reluctant to discuss her.

But Dancy persisted. "Why would anyone want her to leave town?"

Clint could not keep the irritation from his voice. "Hell, I don't know. She was a prostitute. Maybe some man's wife paid the Ku Klux to scare her into leaving."

Hesitantly she advised, "Well, I think you should know some people suspect you had something to do with it. After all, she wasn't the only prostitute working there. They think maybe you wanted her out of the way so she wouldn't make trouble while you try to talk me into leaving and getting out of your way, and—"

"Stop it, Dancy."

She blinked and fell silent, awed by the intensity of his anger.

"I didn't have anything to do with the goddamn Klan going after Lila Coley, and it was Jordan who put that notion in your head, wasn't it? He told you he thought I was involved."

"He was wondering, that's all, but I told him I didn't agree, and the only reason I said anything now is to let you know others might think as he does."

"I don't give a damn about anybody else, but the fact is, Lila was my friend, and I care about what happens to her. I'm going to ride up to Nashville and see if I can find her and make sure she's all right. She told me once she had a sister there, and I'm thinking that's where she might have headed."

Dancy tried to keep the anxiety from her voice as she asked, "Will you bring her back here?"

"No. She's better off there. I don't think folks realize how dangerous the Klan is becoming. And not just around here. It's spreading all over.

"I'll be back as soon as I can." He started to

walk away, then hesitated, wondering how she'd react if he did what he wanted to do right then, which was hold her and kiss her, and—"Look, about what happened today, Dancy . . ." He faltered, drinking in the sight of her lovely face as desire welled once more. "I don't want you to think I'll be coming around and creeping in your bed, expecting more. Unless you want it, too, it won't happen again. Remember that."

Despite the maelstrom of emotions within, Dancy fired back with a forced but saucy grin, "I'm not worried, Clint, because it wouldn't have happened in the first place if I hadn't wanted it to. *You* remember *that*."

She turned on her heel and left the tranquil place—and Clint, staring after her in bemused wonder.

It had been wonderful. Dancy still tingled from head to toe with the touch of his strongly possessive hands. And never would she forget how he'd made her feel when everything within her exploded in ecstasy too wondrous to describe. He had promised her only the glory of the moment, but he'd left her with a splendorous awareness of her own being.

Yet, she promised herself as she made her way home, there was no harm in his momentary possession of her body—as long as she retained custody of her heart.

And that, she knew, was going to be very hard to do.

Clint stood with hands on his hips, legs apart, thinking how Dancy could switch from fire and passion to demureness and indifference with a blink of those long, silky lashes.

She was one hell of a woman, in so many ways, and he knew he had to be real careful lest he find himself genuinely bewitched.

She had possession of his land, and he knew it was time to get her out of his life—before she took possession of his heart, as well.

13

As soon as Dancy arrived in Pinetops, she headed straight for the dry goods store. She wanted a new dress to wear to the bank and was sure if she found something to fit, Emmett would let her change in the storage room.

After tying her horse to the hitching post outside, Dancy started to enter the store but paused in the doorway to allow her eyes to adjust to the light within. Several ladies were gathered around a table laden with a new shipment of cotton bolts, and she wondered if Emmett even carried any ready-to-wear dresses. She just didn't want to take the time to go all the way to Nashville to the shops there.

Aware that all eyes were turning in her direction, Dancy stepped on in and was relieved to spy a rack of clothes toward the rear. She selected a soft blue gingham and held it up to her, satisfied it would be the right size.

"May I help you?"

The woman was looking at her with obvious hostility, but Dancy was determined to be friendly. "I hope so," she said brightly. "I'd like to buy this dress, but I need to put it on now. As you can see, I'm near to desperate. . . ." She gestured at the garment she was wearing.

The woman's eyes narrowed. "That's obvious. So how do you intend to pay for it? You just put it back before you get it mussed, young lady."

Dancy saw the other women gathering, and they didn't look friendly, either. "Well, actually, Mr. McCabe over at the bank arranged for me to have credit here. My name is Dancy O'Neal." She glanced about anxiously in hopes of spotting Emmett, who would surely remember her.

"Oh, I know who you are," the woman said with a sneer, folding her arms across her bosom as the others gathered behind her. "Everybody in town knows how you're living in sin with that no-good turncoat, Clint McCabe."

Dancy instinctively took a step backward, at the same time trying to put the dress back on the rack. In her haste and nervousness, it fell to the floor in a heap.

The woman quickly picked it up. "See what you've done? If you've got it dirty, you'll pay for it."

One of the others snickered, "Maybe now that his whore got run out of town, and he don't have to pay her anymore, he'll start keeping you up, and you can buy some decent clothes."

"No, ma'am, that's not going to happen," Dancy responded calmly, not about to let them rile her. "You see, it's not like you think. The fact is, I inherited that place from my uncle, Dooley O'Neal, and Clint works for me now. He sleeps in the barn, when he's there, but he's out of town for a few days. I know it might not look nice to a lot of folks," she went on, noting the way the women were exchanging uneasy glances. No doubt they had expected her to retreat in tears, not stand up to them. "But the fact is, I don't have any choice. I'm trying to fix the place up, and just like everybody else in the South, unless they're lucky enough to have money, I need all the help I can get."

She turned back to the woman who had first spoken and politely requested, "Now if you'll direct me to Emmett, I'm sure he'll be glad to put that dress on my account."

"Well, I never . . ." the woman sputtered amid the clucking sounds of her friends. "For your information, you arrogant little upstart, I happen to be Mrs. Emmett Peabody, and I can assure you that you do not have an account here. Now I want you to leave."

"You're no more welcome here than your Yankee-lovin' uncle would be," someone shouted.

Dancy knew that for the moment she was beaten, and she was about to leave when suddenly a voice called out from the front of the store, "What is going on in here? What's all this carrying on about?"

Addie McCabe used her parasol to make everyone move aside. Seeing Dancy, she said, "Well, I might have known the cat would drag you in sooner or later. What have you done now?"

"She wants credit, that's what she wants," Dorothy Peabody said and proceeded to recount everything to Addie.

"Credit, does she? Well, folks in hell are going to want ice water, too." Addie snapped her fingers under Dancy's nose. "We don't want your business, you little tart. Now get out of here."

Dancy shook her head firmly from side to side in refusal and commenced to assert herself. "Now, Miss Addie, that's no way for you to be treating me, especially when I'd like so much to be your friend, and everybody else's, too, if you'd let me." She swept them each in turn with an assuring smile before focusing once more on Addie. "But I have to say, I'm not going to let anybody walk all over me. Now I know for a fact I've got an account here, because I charged some things to it just the other day, after your son, Jordan, was kind enough to send word to Emmett to help me out. And if you don't honor that, well . . ." She shrugged. "I guess I'll have to go over to the bank and roll Jordan over here in his wheelchair and let him take care of it."

At that Addie swung her parasol menacingly. "Why, you little upstart. How dare you threaten me?"

Dancy ducked, protesting, "Miss Addie, I'm not threatening you. I told you. I want to be your friend. I was going to come and visit you later today and tell you that. I've known you since I was a little girl, an—"

"And I've known you, too, for the troublemaker you are. Now you'd best leave and keep on going."

Dancy stood her ground. "No, ma'am, I already told you, I intend to buy this dress, and a few other things, too, but since you all keep refusing, I suppose I'll just have to go get Jordan."

The others were all looking at Addie, waiting to see what she would do.

Addie was so angry her knees were knocking together. The thought of Jordan being brought in to defend this little trollop, especially in front of Dorothy Peabody, his future mother-in-law, was just too much. "Oh, go ahead and let her have the dress. Sooner or later she'll realize she's not welcome here and leave."

Addie knew she had made a weak argument, but she wanted the confrontation to end, so she hurried out of the store.

Dancy took the dress and found the storage room herself and quickly changed. Returning a few moments later, she was relieved to see that attention had turned from her to the arrival of a wagon from Nashville, bringing a small and much needed load of coffee beans.

She watched the women jostling each other in their haste to have Dorothy weigh the coffee in bags; in no time at all, the supply was almost completely gone.

Dancy overheard someone ask, in an amused tone, "Are you going to save some for Addie, Dorothy? There's not much left."

"No," came the reply. "She shouldn't have got so upset and left when she did. First come, first served, that's my motto."

Dancy stepped forward then and handed the tag from the dress she was wearing to Dorothy Peabody. "Put this on my account, please," she requested politely, ignoring the glares. She started to turn away, then on impulse said, "Weigh up the rest of that coffee and put that on there, also."

"Well, of all the nerve," someone whispered harshly as Dorothy had no choice but to oblige.

Jordan's greeting was warm and eager as he held out his hand across the desk to Dancy. "It's moments like this when I really curse these legs of mine, because I'd like to give you a big hug, Dancy. You are absolutely ravishing in blue gingham."

"Maybe you'll feel different when I ask you for the money to pay for it," she said lightly, taking a seat.

"I told you I'm willing to help you any way I can."

"I don't think your mother shares your benevolent attitude." She recounted the incident at the store.

Jordan listened, shaking his head now and then in disgust. When Dancy had finished, he assured her his mother would not be able to change his mind. "Besides," he went on, "I think it's only fair to tell you Dorothy Peabody had another motive for being so nasty. They both have their minds made up that I'm going to marry Dorothy and Emmett's daughter, Felicia, and they're no doubt worried about my childhood sweetheart showing up to claim my heart after all these years."

Dancy did not want to look at him just then, afraid it might encourage him if she met his hopeful gaze. After all, her lips were still warm from Clint's kisses, and despite telling herself not to, she knew she was looking forward to the next time he took her in his arms. So it seemed terribly hypocritical for her even to banter good-naturedly with a man who had made his romantic intentions known. And neither did she want him ever to be able to say she'd used his emotions for personal gain.

"I really do need a loan." Dancy glanced about the room, impressed by the rich decor. "I assure you I'll pay it back. I have every reason to be optimistic about my turpentine venture. You've nothing to worry about."

With a sigh of disappointment that she was not more receptive to him personally, he agreed. "Very well." Opening a drawer, he took out a paper and passed it to her, along with quill and ink. "Write in the amount you need and sign it."

Dancy scanned the page, saw the blank line for "security and collateral" and asked, "What about this part? I'm afraid Clint holds title to my land, for a little while, anyway." She confided the bargain they had made.

Jordan's scowl deepened with each word she spoke. "I don't like it." He bit out the words. "I told you, I don't want him hanging around out there. Besides talk of his being involved in the Ku Klux Klan, it's a known fact he's a womanizer. You're young and beautiful, and living out there alone, you're vulnerable. It's just not a good situation."

Dancy was afraid what she was feeling inside might just show on her face, and it wouldn't do for Jordan to suspect anything had already happened between her and Clint.

Opting not to pursue the subject any further, she scribbled a figure on the paper and handed it back.

Jordan looked from it to her in astonishment. "I don't understand. This is such a small amount of money."

"I have an idea," she told him mysteriously, "and if it works, I might not need any more. Just loan me that for now, all right?"

"Well, you know you can get more if you need it. So." He leaned back in his chair, relaxing. "Now that we've taken care of business, perhaps you'll allow me to call on you this Sunday? If the weather is nice, Gabriel could take us for a nice long ride. I might even persuade him to make us a picnic lunch."

"We'll see," she hedged, then asked curiously, "Why would you ask him to prepare food? I should think your mother has plenty of house help. She's practically the only person in the county who can afford to these days."

"True, but the fact is, she has a hard time keeping anyone. The Negroes don't mind working in the fields, but they sure don't last long inside. It was different before the war, when we had slaves and they didn't have any choice. Now they're able to decide some things just aren't worth the money, which includes putting up with my mother's sharp tongue. But don't concern yourself with her. She'll come around to my way of thinking sooner or later. Just like you." He winked at her.

Dancy was uncomfortable with his innuendos and turned the conversation to the many changes in their lives since childhood. Jordan, eager to oblige by sharing anything of possible interest to her, summoned Matilda to bring tea while they talked. When Dancy finally left the bank, she carried with her not only the money she'd requested, but the hope that she and Jordan would become good, close friends, despite her lack of enthusiasm for his romantic intentions.

Dancy hurried toward the stockyard at the edge of town. The poster she'd seen earlier, nailed to a tree, had said the auction would start at two o'clock, and it was nearly that time.

Buoyant with confidence she was doing the right thing, she ignored the curious stares of the men gathered at the stockyard. Standing away from them, Dancy waited patiently for the bidding on the surplus federal army property to begin.

At first she refrained from participating, wanting to learn the procedure. Then, when she made her first bid on a pair of mules, a hush fell over the crowd as everyone in attendance turned to stare. Dancy was undaunted, and when a pompous man nearby irritably raised her bid, she raised his. And when the auctioneer finally pointed to her and cried, "Sold to the lady in the blue dress," she smiled in triumph.

After successfully bidding on six mules, four horses, and two wagons, Dancy decided she had spent enough. Then she approached two Negroes who were standing to one side watching the goings-on. For two bits apiece they eagerly agreed to help her get her purchases home. She gave them the directions, then told them to move slowly, as she had one more errand to do and would have to catch up with them.

She found her way to the McCabe plantation, which was even more magnificent than she remembered. Dancy reined in her team at the gate and stared up the long drive leading to the impressive two-story white brick house. A long columned porch swept across the front, shaded by thick wisteria vines, and the lawn was dotted with pines and a few dogwoods.

Yes, she mused as she drank in the sight of the palatial estate, Miss Addie was truly one of the fortunate southerners after the war.

At the front door, a servant girl in a starched gray dress informed her Miss Addie was not receiving guests because she wasn't feeling well.

"Is it serious?" Dancy wanted to know, genuinely concerned.

The servant shrugged as though she didn't care whether it was or wasn't. "Can't never tell about Miss Addie. Bein' as she don't never have much company no how, I guess she must be feelin' real bad to say she don't want to see 'em if she does."

Dancy held out the bag containing the coffee beans. "Well, just give her this, and tell her Dancy O'Neal came to call, and if I can do anything for her, she's to let me know."

The woman sniffed the bag and grinned. "Coffee. Lordy, she'll sure be glad to get this. Even with her money," she added with the touch of a sneer, "this here is hard to come by." Then she blurted, "I think I've heard your name before. I think I heard Miss Addie and Master Jordan talking about you."

"Arguing is more like it." Dancy laughed, thinking how Jordan had been right about circumstances concerning household servants being so different. When still a slave, this woman would never have dared share a confidence about her mistress and master.

The woman was only too eager to continue. "Yes'm, I guess you could say so. I don't think Miss Addie likes you none too much. You sure you want to leave something so hard to come by?" She held up the bag, eyebrows raised in question.

"Of course. I wouldn't have come all the way out here if I didn't."

When Dancy caught up with the men she'd hired, she rode alongside them, engaging them in conversation. She learned their names were Roscoe and Billy, neither had any family, and both were like so many other freedmen, destitute and eager for work. When she offered them jobs they leaped at the chance, assuring her they could be trusted to perform any task.

"Well, we're going to find out quick enough," she told them bluntly, "because I'm going to trust you to take four of the mules, two of the horses, and one of the wagons to a friend of mine, over near Chattanooga."

The two men exchanged astonished glances. They were not used to white folks entrusting them to do anything so important.

Dancy went on to explain about Ben Caudell,

and how he'd told her there was money to be made on livestock, if the price was right. She would send them with a letter asking him to sell the mules and horses, take out what he had loaned her, and send the rest back with them.

"It'd be real easy, I know, for you to take the money and keep on going," Dancy pointed out, "but after you spent it, what then? You bring it back to me, and you've got a job."

Heads bobbing up and down, they vowed again not to let her down, and somehow Dancy knew they wouldn't.

Later on Billy mentioned he'd noticed that when Dancy sent them on their way, she had turned in the direction of the McCabe farm. "You friends with that woman?" he wanted to know.

Dancy replied, "Not exactly. I knew her a long time ago."

Billy proceeded to tell her his sister worked there. "And gives her a devil of a time, I can tell you. Always screamin' and yellin' at Molly, but Molly don't pay her no mind."

When they got back to the farm, Dancy filled two knapsacks with food, drew yet another map, this time to Ben's place, and promptly sent them on their way so they could cover some distance before darkness fell. "You'll probably be back in three days or so," she advised, "and as soon as

I've got the money Ben will get for you, we're in business."

She waved good-bye, pushing aside thoughts that maybe she was actually a fool and would never see them or the money for the mules and horses again.

Provost Marshal Borden Crenshaw had fought alongside Clint McCabe in the war and had the utmost respect for the man, but for the life of him, he could not understand why Clint was searching for a prostitute. "What happened?" he asked. "Did she have some special talent that drove you crazy?"

Clint did not reply, instead told him about the Klan's visit to Sweeney's place. "I heard she had family in Nashville and figured this is where she'd come, and I just wanted to see if I could find her and make sure she's all right. I also wanted to pay you a visit and find out what the government is doing about these bastards."

Crenshaw's humor quickly faded. "Not as much as it should be, I'm afraid, and you and I both know the reason. Shortage of men. Too many troops mustered out too fast in the first, frantic months when the war finally ended. Last I heard, we only have twenty thousand troops left in the South, and that's hardly enough to keep an eye on a bunch of rowdy, diehard Rebs determined to maintain control over the ex-slaves.

"You have to remember," he went on, "that the war caused people to lose their money, their slaves, and control of their government, and they aren't about to forget who was responsible. And you of all people," he rushed to add, "should understand how there's still strife and hatred between neighbors who fought on different sides, and that hatred didn't die when Lee surrendered. No doubt a lot of the Ku Klux Klan's attacks on whites are fired by old resentments."

Clint didn't agree with that theory and said so. "Lila was just a prostitute. She didn't care what color uniform a man wore, so long as he had the price of his pleasure."

Crenshaw looked at him for a moment in contemplative silence, then suggested, "Maybe it made a difference to some others."

"I'm sure it did, just like I'm sure I'm the real reason they went after her, and that's why I'm trying to find her. I feel obligated to make sure she's all right."

Leaning forward, Crenshaw locked eyes with Clint and proceeded to warn him: "Forget about her, McCabe, and get on out of these parts. Everybody in your hometown hates you, and you know it, so why in hell are you hanging around? It's only going to get worse. We've heard they're growing, forming new dens in other areas, other states. It's going to get a hell of a lot worse before it gets better. And when they start threatening helpless women," he concluded fiercely, "that tells me nothing will stop the bastards from doing as they damn well please, not even the army. So you'd best forget your whore."

Clint regarded him with disgust. "It's a good thing most Union officers didn't have an attitude like yours, or the war wouldn't have been won. I'm not going to belly up to these low-life rowdies. Now if you'll give me the addresses of all the known bawdy houses in Nashville, I'll get out of here and quit wasting your time."

Crenshaw bit back an angry retort. It was best, he decided quickly, to just send McCabe on his way, especially when the devil gleamed in his eyes and he looked mad enough to bite nails. But maybe later some of that wild spirit of his could be used to do battle with the Klan.

The list Clint was given took him down to the teeming riverfront, a bustling underworld jungle of bars, brothels, thieves, and pickpockets. A dangerous place, it was avoided as much as possible even by the army, but no one dared get in Clint's way as he walked along purposefully, his expression ominous.

He found Lila's sister, Annessa, first, who assured him over drinks that Lila was fine.

"Actually, I'm glad it happened," she told him, flicking her tongue across her heavily painted mouth as she thought how she'd like to get him upstairs in her bed for a quick tumble. She'd do it for free, too. "I've been trying to get her to move up here with me, but she wouldn't leave because of you."

"I never asked her to stay, Annessa."

Annessa gave a hearty laugh and slapped him on his shoulder. "Well, now you wouldn't have to ask me to stay, either. With a handsome stud like you, they'd have to chase me away."

He was not in the mood for chatter. "How about telling me where I can find her so I can get out of here?"

Annessa squinted at the clock hanging above the bar. "She should be downstairs soon. She took a customer up there about twenty minutes ago, and she don't usually take longer than that."

He bought her another drink, and before long Lila appeared. She took one look at Clint, screamed out loud with delight, and ran across the room to fling herself in his arms. Then, not caring who saw, she rushed him upstairs. "I can't believe you're here," she told him excitedly.

"I was worried about you, Lila. I wanted to make sure you're all right."

"Well, this is probably the best thing that could've happened, but I admit those men scared me to death. I couldn't get out of there fast enough."

"Did you recognize any of them?"

"Are you kidding?" she hooted, eyes widening. "I took one look at them in those white robes, and I started packing. I don't guess I'll ever know why they picked on me, but I've heard some of the things they've done to the Negroes they wanted to teach a lesson to—floggings, even hanged a few. I wasn't about to argue with them. I just took off."

"Do you need any money?"

She shook her head, and he could see the glimmer of tears as she whispered tremulously, "No. For you it's always free, Clint. You know that."

"I didn't mean—"

"Oh, I know, I know," she assured him with a wan smile, turning away to blink furiously lest she start to cry. "I was teasing you, but it's true just the same. If you get back to Nashville, you come by to see me, you hear?"

He knew it was time to go, because he was hurting her, and damn it, that was the last thing he ever wanted to do. "If you ever need anything—"

Again she cut him off. "I know, but you'd better get on out of here. My new boss isn't as tolerant as Sweeney was. He'll have my hide if I don't get to work."

Clint opened the door, but just as he was about

to step out into the hallway, she called to him.

He turned, but she was facing away from him, and he couldn't see her face as her words tumbled out, as though she were afraid if she didn't speak her mind quickly, she might lose her nerve.

"I know it's only been a few days, Clint, but I saw a look in your eyes I never saw before, a look you sure never had for me. That's when I knew I was only fooling myself to think you could ever love me. It's her you want, and you'd best get back there and look after her. We both know why the Ku Klux went after me: to hurt you. And with me gone, they'll go after her next."

He closed the door and hurried away.

Lila was right.

They would go after Dancy next, and although he wasn't sure who was responsible, he had a strong suspicion either Addie or Jordan was behind it all. Who else wanted his land so desperately?

But something else Lila had said was preying on his mind, the part about him wanting Dancy.

She was right.

He did want her.

But he also wanted her out of danger, and that's why he knew what had to be done.

14

There were times when Slade Hawkins wanted to tell Addie McCabe to go to hell, and this was one of them. She had summoned him to the house, all the way to her bedroom upstairs instead of her parlor, where she usually conducted her business. Propped in bed on pillows, she was, and he could tell she was sick, like the wench Molly had said. Her face was pasty, and her eyes looked glassy, and she kept sipping from a glass of water, then coughing so hard he thought she'd lose her breath. No such luck, however, for she recovered after every spasm to rail out at him again.

"Dragging that casket was an evil thing to do, Slade," she told him for what he figured had to be the fourth time since he'd arrived. "It might work on the superstitious Negroes, who're scared to death of anything to do with a graveyard, but it was sacrilegious and uncalled for in dealing with white people."

Slade stood with his back against the closed door, ever alert for any sounds to indicate one of the servants was eavesdropping. Methodically scraping beneath his nails with his pocketknife, he tonelessly defended himself. "Well, you said to scare her out of town, Miz Addie, and that's sure enough what we did."

"There are other ways. Those costumes you wear, the torches you carry. That in itself should be enough to scare anyone half to death."

"We figured the part about the coffin would spread among the Negroes, which would increase their fear of us."

Addie reminded him sharply, "I don't pay you to *figure*, Slade Hawkins. I don't pay you to even think, damn it. I pay you to follow my orders and keep your mouth shut. And if I find out you're involved with the real Ku Klux Klan, I'll have your head, do you understand me?"

He kept his head down, continued to clean his nails as he mumbled, "Yes, ma'am, I understand."

"You'd better," she warned. "Those hoodlums are killing and hurting people, and I want no part of them. All I intend for you and your men to do is maintain law and order in this county by frightening the freed slaves into submission. I'll not tolerate the rebellion other areas are having. It's bad enough I have to pay them wages without putting up with their arrogance. But I don't want any of them hurt," she ordered adamantly. "Not ever."

"Oh, yes, ma'am, yes, ma'am, I agree." His head bobbed up and down obediently. It was all he could do to keep from laughing. "There's no need for violence, and I apologize for the casket. We probably shouldn't have done it. Real disrespectful, I guess."

"It certainly was. Where did you get it, anyway?"

"Lem, the undertaker, has a storage shed behind his place. We already put it back."

"Damaged, no doubt," Addie opined, disgusted. "Well, I'll see that it's paid for, anonymously, of course. Probably cost Lem fifty cents in lumber, and he can't stand a loss."

Slade sought to get her in a better mood. "I hear Clint took off. Looks like you were right about him falling for Lila. He'll try to get her to come back, but she won't, 'cause she's too scared, so he'll stay with her."

"Well, if he does, we now have to contend with Dooley O'Neal's niece."

Slade had heard all about Dancy's claim on the land and also how it was said she was a real fine-looking woman. He'd seen her from a distance, and Lord, how he'd love to bed up with such a fine piece of womanflesh. "You want us to ride on her?" he asked casually, trying not to sound too hopeful. He had some real good ideas as to how to frighten her away, and give her something to remember him by, too, he thought with a warm shudder in his loins.

"I'll think about it. It might be best to wait and see what happens with Clinton. If we can get rid of him, Dancy won't be a problem. She'll run faster than Lila did once she realizes she's all alone."

Slade was impatient. "What would it hurt to scare her a bit now? If he does come back, we'll be right back where we started from, and we don't need to worry with her."

"I'm afraid when Jordan hears about it, he'll be upset, and I don't want him feeling protective toward her. They were close when they were children, and I'm afraid he's still sweet on her. I've got to nip that in the bud before he gets too involved. Still, you might be right. She's all alone out there now, and it would be unnerving to have the Ku Klux pay her a visit.

"Let me think about it when I'm feeling better," she said with a wave of dismissal. "Now get back to work."

Slade waited till he was all the way out of the house before bursting into laughter. He and his men weren't involved with the "other" Ku Klux Klan, they *were* the Ku Klux Klan, by damn, and the old bat would croak if she ever found out.

In fact, there were lots of things it wouldn't do for her to know, and despite his humor over the situation, he knew it was best to keep everything secret. In addition to providing food and shelter and extra money for the occasional night rides she ordered, Addie also provided him with cover. He had a job as overseer and a shack to live in back in the woods. He worked hard, minded his own business, and no one had any reason to suspect he was the leader of the vigilantes.

Lord, how he loved it. Like the rest of his band, he saw it as a way of getting back for losing the war, a way of salvaging some Rebel pride. He enjoyed teaching the freed slaves a lesson, reminding them that no matter what the government said, they'd better stay in their place.

But most of all, Slade was looking forward to the day he got the orders to do away with Clint McCabe. It would be more than a night ride to scare him, too, because no matter what Addie McCabe said, Slade and his boys were itching to take revenge on a traitor who'd had the nerve to come back home and flaunt what he'd done.

Yes, Slade was looking forward to taking care of McCabe almost as much as he anticipated getting his hands on Dancy O'Neal.

All he had to do was wait till the time was right.

* * *

Dancy was crossing her fingers that Billy and Roscoe returned before Clint. It would be bad enough if the two Negroes took off with either the mules and horses or the money Ben gave them, without having to listen to Clint rant and rave over her stupidity in trusting complete strangers.

Still, she could not deny being anxious for Clint to come back.

The glory of the moment, that's all he'd promised, but oh, dear Lord, he had kept that vow in the most wonderful ways.

But she was missing him for other reasons besides the fierce desire and passion that had ignited between them. Dancy missed how time flew by when they worked together, thanks to their playful bantering. As a child Clint had been a pesky, exasperating boy, whom she had despised. Now, however, she found herself adoring his good-natured humor.

Yet, despite the lightness of moments shared, Clint exuded power and strength, and yes, ever an awareness that he was not a man to rile. She felt completely safe and protected from all harm in his presence, the only danger from her own heart as it sought to betray her.

Three days had passed since Clint had gone to Nashville and she'd sent Roscoe and Billy to Ben.

Jordan had been out this day and the one before, with Gabriel bringing a basket lunch, despite her protests there was work to be done. Boldly, however, Jordan had said if she'd become his wife, she'd never have to work again.

"But I want to work." She'd endeavored to make him understand. "I have a dream, Jordan, to make a home of my own, here, where I was once so happy. With Uncle Dooley dead, I want it more than ever to honor his memory."

"But that's the dream of a child," he had scoffed lightly, reaching to twine his fingers lovingly in her long hair. "You're a woman now, Dancy. A very beautiful woman. You need a husband to take care of you, to give you children of your own."

He had kissed her then, but only briefly, for she'd wriggled away to scold how it wasn't proper, how they shouldn't even be alone together. They were sitting on a grassy knoll, and, as always, her heart had gone out to him as she'd watched Gabriel carry him like an infant. She could feel his humiliation.

Jordan had continued his argument that she should stop being so stubborn, that they were right for each other.

"And what about Felicia?" she had reminded him saucily, not that she really cared. She sought only to get his mind on something else.

Jordan had sighed, lowering himself to lie on his side as he stared up at her adoringly. "I've told you, darling. That's my mother's wish, not mine. Felicia means nothing to me. No woman does— except you . . ."

He had held out his arms to her, wanting her to lie beside him, but Dancy had moved farther away.

With a hurt expression, he had asked, "How can you forget how close we used to be?" His arm snaked out, hand closing about her arm to yank her down beside him. Tersely, angrily, he accused, "Is it Clint? Oh, I know what a charmer he is with the women. A real regular over at Sweeney's place, they say. He's not for you, Dancy. You deserve a good man, a gentleman. Someone who'll respect you and treat you like the lady you are—"

"Stop it, Jordan. I won't listen to this kind of talk. Clint works for me, and that's none of your business." She wrestled away from him, chafed by his boldness, all the while aware he'd struck a nerve by mentioning Clint. Perhaps if Clint had not been around, she might have been inclined to regard Jordan in a romantic way. After all, he was right in saying they'd meant something to each other once, and no matter that they had been children then. Sometimes young and foolish idyllic emotions could last, but the reality was, she could not help being drawn to Clint in every possible way. Still, the last thing she wanted to do was hurt Jordan, so she tried once more to make him see she could feel nothing for him beyond friendship.

He rolled to lie on his back and gaze petulantly at lazy clouds in an azure sky. Finally he told her stiffly that maybe he'd been too good to her. "Even my mother is saying your only interest in me is to get me to loan you money," he lied. Actually Addie didn't know about the loan. Also, she hadn't said anything about Dancy since taking to her bed with some mysterious malady, refusing to allow him to summon a doctor.

"I'm hoping to pay you back soon, Jordan."

Instantly contrite, he reached over to clasp her hands. "Oh, Dancy, forgive me. I shouldn't have said that. It's just that I love you so much. I always have. If you only knew how I'd thought of you all these years, praying you'd come back to me. And when you did, I knew God had heard me."

Dancy found herself wishing it was not necessary to do business with Jordan. Far better it would be if she could sever the relationship, for now she was convinced he was not going to give up easily. A shame, she mused, that his mother had not already manipulated him into marrying Felicia Peabody. Then there would be no tension between them.

Jordan had finally left, disgruntled and vowing to leave her alone for a while and let her come to her senses. She'd see what it was like to be a woman alone in the wilderness, with no friends. If Clint even returned, he'd taunted, she could never depend on him for anything, because he was no good, a carouser, and everyone around hated and despised him. If she didn't run him off, or accept help in legally taking the land she, too, would bear the brunt of animosity from her neighbors.

"No," Dancy said out loud, snapping from her reverie. "This is my home. I belong here." She was sitting at the table, over a hardly touched supper of bacon and potatoes. Outside, the wind was blowing, and the gentle day was yielding to a possibly stormy night. As shadows crept from the corners of the cabin, she shuddered and wished Clint were there.

"Besides," she murmured, feeling a tear trickle down her cheek as she pushed the plate away and got to her feet, "I don't have anyplace else to go."

She stood in the doorway and stared out into the pale violet hue of gathering dusk. The limbs of the trees bent to the ground in protest as the gales intensified. On the far horizon, forks of lightning split the darkening sky. It had been a terribly hot day, and as the first drops of rain began to fall, the air cooled almost instantaneously.

Finally she went to bed, hoping the night would pass quickly. Her gun was nearby, but it wasn't altogether uneasiness over being alone that rankled. She just wanted morning to come so she could once more anticipate Clint's return. Billy and Roscoe's, too.

But it was Clint she yearned for, and with thoughts of him to cheer her in the long, lonely night, Dancy closed her eyes and slept.

It came at first like the mournful wail of an animal seeking its mate in the wilderness. Then, as she struggled to escape the clutching web of slumber, she became aware it was a human sound, a voice, calling her name.

"Dancy . . . Dancy, child. Can you hear me?"

Scrambling from the bed, she fumbled for the holster hanging on the bedpost. Only when her hand closed about it did she move forward, toward the door.

"Dancy . . . Dancy . . ."

A man's voice, pleading, desperate.

With heart pounding so fast she scarcely could get her breath, with every nerve raw and shrieking, Dancy eased the door open to peer out fearfully. The storm had moved on after a brief shower, and though the wind was still lusty and strong, the air was sweet with the pungent smell of pine.

All was quiet, and she told herself she'd been

hearing things. It had been a bird, an owl, certainly not someone calling her name, for heaven's sake, and—

"Dancy. Dancy, my love . . ."

A cry escaped her throat as she turned toward the knoll that eventually led up to the secret place. For one stunning instant she thought she'd actually seen someone, on horseback, beneath the whipping fronds of the willow tree. Now, however, dancing, cloudlike fingers held back the light of a half-moon, and she could make out neither shadow nor form.

Then, in a twinkling, the fingers parted and at the same instant the voice called to her again as the world became washed by moonglow.

She dared move only a few steps farther across the porch, finger tightening around the trigger, ready to fire.

"You must leave this place."

Dancy strained to see his face, but he was obscured by shadow. However, it appeared he was wearing dark clothes, a uniform of some sort, tattered, ragged. "Who are you?" she demanded in a voice much braver than she felt. "What do you want with me?"

"Leave," he called mournfully. "Forget this place."

Hearing that, Dancy exploded, "Clint, is that you? Is this your idea of a joke? It's not working, and you damn well better stop it." With an ominous click that seemed to slice into the stillness, she pulled back the gun hammer.

Just then the moon was again snatched away by the claws of darkness, and she thought she heard him say, "It's your uncle Dooley, Dancy. Don't you know me?"

And when the clouds opened again, he was gone.

It had to have been Clint, she told herself, cautiously making her way down the steps and across the yard. If not, then who? The Ku Klux Klan? She damn well intended to find out.

After looking around the area for nearly ten minutes, Dancy gave up and went back inside to wait for sunrise.

For the rest of the night, she did not close her eyes. Tense, alert, she was ready to rush outside at first light to scrutinize the area where the "ghost" had appeared.

But there was nothing.

She told herself, all the while cringing within, that she had not been dreaming. She had seen and heard someone. And since there was no evidence, it would be very easy to believe it had been a ghost.

But Dancy did not believe in ghosts. With a deep breath of resolve, she decided that whoever was responsible was quite clever. No doubt they'd be back when they realized their cruel trick had not worked.

And their next visit, she vowed fiercely, just might be their last.

She was hard at work, pulling six years' growth of weeds from the garden plot next to the cabin, when Billy and Roscoe returned. She threw down the hoe and ran all the way to the road to meet them, waving happily. Not only was she ecstatic over the money they turned over, telling her Ben had sold the surplus army property at a tidy profit, but she was relieved to feel she had found two trusted workers.

Roscoe relayed the message from Ben that any time she had more horses or mules, he knew plenty of farmers anxious to buy. Individual prices at auctions were too high for them to afford, and Dancy was obviously fortunate to be able to procure them in lots.

Dancy counted the money, hopping up and down in delight. "The next horses and mules I buy will be for myself. Gentlemen"—she grinned at them—"if you want a job making turpentine, you've got one. And any of your friends, too."

Billy and Roscoe exchanged incredulous looks, then broke into wide smiles themselves as they assured her they knew lots of men looking for work and would start spreading the word.

"I'll ride into town and get some tools and equipment," Dancy cried. "I'm sure glad you boys got back in time for me to go do that today."

Billy explained, "We'd have been here a lot sooner, but we cut over by the McCabe place, so's I could see my sister. I wanted to tell her I ran into one of our cousins on the road and pass along the word one of our kin died. She won't there, so I had to run her down at a cousin's house. I hope you don't mind, Miss Dancy."

"No, of course not. I've got plenty of time." She started toward the cabin, then thought to ask, "Why wasn't Molly at Miss Addie's? When I was over there the other day, she wasn't feeling well."

Billy shifted uncomfortably from one foot to the other. He had never known anything in his life but slavery, and it still seemed strange to see his kind stand up to white folks. So what Molly had done filled him with a bit of dread. "She quit her," he said finally, noting Roscoe had drifted away, not wanting to be involved.

"Quit? But why? You told me Molly didn't let Miss Addie's crankiness bother her, that she needed the money. So why would she quit?"

Billy hedged, "Well, she didn't want to."

"Billy," Dancy said firmly, walking over to put her hand on his shoulder and give him a gentle shake. "What's this all about? Tell me."

"Molly said . . ." He paused and swallowed hard, not wanting to relate the dreaded news. "Molly said Miss Addie may have the pox."

Dancy gasped, "Smallpox?"

Roscoe disappeared behind the barn.

"Yes'm," Billy went on, twisting his straw hat in his hands. "I don't know if you know it or not, but the last year of the war, it was, there was lots of the pox up in Nashville. Lots of folks died. Molly, she said she remembered our granny talkin' about it, and she thinks Miss Addie got the same thing. So Molly, she won't about to stay there and tend to her."

"Is anyone with her now?"

"I don't know. Molly said she was up with her all night, and she was burnin' with fever and talkin' out of her head. That's when she got to thinkin' she had the pox, so she took off. She said won't nobody else home then, 'cause Mastah Jordan had done already left to go to the bank."

Dancy's eyes widened with the fearful implication of all she was hearing. "You mean to tell me Molly just left without telling anybody?"

"She said she did stop by the store and tell Miz Dorothy."

"Then she probably sent for a doctor and then went out there herself to look after her."

"Well, I wouldn't know about that, Miz Dancy, but . . ." Billy fell silent. Dancy was running toward the cabin and not listening, which was just as well, because he didn't want to be the one to tell her.

The truth was, folks didn't like the pox, and they didn't like Miss Addie, and he had all ideas nobody had gone out to see to her.

And that's just the way it was.

15

*When Dancy learned t*hat Dorothy Peabody had done nothing more than send a message to the local doctor, she was appalled. "You mean to tell me Miss Addie is out there all alone?"

Dorothy's chin lifted in defiance. "Don't you get snippity with me, Dancy O'Neal. Nobody wants to be around smallpox."

"What about Jordan? Did you bother to let him know how sick his mother is?"

"Not that it's any of your business, but, yes, I did send word to the bank. Matilda said he was out of town for the day on business. Won't be back till late tonight. Just like Doc Casper. I hear he had to go near 'bout to Nashville to deliver a baby."

Dancy threw up her hands in frustration, glanced about at the faces of those observing, to see the same arrogance mirrored there. "Well, I'm going out there," she said to no one in particular.

Chuckles rippled through the crowd, and Dorothy said, "Addie would rather die than be in the company of the likes of you."

Dancy let the remark pass and hurried on her way.

When she got to the house, she opened the door and walked right in. No need to knock when no one was about to respond.

Upstairs, there was no response as she walked down the hallway, calling to Addie; so, there was nothing to do but open each and every door till she found her. When she did, she was horrified to find her unconscious and burning with fever. Quickly she went in search of rags and a basin of cool water and began to sponge her face.

After a time Addie's lashes fluttered open, and Dancy could see her glassy eyes, knew she was, indeed, out of her head when she protested feebly, "Molly, you're getting me all wet. . . ."

She faded away once more, but Dancy was relieved that she'd come around at least a little. Continuing to sponge her face, she noted there was no sign of any pox as far as she could tell. She started thinking about the time her great-aunt in Dublin had been similarly ill. She had not had the pox, either; instead, it was her kidneys. Bright's disease, it was called.

Dancy looked at her face, saw it was puffy,

swollen. There was also evidence she had been nauseated, and a quick check of the chamber pot beneath the bed revealed it had not been used recently, probably not since the day before.

Slipping a hand under Addie, Dancy pressed gently on her lower back. There was no mistaking the way Addie's face winced or how she seemed to stiffen with discomfort.

"Bright's disease," Dancy said out loud. "I'm sure of it."

She found her way to the kitchen building, which was located outside and away from the main house. There, in the herb cabinet, she discovered what she was looking for—quince and mustard seeds. Using a wooden bowl and pestle, she ground them separately to a fine powder. She made a pot of hot tea from the quince and mixed the mustard in cold water to make a poultice.

Back in Addie's room, she maneuvered her patient onto her stomach and pulled up her gown. She applied the warm concoction against the small of her back till it cooled, then replaced it with a rag dipped in oil and water, so as not to blister the skin with the mustard.

The day wore on. Dancy lost count of her numerous trips out to the kitchen to heat more water for the mustard plaster. Tirelessly she ministered to Addie, now and then sponging her face with cool water, relieved that the fever seemed to be coming down.

Long shadows had just begun to creep across the room when Addie stirred. Eyes fluttering open, she screeched, "Molly, what in thunderation are you doing? What's that mess you've got on my back? What—" She rolled over, saw Dancy, and sat straight up. "What the hell are you doing here?"

Dancy backed away from her. Holding the pan of mustard plaster and wet rags, she commenced to explain everything.

"The pox? Molly dared tell folks I had the pox?" Addie cried. "How stupid. . . ." Her gaze swept over Dancy, first with incredulity, then with anger. "You still haven't told me what you're doing here, in my house, yanking my nightgown up, smearing that mess on me. How dare you?"

Dancy again attempted to make her see she was only trying to help. "Molly stopped by the store to tell Dorothy Peabody you were all alone, and Dorothy sent word to Jordan, but he's out of town. I knew you were alone, so I came to do what I could. I think it's your kidneys. Bright's disease, Miss Addie." She told her about her relative in Dublin, how she'd noticed her face was swollen just like hers and how the poultice had helped.

When she had finished, Addie continued to stare in muted fury. "I think," she said finally, tightly, "that you are out of your mind. What do you think you are, a doctor? I'll probably catch my death of cold from having you expose my backsides all day and soaking me with your weird concoctions. Now you get out of here, or so help me I'll send for the marshal and have you arrested. You can't go barging into people's houses this way. Didn't I make myself clear the other day?" She reached for her parasol, which she always kept near the bed. Swinging menacingly she shouted, "You were a little hellion when last I knew you, and you've grown up to be a big hellion. Now get out, I say."

"No, ma'am." Dancy shook her head. Lord, Miss Addie had to be the most cantankerous woman she'd ever encountered. "I'm afraid I can't do that. And since you're obviously feeling better from the mustard plaster, I'm going to go out to the kitchen and heat that quince tea I made earlier. Then I'm going to the henhouse and get some eggs and fix you something to eat."

"Won't eat it!" Addie called after her. "And you'd better get out of here. I mean it. I won't have the likes of you in my house. Just like your mother you are, always trying to make folks like you. But they won't. They'll see you for what you are. . . ."

Dancy kept on going and did what she'd said she would. When she returned with a tray, Addie had fallen asleep. After touching her face, she knew her fever was gone, so she was definitely better.

It was nearly night. Dancy was just about to settle down, not about to leave Addie, when she heard the sound of a carriage approaching. Hurrying downstairs, she saw a man coming up the steps carrying a worn brown bag and knew it had to be Dr. Casper.

"I hear it's the pox," he said warily. "How far gone is she?"

"It's not the pox, thank goodness." While she led him upstairs, she told him of her own diagnosis and the treatment she'd administered. "I'm no doctor, but I know she had the symptoms of Bright's disease, and that's what I treated her for, and she seems a lot better."

His sigh of relief echoed in the stillness around them. "That's probably what it is all right. Addie was complaining not long ago of some back pain and looked kind of swollen. Tried to get her to tell me if she'd been having trouble making her water, but she puffed up like a guinea hen and said I was getting too damn personal to suit her. That a person's water making is their own private business and nobody else's."

Dancy laughed. That sounded like Miss Addie, for sure.

Just as they got to Addie's room, Dancy heard

the sound of another carriage, this one coming in hard and fast. "I'll leave you with her," she said, turning to go back downstairs.

It was Jordan, and he yelled at Gabriel to hurry up and get him down and in the house. Dancy rushed to let him know there was no smallpox, only kidney problems.

"Thank God." He breathed in deeply, then smiled down at her gratefully from the carriage. "It was nice of you to come out here, Dancy. I hope you know how much I appreciate it."

Gabriel took him inside, carrying him all the way upstairs, with Dancy walking alongside.

"I really need to be getting back now," she said.

"Why, no, not at this time of night." He turned his head to look at her sharply over Gabriel's shoulder. "I'll not hear of you leaving. It's not safe. Gabriel will fix us some supper, and you can stay the night. I insist."

Dancy did not protest. She was tired, and it sounded wonderful to just be able to relax and accept his hospitality.

"She's going to be fine." Doc Casper assured Jordan with a chuckle. "You should have heard her ranting and raving about 'that hellish girl' trying to kill her. She's back to her old self.

"And I agree it's Bright's disease. I'll come by tomorrow to see how she's doing and try to make her see how serious it can be."

After he'd gone, Dancy and Jordan sat on the divan in the parlor adjacent to his room, sipping glasses of sherry while Gabriel prepared supper. It was a mellow, cozy time, and Dancy was grateful he was allowing her just to relax, not continuing his plea to court her. They talked of olden days and places, reminiscing, getting to know each other all over again. Glancing around at the opulent furnishings, warm mahoganies, rich, imported rugs and tapestries, Dancy was moved to ask, "Did a lot of people get angry when they found out your mother was able to come out of the war rich, while they're poor?"

"Probably. But it doesn't matter. After all, between the two of us, we own practically the whole town."

"Well, I have to say I was surprised none of her friends came out here when they heard she was sick."

"Oh, that doesn't surprise me at all. She doesn't have any."

Dancy was stunned.

"Oh, it's true," he continued. "Sad, but true. To her face, people treat Mother in the queenly way she expects, but they say terrible things about her behind her back, and as you saw today, they don't care anything at all about her. She could lie here and die, and they wouldn't care."

Dancy was glad when he began relating how

the house had been remodeled after the war. She didn't want to hear such sad things about Addie McCabe, because she'd never been able to forget how her uncle Dooley had said she only pretended to be mean, that she really wasn't. So she concentrated on listening to Jordan describe how he'd taken one whole end of the hallway and transformed it into a wing for him, encompassing the master suite formerly used by his parents.

"Being crippled"—he gestured to his legs—"I don't like to be moved around a lot. Mother and I eat in here most of the time, and I have a small office next to this parlor. It's all quite comfortable.

"And . . ." He reached for the bottle to pour them each another sherry. "I made guest quarters out of Clint's old room." He watched her face for any reaction.

Dancy lifted the glass to her lips and swallowed against the sudden skip of her heart. Clint would be back soon, she knew, *hoped*. She had missed him but was also anxious to gauge his reaction when she told him about her mysterious visitor the night before. She was still not convinced he wasn't responsible and hoped he wasn't, especially after what they had shared.

Gabriel brought supper—crispy fried chicken and turnips. Dancy was enjoying herself, for she'd not had such a good meal in a long time.

Finally she could hold back her yawns no

longer. The day had been long and arduous.

"I'm keeping you up," Jordan said reluctantly, not wanting the evening to end. He picked up the bell on the table and gave it a jingle. "Gabriel will show you to your room, and I'll see you for breakfast in the morning."

She was almost to the door when he suddenly asked how she liked his home.

"It's lovely," she said, glancing about appreciatively. "I've never been in such a beautiful house."

"It can be yours, you know," he said, with such longing in his voice that Dancy felt a wave of pity. "And if there's anything you want to change, anything at all, we will. You belong in a fine house like this, Dancy."

She did not know what to say, could only offer a halfhearted smile as she hurried to catch up with Gabriel.

She wished Jordan had not said anything. Their time together had been pleasant, friendly, the way she wanted it always to be. Now she dreaded breakfast, wondering if he'd bring it up again.

"So this was Clint's room," Dancy said more to herself than Gabriel as he ushered her inside, holding a lantern. The furnishings, she noted, were not nearly as sumptuous as those of the other rooms she'd seen. There were no objets d'art, no paintings on the walls. Everything was bold, masculine. "Didn't the Yankees strip it?"

"Oh, no, ma'am. The Yankees didn't do damage to nothing. Miss Addie, she was real quick to sign the loyalty oath when they got here, so's they wouldn't. This room has always looked like this, 'cause it's the room Master Angus growed up in and nobody ever wanted to change it. 'Specially Master Clint."

"You've been here that long?" Dancy marveled.

He was proud to confirm, "Oh, yes, ma'am. I was born here. About the same time as Master Angus. My momma and daddy was among the first slaves in the McCabe family.

"Master Clint," he went on to share, "he didn't change nothing in here. 'Course he was never around a whole lot. Always off ridin' and huntin' when he was a boy, and when he growed up, he was the overseer for a time. Master Jordan, he didn't care nothin' about that kind of work. He was always readin' and studyin'. But I guess you knowed what happened with Master Clint and Miss Addie and the war."

Dancy nodded.

"I'm real glad I'm too old to work the fields, and poor Master Jordan bein' crippled like he is, he needs somebody to look after him."

He laid a gown borrowed from Miss Addie on the bed and left her.

When he was gone, Dancy gratefully snuggled beneath the covers of the bed, weary and exhausted but also filled with a warm glow to think here was where Clint had slept.

Cradling a pillow in her arms, she drifted off to sleep, swept away by tender memories.

Clint stood at the edge of the woods and smiled as he saw the windows of his room darken. Dancy would be bedded down there; he knew Jordan had divided up the other quarters between himself and Addie, leaving his old quarters for occasional guests.

He crossed the lawn and climbed up to the verandah with ease. He'd done it so many times as a boy, sneaking out and back at night whenever there was a girl in town he was sweet on.

The window was open, and he stepped inside.

Fearing Dancy would scream before she recognized him, he clamped a hand over her mouth, at the same time whispering, "It's me. Don't be afraid."

Dancy's eyes flashed open, but she could not see anything in the dark. Still, she recognized his voice and relaxed.

He removed his hand and sat down beside her. "What I want to know is, how come I keep finding you in my bed?

She pretended annoyance, though her insides were churning with excitement. "You seem to make a habit of sneaking around at night, don't you?"

"It's my room," he reminded her, and she could sense his insolent grin.

"How did you know I was here?"

"Billy told me you took off when you heard Addie was sick. I rode over, and I've been hanging around outside, thinking you'd leave. Then when I saw everything get dark, I knew you were staying the night. I took a chance you'd be in here instead of Jordan's bedroom."

She did not miss the sarcasm.

"How is she?" he asked. "Is it the pox?"

She told him everything, and he listened quietly, relaxing as he learned things weren't as serious as he'd thought. By the time she'd finished, his hands had crept beneath the sheet.

Clint decided that if she stopped him, he would not try to force her. But, God, he wanted her. "Should I leave?" he asked, beginning to nibble at her ear.

The feel of his tongue against her skin was causing delicious little tremors to quake through her body. For answer, she drew back the covers for him, and he slid easily beneath as she reminded him huskily, "It's your bed, mister. I'm just a visitor."

He easily removed the gown. His hands maneuvered their way between their bodies and closed
about her breasts. He fondled them eagerly, mar-
veling at the plump fullness as he stroked the
flesh. He touched the nipples, which hardened
against his thumbs.

Swiftly he lowered his head, and his mouth
began to move about with caresses until finally
his lips fastened upon a nipple. His tongue
delighted in fleeting licks, then he began to suck
gently, drawing all of it inside his mouth to taste
and savor.

Dancy moaned with pleasure, her fingers
twined in his thick hair to clutch him yet closer.
No doubt Addie might be justified in denouncing
her now. No matter that each time with Clint
might be the last, that he could ride out of her life
on the morrow and never look back. This was
here. This was now. And if, God forbid, it should
be her one and only hour of glory, then she would
revel and savor and have no regrets.

His head came up, and he fused his mouth
against hers until he could stand the heat no
longer. Tongue mating with hers, lips almost
abrading, he felt fire in his loins consuming, tormenting.

He reached down to part her thighs, and she
yielded. Dancy's breathing was labored; she was
almost gasping. He lifted himself on top of her,

still holding her imprisoned by his kiss. He held her hips firmly as he slowly penetrated her with a long, steady stroke.

Dancy knew she was feeling something besides overwhelming passion. It was not only the ecstatic emotions he provoked in her body, but the exaltations within her heart that told her she had, somehow, tossed all reserves to the wind and fallen in love. She felt the quickening within, and with a shudder that swept from head to toe, she exploded.

Clint had been holding back his own surrender, and as he felt the beginnings of her own release, he drove into her with all his might, taking them both to simultaneous joy.

Afterward they lay side by side in quiet awe of the wonders just transpired.

Dancy may have been inexperienced, but she could envision no greater bliss. Clint, however, had known many women, in many different ways, and he was struck once again to realize that lovemaking had never been as satisfying. He did not want to let Dancy go, for the aura of rapture refused to diminish.

After a time Dancy dared ask, "Should we stay here? I mean, if someone should come—"

He got up and locked the door, then returned to gather her in his arms once more. "Maybe I'm not welcome here anymore, but it's still my home, as it was before my father married Addie, and believe me, the only reason I left was that I really didn't give a damn about staying."

Arms wrapped about each other, snuggled close, they talked on into the night.

He told her about finding Lila. Dancy secretly, jealously, wondered if he'd made love to her but was not about to ask. Then she shared her own news about making a profit on the auction and was disappointed, but not surprised, when he was unimpressed. "So now I suppose you'll go through with your plans."

"Why wouldn't I?" she challenged stiffly.

He rolled away from her then, to fold his arms behind his head and stare into the darkness. "I went to army headquarters in Nashville and talked to someone who confirmed my fears that the activities of the Ku Klux Klan are spreading, getting bigger. As I told you before, you're asking for trouble hiring freedmen when so many whites need jobs. Mind you, I agree that if they're willing to work for less, hire them, but I just don't like the idea. You're courting trouble with those hooded bastards, Dancy, and I can't always be around to look out for you."

"I won't live my life to suit other people, Clint. You should know that about me by now."

"I know you're stubborn, obstinate, and bullheaded," he said matter-of-factly, "but you always have been. I guess all I can do is stick around and do what I can."

That made her feel better, but she wasn't about to let him get the wrong idea. "We have an agreement, and I'm confident I'll live up to my end and be able to reimburse you for the taxes. But meanwhile, remember, *I'm* the boss."

"Sometimes," he murmured huskily before claiming her mouth once again.

Much later Dancy drifted off to sleep, and when she awoke early the next morning, Clint was gone. She decided also to leave quietly, rather than endure breakfast with Jordan when her lips were still kiss-swollen, her body yet warm and tingling.

Jordan squeezed the note into a tight ball and flung it angrily across the room. Anxious to get home and get to her chores, she'd written, she had decided to leave at first light.

She wasn't fooling him. He hadn't missed the look that had come into her eyes when he'd mentioned Clint the night before. She was hurrying back to see if he'd returned.

He had to admit his mother was right about a few things, like how it was wrong for Dancy and Clint to be out there together. If he intended to make her his wife, he was going to have to put a stop to it as soon as possible.

It was time for her to realize he was a better man than his half brother.

16

In the following weeks, Dancy hired additional freedmen who were pleased to get the wages she offered. In addition she spent part of the money Roscoe and Billy brought back at another auction. This time she was able to buy twice as many mules and several carts for hauling. Already nearly a hundred pines had been properly spliced, the sap running into buckets to begin the process of making turpentine. She was ecstatic with the way things were going, even though Jordan's almost daily visits were becoming more and more unnerving.

"He invited me to supper tonight," she told Clint one afternoon right after Jordan had left. "He says Miss Addie is feeling better now and wants to thank me for helping her."

Clint was not in a good mood. Crouched beside an old cart Dancy had bought at auction, he was trying to repair a wheel and had just gouged himself with a splinter, on top of mashing his thumb. "I can't remember Addie ever thanking anybody for anything in her whole life. He's probably going to want some kind of payment on your loan," he added irritably.

"It's not really past due."

"How much?" He stood, wiping his hands on his denim pants, ignoring the pain from his wounds.

He was bare-chested, reminding Dancy how good it felt to lay her cheek against the thick mat of hair when he held her. Keeping her voice even, she hedged, "It doesn't matter. When the first batch of pine sap is sold, I'll have enough to pay it."

"How much, Dancy?"

She told him, and he cursed, "Damn it, if I could, I'd pay it for you, but there's only one thing to do. I'll take some of the mules you bought last week up to Nashville and see if I can sell them there."

"You don't have to go. Billy and Roscoe can do it." Though she wasn't about to admit it, Dancy did not relish the idea of his going to Nashville. Lila was there.

"You can't ask them to do that. Too risky. There was another lynching last week north of Nashville. The Klan grabbed two Negroes on their way back from selling a crop they'd raised on land that used to belong to whites. Robbed and murdered them. I'm not about to let Billy and Roscoe head up there by themselves. I doubt they'd agree to go, anyway. Things have got a lot worse since you sent them to Chattanooga last month."

Dancy felt a little uneasy about being alone at night, even though she and Clint did not openly sleep together. Some of the workers were bedding down in the barn because they had no place else to go, and she was not about to provide fodder for gossip among them. She also needed their respect. So Clint could not come to her bed as often as either of them wanted, only when he felt he could slip out of the tack room he'd turned into personal quarters and creep through the night to the cabin. Still, it was comforting to know he was within shouting distance if there was any trouble.

It was also disconcerting to acknowledge that he had convinced her he had nothing to do with the nocturnal visit from someone pretending to be Dooley. The storm, he'd pointed out, along with her imagination running wild, had caused the ridiculous illusion.

But even though she believed Clint was innocent, she was sure someone, or something, had been there, and she would like to be able to call on him to investigate should it happen again. The workers were far too superstitious to investigate anything resembling the ghost of a dead soldier.

"Well, if that's what you have to do . . ." she murmured with a shrug.

Annoyed, irritated, not only over the need to leave her in order to scrape up money to pay a debt he'd warned her against, but about the increasing violence of the countryside as well, Clint snapped, "You know, if you'd accept Jordan's proposal, you wouldn't have to be bothered with any of this."

"Oh, you'd like that, wouldn't you?" she flared. The sun was boiling down. Sweat was making her eyes burn, every stitch she had on was damp with perspiration, and gnats were buzzing around her head. It was a miserable time, and the last thing she was in the mood for was Clint's sarcasm.

In a flash, his own ire boiled over. The reality was, he wouldn't like it. Not at all. But damn it, he was mad. "As a matter of fact, it *would* be nice to take over my own land again, instead of breaking my back for your harebrained ideas, waiting for you to get a bellyful and realize a woman has no business trying to run a farm, especially one this size."

"Oh, is that so? Well, I think the real reason you've got your dander up is because you regret agreeing to get the hell out of here if I prove I can succeed, because you know now there's a good chance I will. And we both know you have no right to claim this land anyway, because Uncle Dooley wanted me to have it."

"That's your story."

Hands on her hips, eyes narrowed, every nerve taut with fury, Dancy demanded, "Are you calling me a liar, Clint McCabe?"

"Nobody ever saw that letter but you."

"I told you it was stolen."

"So you say."

Their gazes locked.

"Maybe," Dancy said finally, coldly, "you'd better just get out of here now. I can manage just fine without you."

He had picked up the hammer, about to get back to work on the wheel, but instead he threw it to the ground. "No, you aren't getting your way this time, Dancy. I'm taking those mules to Nashville and get what I can for them. I don't need a bank lien against this place when you finally do get enough and decide to sashay out of here. And you can damn well believe Jordan would try something like that, even though title is still in my name.

"Yes," he added, "it sure would make my life a lot easier if you'd go on and marry him."

"Why? So you can move your whore in here?

No doubt she's the reason you're willing to go to Nashville."

His mustache twitched, and he raised one brow sardonically. "Hadn't really thought about it, but now that you mention it, sounds like a good idea. She's not a spoiled brat." He turned on his heel and started walking toward the barn.

"Damn you, Clint McCabe," Dancy cursed between clenched teeth, blinking furiously to hold back the tears. "I hope you *never* come back!"

"You won't be that lucky, sweetheart." He continued on his way, whistling, his step jaunty.

In that moment Dancy hated him. Arrogant, smug, he was just waiting for her to fail, and meanwhile she was a fool to allow him to come to her bed any time he wanted. At least Lila got paid for her services, but she'd been fool enough to pleasure him for free.

"No more," she promised herself out loud, heading for the cabin to get ready for the evening ahead.

If only she didn't need so much to get things going, she could afford to borrow enough from Jordan to pay off Clint. But she was afraid to put herself in his debt any deeper than she already was. So far she'd made nothing on the sap, for there wasn't enough to sell and it would be a while till there was. Until then she had to have money not only to pay the workers, but to provide food as well. There was just no way she could pay Clint back for the taxes any time soon.

She slowed her pace, shoulders slumping as dejection washed through her. Though she didn't like admitting it, the fact was she cared for him deeply. But she was no more than a folly to him, and it was hopeless to think he could ever feel otherwise.

Clint McCabe was not the sort to settle down with one woman . . . and she was not the kind to share a man.

She had splurged and bought a nice gown, a soft peach taffeta, hoping an occasion to wear it would eventually come along. The bodice dipped lower than she'd have liked, but it was the only thing available at the dry goods store that even came near fitting her. Though a warm evening, she draped a shawl about her bare shoulders, covering much of the revealing décolletage.

The wagon was a bit rickety, one Clint had found abandoned in a field and repaired. Jordan had offered to send Gabriel for her, but she had refused.

Addie was not present for the drinks served in the parlor. Jordan, in his wheelchair, attractively dressed in a white suit, explained that she was still a bit weak.

"Maybe she's rushing things," Dancy said.

He slapped the air with his hand. "No, no. It will do her good to dress and come downstairs. Molly is helping her."

"Molly came back?"

"Oh, yes, and she apologized and promised it would never happen again."

"And your mother is better?"

"Much. Doc Casper seems very pleased with her recovery. As a matter of fact"—he paused to smile—"it was her idea to invite you tonight."

Dancy shook her head in uncertainty. "I'm sorry, Jordan, but I really find that hard to believe. Your mother can't stand me, and you know it."

She was sitting on the divan, and he rolled his chair closer so he could reach out and clasp her hands in his. "Mother can't stand anybody, Dancy, but she has nothing to do with us. I've told her how I feel about you," he lied, "how I intend to marry you, and she knows she has to accept it, and eventually she will. Trust me.

"It's Clint she's upset about." He frowned. "His presence around here is an embarrassment. It reminds people we have a traitor in the family. She wants him to go away, so everyone can start to forget. I have my own reasons," he went on soberly, releasing her to accept a fresh drink from the tray Gabriel offered. "I don't want him around you. Where is he tonight, anyway?"

"I don't know." She didn't want to confide anything.

"It doesn't look nice. No doubt others feel the same. I don't want gossip about the woman I want to marry."

"And I've told you," she responded, an edge to her voice, "I intend to run my life, my business, the way I want to, and besides, I'm not ready to even think about marriage, Jordan. How many times do I have to tell you I want your friendship and nothing more?"

He managed to remain expressionless as he gave a polite nod of assent, but inside, he was seething. If not for Clint, he was sure she'd be desperate to accept his proposal.

Dancy decided it was a good time to remind Jordan he'd promised an early supper, so she could leave in time to get home before dark. Having refused his invitation to stay the night, she suspected he was now deliberately stalling, thinking she would be afraid to be on the road after dark. Well, she mused with a determined lift of her chin, he'd find out otherwise.

The table was lovely, complemented by the crystal and china Addie had cleverly hid from the Yankees. Dancy still marveled at the grand way the McCabes were able to live amid the poverty and destitution of their fellow southerners.

Gabriel and Molly assisted Addie into the dining room, supporting her as she shuffled along between them. She was wearing a dress of cream-colored silk, her hair pulled back in a snood. She was pale, her skin almost translucent in the mellow glow of candlelight. Dancy didn't think she looked at all as if she should be up and about. "Miss Addie, are you sure you're well enough to join us?"

"I wouldn't be here if I wasn't," Addie replied curtly. "I guess I've got sense enough to know what I can and can't do."

Gingerly Dancy offered, "Well, if you get to feeling poorly and want to go back to bed, we'll certainly understand."

Addie shot an angry glance at Jordan. The roof had practically flown off the house when he'd announced he was inviting Dancy O'Neal for supper, but he had sworn that if Addie did not behave herself, he'd have her taken to a hospital in Nashville, as Dr. Casper wanted. She was not about to let that happen. Weak as she was, Addie knew that for the time being she was at his mercy; but when she was stronger, he'd be sorry, by God, even though she had secretly worked something out so the evening would not be a total loss.

She felt Jordan's foot nudging her leg and proceeded to obey the rest of his edict. "I wanted to thank you for coming to take care of me."

He kicked her again.

"And thank you for the coffee." She flashed a look that warned her son enough was enough. She'd go just so far, and—

He kicked her harder.

"And I'm sorry," she mumbled, reaching for her glass and taking a big gulp of wine before speaking her next words. "I shouldn't have said what I did when I called on you."

Dancy was so grateful for Addie's apology that she failed to notice the increasing tension and began happily to babble, "Oh, Miss Addie, I really appreciate your saying that. Clint works for me like everybody else, and—"

As if on cue, Addie exploded, "I'll not have his name mentioned in my house!" Despite the shuddering wave of weakness, she managed to slam her hands on the table so hard that her glass spilled. As white lace turned crimson in the spreading stain, she cried, "He's a coward. A traitor. A liar and a whoremonger. He's no son of mine and never was."

"Mother, that's enough." Jordan also banged the table, much harder, which caused both his and Dancy's glasses to turn over. Dancy quickly pushed back her chair and stood up to escape getting wine all over her one decent gown.

"I'll not tolerate such rudeness, Mother," he railed, for the moment forgetting Dancy.

Addie fired back, "I still rule this house, you ingrate, even if I have been sick, and you're going to find that out. I'll have you know I can disown you and kick your butt out just like I did *him*." She was feeling sicker by the moment and gripped the edge of the table. "It's one thing for me to eat crow and apologize, but I won't sit here and listen to the likes of her sing the praises of a turncoat."

Dancy backed away as they both began to shout at each other. Jordan was saying something about how she had dominated him his whole life, but that was over now, and Addie was yelling incoherently. Molly and Gabriel had rushed in— Gabriel to clean up the mess on the table, Molly to urge Addie upstairs to bed.

By the time Jordan noticed that Dancy had retreated, she was out the front door and scrambling into her wagon to pop the reins over the horses' rumps and send them in a fast gallop down the road.

Eventually, she slowed them to a steady trot. Beneath the canopy of trees lining the road, the shadows were dark and ominous— she knew she'd misjudged when nightfall would come.

To take her mind off of her creeping uneasiness, Dancy concentrated on the miserable evening. She had been disappointed by Addie's outburst, but not truly surprised. It was Jordan's behavior that astonished her. Never had she known him to be anything but tolerant and patient, and tonight she'd seen a different side of him. Maybe Clint had been right. Maybe she shouldn't have put herself in Jordan's debt. But what other choice did she have?

Now she was starting to feel bad about the earlier argument with Clint, which no doubt had sent him straight to Lila Coley's arms.

With a deep, shuddering sigh, Dancy decided it had been a wretched day, and she was glad it would soon be over. All she had to do was make it safely home and . . .

In the hovering darkness, she almost missed the two men on horseback blocking her path. She nearly tumbled out as her own horses came to an abrupt halt. "What do you think you're doing . . ." she began furiously, but was struck with smothering terror to see they had bandanas pulled across the lower part of their faces.

Hand shaking, she snaked her fingers toward the gun lying next to her. It was beneath the shawl that had fallen from her shoulders during her hasty departure. "Get out of my way, I warn you."

As they threw back their heads to laugh raucously, a third man leaped onto the back of the cart to grab her and pull her backward. "Where's your purse, little lady? We heard you got all kinds of money, being as you bought that traitor's place."

Dancy struggled futilely as he held her and yelled to his friends, "Search the wagon. If you don't find her bag, we'll search her."

"Hey, sounds like somebody's coming," one of the men yelled.

Dancy was released, but was given a rough shove that sent her sprawling to the floor as her attacker leaped to a waiting horse.

"Next time, there won't be no interruptions," he warned. "Maybe we'll just ride out and pay you a cozy visit in the middle of the night. We'll get your money . . . and more," he promised with an ominous cackle as he took off through the woods behind the others.

By the time Dancy had scrambled to get her gun, they were lost among the trees and foliage. Shaken and angry, she waited a few moments, but no one appeared, which meant the hooligans had only thought they'd heard someone. Fortunate for her that they had, because she had let her guard down. Usually, she rode with her gun in her lap, but her mind had been on other things, and she had gotten careless.

Grimly, Dancy decided she might just have to shoot somebody to send a warning to leave her alone.

"Gotta hand it to you, Slade." Pete Dugan laughed. "If it'd been me with my hands on that pretty little filly, I don't think I could've gone along with orders and quit. I'd have had to taste me some of that honey."

Buck Sweeney chimed in to goad, "Me, too. You reckon he just really didn't want none, Pete?"

"Shut up, both of you." Slade felt like slamming his fist in their taunting faces. "Next time I ain't backing off. I don't care what I'm told to do. A man can stand just so much."

Pete spat a wad of tobacco juice, grinned at Buck before prodding, "Who was it, Slade? Who's giving you orders?"

"None of your business," Slade fired back promptly. "You just follow mine."

Buck had asked the same question many times and always received the same answer, so he wasn't surprised. He shrugged. "Seems to me whoever it is, they ain't very smart."

"I don't ask questions. I was told to just give her a good scare and then back off."

Pete remarked, "Seems to me, she's had enough

for one night." They had reached the area where their fellow Klansmen gathered, and they could see that some of them had already donned robes and hoods. "You sure you want to burn her out?" he asked Slade.

"That's what we were told to do. Now stop your jawing." He dismounted and started walking toward the dilapidated cabin to get his own costume.

"How'd it go?"

Slade looked around and tried to figure whose eyes were peering at him from behind the slitted, pointed hood. Then it dawned on him it was Frank Cox, a local farmer who'd hypocritically signed the Union loyalty oath to get himself appointed marshal as the troops were withdrawing the previous year. Slade liked Frank. He did a good job of pretending to be hell-bent to enforce law and order, all the while actively working with the Ku Klux Klan to maintain white supremacy. He didn't mind confiding in him at all, and told him everything had gone real well. "She was proper scared. I think after tonight, she'll be leaving these parts. And it's a good thing," Slade hastened to add, "that one of your men happened to see McCabe and that black boy heading toward Nashville. We've been waiting for a chance to catch her alone out there."

"Don't worry. I'll be waiting to ambush him on

his way back. With him dead, and her cabin burned down, Dancy O'Neal will be on her knees."

Slade's laugh was guttural. "With me right behind her, waitin'."

17

Hours later Dancy was still shaken over the attack. She had stripped off the ruined dress, stuffed it in the grate, and set fire to it. Never again would she have been able to wear it without remembering the way that bastard had ripped it open.

She had gone to bed, her gun tucked beneath the pillow. She'd lain awake for a long, long time, unable to sleep as she brooded over all the upheaval of her life. At times like this it all seemed so hopeless, and she found herself thinking maybe she had been wrong to try to make it on her own.

Finally she drifted away, but sleep was not deep or peaceful, and she was wide awake at the first thundering sound of horses approaching. She knew it wasn't Clint and Roscoe returning, for there were too many horses.

Snatching the gun out from under the pillow, she raced to the window and peered out. Terror closed an icy fist about her heart as she saw torches casting eerie, ghostly shadows at the edge of the forest. White things seemed to be floating about, and then she realized there were men out there, dressed in flowing white robes. She could not make out their faces, for, as the others had, they wore hoods, with slits cut for their eyes, nose, and mouth.

And she knew, in that frozen moment of horror, she had to be looking at the evil and loathsome Ku Klux Klan.

She estimated there were at least twenty of them, spectral in their white garb, as they fanned out in a semicircle before the cabin. Each held a blazing torch aloft. From the corner of her eye, she could see the workers lodged in the barn scurrying to disappear into the woods, not about to get involved.

With wide, fearful eyes, Dancy held the gun ready as she watched one man, different from the others in bright red satin, maneuver his horse to the center.

"Dancy O'Neal, come out," his stern voice rang out in the mantling night. "We're not gonna hurt you. We just want to talk."

"I can hear you," she called back, amazed at the strength in her tone, because despite the fact that she held a gun and knew how to use it, her knees were all but knocking together.

"You been hirin' slaves to work for you. White men need the jobs."

"When white men are willing to work for the same wages, I'll hire them, too."

"You need to learn a lesson. You need to learn we don't tolerate your kind around here."

Things happened fast then.

Dancy fired twice into the air in warning. She expected them to panic and retreat, which they did, except for one. Brazenly he drew back his arm and made ready to fling his torch onto the roof.

Dancy shot him in time to stop him, the bullet striking his shoulder exactly where she aimed. As he fell from his horse, she fired again in the direction of the man in red, splintering the torch he also appeared about to throw.

When the echoes of their retreat faded, Dancy slipped on her boots and cautiously went outside.

"Miss Dancy, are they gone? Are you all right? Is he dead?"

It was Billy, bless him. He had not completely deserted her with the others. Now he stepped from the shadows, carrying a big stick.

"I'm fine, and he isn't dead." She picked up the still-burning torch from where the man had dropped it when he was shot. "I hit him in his shoulder. He must have hit his head when he fell and got knocked out. Take off his hood and see if you know who he is." She held the torch in one hand, her gun steady in the other, lest the wounded man be merely pretending to be unconscious.

Cautiously Billy obliged, then leaped back and cried, "Lordy, Miss Dancy, this here is Frank Cox. You done shot the marshal himself."

Dancy bit down on her lower lip. It seemed as though all the misery of her life came crashing down at once. One day she'd had her mother to lean on; then before she knew it she had set sail for a new life in America, and ever since it seemed she'd been faced with trial and tribulation.

And now she had shot a man.

No matter he had been about to burn down her home.

All she knew in this wretched moment was that her life had all come down to this—a hell-bent struggle to survive. Destroy or be destroyed. Kill or be killed. She didn't want it that way, but she had no choice.

Dully, she told Billy, "The wound isn't serious, but he needs a doctor. I can't take him, because they might come back, and I'm sure not going to let you or any of the others get caught with a wounded white man. That would only be asking for trouble. So what I want you to do is get him into the barn, tie him up, then ride like hell to Pinetops and fetch Doc Casper. Maybe we can trust him," she said wearily. "For all we know the whole town might be hiding under those hoods."

Billy argued, "I bet I know one who don't ride with 'em."

Dancy wasn't listening. She was already on her way back inside, too exhausted and overwrought to think clearly. Despite doubting the savages would come back, she was taking no chances. She would have to sit up the rest of the night, gun ready, just in case. It was just as well, she decided. She had a feeling she'd never relax enough to sleep, anyway.

Finally, after darkness that seemed never to end, a soft pink haze began to permeate the forest. And with daylight came the sound of wagons approaching.

Rushing out, expecting to see Doc Casper, Dancy was surprised to see Jordan's carriage. Close behind was a buckboard carrying two men she did not know. "I sent Billy for the doctor," she greeted him, disappointed.

Jordan gestured to his legs. "Billy said he figured I was the only man he could be sure wasn't riding with the Klan last night, so he came to me for help."

"And them?" She nodded warily to the others.

"My overseer, Slade Hawkins, and one of our hands. They're going to take the marshal to Nashville to the doctor."

"I don't understand."

"It's not safe in Pinetops. We don't know whom to trust now," he said grimly. "It's best he be taken to army headquarters. They'll see he gets care and also goes to jail. Is he still alive? And where is he? Inside?"

"In the barn. I only winged him in the shoulder. It's not serious."

The two men in the buckboard had climbed down and walked over. Jordan told them where to find the marshal and ordered them to get him and be on their way. "Be sure to tell the provost marshal I'll be in to see him later today to get some law and order set up here."

Dancy took an instant dislike of the one called Slade. There was something ominous about him, and as they started toward the barn she noted he wore a low-slung, double holster and swaggered pompously.

"You look terrible, Dancy, like you might collapse any minute," Jordan said worriedly. "Come home with me and rest. I insist. Those hoodlums might decide to come back, and there's no one here to take care of you."

Her mouth curved in a confident smile. "I think

I proved last night I can take care of myself, though I have to admit it was a stroke of luck I was saved from being raped and beaten earlier."

"What did you say?" Jordan cried, aghast. "You mean they attacked you? I thought from what Billy said that they never got off their horses, and—"

"No, no, not the Ku Klux Klan," She waved a hand in denial, then quickly recounted what had happened not long after she'd left his house. The skin around Jordan's mouth seemed to turn white, she noticed, and the nerves in his jaw began to pulsate wildly.

"I'm sorry," he offered when she'd finished. "I should have made sure you left before dark. I'm sorry for so many things, Dancy." He lifted eyes mirroring his self-admonishment. "I never thought Mother would behave so disgracefully."

"That's the least of my worries," she countered honestly. "I know how cantankerous she can be. Forget it. I only want to see some law and order around here."

"And you will, as soon as I go to Nashville and raise holy hell with the army. Meanwhile, I can't rest knowing you're out here by yourself."

"Clint will be back soon," she told him, anticipating his bitter reaction.

"All the more reason for you to get away. Dancy, how can you not believe he's involved with those bastards? He's never around here when they're out on their raids, is he?"

"I know where he was," she said defensively.

"Well, then, tell me."

Dancy was fast becoming annoyed. "It's none of your concern, Jordan. He was taking care of some business for me."

"Your business *is* mine," he fired back, "as long as you owe my bank money, and—" He was instantly ashamed. "Seems I'm always saying the wrong thing, but I'm so worried about you."

"I know, I know," she murmured, trying to understand but miffed all the same. The sooner she paid him back, and Clint, the better. She was anxious to be free of all obligations.

"They're going to conduct an investigation, you know."

Something in his voice made her apprehensive. "What are you talking about?"

"The army. They're going to ask you a lot of questions about what happened here last night. I'll tell them you were attacked earlier, so they'll know why you were so eager to shoot. But this is going to stop, Dancy. It's got to. If only I weren't so useless . . ." He slapped viciously at his legs, blinking back tears of frustration.

Dancy's heart went out to him. After all, if not for his help, she'd have been at Clint's mercy with no chance at all to claim what was rightfully hers.

She scrambled up onto the seat beside him, lifted his clenched fists from his knees, and placed them in her lap to hold gently and caress. "You aren't useless, Jordan. You're a wonderful man, and you have nothing to apologize for."

He leaned to rest his head on her bosom. "Don't you know how it's killing me not to be able to take care of you, Dancy? I think about you out here, all alone, and those savages in their robes and hoods terrorizing you. I think about you almost being raped, or killed, and it tears me apart because I love you, and I'm not around to protect you."

He sat up to look her straight in the eye. "I want you to go home with me and let me look after you. If you don't, then I'll move in here with you, I swear."

She gave a ragged, weary sigh. "Oh, Jordan."

"Only for a few days. Till all this is straightened out, and the army gets a new marshal down here. Please, Dancy," he begged. "You can't even be sure Clint will show up. He might have found another woman and taken off. You can't depend on him. I know him much better than you."

Dancy was pained to admit he might be right and was much too tired to rationalize about anything anyway. Billy and the others would run away at the first sign of a Klansman, so she couldn't depend on them to keep watch while she slept, and dear God, she was so very, very tired.

Her whole body ached, from head to toe, and her eyes burned as if they'd been sprinkled with salt. She knew she had to get some sleep or she was going to pass out from exhaustion, and heaven help her if she did and there was no one else around.

"Please," Jordan persisted. "Just till things settle down."

She saw them bringing Marshal Cox from the barn and did not want to watch. Instead she rested her head on Jordan's shoulder. "What about your mother? She won't like it."

"She won't even know you're in the house." To Gabriel he said, "Go find Billy. I saw him ride in a minute ago. Tell him Miss Dancy is going home with us. Tell him it's best he and the other workers keep out of sight for a while. Scatter. Find somewhere else to stay for a day or two. Then get back here, and let's be on our way."

He turned to Dancy to ask if there was anything she wanted to take with her, and his heart quickened. Her eyes were closed, her long, thick lashes lying like copper fans, casting shadows on her smooth cheeks. His adoring gaze dropped to her lips, soft and inviting. He ached to kiss her but dared not, lest others be watching.

"But soon," he whispered, taking the carriage robe from his legs and tucking it about her. "Soon, my darling, you'll be mine to kiss whenever I want to, forever and always."

Molly assisted Dancy in changing into a gown, then pulled back the bedcovers before offering the cup of tea Gabriel had brought. "You drink this and get some rest, and when you wake up, I'll fix something for you to eat."

Molly tiptoed out, satisfied Miss Dancy was drinking the tea. Gabriel had brought in a pot and said to make sure she had plenty of it.

The house was quiet and still. Molly was relieved Miss Addie wasn't awake and jingling that annoying bell of hers, yelling irritably for something, but then she'd had a restless night. Several times, as Molly lay on a pallet on the floor, she'd heard Miss Addie up moving about. Yet whenever Molly had asked if there was anything she could do for her, Miss Addie had snapped at her to go back to sleep and leave her alone. So now weariness had, no doubt, caught up with her.

Molly went on downstairs and out to the kitchen. Miss Dancy hadn't stayed long enough to eat supper the night before, and judging from what Billy had said about all that had happened since, Molly knew she was bound to be terribly hungry. And though it would be a lot of work, having to chase down a hen, wring its neck, and pluck and clean it, she was sure Miss Dancy would really appreciate some nice chicken when she woke up.

After making sure Molly had everything in the house under control, Gabriel returned to the carriage.

"Everything is taken care of?" Jordan asked.

"Yes, sir. Molly, she got Miss Dancy all tucked in, and now she's fixin' to start cookin'."

"And you made sure you fixed the tea like I wanted?"

"Sure did. I used the powder from the jar in your room and stirred it in good. Molly said Miss Dancy took some good swallows while she was with her."

Jordan leaned back against the smooth leather seat and relaxed. Everything was taken care of. The laudanum he sometimes used when he wanted his mother out of the way for a while would ensure Dancy would not awaken till he returned late in the day. Perhaps she would sleep even longer. Good. He was already tired, and the day had hardly begun. He needed time to rest himself and plan what to do now since things had taken an unexpected turn.

Innocently Gabriel inquired, "You all comfortable and ready to go to Nashville, Master Jordan?"

"We aren't going to Nashville, you idiot."

"But you said—"

"Don't worry about what I said. I didn't say it to you, did I? Now get me to my office. I've got a foreclosure this morning."

Gabriel mumbled, "Yes, sir," and started the horses moving.

Neither Gabriel nor Jordan noticed the curtains moving at the corner window upstairs as they left.

Addie had been a witness to it all.

Early that morning she had been sleeping only lightly when Gabriel came to tell Molly her brother Billy was downstairs. He was demanding to see Jordan, but Gabriel wasn't about to wake him up and wanted Molly to find out what was wrong.

Addie had followed quietly, tiptoeing all the way downstairs to listen in wide-eyed horror as Billy stood on the back porch and recounted what had happened at Dooley's place.

She heard Gabriel say he'd better wake up Master Jordan after all, and she had hurried back to her room, anxious to find out what would happen next. Finally she had heard Jordan returning and saw that Dancy was with him. Peeking out into the hallway, she had seen Gabriel carry her into Clint's room.

For the remainder of the day she raged inwardly over how things were getting out of hand. Her orders were not being followed. Then, right before dusk, she saw Slade riding in. Not wanting Jordan to find him in the house, she waited until Molly wasn't looking, then hurried out to his shack in the rear.

He was sitting at the table, a jug of whiskey turned up to his lips. Even after spying her over the rim, he continued to drink, expressionless.

"You best put that down and explain yourself, you ninny. You've really messed things up this time."

Slade set aside the jug and wiped his mouth with the back of his hand before responding with a lazy grin, "Now what's got you all riled up this time, Miz McCabe?"

"Don't you get smart with me. You didn't follow my orders. You were supposed to scare that girl, not try to burn her out. I never told you to do that."

Slade raised his eyebrows in a gesture of innocence. "I don't know what you're talking about. I did exactly what you told me to. We waylaid her, scared her half to death, then made like we heard somebody coming and took off. Did some somebody try to burn her out?" he asked with pretended concern.

Addie's knees were feeling terribly weak. She was still feeling poorly. Sinking onto the chair opposite him, she said, "You're telling me your men weren't involved with the Klan going out to Dooley's place last night?"

"Oh, no, ma'am." He mustered a look of hurt surprise that she could even think such a thing. "We do what you tell us to do, and we're not about to get involved with them, even if we knew who they were. But you got to remember we don't have no control over them outsiders coming in here, and we don't want no trouble with them, so we try to stay out of their way."

"See you do. I won't be a party to anybody getting hurt or property being destroyed. We can maintain control by scaring folks, and that's not exactly breaking the law the way *I* see it."

"We think the reason the real Klan is after Miss Dancy is because she's hiring coloreds instead of whites."

"Well, that's too bad. If they aren't willing to work for the wages she can afford to pay, and the colored are, it's not her fault. I guess I've been lucky to hire both and not get anybody riled with me, because if I had to, I'd do the same damn thing."

"Sounds like you're defending her," he remarked suspiciously. "I thought you wanted to run her off."

"Don't be ridiculous. Of course I want her out of there. Clinton, too. All I'm saying is times are hard, and work is work, no matter the wages. Now what's this about Frank Cox getting shot? I can't believe he's involved with them."

"He isn't. He went out there, so I hear, because he got a report there was trouble. He was planning to stop it, but when he got there, she went crazy and started shooting. Gunned him down, she did, then—"

"Well, we'll hear the full story when he recovers," Addie interrupted. She had to get back to the house before Jordan came home. Besides, she had heard enough. Slade, unscrupulous character though he was, had followed his orders. What outside vigilantes did could not be helped, and she had never cared for Frank Cox anyway. He and his heathenish wife, Dorcas, thought they could fool people into thinking their first child had come early, but Addie knew better. He'd been born with hot feet, trying to get to the wedding on time. So she didn't care about sinful folks like Dorcas and Frank and wasn't at all surprised to hear he was mixed up with the Klan.

What did astonish her, however, was Dancy being a good enough shot even to hit the man.

She was almost to the door when it dawned on her that Slade had suddenly become very quiet. Turning, she saw him watching her in a kind of cold, defiant fury. "What's wrong with you? Why are you looking at me that way?"

"I figured you knew."

"Knew what?" Impatience was mounting. "Stop fooling around, Slade. Say what you've got to say and be done with it."

He paused to draw a deep breath and let it out slowly, enjoying the moment. "Well, the fact is, Miss Addie," he drawled, "Frank Cox is dead. Looks like Dancy O'Neal done killed herself a federal marshal."

18

After returning from a busy day at the bank, Jordan had wheeled himself in to check on Dancy and was satisfied to find her still sleeping soundly. And according to Molly, his mother had taken supper in her room and asked not to be disturbed. So all was quiet.

Relaxing in his bedroom parlor with a large glass of brandy, Jordan mused smugly over how well everything seemed to be going, despite a few unexpected developments. Perhaps they would actually hasten his ultimate goal. Dancy's feisty spirit was bound to diminish in the wake of community furor over her gunning down the marshal. And sooner or later, Jordan was confident, she'd turn to him. He would then have the woman he wanted for his wife, as well as control of the vast timberland of the Dooley O'Neal estate.

That left only his mother to contend with. But he had plans for her, too.

One thing at a time, he thought, smiling, and lifted his glass to his lips. Soon no one would dare laugh at him behind his back, calling him Addie McCabe's puppet. They would see he was capable of making his own decisions, running a successful business, and he would no longer be haunted by feelings of inadequacy because of his mother's dominance.

There were lots of things Jordan wanted to forget, such as the way his father had looked upon him so contemptuously because he couldn't go hunting or riding with him or do any of the manly father-son things Angus had enjoyed with Clint. Clint was the one who got to do everything, go everywhere, while Jordan was forced to be in his mother's shadow. He had actually been glad when the war broke out, anxious to join the fight just to get away from her.

But never had Dancy laughed at him, he recalled with a wave of tenderness. She would take up for him, especially when Clint egged on the other children to call him sissy and "Mommy's baby."

Jordan knew beyond a doubt that he had loved her then, as he did now. So often he'd thought of her during the years, wondering where she was, how she was, dreaming about how things might have been had she never left. Perhaps so much sadness could have been avoided.

But it was over. He grinned in triumph, tossing down the rest of his drink and quickly pouring another. It would be his turn to gloat and laugh, because Dancy was going to be his wife, and he was going to own this goddamn county one day, and everyone who'd dared snicker and call him names would be on their knees to him, and—

He froze, hand in mid-air as he was lifting the glass to his lips. Someone was pounding on the front door. He wondered who the hell it was, at the same time fearing the racket would wake up Dancy. He wanted her to sleep through till morning, so she'd be refreshed and receptive when he tried to persuade her to move in, where she would be safe.

Exasperated, he wheeled himself next to the fireplace mantel and pulled the bell cord that connected with the house servants' quarters back of the house. Then he rolled the chair to the door, opened it, and maneuvered himself into the hallway.

Gabriel had left lanterns burning as always, and as Jordan approached the landing, he could see his mother coming from the opposite direction, looking quite ridiculous in flannel gown and stocking cap and carrying that infernal parasol of hers. "Go back to bed, Mother," he said irritably, "I'll handle this."

"And how are you going to get downstairs to handle anything? This is what happens when you don't allow the servants to sleep in the house at night." At the railing, she peered down and yelled above the din, "Gabriel, where are you, damn it? See who it is before they break the door down."

Gabriel finally appeared to slide back the bolt and open the door. In sleepy surprise, he saw it was Master Clint.

"Miss Dancy is here, isn't she, Gabriel?"

"Why, yes, sir." It never occurred to him to lie.

Jordan, at the head of the stairs, shouted, "That's none of your business, Clint. Now get out of here."

"That's right," Addie chimed in, swinging her parasol over the railing. "You get out of here right now. Gabriel, throw him out."

Gabriel stood there, not knowing what to do. He was no match for Master Clint and wasn't about to try and force him out. "Maybe you'd better leave," he suggested timidly.

"Go back to bed, Gabriel." Clint strode to the foot of the steps and declared, "I'm not going anywhere till I see Dancy. Now are you going to send her down here, or am I going to have to come up?" Actually he would have preferred to sneak in and take her out, but the blasted shutters on the window had been locked from the inside.

"What you're going to do"—Jordan was already twisting his chair around, intending to head back to his room for his pistol—"is leave. You're going to learn you can't come barging in here like this."

"He's right, you hellish boy." Addie swung the parasol again, then gasped in horror as she dropped it, watching with wide eyes as it fell to the foyer to land with a clatter.

With a chuckle, Clint walked over and picked it up, then took it and jammed it in the stand by the door with the rest of the umbrellas. "Addie, Addie." He shook his head. "If you're going to use that thing as a weapon, you need to keep a better hold on it. You're always losing it."

"Damn you, Clinton."

Jordan clutched the wheels of his chair, bringing himself to such an abrupt halt that he pitched forward, almost falling. "Dancy, I almost ran over you," he gasped.

She was gripping the railing with both hands, legs wobbly as she fought to remain standing. "I heard all the shouting," she said groggily. "What's going on?"

From below, Clint saw her and without hesitation raced up the stairs. Addie moved to bar his way, but he managed to get by her without knocking her down. Grabbing Dancy as she collapsed in his arms, he knew at once she had to have been drugged. "What the hell did you give her, Jordan?"

Jordan raised his brows in innocence. "Why, nothing. She's just exhausted. In case you didn't know, she's had a harrowing experience. That's why I brought her here. Where she'd be looked after and safe."

"Well, she can leave now," Addie was quick to declare. "I don't want her here. Not after . . ." She fell silent as Jordan suddenly looked at her in question. She was not supposed to know anything, she reminded herself. "After . . . after the way she's been misbehaving, living in sin. Take her and go."

Suspicion appeased, Jordan turned his attention back to Clint. "You aren't taking her anywhere."

Dancy was terribly sleepy but alert enough to feel relief that Clint was back.

"Do you feel up to going home, Dancy?"

Blinking, she rubbed her eyes, tried to focus. Gabriel had left one chandelier softly aglow with candles, and she could see Clint's face, see the concern and apprehension etched there. Obviously he didn't want to talk in front of Jordan and Addie, and she had so much to tell him, too. "I'll get dressed and be with you in a minute."

"Don't bother. You can get your clothes later.

Let's get out of here." He lifted her up and started toward the stairs.

Jordan swung his chair to block them, fury exploding. "You aren't taking her out of here, Clint. I mean it."

Addie chirped, "Oh, yes, he is."

"No, he's not!" Jordan roared.

Clint was tired of arguing. Maneuvering to hang on to Dancy, he reached out and spun Jordan's chair around, then, with a mighty push, sent him careering down the hall.

Jordan fought for control, yelling and cursing as he was helplessly propelled, while Addie ran after him.

Clint proceeded down the steps and out. After getting in the saddle, he hoisted Dancy in front of him, then took off into the night.

Her head resting cozily against him, Dancy drifted back to sleep. Clint had an idea that the drug Jordan had given her was laudanum, which would take time to wear off.

When they reached the cabin he took her inside and tucked her in bed. He got a fire going, boiled a pot of strong coffee, poured her a cup, then shook her awake. "Sit up and drink this," he urged. "We need to talk."

The coffee was scalding. She blew on it, then took a few sips before saying dully, "Obviously you already know what happened."

"I know what I heard. Now I want to hear your side. Tell me everything."

And she did so, becoming more and more unnerved as she watched his face in the glow of the lantern. He seemed to become more worried with each word she spoke. Finally she could stand it no longer. "Clint, why are you looking like that? I didn't do anything wrong. I had every right to shoot a man who was about to burn my cabin down. And I only wounded him, for heaven's sake."

Clint hated having to tell her, but he had no choice. "Frank Cox is dead, Dancy."

She sat up so quickly, the coffee sloshed over the rim, but she paid no attention as she cried in protest, "I hit him in the shoulder. A wound like that isn't going to kill a man. He wasn't even bleeding bad."

"It looks like he hit his head on a rock when he fell."

Dazed, Dancy leaned back and rationalized out loud. "I figured he did, because he was knocked out, but for the life of me, he didn't seem badly hurt. But I have to admit I didn't bother to look at him carefully. I do know he was breathing when Billy rolled him over to take off his mask."

"There's something else, Dancy," Clint said grimly.

She raised wary eyes.

"Cox's wife is saying he wasn't involved in the Klan, and the reason he was out here was that he'd heard a rumor there was going to be trouble. He rode out to investigate, and you were so hysterical you shot him by mistake."

Dancy felt the heat of indignant fury spread through her body. "That's a lie. He was wearing a white costume. They all were. Except for one in red. Billy pulled his hood off. He can tell you—"

"Billy isn't saying anything, Dancy. He's scared to. Like all the other Negroes. And even if he did, it wouldn't hold up in court. A black man can't testify for, or against, a white. It's the law."

"But the costume . . ."

"It's not to be found."

"Wait a minute, it has to be!" She snapped her fingers, started to scramble out of bed, but he held her back as she argued, "I remember now. When those men Jordan brought with him carried the marshal out of the barn, I distinctly remember not seeing the white robe. It has to still be in the barn."

"I looked. It isn't there."

"But Billy will—"

"I told you, Dancy, Billy isn't going to tell me or anybody anything. He's afraid of what the Klan will do to him if he does. I can't convince him otherwise."

She slumped against the pillows again. "Then

you're telling me I'll probably hang for killing a marshal."

"No, because there's no one to dispute what you're saying, but unless we come up with a robe and a hood to prove he was in fact a member of the Klan, I'm afraid there's going to be a lot of trouble over this. But tell me what happened when Jordan got here," he asked suddenly.

"He brought two men with him and told them to take the marshal into Nashville to a doctor there. Evidently he expected him to be arrested. He convinced me to go home with him and stay while he went to Nashville to talk to the provost marshal and have him send a new marshal to take over here and get things calmed down."

"Jordan never showed up in Nashville. The provost marshal is a friend of mine. We fought together in the war. I always stop by to see him when I'm in town, and I happened to be there when the telegram came from Pinetops reporting Cox's death. Seems everyone is real upset."

Furiously Dancy spoke through tightly clenched teeth. "I don't care if Frank Cox was the governor of Tennessee. I know what I saw, and he was one of those hooded bastards."

"I believe you. . . ." He pulled her into his arms and held her close, could feel her trembling. "Now we've got to make everybody else believe you, too."

"So what happens now?" she asked warily.

"We get some rest till daylight." He pushed her back on the bed and lay down beside her, pulling her close in his arms.

And, as always, Dancy felt safe, if only for the time at hand.

Clint watched as pink shadows of dawn slithered through the windows to bathe Dancy in a soft, ethereal light. He had pulled back the sheet to drink in the sight of her. He hadn't planned to make love to her. All he wanted was to hold her as she slept, dreading the moment when he had to tell her it was his job to conduct a full investigation of the incident leading to the death of Marshal Frank Cox. He believed her story, but it had fallen upon him to convince everyone else. Now, however, with desire welling, priorities were fast slipping away.

Slowly, gently, he raised her gown. At the sight of her in all her naked splendor, his breath caught. The tender perfection of her lush, rose-tipped breasts, her tiny waist, luscious rounded hips, and long, smooth and shapely legs—all conspired to evoke a rush of longing akin to pain, deep in his loins. Her tawny, red-gold hair was fanned luxuriantly across the pillows, and he marveled once again what a truly beautiful creature she was.

His fingers, softly caressing, slid to her nipple and brushed it lightly, back and forth. He moved his hand downward.

Dancy awoke. His tongue began to brush her lips, easily coaxing them apart as he tortured with teasing tenderness.

Her fingers slipped about his neck, and boldly she brought him closer, offering him her mouth, moving against him to receive his kiss hungrily, deeply. Her hands moved onward to the rock-hard muscles of his shoulders and chest. He was still wearing his clothes, and she worked at the buttons with nimble fingers.

He assisted her, quickly rendering himself naked, his mouth against hers all the while. Dancy felt the heated rush building, pulsing through her veins, up and down her spine, fired by the thundering beat of her heart.

Drawing away, she gazed up into his scorching brown eyes. Lovingly she touched his face, tracing the lines of his cheek, across his mustache, onward to his smooth lips. He was rugged, he was rough. In some ways he was savage. She could feel the danger smoldering in him when he held her. She did not care what tomorrow held or whether their union was a sin. Nothing concerned her except the magic of the moment, the splendor of this glorious hour when he made her revel in her womanhood, joyous to be possessed by a man who brought her senses alive in a way she never dreamed possible.

Clint gazed into her intoxicating green eyes, desire raging till he felt he would surely explode without even entering her. "I want you," he whispered huskily, "but only if you want me, Dancy. Tell me, show me. . . ."

And she did so.

Slowly he inched his eager shaft into her extraordinary warmth, knowing each time he took her would be easier—and Lord, he planned to take her as much as she'd allow, for never, ever would he tire of such delight. He felt her silken heat sheathing him, yielding to envelop him. Finally he was able to penetrate fully, and she wrapped her legs about him, heels digging into his buttocks as she whispered, "You aren't hurting me now, Clint. I'm all yours. . . ."

He began possessive, rhythmic strokes, and Dancy knew she wanted it never to end. As long as he held her, as long as they were held captives of ecstasy, all was bliss.

Fully aroused, desperate for relief, Clint struggled to hold back. The pleasure was startling in its intensity, the gentle torture of her instinctive response as she clasped about his hardness excruciating in its sweetness.

She felt it from deep within, the first, stabbing quakes heralding the ultimate explosion. Her fingers dug into his strong back, clutching, squeezing, as she sought to enter him completely, become a part of him and never, ever leave.

Clint could sense her pending release, and his entry became harder, mightier, stronger. No longer did he fear he was hurting her, for she was meeting his every thrust with a roll of her hips.

They exploded together, both gasping out loud in wonder as their bodies fused, held, pressed, continued to undulate in the wild, reckless zenith. Yet what truly overwhelmed them was the silent, mutual realization that their coupling had not been mere lust of the flesh, but solace of the heart.

As they lay side by side, bodies soaked in perspiration, hearts pounding fiercely, Dancy acknowledged to herself that she was deeply in love. Yet there was a sadness shadowing the revelation. Kindred souls, they seemed to bring out the wild, stubborn streak in each other as they had when they were children. But now it was serious, because their lives, their futures, were at stake. And she knew she had to move slowly, lest she wind up with a broken heart that would not heal, spirit forever crushed and destroyed.

"I think," Clint said reluctantly, "we'd better get up and get ourselves decent. I've got a feeling we'll be having visitors soon."

Dancy forced herself back to reality. "No doubt.

It seems I've suddenly got to prove not only that I didn't shoot a federal marshal due to hysteria, but also that he was a member of the Ku Klux Klan. Should I ride into Nashville this morning and talk to the provost marshal?"

"That won't be necessary."

She raised up on one elbow to stare at him. Something in his voice, the way he met her questioning gaze, was unnerving. Frightening. "Why?" she asked.

"I'm conducting the investigation, Dancy."

"You?" She blinked, not understanding. "You mean the provost marshal asked you to investigate *me*?" The idea was ludicrous, and she could not help smiling.

But amusement faded with his next words.

"More than that. He's appointed me the new marshal."

Her eyes saw then what they'd failed to notice the night before.

He had removed his shirt, hung it on the bedpost. And for some reason she did not yet understand she found the flash of the tin badge in the early morning light not only intimidating, but ominous as well.

She moved away from him, trying to grasp what it all meant. Still heavy-headed from the laudanum, she went to the door, seeking fresh and cooling air to clear her brain.

And that was when she saw it, the neatly folded bundle lying on the porch.

Clint heard her soft, startled gasp. He saw how she clutched her throat with both hands as she began to laugh and cry at the same time.

"Dancy, what is it?"

He rushed to her side and snatched up the garments. Shaking them out, he found himself looking at a white robe and slitted hood—the dastardly garb of the Ku Klux Klan.

19

Clint gave his report on the death of Frank Cox to the authorities in Nashville. Indications were, he summarized, that Cox was indeed riding with the Ku Klux Klan that night, and Dancy had justifiably shot him in the act of attempting to burn down her home.

Dancy went about her business, trying not to be upset over how the townspeople continued to blame her. Dorcas Cox took her children and moved to live with relatives in Atlanta, and eventually gossip turned from Dancy to concern over the growing terrorism of the Klan all around.

The first batch of sap was harvested from her trees, and Dancy was elated. Clint insisted on going with her to lead the convoy of wagons and carts to the turpentine distillery in Nashville, afraid she might still be in danger of retaliation from the Klan, or others, for killing Cox. Dancy, however, felt she had exhibited to everyone that she had no intention of being intimidated. She didn't like having killed a man but bore no guilt over having done so accidentally.

"I don't like leaving you here alone again," Clint told her when they returned from the profitable trip to Nashville. "I've got an important job to do, Dancy, and it's going to take up a lot of my time. The Klan is spreading to other states besides Tennessee, and things are getting worse all the time."

They were sitting on the front porch steps. It was a peaceful time, with fireflies playfully twinkling in the shadows of the blackberry bushes by the barn and no sound save the distant hooting of an owl.

Dancy reached in her pocket and took out the money she'd set aside. Handing it to him, she tried not to sound gloating as she told him, "This pays you back for the taxes, Clint. I've kept my part of our bargain. I expect you to keep yours."

He looked from her outstretched palm to her expectant face and informed her solemnly, "Not till you've paid back Jordan. As long as he's got a lien on the place, I keep the title."

Despite deep personal feelings, Dancy was incensed. "I don't think that's any of your business. I know how you feel about him, but what's to stop me from borrowing from him again once you do give me title?"

"Then that will be *your* business. If he has to foreclose and takes the land, he'll be taking it away from you, not me. I'll be damned if I ever see him have the satisfaction."

Dancy crushed the bills in an angry fist, stuffed them back in her pocket. "Damn it, Clint, I don't have enough to pay both of you, not with all the supplies I need to double sap production, and you know it. You aren't being fair."

"I'm doing you a favor, but you won't see it because you're trapped in childhood memories of the way he used to be. He's changed, Dancy. He's mean. He revels in loaning people money and then foreclosing the first time they run into hard times. He's gathering a nice fortune for himself and slowly taking control of Addie's interests. But she's blind to him, like you are."

"And how do you know all this?"

"I've talked to some of the people whose property he's taken. They said he jumped at the chance to foreclose and wouldn't give them even a day's extension to come up with the money.

"And the Klan makes it all worse," he went on. "Their infernal raids are intimidating the freed slaves into moving away from here. People have to pay whites more money, and they can't afford it. With no labor, they can't get their crops in, and they go under. Jordan is right there, like a buzzard, waiting to pick their bones clean."

"You two really hate each other, don't you?" she remarked in wonder. "He tries to convince me you're actually a part of the Ku Klux Klan, and you try to make me see him as a hardhearted villain, out to take control of the entire county, no matter whom he destroys."

"You refuse to see him as anything but a charming little boy, don't you? Sure, I think it was wrong the way Addie raised him, never letting him do things other boys his age did, making a sissy out of him. And I admit I did my share of teasing, like brothers do. But I don't think it gives him the right to grow up and take out his resentment on everybody else."

Dancy admonished, "I don't think you're being fair. The man is a cripple. He'll be in a wheelchair the rest of his life."

"If that's the way you see him, I can't make you change your mind."

"No, you can't."

Several moments passed in tense silence, then Dancy, not wanting to part in anger, offered, "Let's not talk about Jordan. It's you I'm worried about. You disappear for days at a time, and you won't tell me where you go, what you do."

"The less you know, the better," he explained

gently. "My job is to try to bust up the Klan, at least around here. The civil authorities, like most of the white people, are either in sympathy with them or intimidated, so it's not going to be easy."

"It was an accident we even found out about Marshal Cox. A shame he didn't live long enough to tell you something," she lamented.

"I think they made sure he didn't. I believe he was killed to make sure he didn't talk and tell who else was riding with him that night."

"Murdered?"

"Exactly. But I can't prove a damn thing. I questioned Slade and his sidekick, but they swore up and down he died right after they left here, so they turned around and took him into town, and Doc Casper said his skull was busted when he fell, like I told you."

Dancy pressed her fingertips to his cheek. "Be careful," she urged. "Your life could be in danger, Clint."

"Yours, too, and that's the main reason I accepted the provost marshal's appointment. I want to rid this county of anybody who might harm you. Let me tell you something." He pulled her almost roughly into his arms. "Maybe I can be called a traitor to the South for fighting with the North, but Dooley O'Neal helped me see I was wrong in defending slavery. I owe him something for that—I intend to see that nothing happens to you."

His mouth claimed hers, and she twined her arms about his neck, reveling in the feel, the touch, the closeness, of his body. He lifted her in his arms and carried her inside to shut out the world as they found heaven and peace in each other's arms once again.

But even as desire raged and turned Dancy's blood to fire, she could not help wishing Clint McCabe's devotion were sired not by her uncle's love for her . . . but by his own.

Likewise plagued with doubts, Clint was needled with suspicion to think he was nothing more to Dancy than someone to be used to help with her dreams for the farm and occasionally fulfill needs he had awakened within her. And even though he wanted her as no other, he silently, fervently vowed to continue to keep a tight rein on his heart.

When once again they had climbed to the stars to soar through the heavens in bliss, they lay together for long, tender moments. Finally, reluctantly, Clint told her he'd be leaving the next morning. "I don't like leaving you, but I have no choice. I wish I could persuade you to go where it's safe."

"Do I have to remind you I've already proved I can take care of myself? God help those bastards if they dare ride on me again. And I've got more weapons now, remember? A breech-loading shotgun and a Spencer repeating carbine."

Clint knew about the new guns she'd purchased and was confident she knew how to use them, but she'd taken the Klan by surprise with her marksmanship before. If there was a next time, he feared they would be ready.

Concerning him, also, was the welfare of those around her. All freedmen, they were as vulnerable to violence as she was.

In the morning, when Dancy awoke to the sun streaming through the cabin windows, Clint was gone, and she realized she'd never felt more alone.

The next few weeks were extremely busy as she hired more workers to tend the trees, increasing production. With so much to do, she didn't have time to go into town, and even though Jordan still made frequent visits, often she was nowhere around when he came. Sometimes he left flowers he'd had Gabriel pick along the road, and a few times he brought gifts of food items still in short supply—coffee, tea, sugar, and spices. Though grateful, she was relieved on those occasions when she missed him, for he was becoming bolder and bolder in his insistence that she accept his proposal.

Then came time to make the payment on her

loan, and she knew it was no coincidence that Jordan made no appearance for a few days prior. He did not want her to think he was coming around solely to collect the money, and Dancy suspected he was hoping she wouldn't have it anyway.

When she had received payment for the sap at the turpentine distillery, she had gone shopping in Nashville and bought much needed clothes. Wanting to look nice for her trip into Pinetops, she chose her favorite of the new gowns, a white-and-yellow-patterned cotton. It had a fitted bodice with a shawl collar and sleeves with double puffs, and the flounces of the skirt were edged with embroidery. On top of her flame red hair, she positioned the delicate batiste cap trimmed with ribbon rosettes and lace.

After pulling on kid gloves, she picked up her matching parasol and smiled, thinking how Addie McCabe would consider that alone protection and would regard the pistol hidden in her bag unnecessary.

First she went to the store to leave her list, so Emmett could get everything ready while she took care of business at the bank. Seeing Dorothy behind the counter, Dancy felt her cheerful mood begin to dissipate.

Coldly, Dorothy took the list and scanned it, then, over the rims of her owlish glasses, grunted and said, "Quite an order here, missy. You got the money to pay for it? I don't care what Jordan McCabe told Emmett, I'm not going to let you keep on running up your credit."

Politely Dancy informed her, "I'll pay cash for it today, Miss Dorothy, as well as everything I owe you."

Stepping out of the shadows, Lucille Byrnes cut in sarcastically, "Well, well, where would you get that kind of money, Dancy O'Neal? Is the new marshal paying you well these days?"

The woman was familiar, Dancy realized, although she couldn't place her. "I beg your pardon, ma'am, but you have no right to say such things to me. And don't I know you?"

Lucille pulled herself to her full height, glad she could look down on the red-haired heathen. "No, you don't, but I know you all right. Your mother, too. I was there when your brother was born. Saw you in church, too. Always talking instead of listening to the preacher. Fighting in the yard, too, like a rowdy boy. Not surprised at all to hear you grew up to gun down a man," she finished with a sniff of contempt and a haughty lift of her chin.

Dancy's mouth actually opened to respond, but she closed it quickly and turned back to Dorothy. No good would come of confrontation, she had told herself over and over. These women would always dislike her, and nothing she could do would change their feelings. "I'll be back in a little while. If you'll have those things ready, I'd appreciate it."

She was almost out the door when Lucille called shrilly, "It's real interesting when a feud keeps going on into the next generation. You've got the McCabe boys at each other's throats, like your ma had the O'Neals."

"Bad blood will out," someone shouted from the back of the door.

"Amen, sister," came several responses at once.

Dancy kept on going, head high, heart pounding. So, the way her mother and Dooley felt about each other had not been a true secret after all. Others had suspected as well. But it doesn't matter now, she told herself adamantly, and if people blamed her for the animosity between Clint and Jordan, they were dead wrong. Those two had been at odds with each other their whole lives, and now it was exacerbated because of the war. She had nothing to do with that.

Matilda Warren gave Dancy a curt nod and motioned her to go right into Jordan's office.

"Dancy." He greeted her effusively, rolling his chair from behind his desk and holding out his hands to her. She gave an obligatory squeeze with her fingertips but did not enter into an embrace.

"Is something wrong?" He regarded her in alarm as he backed up his chair.

"Not at all." She managed a tight smile. The truth was, she had been annoyed with him ever since he'd admitted giving her laudanum that night to make her sleep. He'd had no right to take control in such a way, and she'd told him so.

"Well, I don't believe you," he was saying. "I know all this has been hard on you, my dear. It has to be a terrible burden to bear, knowing you killed a man, especially one with a wife and two little boys, and—"

"No, Jordan, as a matter of fact, it isn't. I was defending myself. I shot—in the shoulder—a man who was not only a member of the Ku Klux Klan and guilty of God only knows how many other crimes of injustice, but was also a hypocrite, sworn to uphold the law, not break it. As for his wife and children, I'm sorry they had the misfortune to call him husband and father. Perhaps they'll even be better off without him in their life."

Jordan blanched. This was a side to Dancy he hadn't seen before. Indignation and temper, yes, but never so much unbridled fire and ice. "I'm sorry. I had no idea you'd come to terms so rapidly with what you did. Perhaps the way you're living is causing you to become hardened. I hate to see it."

"Well, you won't hate to see this." She made her tone light and forced a smile as she opened her bag and laid out the money on the desk. "The money you loaned me. All of it. I'm now out of your debt, Jordan."

For a moment all he could do was look at the bills in disbelief, then slowly he lifted his gaze and whispered, "Monetarily, perhaps, but you've yet to reimburse me for stealing my heart."

"Jordan, no—"

"No, you listen." He was whirling about the desk in a flash. "I love you. I always have. And if you weren't so hell-bent on proving you can make a go of that infernal land, you'd admit you love me, too. Give me a chance. That's all I ask.

"It's Clint, isn't it?" he rushed on, eyes wide with fury, nostrils flaring as he flailed at the air with his fists. "Damn him. Can't you see he's making a fool of you? He's using you, Dancy, like he's used all the women in his life. He still visits that whore of his in Nashville. I hear things. I know what goes on. As for him being marshal, everybody but you knows he's only hiding behind his badge to get even with everybody who holds him in contempt for being a traitor to the South."

"Jordan, I don't want to hear any of this," Dancy protested, "It's not true, and—"

"It *is* true, damn it. You're too blind to see it.

And he's also a womanizer. Someone told me three days ago he was in Pulaski, and they saw him at a saloon, headed upstairs with some whore hanging on his arm. It's the truth, I swear it."

Exasperated, she cried, "Why do you say such things about your brother?"

"Brother," he sneered. "He's no brother of mine. And he's not good enough for you. You need a good man, a gentleman, someone with breeding and intelligence. And I *can* be a husband to you." He reached for her, tried to pull her into his arms, but she struggled against him. "I'll prove it to you, if that's what you're worried about. And I can put a baby inside you, our baby, Dancy. I swear it."

He held her face between his hands in a vise-like grip as he claimed her mouth roughly. In panic, Dancy clutched his wrists, trying to make him release his hold without causing him to topple over in his chair.

But to an outsider, in that frozen moment, it could have appeared that Dancy was merely caressing him as he held her, enjoying his kiss.

And, in fact, that's exactly what it did look like to Addie McCabe as she walked into the room.

"Stop that!" She rushed to beat on Jordan's back with her parasol. Startled, he pulled away and threw up his arms to fend off her attack. She then turned her attention to Dancy.

"Mother, get away!" he yelled, lashing out to grab the annoying weapon and yank it away from her. But she had a good grip and wound up being jerked across his lap.

Dancy scrambled to her feet and backed away from both of them. She dimly was aware of Matilda Warren's curiously staring face at the door, along with a few customers.

"You . . . you Jezebel!" Addie screamed. "You whore of Babylon. How dare you come in here and bewitch my son? Isn't it enough you killed the father of two innocent children? Do you have to keep on wrecking lives? You're just like your—"

Then, Dancy and Jordan, along with the bank's customers gathered in the doorway, watched in momentary shock as Addie, with a gasp, suddenly slumped to the floor.

Matilda said, "My God, she's had a stroke. . ."

"Get a doctor," Dancy yelled, dropping to her knees to cradle Addie in her arms. "She's still breathing. Hurry."

"Oh, she's had these spells before," Jordan said airily, rolling himself behind his desk. Then, glancing up to see people watching, he cried, "What's wrong with you? This is none of your business. Get out of here, all of you, or I'll remember your inconsideration the next time you're in arrears on your loans, I warn you." He shook a finger, and the crowd quickly disappeared.

Dancy was still kneeling beside Addie when Doc Casper arrived a few moments later. Swearing under his breath, he opened his worn leather bag and took out the stethoscope. Pressing it against her chest, he said to no one in particular, "Heart sounds good. I don't think we need worry she's had a stroke. Probably just fainted. I told her she shouldn't be up and about so much. Kidney troubles can make a person awful weak, but she's a stubborn old bird. Can't tell her anything."

"That's a fact." Jordan was behind his desk once more, counting money, unconcerned. "I was telling Dancy she's had these spells before. She gets mad and faints. Sometimes I wonder if she's really unconscious or faking to get attention."

Addie did not move, though it was all she could do to keep from bristling from head to toe as she witnessed her son's insolence. She had not faked anything. All of a sudden the world had started spinning, and she'd felt herself being sucked into a great, dark void. She had come around as Doc Casper arrived, but no one saw her open her eyes, and she had quickly closed them, wanting to hear what was said about her.

The doctor straightened. "I wouldn't know about that, Jordan, but your mother is going to have to take better care of herself."

Jordan remarked, "I thought Bright's disease was fatal."

Dancy glanced at him sharply, stunned he could sound so uncaring about his own mother.

"*Life* is fatal, Jordan," Doc Casper responded dryly, "but your mother's does not have to end any time soon, not if she gets good care."

"Well, I've told you I'm willing to bear any expense to send her to a hospital somewhere and let them take care of her."

"She doesn't want to go, and they can't give her any better care than she can get at home."

Jordan did look at him then, and the air was nearly crackling with tension as he said tartly, "She's getting to be quite a burden, doctor. I have enough to worry about with my own handicap without trying to cope with hers. I also fear she's losing her mind. There are places to put people like her."

"Oh, is that so?" Addie sat up.

Dancy was so shocked that she lost her balance and fell backward on her bottom. Addie struggled to her feet, while Dancy, Jordan, and the doctor could only stare in stunned silence.

"You'd like that, wouldn't you?" She directed her fury at Jordan. "You'd like to have me locked away in one of those places where they put crazy people. Then you could take over. Well, it won't happen."

Parasol in hand, she jabbed Doc Casper in the chest with the tip as he reflexively raised his arms in surrender. "And you better not be in cahoots with him, either. Nobody is getting rid of Addie McCabe, and God help anybody who tries."

With a swish, the papers on Jordan's desk scattered. "We'll talk later about what happened here today, boy. You count on it."

Dancy had already scrambled to her feet and was retreating toward the door, knowing she was next in line for castigation.

"And you," Addie raged. "I want you to get out of town and leave my son alone, you hear me?"

Instead of withering before her as Jordan and Doc Casper had done, Dancy suddenly halted. "I haven't done anything to invite Jordan's interest in me, Miss Addie. You're wrong if you think I have. Frankly, I think you're wrong about a lot of things. Especially about me. I want to be your friend, if you'll let me. I thought I proved that by nursing you when everyone else stayed away, thinking you had the pox."

"That's right," Doc Casper dared to agree.

"Shut your mouth," Addie ordered, then said to Dancy, "You thought you could butter me up, so's I'd approve of your marrying my son—"

"That's a lie." It was Dancy's turn to interrupt, and she did so with gusto. "I don't want to marry Jordan, and I am not going to marry him. All I want is to farm the land my uncle left me, to make a home for myself here. And I'd like to be friends with you, Miss Addie, if you'll let me, and everyone else in this town. Because the truth is," she finished, blinking back tears of loneliness, "I don't have anywhere else to go."

She turned on her heel and ran from the office.

Doc Casper nodded with admiration and murmured, "Now that's a spunky girl, if I ever saw one."

Addie sniffed. "She's a sassy, hellish girl. Always was. Always will be."

Secretly, however, Addie was taken aback by Dancy's grit. Nobody had ever stood up to her that way and admittedly it was a shock to hear her come right out and say she didn't have any notions about marrying Jordan. He was rich and handsome, despite being a cripple, and there wasn't an unmarried girl in middle Tennessee who wouldn't jump at the chance to land a husband like him. No doubt she was smitten with Clint. Good, Addie opined with a quick nod. The two scalawags deserved each other.

Jordan said nothing, merely leaned back in his chair and templed his fingers as rage worked its way through his body.

Dancy had made a fool of him by declaring in front of witnesses that she did not want to marry him. But no one, by God, made a fool of Jordan McCabe and got away with it.

Dancy would come to realize that, just as she'd see she was wrong in thinking she'd never be his wife.

20

Clint downed the last of his whiskey and smiled gratefully at the woman sitting on the edge of the bed. She was wearing a black silk robe edged in white feathers, opened just enough to reveal the curve of her generous breasts. Her cheeks, like her lips, were painted bright orange, the same color as her hair, which was a mass of ringlets. She reeked of perfume. "You've been a big help, Lucy," he told her appreciatively as he laid several bills on the bedside table.

They were in her room, above a saloon in Pulaski, Tennessee. It was late, after midnight, and she reached out and placed her hand on his thigh and gently squeezed. "I could help you in a lot of other ways, Marshal, and from the looks of the money you laid down, I'd say you've already paid for it."

Clint knew any other time he'd have fallen

right on top of her, but things had changed. *He* had changed. "Another time. I'm going to slip on out of here. I've got to be heading home."

"Well, remember you've got some free lovin', whenever you want it." With a sudden frown she warned, "Don't forget you swore you wouldn't say nothing about talking to me."

He was quick to assure her, "You don't have to worry, Lucy. If it weren't for you girls keeping your eyes and ears open, I'd never pick up any clues as to who's in the Klan. Nobody else is willing to talk to a *traitor*," he reminded her with a wink.

Lucy giggled. "You use them big words, Marshal, and make being a whore sound real respectable. Besides," she added with a sudden flash of ire, "I don't like them bastards, the way they hide behind their masks to torment people. They beat my brother real bad, they did, 'cause he befriended an ex-slave. I hope you catch every one of them."

"I'll see you soon, Lucy." He patted her cheek fondly. "Keep up the good work."

He left her, leaving by the back door so the owner of the place would think he was staying the night. Usually Clint hung around long after he'd obtained whatever information there was to be had, but it got awkward after a time. The whores felt guilty, he supposed, not to be doing what they were paid to do, and sometimes it got hard to turn down their offers, but he no longer found a quick tumble in bed, with someone he felt nothing for, satisfying.

The fact was, he had broken his own vow by falling in love, and now he wanted no one but Dancy.

Dancy had made up her mind not to go into Pinetops again until things calmed down. With the exception of Clint, and Jordan, who admitted he'd believe anything she said anyway because of the way he felt about her, no one else accepted her claim that the marshal had actually been riding with the Klan. Feelings were running extremely high against her.

She threw herself into her work. Up at dawn to oversee whatever chores needed to be done, she was ready by midmorning to ride the woods and check the progress of the sap collection. In addition, she had men building new fences to keep out trespassers, as she had found stumps on remote borders where trees had been chopped down and stolen.

With chickens and a few cows and hogs purchased, there was much to be done. Already she was having clearings tilled in preparation for planting more cotton next spring.

"Miz Dancy, you got one of the best farms in Tennessee," Billy complimented her one day as she was watching him build a new henhouse. "Most of the land hereabouts is too rocky and steep for tilling and planting, but you got lots of level ground, and folks say cotton is gonna really go up in price. No wonder Master Clint wanted this place."

"He's not the only one," she stated flatly, thinking about Jordan and his mother. "But it's mine now."

She stood there a few moments and finally decided she had to say it. "Billy, I want you to know how much I appreciate what you did for me."

He was digging a post hole and did not glance up, but she noted how he gripped the shovel tighter.

"Don't rightly know what you're talkin' about, Miss Dancy."

"Yes, you do. The robe and hood Marshal Cox was wearing the night I shot him. You were the one who found it and left it on the porch for Clint to see. If you hadn't, there'd have been no proof I was telling the truth. That was good of you, Billy. I'll never forget you for it."

He continued to dig, keeping his head down. "I'm afraid you're wrong, missy. I don't know nothin' about no robe."

She knew he was lying but went along with him. "Well, how do you suppose those things got on my porch?"

He paused as though seriously considering her question, then, with a twinkle in his eyes, said, "Well, there just ain't no telling. But what I do know is when I got back from fetchin' Master Jordan, when me and those two men of his went out to the barn, the marshal, he was laying there, just like I left him, but there won't no robe around. Somebody had done stripped it off him. Nobody said nothin', so I didn't, either. I made like I didn't know a thing."

With a warm smile she told him, "Well, if you ever do find out who was responsible, tell them I'll always be grateful."

She was starting to worry over not having heard from Clint. At night she'd lie awake as long as possible, hoping he'd use the cloak of darkness to slip in to see her. But as time passed and he did not come, she was plagued by Jordan's taunts and began to wonder if maybe she were merely a folly to Clint. She had proved to him she could take care of herself, make a living off the land and had no intention of leaving, so perhaps he'd tired of their wager and used his appointment to marshal to rid himself of her. Then, when Billy told her he'd seen him in town, she really got mad.

Therefore she was not in the best of moods

when Jordan arrived late one afternoon. She had just returned from the falls after a bath and swim. She dressed quickly.

"I wasn't expecting you," she informed him brusquely as she stood in the doorway, watching as Gabriel carried him up the steps.

"You're beautiful, as always." His expression was adoring as he motioned Gabriel to carry him inside.

Dancy followed, protesting, "Really, Jordan, I find this an imposition, and—"

"Nonsense. We're friends, aren't we?" He indicated Gabriel should place him on the bed. "The road was unusually bumpy today. Must be the rains. My back is hurting. I need to prop myself on the pillows."

Gabriel obliged, while Dancy stood watching, frowning, hands on her hips.

"You can't stay. I'd planned to go to bed early, Jordan. It's been a very hard day."

"I've been worried about you. You haven't been in to see me."

"There was no reason to. I paid back the money you loaned me, remember?"

He nodded and reached into his coat pocket, took out a piece of paper and handed it to her. "Your receipt. Paid in full. You were in such a hurry to leave, you forgot it.

"But that means you trust me, doesn't it?" he

went on complacently. "And it pleases me. More than you know."

Dancy saw he was removing his coat, folding it neatly on the chair beside the bed, then loosening his cravat. "What do you think you're doing? I told you—" She stopped at the sound of a carriage and ran to the window to see that Gabriel was leaving. Whirling around to see Jordan's smug grin, she cried, "Why did you send him away? I told you, you can't stay."

"Don't be upset, Dancy, please. I told him to take a little ride and give us some privacy. I have to talk to you."

"We've nothing to talk about."

He gave a helpless sigh. "Dancy, why are you so angry with me? I helped you, remember? If not for me—"

"And I'm grateful," she assured him, "but I've paid you back in full, with interest. I can't see where I owe you anything else."

"How about friendship?"

"You want more than that, and you know it. And it can't be."

"You thought so once. We used to play Mommy and Daddy, remember? And we grieved together when Clint drowned our baby, and—"

"Stop it, Jordan. I won't keep listening to this childish drivel." She went to the side of the bed to tower over him, losing all patience. "We were children, for God's sake. A lot has happened since then. I've been through hell to get where I am now—self-supporting, free from anyone dictating to me how to live my life. And I'll not have you or anyone else badgering me. I offered you friendship, but you didn't want it. Neither did your mother. And I think the way you treat her is terribly disrespectful. Maybe she is cantankerous and hard to get along with, but she's still your mother and deserves your respect."

He hung his head as though contrite. "Yes, yes, you're probably right. I should have more patience with her. God only knows Clint has hurt her enough. Did you know he's in town?" he asked suddenly, looking up at her with a taunting gleam. "When Gabriel and I passed by Sweeney's place, we saw him. Standing on the porch, talking to one of those debauched women."

Lest he see the distress on her face, Dancy turned away. "What Clint does is his business. I'm not interested."

"I can understand that. He's caused grief to so many people, Dancy. I just don't want you mad at me. God knows I've got my own pain to bear—" He gasped and groaned, lunging forward to clutch at his right leg.

Dancy whipped about in alarm. "What is it? What's wrong?"

"Cramps." His face twisted in anguish. "Happens sometimes. Help me, please."

"Of course, of course." She sat beside him. "Just tell me what to do."

"Massage my leg, please. Rub the calf. Work it out. My back is hurting so bad from the carriage ride, I can't do it hard enough. I'm sorry."

"You've nothing to be sorry for. You can't help it." After pushing his trousers leg above his knee, she began nimbly to rub and knead.

He arched his back against the pillows and moaned softly as she worked. "That's good. That's better. Yes, yes, Dancy, thank you. I hate being a bother, but the pain is terrible."

"Relax," she urged, feeling terribly sorry for him.

"Sometimes I wish I'd died right on the battlefield. What do I have to live for, anyway? I'm not paralyzed. I can move my legs, but I still can't walk, because the ball damaged my spine. I can't do anything except sit behind a desk all day, trying to run a bank, despite my mother driving customers away with her nasty disposition.

"When you came back into my life"—his tone suddenly became reverent, tender—"I thought God had sent me a special blessing, and it was His way of giving me happiness despite losing my ability to walk. But you didn't think I was man enough for you—"

"Jordan, stop it, please," Dancy pleaded. "I'm trying to help you with the pain, but I'm not going to sit here and listen to nonsense."

"No, don't listen to it," he cried suddenly, lunging to grab her and swing her down beside him. "I'll make you see you're wrong. You think because Clint can walk he's better than I, but it doesn't matter in bed. I'm able to give you anything he or any other man can."

His hands seemed to be everywhere at once. Dancy screamed in protest.

"I'll show you, damn it." He covered her face with moist, eager kisses, her cheeks, her eyelids, her ears, as she twisted beneath him. "I'll make you see I *am* a man, and then you'll marry me, and I swear, Dancy, you'll be the happiest and richest woman in all of Tennessee. You and I, we'll run this state."

She beat upon his back with her fists and then, in desperation, clawed at his face. "You're making me hate you, Jordan," she raged. "Do you really think I'd marry you after this? I'd hate you till the day I die."

He froze. Then he raised his head to stare down at her as her words washed over him. "Don't, Dancy," he whispered miserably. "Don't hate me. I love you, and I only want to show you how much."

"Then let me go," she commanded, "because if

you do this, I swear I will never forgive you. You don't have to prove anything," she added, buoyed by the way his hold upon her slackened somewhat. "Give me time, Jordan. Give *us* time. You're rushing me, and I'm not ready. God knows I've been through so much." She made her voice crack, as though about to burst into tears, daring to inspire compassion and pity.

"I thought," she whispered as he stared down at her with tormented eyes, "you were my friend. I never thought you'd hurt me this way."

He tore away from her then, covering his face with his hands as he rolled onto his back and cried, "Oh, God, what have I done? I love you so much it's driving me crazy."

Dancy eased from the bed, keeping a wary eye upon him as she distanced herself. Then she ran from the cabin and out to the barn, leaving him to await Gabriel's return.

The barn was empty. The workers were either still in the fields or busy with other chores. He'd had it planned. She knew that now and felt like such a fool. The cramps in his leg had been faked. He had wanted only to get her on the bed and into his clutches, and she was fortunate to have escaped.

Rage burned in her veins like molten lava. She stared out the window, hoping to see Gabriel coming back. Her heart was pounding furiously, and she shook from head to toe to think of him there, in her house, while she was forced to retreat.

Finally, unable to stand the tension any longer, she saddled a horse and charged out of the barn, thundering down toward the main road. She didn't know where she was going, nor did she care. She merely rode toward the sinking sun, as though pleading to be taken with it, to the other side of the world, away from the madness.

She didn't realize she'd gone so far till the church loomed ahead. Beyond was the graveyard, dotted with tombstones. An aura of peace spread like an invisible shroud amid the hallowed glow of dusk, and she found herself dismounting and entering the gate. She had meant to visit since returning but had never found the time. To do so now seemed strangely appropriate.

She wandered among the monuments, memory jogged now and then by familiar names not thought of for so many years.

At first Dancy did not see her, for the grave was obscured by the trunk of the massive oak tree. The woman's back was to her as she knelt, and Dancy halted where she stood, respectful of her mourning. Then, slowly, the name on the stone became clear.

O'Neal.

Dancy ventured closer, footsteps muffled by the thick grass as she walked gingerly on top of a grave to keep from being seen. That was when she noticed what she'd failed to before—the horse and carriage hidden from view behind the church.

Addie McCabe's carriage.

But why was Addie visiting her father's grave? Dancy wondered. Across the path, in the very middle of the cemetery, as befitting someone so prominent, a tall marker stretched toward the sky—a marker carved with the name *McCabe* in bold letters. That was where Addie should be doing her grieving, not at the O'Neal site.

Another jolt as Dancy drew closer and saw it was not her father's grave Addie knelt beside, but Dooley's. A soft gasp of surprise escaped her, and Addie heard and whipped about to stare in embarrassed horror.

"What . . . what are you doing here?" she cried, struggling to stand as surprise yielded to anger. "Spying on me, are you? How dare you?"

Calmly Dancy responded, "I wasn't spying. I was looking for my family's graves. My father. My little brother. My *uncle*," she added pointedly, almost accusingly.

"Well, there he is." Addie pointed with a hastily conjured flash of contempt. "Better visit all you can, because I wouldn't be surprised sometime to come out here and find him dug up."

She hastened to add, "I was paying my respects

to your father, like I promised my cousin I'd do when she moved away."

Dancy suspected she was lying but wasn't about to say so. "Well, that's real nice of you, Miss Addie. Now what was it you were saying about my uncle's grave?"

"There're brave Confederate soldiers buried on these sacred grounds. Some of their families don't like the idea of a Union soldier being buried amongst them. Especially one who was a traitor to the South."

"And you think someone would be evil enough to dig up his body?" Dancy was horrified.

"You never know what folks will do when they get riled." She leaned over to pick up her bag and parasol.

"Are you feeling better these days?"

Addie turned to stare at her, struck by how it sounded as though she really cared, but indignant all the same. "Can't see it's any of your business, but as a matter of fact, yes, I am. You and Jordan can scheme all you want to get rid of me, but I'm not going anywhere. And God help anybody who tries to make me."

Dancy could not help smiling. Thin, wiry Addie McCabe looked anything but threatening. "Miss Addie, I'd never do anything to hurt you, and I do wish you'd get the notion out of your head that I've got any thoughts of marrying Jordan."

"Well, he's got different ideas, and he didn't get them by himself. You must have done something to encourage him."

"No ma'am," Dancy shook her head solemnly. "I swear I haven't done anything. The fact is, I left my cabin just now to get away from him."

"You did what?" Addie's eyes widened.

"He won't take no for an answer, so I left him back at my place. Gabriel will take him home soon, I'm sure. I didn't want to keep arguing with him."

"For some reason, I'm starting to believe you," Addie said in wonder, then added coldly, "But it doesn't change anything. You're still on land I want, land I'm willing to buy from you, and you're being stubborn, like Clinton, wanting to hurt me."

"No, ma'am," Dancy denied once more. "It's my home now, and I'm staying."

"Even after killing an innocent man? Leaving two little boys without a father?"

"Marshal Cox was not innocent. He was a member of the Klan. But you won't believe me. Nobody will, except Clint. Jordan says he does, but sometimes I'm not so sure."

"Clinton. What does he know?" Addie scoffed. "He'll tell you anything to get his way. He always was a conniver and a liar."

Dancy surprised her by inquiring innocently, "Have you always despised him?"

"What are you talking about?"

"He was only a year old when you married his father, wasn't he? Still a baby. Did you resent him even then? I can't believe you couldn't love a helpless, motherless child."

"Why . . . why . . ." Addie stammered, unaccustomed to scrutiny from anyone. "You've got a lot of nerve, young lady."

"And another thing," Dancy continued after pausing to bestow a genuinely compassionate smile, "I don't believe you're as mean and ornery as you'd have everybody believe. I think somebody hurt you real bad, a long time ago, and you act like you do to keep folks from knowing you're crying on the inside."

Addie paled, then swayed ever so slightly. "That . . . that's absurd. You're an insolent girl, that's what you are. You have no respect for your elders."

"No, ma'am," Dancy disputed in her most respectful tone. "That's not true at all. I do respect you, but I also feel sorry for you."

Addie was quick to cry, "I don't want your pity, damn you."

"Uncle Dooley said the same thing."

Addie's stiffened. "What are you talking about?"

"I was mad at you about something. I can't remember exactly. I think it was the day Clint put my doll in the creek and said he was drowning her." She smiled to recall the childish incident that had so infuriated her at the time. "And then I punched him in the eye. Anyway, you scolded me, and I told Uncle Dooley I hated you, and he said I shouldn't, because sometimes people get disappointed and hurt in life, and they take it out on others, and you have to look inside them to see how good they really are. That's what I've tried to do for you, Miss Addie." She reached out to touch her shoulder in a gesture of kindness.

Addie jerked away. "You don't know what you're talking about, and—"

"Oh, look," Dancy said suddenly, hurrying to where a patch of daisies bloomed profusely. She knelt and ran her fingers lovingly through the gentle white blossoms. "My baby brother is buried here."

"Oh, land's sakes," Addie said, exasperated. "How can you know? There's no marker. Carlin never put one up after your mother took you and ran off. No doubt he just wanted to forget anything to do with her."

"Uncle Dooley must have planted them."

"Don't be ridiculous."

Dancy was not about to confide the tender memories of the day of her brother's burial, when her uncle had shared the sweet story about the forever kind of flowers. But she was sure he had planted them on top of the grave, and she vowed to return soon and do the same for his.

She straightened and turned, intending to try once again to make Miss Addie see she wanted only to be her friend. But the older woman was stalking away, leaning to poke her parasol into the ground to help support her as she made her way back to the carriage.

Darkness had fallen by the time Dancy returned to the cabin. There was no sign of Jordan, and she went inside gratefully. Then, after a quick supper of buttermilk and cornbread, she went to bed, wearily falling asleep right away.

From somewhere far, far away, she heard the sound of someone calling her name frantically. She struggled to awaken, to escape the nebulous web of slumber.

"Miss Dancy, you gotta come quick. Please."

She bolted upright, instinctively reaching for her gun.

"Miss Dancy . . ."

It was Roscoe's voice, and he sounded terrified. She bounded out of bed, ran to the door, and yanked it open. She could barely see his face in the darkness as he wailed, "Oh, Miss Dancy, it's awful. They beat him real bad. You gotta help him."

"Who, Roscoe? Who was beaten?" Already she was backing inside the cabin, fumbling for her robe, grabbing her gun and fighting to remain calm amid the prickling needles of terror. "Tell me what happened."

"Just hurry," he urged hysterically, already down the steps and racing toward the barn.

Dancy was close on his heels. "Roscoe, for God's sake, tell me."

"It's Billy," he yelled over his shoulder. "The Ku Klux Klanners beat him bad."

And Dancy kept on running, despite the quaking horror that shook her from head to toe.

21

They had carried Billy into the barn and placed him on a bed of straw in one of the stalls. He was barely conscious. The other blacks had gathered around him, several holding lanterns, and they parted to let Dancy through.

Dropping to her knees, she saw there was no visible sign of injury on his face. She clutched one of his hands as he looked up at her with pain-dimmed eyes. "Where are you hurt, Billy?" she asked. "What did they do to you?"

Billy moaned softly and closed his eyes, in too much pain to speak.

Roscoe exploded. "They kicked him. Must've broke some ribs."

"We couldn't help him," someone else chimed in. "We wanted to, Lord knows, but they had guns, Miz Dancy."

She rocked back on her heels and stared at him

worriedly. They had stripped off his shirt. There seemed to be no bleeding, so obviously all they had done was punch and kick. No doubt, some bones were broken, or, at the very least, cracked. He'd be sore for a while, but nothing could be done other than see that he got plenty of rest. Binding him with soft rags might give some relief, so she instructed one of the workers to go to the cabin for a sheet to tear into strips.

Then she asked of no one in particular, "Tell me what happened."

They recounted to her how they had been returning from changing sap buckets at the stand of pines on the other side of the pointed ridge. It was nearly dark, so no one had seen the "ghosts," as they called them, till they'd converged from the woods, on foot, all carrying guns. They'd demanded to know which one of them was called Billy.

"At first he didn't say nothin', and we didn't, either," one worker offered. "Then they said if Billy didn't speak up and identify himself, they was gonna hang all of us. So Billy, he stepped forward."

Dancy was swept with admiration for the man and touched tender fingertips to his brow in a gesture of respect. "It's a wonder they didn't kill him."

His eyes fluttered open momentarily, and he smiled wanly.

Roscoe spoke angrily between clenched teeth. "They said it was just a warning, that Billy better learn to stay out of white folks' business, and all of us better ride on and find other jobs, 'cause you're gonna pay for what you did."

Dancy wasn't frightened about their threats concerning her. What disturbed her, however, was how the Klan obviously held Billy responsible for the mysterious appearance of Frank Cox's costume. "But how could they have known?" she wondered aloud.

Roscoe offered his theory. "Maybe they was still close by and watching when Billy came out of the woods and heard you call his name."

"Maybe," she agreed, but something was beginning to needle at her, something she couldn't quite put her finger on.

She got to her feet. "I want you to listen to me, all of you," she began slowly, evenly, wanting to underscore each and every word. "I don't want you to be afraid of those hooligans, understand? Don't let them make you run away. You've got a job here. A place to live. I'll look after you the best I can, I swear it. And from now on, you'll quit the fields early, and be back before dark, and you won't go out again until daylight, understand? I don't think they'll come during the day," she rushed on. "They never do. They're afraid someone might recognize something about them, tell who they are, because, I promise you, the law is after them.

"They know I'll shoot. I didn't mean to kill Marshal Cox, but I promise you, I won't bat an eye at blowing all of them straight to hell if they dare ride on this farm again." She shook her fist for emphasis.

The Negroes exchanged glances, nodding at each other as if agreeing that Miss Dancy meant what she said.

"I'll sit up a spell with Billy and make sure he's not seriously hurt," she went on. "The rest of you get some sleep. If you're going to quit work before dark, you're going to have to start at first light."

Dancy tried to stay awake but weariness took command, and with Billy sleeping soundly, she was soon nodding herself, leaning back against the stall railings with eyes closed.

Sometime later a gentle hand shook her awake, and she jumped, startled. At once she was swept with relief to see Clint. "Thank God, you're back," she whispered.

"Roscoe told me what happened," he said darkly. "I examined Billy, and he's not hurt too bad. He'll be all right in a few days. They could've killed him. Let's go back to the cabin where we can talk."

Dancy waited till they were seated at the table with steaming mugs of coffee before asking,

"Have you been able to find out anything? Anything at all?"

He had, but he was not prepared to tell her, not till he had proof. For the time being all he had were his suspicions. "No," he lied. "Not yet."

"It's getting worse. Where's it all going to lead? How many helpless people like Billy are going to be hurt? How many of those bastards am I going to have to shoot before they learn to leave me alone?"

"Stop it, Dancy." Angry himself, he charged, "When are you going to learn these bastards are nothing to fool around with? After all they've done, do you think they're going to let a woman stand up to them? You only aggravated the situation by shooting Cox. You haven't scared them off for good."

"Well, what in the hell was I supposed to do?" she fired back. "Stand there and let them burn my cabin down? No, Clint, I won't cower before someone hiding behind a sheet, and you can be sure I'll be waiting for them if they come back."

Exasperated, he pleaded, "When are you going to understand you can't fight them? Get out and let the law take care of it."

"Where would I go? As long as evil is allowed to run rampant, it isn't safe anywhere. And just what is the law doing to take care of it? You say you haven't been able to find out anything, so what have you been doing all this time?

"I know what I've *heard* you're doing," she added hotly, not about to come right out and tell him what Jordan had said. She wanted him to admit it himself and offer an explanation.

"I can't help what you've heard, and I don't give a damn." His jaw tightened. He suspected that Jordan was filling her head with lies. "I'm doing my job the best I know how. If it's not good enough for you, I'm sorry."

Dancy couldn't keep her frustrations inside any longer. "Were you in town a few days ago?"

He wasn't about to divulge why he hadn't come out to see her. The truth was, he'd been trying to stay away, because when he was with her all he could think of was how much he wanted her, how much he cared. She had the workers staying in the barn now, and she did know how to use a gun. He felt as if he were keeping an eye on things, but he kept his distance for personal reasons.

"Yes, I was," he finally admitted, but gave the excuse he already knew was flimsy. "I didn't come out because I was busy."

"With your whores?" Dancy figured if she was going to open her mouth and make a fool of herself, she might as well go all the way. "You've been seen at bawdy houses, Clint. Is that all I mean to you?"

Clint felt rage creeping, but not with her, for under other circumstances her jealousy would please him. What worried him was that he'd been seen. He only hoped somebody didn't figure out why he was questioning the prostitutes.

Right then, however, he didn't know what to say to appease Dancy without letting her know what he was up to. So, with heavy heart he made his tone flippant as he gave her the same response he'd used with women in the past. Only those women had meant nothing to him, and it actually stabbed his gut to have to face her hurt-filled eyes and say, "I never promised you anything but the glory of the moment, Dancy."

She felt like a dandelion, blown to the wind, emotionally torn. "I think . . ." she said, biting back tears, "you'd best get out of here. I don't think we've got anything else to say to each other."

He hated leaving her but knew, for the moment, it was best. Later, when it was over, he could only hope she would understand. "I'll question Roscoe and the others again and see if they remember anything that might help."

He got up and walked out.

Dancy was enraged, not only with Clint, but with herself, for being stupid enough as to fall in love with him. And he, womanizer that he was, couldn't do his job as marshal because he couldn't leave his whores alone.

"But by God, *I'll* do something," she vowed fiercely, dressing, shaking with anger and determination. "Somebody's got to."

While she had no idea exactly how to go about it, Dancy made up her mind she was declaring war on the Ku Klux Klan.

When she returned to the barn to see how Billy was doing, she found his sister kneeling beside him.

Lifting tear-filled eyes, Molly looked up at her and whispered brokenly, "When's it all gonna stop? What did my brother do to deserve this?"

Billy was sleeping. Dancy knelt beside her to confide, "I think it's because he stood up for me, Molly. The law never would have believed Frank Cox was a member of the Klan if his robe and mask hadn't been found."

Molly blinked, confused. "But what did Billy have to do with that?"

Dancy told her.

"Lordy. It's a wonder they didn't kill him."

"I know." Dancy patted her hand. "But don't you worry. From now on we're going to watch for them, and if they come back, we'll be ready."

"But it's not enough. Sooner or later they'll catch Billy, or Roscoe, or whoever they're after, off by themselves, and then they'll whip 'em, or kill 'em, whatever they want to do, 'cause that's the way it is, Miss Dancy. Till the law steps in and puts those evil folks in jail, it's going to keep on. And it's gonna get worse. You can't stop 'em."

"And neither can the law, as long as they don't know who they are." Dancy sighed, plopped down in the straw, and leaned back against a post. "Marshal McCabe says he's trying, but the Klan is so secretive, nobody knows anything."

"And those that do won't tell him, anyway. None of us know who to trust. How do we know he ain't one of 'em, too?"

Despite her personal rage, Dancy said, "I'll never believe that. Besides, why would a man who gave up friends and family to put an end to slavery turn around and join a secret organization that's hell-bent to maintain white supremacy? It doesn't make sense."

Molly was not entirely convinced. "Well, others don't see it like you do. Nobody knows who to trust anymore."

"Do you think your friends trust me? If they knew anything that might help, would they tell me?" She held her breath, waiting, hoping, because something told her Molly knew more than she let on.

Molly gave her a suspicious glance. "What could you do if they did?"

"I can't make any promises, except to try to

learn the names of those involved and turn them over to the authorities. In Nashville," she was quick to add, to let her know she'd see the information got beyond Clint.

Molly became very quiet. Dancy allowed her the time for deliberation. Anything would be a start. Finally, Molly cleared her throat, and after glancing about to ensure they were all alone, save for Billy who continued to sleep soundly, she confided, "I've heard stories about where they meet."

Dancy could contain herself no longer. Reaching to clutch Molly's arm, she pleaded, "You've got to tell me. I won't tell a soul, I swear it. No one will ever know you told me anything."

Molly looked from Dancy's frantic grip to her anxious face. "What will you do? You ain't gonna go there, are you?"

"I'm not sure," Dancy hedged, knowing full well that was exactly what she intended to do. "Just tell me the location, Molly, please."

"They say," she began slowly, lowering her voice until it was barely audible, "the reason the Slocumb family moved out of that old shack by the creek that disappears inside Honey Mountain was that they saw ghosts dancing in the woods. They were floating through the trees, and fires from hell were burning all around. So they run off to Georgia. At least, that's what they say." Eyes riveted upon Dancy, she watched for her reaction.

Dancy patted Molly's shoulder, then leaned back again, smiling to herself. Honey Mountain. The dividing ridge between what was once her father's land and Dooley's, where a secret tunnel went all the way through.

"If a body don't believe in ghosts," Molly said with a twisted, cynical smile, "I'd say that's the place they get together to plan the devil's work."

A slow grin of triumph spread across Dancy's face. "And I reckon," she drawled mockingly, "you just might be right."

22

Clint tried to push thoughts of Dancy from his mind, without success. He was worried that she might, in her anger and frustration, do something impulsive and foolish, but for the time being, he was helpless. Besides, he was hoping his investigation was leading him the wrong way, that his suspicions were unjustified.

Damn it, he didn't like thinking his own family was involved. But more and more it was sure as hell starting to look that way.

He had never liked Slade Hawkins. As a boy, growing up, Slade was always in trouble. When Addie hired Slade, Clint felt she did it to spite him, knowing how the two had never got along.

Lately a few things had started bothering Clint, such as how it was Slade and one of his sidekicks Jordan had ordered to take Cox to Nashville. Therefore they knew Billy was the one who had gone to get Jordan and was the likely one to have removed Cox's hood and robe. That pointed the finger at Billy for the mysterious appearance of the costume.

Clint reasoned Slade might be involved with the Ku Klux Klan. However, Slade was not smart enough to be the leader, and since he worked for Addie, it stood to reason she might actually be the one doling out orders.

He was not, however, ready to reach that conclusion, because despite her cantankerous ways and peevish disposition, he couldn't quite make himself believe she was capable of ordering mayhem, which turned his attention to Jordan. True, he was crippled, but that would not prevent him from issuing commands.

Riding into Pinetops, Clint headed straight to the bank. He strode by the staring woman behind the counter and entered Jordan's office.

"How dare you barge in this way?" Jordan exploded. "Get out of here."

"What will you do if I don't, brother dear? Yell for the law?" Clint lowered himself onto a chair.

Jordan grimaced. "Never call me your brother. I claim no kinship with traitors."

Clint shrugged, unmoved by the barb, then proceeded to say coolly, "The war is over."

"That doesn't change the fact that you refused to fight for your fellow countrymen."

"I consider all of America one country. I wanted to keep it that way. But I'm not here to flog the issues."

Jordan leaned back in his chair. "Then get to it and get out. I don't want my customers seeing the likes of you in my bank."

Clint raised an eyebrow. "*Your* bank, did you say? Did Addie die and get herself buried without my knowing about it? Her passing on is the only way you'll ever be able to claim ownership of anything of hers."

Jordan told himself to be calm, not let Clint get him riled. "Well, there's a lot of things you don't know, things that are none of your business."

Taking a cheroot from his pocket, Clint responded, "Actually, I'm here to talk about what *is* my business, and"—he paused to light his cigar and blow a perfect smoke ring—"the things I don't know will likely fall into place."

The gray spiral drifted across the desk to hover before Jordan's face. Destroying it with an angry swipe, he snapped, "Get to the point, Clint. How many times do I have to tell you I don't want you here?"

"You know," Clint remarked, pretending to be in deep thought, "I can't, for the life of me, remember what I ever did to make you hate me like you do."

"Oh, really? Well, I don't have time to go back

through the years and remind you how you were always Father's favorite."

"As I recall, that wasn't my doing. Addie wouldn't let you go, and he learned early on it didn't pay to argue with her. She never gave a damn about me, so she never opposed my going with him. I'd say since the way we were raised wasn't our fault, you're wrong to hold it against me."

"Oh, for heaven's sake," Jordan said impatiently, "get to the point. If you came here to talk me into persuading Addie to return you to her favor, you're wasting your time. I like things as they are. And believe me," he added, "things are only going to get better. Now go. I'm too busy to be bothered with you." He began to shuffle papers around on his desk, dismissing his half brother.

Watching for his reaction, Clint asked, "Have you heard the Ku Klux Klan beat one of Dancy's workers last night?"

Jordan looked up to ask sharply "Is she all right? They didn't do it at her place, did they?"

Clint couldn't tell if he was faking concern. "She's fine. It was on the land but she didn't know anything about it till it was all over."

"If you don't start doing your job, sooner or later, she *will* be hurt," Jordan accused. "When are you going to find out who's responsible for wreaking havoc around here, *Marshal*?"

"I thought maybe you might have some information to help me along."

"Such as?"

"Such as why the Klan seems to be targeting Dancy. She's told me you want to marry her. And we both know Addie wants Dooley's land real bad. Seems to me the two of you have reasons for wanting her scared off."

"Let me tell you something, damn you." Jordan leaned forward, fists clenched, face pasty white with rage. "I won't stand for you accusing either me or my mother of being involved in something as despicable as the Ku Klux Klan."

Clint merely smiled, which further infuriated Jordan, who waved his arms angrily. "Get out. If I could, I'd throw you out myself."

Clint stood slowly, deliberately taking his time. He sauntered to the door, then paused and, still smiling, advised, "I'll be watching you, Jordan. Don't make any mistakes. Pass the message along to Addie. If I find either one of you is involved, believe me, I'll give no leniency because you're family."

"We aren't family to the likes of you, goddamn it—-"

Clint closed the door just before the inkwell Jordan had hurled across the room smashed against it. With a polite nod to the terrified woman watching from behind the counter, he walked out of the bank.

Clint had accomplished what he'd set out to do—unnerve Jordan, which might make him careless if he was indeed the secret leader of the Klan. And if Addie was actually the one responsible, Jordan would see she got the message as well.

He went to his office to see if there were any messages of importance, but there was nothing. The townspeople avoided him. He knew better than to expect cooperation from any of them.

Pacing restlessly around the tiny room, Clint found it hard to concentrate on anything except Dancy. He didn't like the way they'd parted. From his childhood years, he knew she was capable of doing foolish things when she was mad. And these were dangerous times. He didn't want her taking any chances. Maybe, he pondered, he should ride back out to the farm and try to reason with her.

He jumped at the sound of the door opening and whirled around, hand on his gun, ready to draw.

"Don't you dare shoot me, Marshal McCabe. You'd never forgive yourself."

Clint warmed at the sight of Lila Coley, lovely in a gown of bright orange satin, cut low in the bodice.

Twirling a lacy, matching parasol, she cooed,

"Well, aren't you going to invite me in?"

Genuinely glad to see her, he drew her inside and closed the door. "Lila, I never thought you'd set foot in this town again."

"Well, I wasn't going to. Not after getting chased out by ghosts." She forced a laugh. "But I came to visit my sick cousin and decided to see if you were in town before going home. I figured as long as you're the marshal, I'm safe." She winked. Her cheerful demeanor, however, was forced; in fact, it was all she could do to keep from throwing herself in his arms.

The office was sparsely furnished with only a desk and two chairs. He motioned her to sit down. "I'm glad you came by. I heard you were doing all right, though. Since you got in touch with your friend over at Sweeney's, she keeps me informed on how you're doing."

"Ramona? Yes, she comes to Nashville now and then." Suddenly her expression became grim. "Actually she's the real reason I'm here, Clint. She told me something I thought you should know about."

He felt a rush of excitement. "Go on," he urged.

"Do you know your stepmother's overseer? Slade Hawkins?"

Clint tensed, nodded.

"Ramona told me something strange. See, she and Buck Sweeney sleep together sometimes, after the regular customers go home, and she was telling me how annoying it is when Slade signals Buck to go out and meet him at odd hours of the night."

Clint hoped the flush of excitement sweeping over him didn't show, well aware if he revealed any sign of the possible significance of what she was saying, Lila would get spooked and clam up. "So?" He gave a careless shrug. "Slade signals Buck to have a drink with him. Why should it upset Ramona?"

"You don't understand. It's the *way* Slade signals. With a whistle."

"A whistle?" Clint echoed, baffled.

"That's right. Ramona said more than once she's been lying there, not asleep yet, and she hears this long sound like a whistle, from way off somewheres. Then Buck leaps out of bed, wide awake, no matter how hard he was snoring, and he throws his clothes on and takes off. Then he's out the rest of the night."

Cautiously Clint pressed, "And how does Ramona know it's actually Slade doing it?"

"One night she heard him grumbling, saying something about 'that damn Hawkins.' So . . ." She looked at him expectantly. "What do you suppose it all means? Could it have something to do with the Klan? Could it be the way they're signaling their members to get together?"

Clint was grinding his teeth together so hard his jaw ached as he cursed himself silently. Damn it, he had heard the whistle sound himself, nights when he'd slept with Lila at Sweeney's. But at the time he'd been too exhausted or befuddled by drink to take notice. But now he knew, beyond doubt, that Lila's guess was right—it was the Klan signal to rally.

But he was not about to let Lila know any of this. She might be tempted to tell Ramona, and then it would spread among all the prostitutes like wildfire. Sooner or later it would get back to the men. He would take no chances.

He scoffed, "Of course not, Lila. That's ridiculous. I've heard it before, myself. It's somebody calling his dog, and it wakes up Buck and he gets annoyed because he can't get back to sleep."

"But why was he cussing Slade?"

"Who knows?" He sat behind his desk, picked up a paper, and glanced over it, dismissing her. "Lila, I'm real glad to see you, but I've got an awful lot of work to do."

"Oh, of course, of course." She was suddenly embarrassed to have bothered him with such absurd notions and started to leave. Then, yielding to her heart, she paused to say softly, "Remember, if you're ever in Nashville, you know where to find me. The door is always open."

His smile was genuine, and he made a vow then and there that one day, when it was all over, he'd pay her a visit and tell her how valuable her information had actually been. For the moment, however, he could only say, "Thanks for coming by, Lila. Be careful going back."

She was almost out the door when impulse took over, and she whirled about to look at his dear, handsome face one last time. With heavy heart she whispered, "Damn it, Clint McCabe, I just hope your redheaded woman knows how lucky she is."

She ran out then, not wanting him to see the tears she could no longer hide.

Clint stared after her pensively. He could have told her Dancy O'Neal considered herself anything but lucky where he was concerned. But he forced himself not to think about that situation for the moment. He had other things to worry about, like keeping an eye on Buck Sweeney. Because now he knew—when the whistle blew, and Buck moved, *so did the Ku Klux Klan.*

Two doors down, Dancy paused on her way into Emmett's store. With a jolt she recognized the heavily made-up woman as the one who had come to see Clint that day. And, she was further needled to recall, the one he had mistaken for *her.*

She stood rooted, unable to tear her eyes away as Lila got into her buggy and headed in the direction of Sweeney's. Then, telling herself she didn't care, she took a deep breath and went on into the store. She had more important things to concern herself with—like buying needle and thread and going home to do a little sewing.

She had a costume to make, because some night very, very soon she had a meeting to attend.

Someone else was also watching.

From his office window, Jordan saw everything. He was still furious over the way his last visit with Dancy had turned out. She wasn't giving him a chance, because obviously she was smitten with Clint.

With teeth ground together so tightly his jaw ached, Jordan knew he had to do something—and soon.

Addie sat on the side of the canopied bed, watching impatiently as Dr. Casper packed his worn leather bag.

"Well, your heart sounds good," he announced, folding the stethoscope and placing it in the bag. "If it weren't for your kidneys, you'd probably outlive all of us."

"Are you saying I'm going to die?" she asked flatly.

He turned grave eyes upon her. "If you don't take better care of yourself, you might."

"Everybody does. It's only a matter of when."

"Some sooner than others. And some more painfully. Bright's disease is not a pleasant way to die, Addie. And I've told you. We don't know much about kidney disease but getting plenty of rest and taking your medicine can only help. You aren't doing either, are you."

"Oh, what do you know? I'll go when the good Lord calls me and not before." She waved him away. "Now off with you. I've no time for your lectures."

He snapped the bag closed but stood there, making no move to leave.

"Well?" Addie glared. "What are you waiting for?"

He gave a sigh of resolution, hating to have to broach the subject, but Jordan had insisted. He walked to the window and stared out, not wanting to look at her as he spoke. "Jordan and I had a long talk about your not taking care of yourself. He thinks, and I agree, you need to be in a sanatorium for a while, to get your strength back. There's a good one in Nashville. You'd be close to home. But Jordan wants the best. So I wrote to the one in Philadelphia. It's much nicer, because it's in the North, where economic conditions are better, of course. And it's understood money is no object here anyway. Jordan wants you to have the best—"

"Jordan wants me out of the way, you idiot, so he can take over all my money, but I'll be damned if I'll let anybody put me anywhere." She slid off the edge of the bed, dropping the few inches to the floor rather than use the stepstool.

She began to peel out of her gown. If the old fool wanted to stand and watch her get dressed, so be it. Time was wasting. He'd seen everything she had anyway, and if he hadn't, he wouldn't know what he was looking at, so what difference did it make.

"Addie, you have to be reasonable." He turned, saw she was about to pull on her dress. Keeping his eyes averted, he picked up his bag and walked toward the door. "Very well. I'll tell Jordan I tried."

"You tell Jordan to go to hell, the arrogant whippersnapper," she raged. "I made him what he is, and I can damn sure snatch it away. He doesn't own the bank. I do. Just like I own nearly everything in this county. And I didn't get it by letting folks tell me what to do, and the sooner you and him both learn that, the better off you'll be."

But Dr. Casper was not listening, for he was already halfway down the stairs in hasty retreat.

Once dressed, Addie went downstairs and

ordered Molly to send one of the field hands to fetch Slade Hawkins.

Molly scurried to obey, wondering if she should have told Miss Addie about the Klan's attack on Billy, since it seemed to have upset her so. But she had been late getting back from Miss Dancy's, and Miss Addie had been fit to be tied and demanding to know why.

Slade came at once, arrogantly stalking right up the front stairs instead of going the back way, as expected of servants and hired hands. He figured she was already mad anyway, or she wouldn't have risked sending for him so close to the time Jordan was due home.

He knocked on her study door, and she icily told him to enter. He walked in to see her sitting at her desk. With bridled fury she commanded, "Close the door and get over here. I don't want anyone to hear what I've got to say to you."

He did so, and she burst out, "What's this I hear about the Klan beating up one of Dancy's hands last night? I gave no such order. And you know it's my rule there be no physical harm, ever. You frighten. You intimidate." She jabbed the air with angry emphasis. "But you do not hurt anybody."

Lazily he denied, "I don't know what you're talking about. Must've been outsiders again."

"Don't lie to me, boy." Addie shakily got to her

feet. Slade was still standing, and she didn't like him looking down on her. "I know it was you. I think it's been you all the time. I think you enjoy what you're doing, and I'm telling you it's going to stop. As of right now, you're to disband your members. The Klan activity in this county is over."

She pointed to the door. "Now get out of my room, out of my house, and off my land. You are no longer employed here."

It was all Slade could do to keep from laughing right in her indignant face. "Well, now, I reckon Jordan will have something to say about that."

"He doesn't run this place. I do. Now get out, I say." She looked about wildly for her parasol, saw it was propped against the wall, and started after it.

Slade hurried on his way. He wasn't going to hit an old lady, but neither was he going to let her beat him to death with an umbrella, either.

He was almost to the bottom of the steps when the front door opened and Gabriel walked in, carrying Jordan in his arms.

Seeing Slade, Jordan demanded, "What the hell are you doing here?"

Slade didn't hesitate to explain. "Your mother sent for me. She ordered me off the place. Says I'm fired." Then, stiffening with the dignity one would be expected to display over such an affront, he added coldly, "She accused me of being involved with the Ku Klux Klan."

Jordan shook his head in disgust, waited till Gabriel lowered him to the waiting wheelchair, then said, "I'm afraid my mother is getting tetched. I apologize for her and ask you pay her no mind. From now on you report directly to me, and if she should send for you, ignore it.

"I think," he added with a feigned sigh of regret, "it's time I yielded to Dr. Casper's recommendation she be committed to a sanatorium, for her own sake. It's unfortunate, but I would be remiss in my duty as a loving son if I didn't make sure she gets the best possible care."

"Oh, I agree." Slade nodded. "She'll be better off, I'm sure. Good day, sir." He tipped his hat and left.

Gabriel rolled Jordan toward the parlor, where he liked to have his before supper drink.

From the landing above, Addie had seen and heard everything.

"Sanatorium indeed," she scoffed under her breath as she turned to go back to her room. "Hell will freeze over first, you insolent pup."

Dancy crouched behind the bushes. There was a quarter-moon, enough light to see the outline of the men as they gathered outside the dilapidated house, but not sufficient to make out their faces, especially from where she was hiding.

She had entered the bowels of Honey Mountain at the opening near the waterfall, following the trail to the other side. Before stepping out, she'd extinguished the torch she had been carrying, then dropped down among the weeds and overgrowth.

Nearly a half hour had passed, and she had begun to think she was wrong about guessing it was their meeting place. Then suddenly, eerily, she saw movement in the forest. Torches flickering. Voices ringing in the wind.

With every nerve raw and tense, Dancy witnessed the men going to the ruins of the house. When they took their white costumes from beneath the porch, she knew with an excited jolt that this was it.

There were, as best she could count, twenty of them. When they'd donned their robes and hoods, they milled about, as if they were waiting for something. The torches they held aloft made the scene even more terrifying to witness.

Unable to hear what they were saying, she crept closer, taking her own robe and pointed hood with her. It was her intent to don the garb and follow after them if they left, but they had not remounted their horses and were standing in a semicircle. If they were only going to have a meeting, she did not want to miss anything.

A murmur went through the men as a late arrival came out of the woods.

Dancy stifled a gasp. As the man dismounted and walked before them in the flickering lights, she recognized him as the man who had come with Jordan to transport Marshal Cox to Nashville. Slade Hawkins, the McCabe overseer.

He went to the ruins, took out his costume. A few moments later he stood before them, attired in red. Dancy knew she was looking at the leader of the Klan.

"The ride is off for tonight," he announced. "No more raids on the O'Neal place for the time being. We're going to try something else.

"We won't signal with whistles. You know what time to meet here."

She listened in horror as he described how they would attack the families. Billy's mother and father would be first. Their house would be burned, his father lynched, his mother left to deliver the message that if all the workers did not desert Dancy immediately, their families would suffer similar fates.

As she watched them disrobe and return their garments to their hiding places, she knew what she had to do.

The Klan would have two surprises waiting for them tomorrow night. They would know about only one when they discovered their intended victims were nowhere around.

They would not be aware *she* was riding with them.

23

Dancy was too restless to sleep, and the night dragged toward dawn with agonizing slowness. She was anxious to see Molly and explain how she had to move her parents to safety, but she didn't dare go the McCabe plantation till a decent hour. Too many questions would be asked by Addie and Jordan, and everything had to be done quietly, in secret. No one could know anything—not even Billy, who was still recuperating from his injuries and had no business getting involved.

"Dancy . . ."

Recognizing Clint's voice, she got up and jerked on her robe. She let him in, all the while hoping he wouldn't hear her heart pounding. "What do you want?"

"We need to talk." He found matches and lit the lantern.

Her first reaction to his unexpected visit was to suspect he'd come to cajole her into bed, seducing her into forgetting her anger. However, in the suffusing glow of the lantern, she could see the grimness etched on his face, knew lovemaking was the farthest thing from his mind. "So talk. And how did you get in here, anyway? Roscoe has orders to shoot anybody sneaking in here."

"I didn't sneak. I rode right in. He obviously recognized me. Now listen. I came to let you know you need to be careful about what you say around Jordan from now on. Keep your business to yourself. If there's more trouble, if you have any more night riders, come to me. Don't go to him. I don't want you telling him about anything that goes on out here."

She had not planned to but saw no reason to say so. "I think you'd better tell me what this is all about," she said uneasily.

He had anticipated her stubborn reaction, and although he felt it dangerous, for her sake, to tell her too much, he knew he had to divulge a little. "What if I told you I have reason to believe some of Jordan's hired hands are involved with the Klan?"

How, she wondered, had he managed to find out about Slade? But she dared not ask. "What does that have to do with Jordan? If what you say is true, he can't help it."

"The ones I suspect aren't very smart. Jordan might be the mastermind."

She threw up her hands in disgust. "First Jordan tries to make me believe you're involved, and now you sit here accusing him. Maybe you're both wrong. Maybe," she added with mock horror, "it's actually Addie."

"Could be."

She blinked, stunned he could even consider such an absurdity. "She's a woman, Clint, and besides, no matter how cantankerous she is, I can't imagine she would ever condone such atrocities."

"And she didn't survive the war with most of her wealth intact by being weak, Dancy. She's shrewd, and she's smart, and she knows it's to her advantage to keep the freedmen knuckled down, intimidated, dependent on her. It stands to reason she'd be willing to resort to force to do it.

"And remember," he said with a curt nod, "she also wants this land. Frankly, I think she'd do anything to get it."

Suddenly he had her interest. "But why? Why is she so determined? Look what she already owns. Why is this place so special?"

"I've spent a lot of time wondering the same thing, and I've decided she was in love with Dooley."

"But she married your father."

"She was his second wife, remember? And a long time ago, back when you were still living here, I overheard something that really puzzled me, something about how sad it was Dooley wound up alone, with no wife, and while it was a shame things never worked out for him and Addie, it was nice my father found a mother for me. I never thought much about it till one day, when I was about fourteen or fifteen, and Addie made some nasty remark about Dooley, and I couldn't resist asking her if they were ever sweethearts." He laughed at the memory. "She got about as mad as I've ever seen her and chased me out of the house with a broom."

"And if Addie somehow knew Dooley was in love with my mother, then she would naturally blame her for losing him. That might explain her animosity. It could also explain why she wants this land so badly, figuring it rightfully belongs to her, because if it hadn't been for my mother, Dooley would have married her, and then it would have been hers. But I still don't see how it ties her in with the Klan."

"She's using them to run you off, don't you see?"

Regretfully Dancy had to admit his theory made sense. "Well, it explains her motive if she is behind it, but what about Jordan? What reason would he have?"

"Basically, because he's a greedy son of a bitch. And I also think he would like a beautiful wife to share it all with him. You. So, if he manages to intimidate you into giving up here, he'll win in two ways. He gets you for his wife, and he also winds up owning one of the prime farms in the state."

"I'll bear in mind what you've said," she said. "Now if you've don't mind, I'd like to get some sleep. And next time," she added curtly, "come to see me during the day. There's no reason for you to sneak in here after dark."

Clint knew it was her way of informing him that whatever had been between them was over, but he had never been one to give up easily. He reached for her.

She stepped away, holding up her hands to fend him off. "It was a mistake. I thought you'd grown into a man. You haven't. You're still a pesky little boy, and I despise you. Now go."

His breath caught in his throat as he drank in the sheer beauty of her, the lantern's light glinting in the golden-red threads of her hair as it cascaded about her shoulders.

Never, Clint knew, had he desired or loved a woman more, but he had to accept it could never be. To Dancy he was no more than a childhood nemesis, and passion shared was pleasure of the flesh and nothing more.

He went to the door, about to leave; then, fired by poignant emotions churning within, he could not resist whirling about to leave her with one burning thought. "It's sad you have to be your mother's daughter, Dancy."

And he melted into the night, leaving Dancy to stare after him, wondering what he meant.

Dancy was on the road to the McCabe plantation at first light. She dared not go right up to the house and talk with Molly there. Jordan might see, or Addie, and there would be questions. Instead she rode just inside the woods bordering the cotton fields and waited for the workers to appear. Finally she was able to get the attention of one and ask him to get word to Molly to meet her. Warily he agreed.

After what seemed like forever, Molly appeared at the back door of the house. She glanced about nervously to make sure no one was watching, then lifted her skirts above her ankles to run across the yard and disappear among the trees and brush.

Dancy did not mince words as she confided what she had seen and heard. Molly's eyes grew wide with terror.

"Oh, Lordy, Lordy, Miss Dancy, they're gonna kill my mammy and pappy," she wailed, covering her stricken face with her hands.

Dancy clutched her wrists and gave her a gentle shake. "No, they won't. Not if you do as I say." She told her carefully what she had to do, and Molly's head bobbed up and down in fierce assent.

Dancy returned home. The day passed with agonizing slowness, but finally it was time.

She had noticed that some of the Klansmen had put coverings on their horses so they would not be recognized, enveloping them to their lower legs. A few, however, with plain brown horses like Dancy's, did not bother, for no one could tell one from the other, so she made no such garb for hers.

She had fashioned her robe, which reached from head to ankles, from a white bedsheet. Calling on her memory, she copied the headpiece, conical in shape, with slits for eyes and mouth.

After rolling everything into a small bundle and tucking it in her saddlebag, Dancy left quietly. She was not going where the Klan gathered. Molly had given her careful directions to her parents' shack, assuring her there were plenty of woods for her to hide and await the raiders.

Darkness was upon her as she reached the remote cabin, which was situated in a small clearing. The door hung open, and there was no sign of life anywhere. Away from the road, deep in the brush, she slipped on her robe and hood, then settled down to wait for the others to arrive.

There was no moon, and the stars were obscured by thick, drifting clouds. Thunder rumbled in the distance, and now and then wicked forks of lightning split the lampblack sky. It was, Dancy thought as icy fingers of apprehension gripped her spine, a night made for demons to ride.

Suddenly they appeared.

Two by two, down the path, mounted on their horses, ramrod straight. Each carried a burning torch, which bathed them in a macabre, ghastly light. They moved slowly, and Dancy held her breath as they passed by her. Hidden by a thick clump of locust trees, heavy with clumps of white blossoms, she blended right in and was not noticed.

She was scared. Her heart was thudding like a woodpecker on a hollow tree. She could feel the blood running cold in her veins. She found herself thinking that perhaps she had been foolish not to tell Clint, then cursed herself for being so weak. Never would he have done what she was doing—getting to the bottom of things and finding out who was responsible. He would have gone about it the way the law did things—methodically, which meant asking questions instead of getting answers.

Dancy drew a deep breath and let it out slowly as she prepared to join them. As they entered the clearing, she could see they were forming a semi-circle, as she had seen them do in front of her own cabin. She figured to blend right in and leaned to take up the torch she had tucked behind her. All she had to do was light it, step right out, and—

She froze.

Dear God, she hadn't seen him.

Dressed in black, his horse completely draped, the last rider was passing right by her. He carried no torch, and had it not been for the light from the others, he would have gone unnoticed.

Without turning, as though feeling his presence, the others parted to allow him to ride right through and stand before them.

With a vibrant chill, Dancy knew she was looking at the real leader of the Ku Klux Klan.

Quickly she lit her torch and carefully jockeyed into place, and no one so much as turned his head to acknowledge her presence. Intent on waiting for their ultimate leader to give the order to begin, they were oblivious of anything else going on around them.

"What's the Grand Giant of the Province doing here tonight?" she overheard the man closest to her ask the rider beside him. "He hardly ever shows up."

His comrade snickered. "I reckon because we're gonna have a lynching tonight, and he wants to make sure it's done right."

Dancy prayed no one would speak to her, for to respond would mean giving herself away.

"Who do you reckon he is, anyway?" whispered the first man who had spoken.

"Don't know," came the reply. "The Grand Cyclops is the only one who does."

Grand Cyclops, Dancy mouthed silently beneath her hood. That had to be Slade Hawkins. She watched him in his bright red garb, as he walked his horse to stand beside his chum in black.

No one could hear what they were saying. Finally, when everyone was getting restless, the horses stamping about anxiously, Hawkins moved closer to the porch of the shack and shouted, "All right, come on out of there, you sons of bitches. We know you're in there. Come out, or you'll burn."

No sound or movement came from within.

The man dressed in black motioned Hawkins forward, and he obeyed, spurring his horse to send him bolting right up the steps and through the open doorway. There were sounds of crashing within, furniture being knocked over, dishes and pottery smashed. Then he emerged once more to yell, "They're gone, goddamn it. No sign of nobody."

Without fanfare or warning, the rider in black whipped his steed about and lunged toward the nearest rider, yanking the torch from his hand. He then spun and flung it through a window, shattering glass.

Flames began to race up the walls like slithering snakes, and Dancy watched in muted horror as the others joined in to throw their torches. Soon the place was an inferno. But while she grieved for the innocent people she did not even know, for the loss of their home, she could take solace in the knowledge that their lives had been spared.

Still, she was sickened to witness such a spectacle and for long moments could only stare in horror. At last she came alive and began to back away. She had not thrown her torch, instead allowing it to drop to the ground, lest someone notice and wonder why she was not participating.

The others were stamping their horses about, cheering happily as the flames leaped skyward, lighting up the sky.

Dancy allowed the night to swallow her and, once again camouflaged by the foliage, waited for the hooligans to leave. She did not dare try to make her way in the dark through the woods for fear of becoming lost or making noise the others might hear.

Bathed in the glow of the angrily dancing flames, the white-clad phantoms from hell pranced their horses about as they continued to cheer what they had done. And when the tiny cabin finally collapsed in an explosion of sparks, they began to ride away.

When all was quiet save for the last crackles among the ruins, Dancy left her sanctuary and began the long ride home. She did not set her horse into a gallop, for she wanted to give those in front of her ample time to go their separate ways.

As she rode, she pulled off the robe and hood, rolling them once more into a tight ball to jam into the saddlebag. They would be needed later, perhaps many more times, for tonight she had realized it was not going to be as easy as she had thought to expose the members of the Klan. She knew of Slade's involvement, but turning him in, and revealing the other names she might overhear, would not accomplish her goal—the discovery of their leader.

Clint was wrong to suspect either Addie or Jordan. The Grand Giant of the Province was definitely a man and certainly not crippled.

Lost in fury and frustration, Dancy was unaware that she was being followed.

Once orders were given and action commenced, Slade Hawkins always hung back to watch his men and make sure each participated with enthusiasm. One of the cardinal rules was that each member have the willingness and nerve to take part in everything. There was no room for cowards. So Slade had moved back into the shadows to observe, and that was when he'd noticed someone dropping his torch instead of flinging it toward the cabin.

He had tensed, glanced about for the Grand Giant, wanting him to witness such a display of weakness. But, as was his way, the leader had departed to avoid having anyone learn of his identity.

So Slade watched alone, and when he saw the man heading surreptitiously into the woods, his first impulse was to shoot him dead, then and there; but something told him not to. The man might not be a coward after all, but a spy among them, and if so, it was up to Slade to find out who he was, how much he knew, and whether anyone else was working with him.

After removing his red garb, Slade stuffed it in his saddlebag, breaking the rule about leaving all costumes at the meeting place. Generally it was considered too risky to have each member be responsible for hiding his own. Most wives knew of their husbands' involvement, having made their outfits for them, but it was still best to leave everything in one place.

He was annoyed to recall how Cox's garb had been taken away from him. In fact, Slade had been so mad at the time, worrying it would show up to incriminate them all later, that he'd found it easy to bash Frank's head and kill him, just so the son of a bitch wouldn't be tempted to tell what he knew to save his own hide.

Slade stayed a good distance back. It was pitch dark, but he could make out his prey. As soon as he figured out where the man was headed, he would get the jump on him. After making him talk, he would kill him. But where in hell was he going? Certainly not back toward town.

Then, suddenly, Slade sat up in his saddle and strained to see. Sure enough, the rider was turning off at the church. That really baffled him, because the only place beyond there was Dooley O'Neal's, and . . .

Everything within him screamed it could not be, but by damn, it was so. Unless one of her workers had dared dress up like a Klansman, the spy could only be Dancy herself.

When shock subsided, Slade continued to follow. He saw her turn into the trail through the woods leading to Dooley's cabin, then he turned back.

He had seen enough.

A single candle provided scant light to read by, but Addie knew the words of the faded, tattered letter by heart. Even though it was stained with tears and the ink was blurred, she could still make out Dooley's scrawling. He had written it in the early days and given it to her on her birthday, along with a bouquet of daisies. It was not a poem, or even a profession of love, merely a note wishing her a happy day. It was not much, but it was all she had. Even after marrying Angus, she had been unable to bring herself to discard it.

He had smashed her heart to bits and pieces, and though she'd never forgiven him, neither had she been able to stop loving him. And when Edana's daughter had returned, so had all the hurtful reminders of the reason Addie had lost him. If not for Edana, Dooley would have married *her*, Addie was positive.

She tucked the note under her pillow and lay back to stare up at the lace canopy. Wealth and power had been a form of revenge, but she knew now Dooley had never cared what she did.

More and more she was starting to feel that maybe she'd been wrong in her thinking. If Dooley wanted his niece to inherit everything, Addie reasoned maybe she shouldn't try to take it away. Perhaps some of the venomous hatred would leave her, and she could live out the last of her days or months, or however long the Lord gave her, in peace.

Maybe, she contemplated, closing her eyes and starting to drift away, it was high time she acknowledged that if it had been meant to be, if

Dooley had really loved her, then not Edana or any other woman could have taken him away.

What difference did any of it make now, anyway? she asked herself miserably. Jordan was hell-bent to send her away, and fighting that was going to take every shred of strength she could muster.

Besides, Dancy wasn't too terribly awful. A scamp, to be sure, but Addie secretly admired her for her spunk and spirit, because in a lot of ways Dancy reminded her of herself.

Clint was uncomfortable as hell. He didn't dare lie down for fear of falling asleep, so he had been sitting on the ground, his back against a tree, for most of the night. The only noise he heard were owls, whippoorwills, and a bobcat screeching from somewhere on the ridge above. There had been no sound even remotely akin to a whistle.

So the Ku Klux Klan had not gathered this night, he decided with a yawn and a stretch. He got to his feet, stiff, cramped. After dusting off the seat of his pants, he headed to where he'd left his horse tied.

And that was when he saw Buck Sweeney.

Buck rode right down the road and up to his place, which was still brightly lit and going strong. A little Negro boy came running out to take the reins of his horse, and Buck disappeared inside.

He had to have gone out early, Clint reasoned, because he sure as hell had not seen Buck leave while he'd been there.

With a curse, Clint mounted and headed back to town.

Whatever the Ku Klux Klan had been up to this night, Clint fumed, he had missed out on it.

24

Gabriel was astonished to open the front door and find Slade standing there. As overseer, he knew better than anybody else go to around to the back, but from the crazy-mad look on his face, Gabriel wasn't about to tell him so.

"I have to see Mr. McCabe. Right away."

As emphatically as he dared, Gabriel explained, "Master Jordan is having his breakfast, but if you'll wait, I'll tell him you're here."

"I'll tell him myself, damn it." Slade pushed by him, then rushed across the foyer to bound up the steps two at a time.

Gabriel stared after him, then scurried to the rear of the house, where he planned to stay till Master Slade left. Something was brewing, to be sure, and he wanted no part of it.

Jordan was about to sip his coffee, but his hand froze in midair as Slade burst into the room without knocking. "What's the meaning of this?"

Slade quickly closed the door behind him. "We got big trouble."

Jordan glowered at him over the rim of his cup. "This better be serious, Slade. I don't like you coming here like this."

"And I don't like spies riding with us."

Jordan set down the cup with a clatter. "What did you say?"

"We had a spy last night." He recounted how he had observed someone behaving strangely and decided to follow and find out who it was.

"And?" Jordan stared with wide, anxious eyes. "Go on. Who was he?"

"She," Slade drawled. "The spy was a *she.*"

Jordan laughed and relaxed. "Well, we should have known sooner or later my mother would try to find out who else has been giving you boys orders, but it doesn't matter. I'm having her committed to a sanatorium, and I'll see to it everyone thinks she's crazy and won't believe a word she says.

"But I have to say I'm impressed," he added. "I'd have never thought she had the strength to ride a horse, sick as she's been. But she's always been a spunky sort. . . ." He fell silent at the strangely smug expression on Slade's face, then demanded, "What's so funny? I've no time for your jokes."

"Dancy O'Neal is no joke, Jordan."

"You don't mean—"

"I *do* mean. I saw with my own eyes."

White-hot rage descended like a smothering cocoon. Jordan's breath came in quick, ragged gasps as he struggled to get the words past the knot of fury in his throat. "Damn you, Slade, you better be sure."

"Oh, it was her all right. And something else. It's mighty funny those Negroes weren't home. It's like somebody tipped 'em off, and I've got a feeling that somebody was Dancy. But what I *can't* figure out," he pressed on, "is why she's doing this on her own, without Clint. I've heard talk there's something between them."

Jordan felt his innards twist, and a bitter taste filled his mouth. It was the kind of gossip he did not want about the woman he intended to marry. "I don't believe that's true, and even if it were, she's beginning to see him for the scoundrel and womanizer he is. I happened to be watching when she saw Lila Coley come out of his office, and she was mad enough to bite a nail."

"That don't mean she won't run to him with what she knows."

"Eventually she will, but Dancy is smart, and she's also stubborn. No doubt she wants to be able to expose all of you before she goes to him." Jordan's frown deepened. "Is there a way she could have overheard any names last night? Seen any-one's face when they were putting their hoods on or taking them off?"

"No. She wasn't there when we were getting robed up. I'm sure of it. I saw everybody, and there were no strangers. And like I said, I fol-lowed her almost home, so she didn't go back with the others to stash their costumes. Nobody was doing any talking once we got there, so she didn't hear anything. And if she was, in fact, hid-ing in the bushes and spying when we met the other night to go over the plans for the ride, I can't for the life of me recall anything she would have heard that would give her a clue as to who anybody is. You know we don't use anybody's names."

"They do it sometimes anyway," Jordan inter-jected with disgust. "We can't be sure. What I want to know is how she found out anything in the first place."

"So would I, but right now I need to know what you plan to do about her."

Jordan grabbed the wheels of his chair and spun himself about. "Just shut up a minute, will you?" he called irritably over his shoulder as he rolled toward the window. "Let me think."

Slade decided he might as well sit down. And since there was no sense in wasting good food, he helped himself to the rest of Jordan's breakfast.

Let him brood all he wanted, Slade mused as he ate. As far as he was concerned, there was only one thing to do to make sure they were not exposed—Dancy had to die.

In her suite at the opposite end of the hall, Addie had awakened spent and exhausted, a sleep plagued by nightmares. She had dreamed she was in a sanatorium somewhere. Surrounded by insane people, living in humiliation and filth, she had tried to kill herself to escape the misery and horror. At the final moment, however, it had been Dancy who'd saved her.

Shaken, still terrified, Addie knew with painful clarity that part of the awful dream could actually come true, because if Jordan did have her put in one of those places, it would be a nightmare, and she *would* want to die.

Dread and desperation consumed her as she rationalized how anything was preferable to being forced from her home. True, she was bitter and angry over how Jordan had changed, but after glimpsing hell in her dreams, she was willing to do anything to keep from being sent away. Therefore she knew what she had to do—pretend to be completely submissive. If he wanted to be in total control, so be it. What difference did it make anymore, anyway, as long as she continued to live in the manner to which she was accustomed? And if ultimately he persuaded Dancy to marry him, so be it. The house was huge. There was room for both of them. Later, when she got her strength back, she would be clever enough to regain control of everything.

She had been a fool all right, for underestimating Jordan, but *he* had also underestimated *her*. If she had foiled the Yankees, she could damn well best her own son.

Earlier than usual she rang for Molly, wanting to bathe and dress and present herself to Jordan before he left for the bank. Strangely, Molly did not respond, so Addie mustered the energy to take care of herself.

She walked toward Jordan's wing of the house. Passing the closed door to the room that had once been Clint's, Addie suddenly recalled Dancy's question as to whether she had resented him when he was a baby.

The truth was, Clint's existence had been a constant reminder that the only reason Angus had married her was to have a mother for his son; but now she could look back and see the unfairness in taking out her pain on an innocent child. Ironic, also, that the daughter of the woman who'd caused Addie her greatest heartache should be the one to bring her to such a revelation.

Addie even found herself wondering how

things would have turned out if she had not disinherited Clint and run him off. Would he condone Jordan's desire to have her committed, or would he go against him in her defense? There was no way of knowing, but the truth was, despite everything, Clint had always been respectful. He was just a scamp, that was all, invariably in trouble and mischief. It was sad how things had turned out because of the infernal war. In years to come perhaps it wouldn't matter which side anybody fought on, but Addie knew she would not witness such indifference in her lifetime.

Addie also regretted asking Slade to have some of his friends masquerade as the Ku Klux Klan. Jordan had known and approved. Oh, she had never ordered violence, to be sure, only the threat. Now, however, caught up in the misery of her own life, she did not like thinking she had caused even one iota of unhappiness or stress to anyone else.

And the saddest bit, she mused wretchedly as she drew closer to Jordan's suite, was feeling too sick to do anything to make amends.

She was about to knock but hearing a voice from within and realizing it wasn't Gabriel, She paused. Curious she leaned closer. What she heard sent icicles of terror cascading through her veins.

"I want Clint killed. Tonight."

It was Jordan who had spoken, she realized in horror.

The other voice fired back, "I don't see what that's going to solve. It's *her* we got to get rid of. Worry about him later."

"She's not to be harmed," Jordan emphasized. "Understand? And with him out of the way, she'll have no one to turn to except me. I'm going to make her my wife, by God, and then I'll have control of her and the land and that's the way it's going to be. But none of it is any of your business. Your job is to take care of him."

Addie swayed, sick to her soul. With a trembling hand she clutched the door frame, knees growing weaker with each passing second. Frantically she tried to believe it wasn't happening, told herself she was still asleep, the nightmare continuing. Yet all the while, with nausea roiling, she knew that what she was witnessing was reality.

"The boys aren't going to like it," Slade pointed out. "Once they find out she's been spying, they'll want her done away with, too, to save their hides."

Jordan fired back, "Well, don't tell all of them, you idiot. Pick a few who have been with you from the start, like your appointed Night Hawks, Buck and Emmett. They'll follow orders. Keep your mouth shut to the rest. There's no need for them to ever know."

With a furious jolt, Addie heard who else was

in there and who else was involved.

"You sure you can keep her occupied?"

"Of course. I'll pay her a visit tonight. No doubt she'll try to get rid of me so she can go spy on you boys, but I'll refuse to leave."

Slade pointed out, "She probably won't be figuring we'll get together anyway, after hearing about last night. Everybody knows we lay low for a while after a big ride."

Addie winced, wondered sadly who their victims had been.

Jordan went on, "It doesn't matter. I'm not taking any chances. As for Clint, we can be sure he'll be busy all day investigating the fire. All you have to do is leave a note in his office late in the day, supposedly from Dancy, saying she's on to something and to meet her quick out at Honey Mountain. He'll take off like a scalded dog, and you and your Night Hawks will be waiting."

Addie heard Slade agree to the plan. She was about to retreat to her room to think of a way to stop them, but with their next words she lost all control.

Slade remarked with a snicker, "It still puzzles me how you can order your own brother killed."

"Brother?" Jordan spat the word as though it were too vile to have in his mouth. "I've told you before, he's not my brother. We shared a father. Not a womb. He's nothing to me."

Hearing that, she opened the door and burst into the room, screaming, "You will burn in hell for your evil. Both of you. He's your half brother, Jordan, for God's sake, blood kin, and you want to murder him!"

The two men stared, stupefied, as Addie continued to rail.

"You won't get away with it. I'll see to it. You, Slade Hawkins." She focused on him. "You lying devil. You and your cutthroats really *are* the Klan. You've been responsible for all the evil in this county. Not outsiders, like you had me believing. You took my money and my orders, and all the time it was *him . . .*"

She turned on Jordan with a fiery glare and a tongue of fury. "You pretended to go along with me and agreed there was nothing wrong with harmless intimidation of the freedmen to keep them in line, and all along you were condoning Slade's meanness. You'll go to jail for this. I'll see to it. I don't care if you are my own son, I won't stand by you in this."

Slade was surprised to see how quickly Jordan recovered from his initial shock, appearing smugly confident as she ranted and raved. Still, he feared some of the servants were going to hear and asked sharply, "Don't I need to do something about her?"

With a curt nod, Jordan agreed. "Don't hurt

her. Take her to her room and lock her inside."

Addie stopped her yelling then as she saw the heinous look on Slade's face as he came toward her. "Don't you touch me," she warned. "So help me—"

He lunged and slapped a burly hand over her mouth, his other gripping her arms to pin them behind her as she fought against him.

Jordan warned, "I said don't hurt her."

Slade wrestled her out of the room and once out of Jordan's view, cuffed her on the back of her head to knock her out. Carrying her over his shoulder like a sack of potatoes, he took her back to her room and dumped her on the bed. After locking her inside, he rushed back.

"We didn't need this, goddamn it." Jordan ran agitated fingers through his hair. "I'll have to see Doc Casper today and have him make immediate arrangements to get her to the sanatorium. Thank goodness Molly decided yesterday to quit and won't be back. She might not be so willing to believe my mother's lost her mind, which is what everyone else has to think when she tells them you and I are involved in the Klan. Gabriel won't be a problem. He knows his place. I'll tell him she went completely insane," he went on, talking more to himself than Slade. "I'll tell him not to dare let her out, and I'll get one of the women out of the fields to tend her. They'll do anything to escape picking cotton.

I'll have her out of here by tonight, anyway."

Slade didn't say anything. He didn't think Jordan would appreciate being told he would need to kill his mother, too.

Dancy heard a rider coming in and knew instinctively it would be Clint. She was inside the new chicken coop, packing pine straw in the wooden boxes to make laying nests. Walking out into the dazzling midafternoon sun, she shielded her eyes with one hand and waited as he approached. She didn't wave, didn't smile, even though inside she was crying with need—to confide in him, as well as to have him hold her close.

"What brings you out here?" She asked as though she really didn't care.

Clint could not deny a rush of longing as he drank in the sight of her. She looked like a little girl with her hair braided and her slightly turned-up nose red from too much sun. He was moved to think of their childhood days; he'd been enchanted by her even then, although he had not realized it until now. "Is Billy still in the barn?"

Dancy had prepared herself for this moment and coolly presented an innocent and bewildered facade. "Yes, but what do you want him for? He's still terribly sore."

"Is Molly with him?"

Dancy pretended annoyance. "I haven't seen her today. Now what's this all about? I don't want you coming out here and upsetting my workers."

"I'm afraid it can't be helped. Billy needs to know the Klan burned his folks' house down last night."

Dancy displayed obligatory shock, asking the proper questions as to whether anyone was hurt, then expressing relief to hear the cabin was abandoned and the couple had escaped unhurt. "I suppose you'll have to tell him," she conceded finally with a nod toward the barn.

He went inside, and Dancy returned to her chore, cursing herself for trembling at his very nearness. Dear God, how long would it take for her mind to make her heart understand it could never be?

It was not long before he returned, and he stood in the doorway of the coop for a long time without speaking. She knew he was there but pretended not to.

Finally he cleared his throat, and she turned and asked, "How did he take it?"

"He was upset. Now he's worried about Molly, since she hasn't shown up. I told him she was probably helping their folks settle in somewhere else."

She moved by him. "Well, if I hear anything, I'll let you know, Marshal."

He caught her arm and spun her about. "Dancy, you've got to listen," he said thickly, desperately. "Things are only going to get worse. I'm going in to Nashville tomorrow to ask for more deputies. I can't be everywhere at once, which means I can't be here all the time, where I want to be. So for the last time, will you please get out till all of this is over?"

With an adamant shake of her head, Dancy refused. "I can take care of myself. You just do your job and I'll do mine. And when this is truly over," she added tartly, in an attempt to quell the emotions churning within, "you'll either legally give up title to this land or I will see you in court, Marshal. Now let me go."

He allowed her to shake free. Their gazes locked, ablaze with challenge yet shadowed with pain.

As he turned to go, Dancy thought how she had been haunted by his parting words the last time she had seen him. Impulsively she called, "Tell me. What did you mean when you said you were sorry I had to be my mother's daughter?"

He drew a deep breath and let it out slowly, all the while fighting the desire to take her in his arms. "She was stubborn, too, and wound up ruining two lives. Hers and Dooley's. I hate to see you do the same to ours."

After mounting his horse, Clint rode away and did not look back.

He did not see how Dancy lifted her hand in beckoning, lips trembling as she whispered his name, nor did he witness the tears streaming down her cheeks.

25

As Gabriel headed the carriage toward Dancy's place, Jordan continued to dwell on the frustrations of the day. He hadn't liked leaving that nitwit servant girl, Cassie, to look after his mother, but he had no choice. According to Mrs. Casper, her husband had been called out during the night to assist in a difficult birth, and there was nothing anyone could do but wait for his return.

Any other time, Jordan would have taken his mother on up to Nashville and committed her himself. Money talked. He could arrange with the officials at the hospital to have her admitted. Only she knew too much now, and to be on the safe side, he wanted her farther away, in Philadelphia. Dr. Casper could make the necessay arrangements much faster than he.

Jordan supposed it was sad, in a way, that his

mother had to live out her days so wretchedly. But she'd had her glory years, and now it was *his* turn.

Along the way Gabriel had timidly offered, "Maybe when I get you settled at Miss Dancy's, I ought to go back and see to your momma. I just ain't sure Cassie can look after her proper. That youngun don't have a lick of sense, and I can come back and get you whenever you say."

Jordan glared at his back and snapped, "You'll do nothing of the kind. I told you. My mother has lost her mind. No one can help her. She'll be put away where she can't harm herself or anyone else, as soon as possible. Now stop worrying about it."

When they arrived, Dancy was nowhere around. "Carry me in," Jordan ordered, "then bring in the packages and go wait at the end of the road till I call you."

Gabriel lifted him in his arms.

"There,"—Jordan pointed. "At the table this time." He did not like thinking about how his previous visit had turned out.

Gabriel was just setting down the box containing coffee, sugar, and a cured ham, when Dancy, breathless, stormed through the door. She had seen the carriage when she'd come out of the chicken coop and had furiously run all the way to the cabin. "Take that out of here, Gabriel," she cried, pointing first to the box, then to Jordan, "and then take him."

"Go and wait for me like I told you," Jordan said blandly before offering his most charming smile to Dancy. "I thought you might like a few staples. Emmett received a shipment today, and I made sure he set some things aside for you."

Each word was barbed. "I don't want your gifts, Jordan, and I don't want you here. I'd hoped we could be friends, but you've made that extremely difficult. It will take time for me to forgive you for the way you acted the last time you barged in here. Now call Gabriel back in here, please."

"I came to apologize."

"I don't want your apology. I just want you to go." At the sound of the wagon leaving, she ran to the door and shouted, but Gabriel kept on going. Whirling around, she threw up her hands in frustration. "Jordan, why do you do this to me? Why do you make me angry with you? I don't want it this way, but you leave me no choice."

He held his genial expression. "I won't stay long, I promise. I only wanted to personally say I'm sorry for what happened the other day."

In weary defeat, she sat down opposite him at the table. Recalling his strength, how quickly he could move, she kept a safe distance. "All right. I'll accept your apology, but never again, understand?"

Searching her face for some sign that she cared,

even a little, he whispered raggedly, "It's because I love you, Dancy. And I want you so much."

"Please don't talk this way," she murmured. Dear Lord, she didn't want to hurt him.

Pitiably he said, "It's because I'm crippled, isn't it?"

"That's not true," she denied.

"You loved me once," he reminded her.

"But we were children, for heaven's sake."

"I loved you then. I love you now. In time you'll come to realize you feel the same, and believe me, my darling, I'll be waiting. Meanwhile"—he leaned back in his chair and folded his arms across his chest—"if you'll look in that box, you'll find one of Dorothy Peabody's famous plum cakes. If we can share a slice of that, and a cup of coffee, I'll say good night."

Dancy made no move to oblige.

"Please."

Deciding to concede, in hopes he would keep his word, she started making the coffee. "This has to stop, Jordan," she told him bluntly. "I find it rude for you to have Gabriel just bring you in here like this. Don't make me have to ask Roscoe to turn you back."

"As if he'd dare." He laughed airily, then, seeing the shadow cross her face, justified hastily, "You have to understand how it is around here. The war may be over, but the freedmen still respect whites. They'd better, if they know which side their bread's buttered."

Dancy found his attitude offensive. "Then I suppose you don't see anything wrong with the Klan, since their purpose is to frighten them into fearful obedience. Did you know they burned down Molly and Billy's parents' house last night, and it was only through the grace of God they weren't home?"

Jordan struggled to remain expressionless. He did not like the direction the conversation had taken, especially about the previous night, because it rankled deeply to know she had been there and seen everything. Further, he was agitated to wonder how much she actually knew. "Yes, I heard. And it makes me sick. I don't know any of the details. Molly informed me yesterday she wouldn't be working for me anymore, and I haven't seen her. She couldn't have left me at a worse time," he added. "Mother has taken a turn for the worse, and—"

"What happened?" Dancy was slicing the cake but whipped about in alarm. "Doc Casper seemed to think she was going to be all right."

"It's not her kidneys."

"Then what—"

"It's her mind." He covered his face with his hands for a moment, as though too despaired to go on, then smoothly told the story he had made up. "I'd been suspecting it for some time. I even talked to Dr. Casper about it, and he said he hated having to agree with me, but he'd noticed it, too. We'd hoped to convince her to go to a sanatorium on her own, but she wouldn't hear of it. Now we have no choice."

Washed with pity, Dancy felt like bursting into tears.

Jordan could see she was shaken and pressed on. "This morning she went completely crazy, and—-"

"Where is she now?"

"At home, she—"

"But who's with her?" she persisted. "And how could you leave her in that condition?"

"Doc Casper sedated her," he lied. "She's sound asleep, and I have a servant with her. She'll be fine. Tomorrow she'll be taken to where they know how to deal with these things.

"As for leaving her, for God's sake," he implored her, "don't you see I can't bear for you to be angry with me? I had to come out here and apologize and tell you I mean you no harm. These past days have been agony."

Dancy turned away. She didn't want to discuss his feelings for her. Not now. Not ever. She did, however, want to know about Addie, and she began asking questions, which he answered patiently. But when she asked to visit Addie before she was taken away, he refused.

"I don't want you or anybody else seeing her as she is now. She wouldn't want it, either."

Dancy was sad to have to agree, and she finished making the coffee. Gradually, they slipped into an easy conversation about olden days, and she found herself wishing once more he could be satisfied with mere friendship.

Time passed. Dancy thought how she'd planned to ride out to the Klan's den just on the chance there might be a meeting, but she decided it would have been a waste of time. They had done their meanness the night before. A few days would probably pass before they moved again.

Finally she reminded Jordan of his promise to leave after coffee and cake, remarking, "If I don't get to bed soon, I won't feel like doing my chores in the morning."

"Marry me," he pointed out cheerily, "and you'd have no chores. You could live like a queen."

"And I'd be bored silly." She was determined not to discuss anything serious. "I like to work, Jordan. Especially around here, because it's mine."

"Has Clint agreed to that?"

She felt herself tense.

"I had Gabriel take me to the courthouse so I

could look at the records myself. Clint hasn't changed anything."

"He will. He's been busy," she hedged.

Testily Jordan pushed, "No, he won't. He's making a fool of you, Dancy, and you're too blind to see it. He connived to get this land. He knew my mother and I wanted it, and he went behind our backs to get it."

Wearily she reminded him, "I've heard that story." She pushed back her chair and stood. "I really think we should say good night. Now where is Gabriel?"

He told her Gabriel was waiting for a signal, so she went to the door and called. Almost instantly she heard the sound of the carriage approaching, and within moments Gabriel was bounding up the steps.

She walked out on the porch to thank Jordan for the staples, then said coolly, "And from now on, please wait for an invitation before you come to call."

Jordan felt an immediate rush of anger and humiliation to be chastised in front of a servant.

"And don't forget," she urged, oblivious of his discomfiture, "if you need me to help with Addie, send Gabriel to get me. And if she rallies at all, please remember me to her. That must have been terrible this morning when she went insane. I feel so sorry for—"

"Gabriel, let's be on our way," Jordan interrupted sharply. The less for the servants to gossip about, the better.

However, Gabriel was already in deep thought, as he had been since hearing Miss Addie's screams that morning. He had been all the way outside in the kitchen but could hear her, as could the cook and some of the other servants. He had rushed into the house, about to go upstairs, then remembered there'd be the devil to pay if he did. Just about that time, things got quiet. Since then he had heard her moan, but Master Jordan got real upset when he said anything about it, so he supposed it was best to just leave it alone. Still, he had a bad feeling something was wrong. Bad wrong.

When they arrived, Gabriel knew Master Jordan was mad about something when he curtly told him to take him to his room and then get the hell out of the house. "Tell Cassie to get out, too. Mother will sleep till morning, and you know I don't like servants in the house at night."

How well he did know, Gabriel mused. Master Jordan had set that rule right after he came back from the war crippled. Miss Addie had wanted him to sleep outside Master Jordan's door, in the parlor on the floor, in case he needed anything or fell out of bed and couldn't get up. But Master Jordan wouldn't hear of it.

Gabriel was sure Miss Addie would indeed sleep all night, because he had shown Cassie how to fix the laudanum-laced tea himself, and this time Master Jordan had ordered the dose doubled.

Still, Gabriel continued to be plagued with the feeling that something was wrong, and he decided to disobey orders this one night. So he bedded down on the floor at the rear of the house, right near the steps that led up to the outside of Miss Addie's rooms. He would hear her if she needed him, and if nothing else, he could make more tea to ease her suffering.

Maybe she was a cranky old soul, but he knew she had a good side, too. Many times he had known her to sit up with a sick slave. She had also secretly helped some white folks at times, sending him to leave food on their doorstep in the middle of the night and not letting them know who did it.

Yes, he sure had a different opinion of Miss Addie than other people. And it bothered him to see her mistreated, especially by Master Jordan. But then, he had always known Master Jordan to be sneaky. As a boy, so many times Master Clint was the one to get in trouble, because Master Jordan made it look like he was responsible for some devilment. And since the war he'd got worse, but Gabriel had decided that had to do with not being able to walk. He supposed if he lost the use of his legs, he might get mean himself, although he liked to think he wouldn't. . . .

And so he drifted away.

After Jordan finally left, Dancy made sure Roscoe was at his post near the road, then she went to bed. She was weary, not only from the day's chores, but also from the ever-present tension when Jordan was around. And, she was forced to admit, Clint's visit had not helped, for being around him only stirred the pain and made it worse. If only she had not fallen in love with him, if only she could have given her body . . . and not her heart.

At the first sound, her eyes flashed open to the darkness, and as always, she was instantly alert and grabbing for her gun.

"Dannnn . . . ceeeee . . ."

A harsh breeze was blowing, and Dancy told herself she had not really heard her name called, that it was merely the wind whistling through the pines.

"Dancy, me darlin' . . ."

But that, she knew beyond doubt, was real.

On her way to the door, she paused to take down the rifle from the inverted horseshoe rack above. Holding it ready in one hand, the pistol in the other, she stepped onto the porch.

A full moon bathed the landscape in silver, casting an eerie, ethereal glow. As she glanced anxiously about, she was struck with worry over Roscoe. He was a good guard, never falling asleep at his post like some of the others. Ever alert and watchful, he would not have allowed anyone to slip by him, which meant he might be injured.

"Who's out there?" she called into the night wind. "I swear, I'll blow you to hell. Now get off my land."

It was like an icicle to her heart to see the figure emerge slowly from the shadows. He was near the foot of the ridge leading up to the secret spot, and though it was too far to distinguish his face, she could see he was clad in a uniform of dark blue.

Fury flashing, she shouted, "Clint, this isn't funny."

And then he spoke in a voice that seemed to whisper through golden chimes, soft and ringing with a melodious echo. "Ah, Dancy, me darlin'. Surely the angels danced the day you were born."

Her heart slammed into her chest, and she told herself she was crazy even to think such a thing— but, dear God, it sounded like Uncle Dooley, calling from somewhere far, far away. For a dazed moment she dared think it couldn't be Clint, for how would he have knowledge of the way Dooley loved to remind her how she came to be named? Dizzily she rationalized that Dooley had probably told him in those miserable times together during the war. Now she was really getting mad but decided to see just how far Clint would carry his ridiculous prank.

"Who are you? What do you want?" she called

"Addie. Addie needs you, Dancy. Help her, please."

Now she was beginning to wonder if she was losing her mind as she shook her head in vicious denial. She did not believe in ghosts.

"Go to her . . . now."

Dancy continued to stare, frozen where she stood. She thought about firing over his head, but for reasons she could not understand, she hesitated.

"Clint needs you, too, Dancy. Remember the forever. . . ."

Suddenly Roscoe came running from the path and across the yard. Moonlight gleamed off the barrel of the gun he carried. His face was aglow with terror as he waved his arms and yelled, "Miss Dancy, what's wrong? What're you shouting about? Ain't nobody got by me, I swear . . ."

Her attention had been momentarily diverted to Roscoe, and when she looked back the mounted figure was gone.

A war of sanity raged within Dancy. Whoever, whatever, had been there had disappeared without making a sound. "Did you hear that man calling to me?" She pointed to the ridge as Roscoe reached the porch.

Out of breath, he stared wide-eyed in the direction she indicated, then told her nervously, "No, ma'am. I heard you yell, and I started running, and I stopped over there in the woods to peek out and see what kind of trouble you was having, and I saw you, heard you talking, but I didn't hear nobody else.

"Miss Dancy," he said slowly, fearfully, because she looked so strange, "are you all right?"

It could be a trick. The Ku Klux Klan was devious enough to fool her into leaving in the middle of the night and be waiting to ambush. But something deep within was telling her she had to take that chance.

"Go saddle my horse," she said in a rush, going back inside to get dressed.

Roscoe could only stand there, dumbfounded. Finally he came out of his stupor to call after her, "Miss Dancy, what in the world you want to go out this time of night for?"

Dancy paused, wondering how in the world she could explain it to him when she didn't understand herself. Ultimately she added to his bewilderment by saying, "I guess I'm going where my heart leads me, Roscoe. I'll know why when I get there."

He didn't understand, thought maybe it was good he didn't, because Miss Dancy was acting mighty funny.

He ran to the barn to do as she had asked.

Clint stopped inside the door to his office to fire up the lantern hanging there. It was late, and he was exhausted, but despite everything, if he thought he'd be welcome, he knew he'd ride out to Dancy's and spend what was left of the night showing her how much he wanted her, and—

He had crossed the tiny room to his desk, and was about to leaf through the few notes left for him, when one seemed to leap out at him. With pounding heart he read the hastily scrawled lines:

I know where they gather. I'm on my way there now to try to find out who they are. Meet me at Honey Mountain, the old cabin, as soon as you can. Hurry. Dancy.

He rushed out, leaving the lantern burning, the door standing wide open, oblivious of everything except getting out there as quick as possible.

Till that jarring moment, when he realized

Dancy's life was in danger, Clint had not known the true depth of his love for her.

He had to save her, and God help anybody who got in his way.

26

The moon continued to dance playfully in and out among the clouds, but Dancy rode like the wind.

Roscoe had begged to come along, but she had made him see he needed to stay behind, in case it was a trick to get her out of the way so the Klan could attack again. "And if they do," she'd instructed, "don't try to stand up to them. Turn the animals out of the barn and hide till it's over. I can always rebuild if they burn me out, and I won't have you and the others risking your lives."

As the horse thundered through the night, Dancy tried to remember every detail of the spectral scene. It had to have been Clint, she reasoned. But if he wanted her to see Addie, why hadn't he come right out and said so? And while she had no idea why he would pretend to be Dooley's ghost, she intended to find out. This time she wouldn't let him pass it off as a trick of her mind due to exhaustion, the wind, or anything else. She would have the truth, by God.

However, if the phantom was someone in the Klan, she could be in serious danger.

Intending to be prepared should an attack come, she was ever alert, constantly scanning both sides of the road. She held the reins in one hand and her gun in the other, ready to shoot to kill at the first threat. She reasoned if she took several of them down at the very onset of trouble, the others would see she meant business and abandon the chase.

Dancy knew she could have dismissed the incident as either a joke or a trap, which might have been wise. However, something prevented her from doing so. Whatever the motive of whoever was responsible, Clint or the Ku Klux Klan, Dancy was now feeling inexplicably drawn to Addie. Jordan's account of how she had suddenly lost her mind needled. Addie might be sick, and it was a known fact she was cantankerous. But she was also sharp-witted, and Dancy found it hard to believe she'd suddenly become demented beyond recovery.

And though she had not wanted to debate the issue with Jordan, Dancy had planned to see Doc Casper to ask his opinion. It might be none of her business, but she could not help worrying about the woman.

She reached the knoll overlooking the McCabe plantation. The low-hanging clouds parted to allow moonlight to bathe the two-story mansion in a mystical glow. All the windows were dark, and not a sound could be heard.

Dancy shivered, despite the warmth of the summer night. Despite the apparent tranquillity, she sensed something was not right.

She was not about to go to the front door and knock. Jordan had told her once that he didn't like servants prowling, as he called it, around the house at night, which meant Gabriel would not respond. Jordan, of course, was not able to respond, so there would be no one to admit her— unless Addie had a nurse, which Dancy somehow doubted.

Leaving her horse back a ways, she proceeded on foot, entering through the back door.

It was pitch dark. Not a single lantern burned anywhere, which prevented her from moving swiftly. Feeling her way along, lest she bump into something and make noise, Dancy was annoyed to think how, with a sick person in the house, light should have been provided for whatever rea-son needed.

Never having been in the rear of the mansion, Dancy had to open several doors before she located the back stairs. Slowly, stealthily, she headed for the second floor.

Gabriel was awake and alert, having heard the back door open. Washed in a glimpse of silver, Dancy O'Neal was easily recognizable to him. He had no idea why she had come, or why she was sneaking in, but he knew she meant no harm. And he was not about to let her or anybody else know he'd disobeyed orders.

Dancy stepped out into the tiny box hallway and tried to get her bearings. Clint's room, she recalled, was on the same side of the grand stairway as Addie's suite. Locating the railing about the landing, she turned in the right direction.

Groping, she found the right door and quietly turned the knob, cursing softly to find it locked. Holding her breath, she moved her fingers downward, then gasped with thanksgiving to find the key still in place. With a twist, she was inside.

"Ohh, Cassie, is that you?"

The feeble moan came from somewhere to her right in the smothering gloom.

"Help me, please, child. Get me out of here."

Dancy bumped into the bed.

Addie, alarmed that there had been no response to her tearful plea, demanded shakily, "Who is it? Who's there? I won't have you sneaking into my room this way. How dare you?"

Despite the tension, Dancy felt a dash of amusement over Addie's indomitable spirit. She promptly identified herself , hastening to add, "I'm here to help you."

Addie's hand snaked out to find and clutch her wrist with amazing strength. "You've got to find Clinton," she began to babble in desperation. "Tell him he's in danger. They're planning to kill him tonight. . . ."

Dancy shook her head in sad resolve, pulled gently from Addie's grasp, and began to search the top of the bedside table for a match. It was true: the poor woman had lost her mind.

"Believe me, please, child. I heard them talking. Jordan and that wretched man, Slade Hawkins. Jordan is the leader of the Ku Klux Klan, you know, but I never thought there was a real Klan. I thought Slade was only warning my Negroes they'd best stay put, or they'd be tracked down and dealt with. My goal was to keep them here. Not hurt them.

"Only he and Jordan lied to me." Her words were tumbling out in chokes and gasps, making her difficult to understand. "Jordan gave the orders. Slade only pretended to follow mine.

"Like the night you were attacked," she rushed on, "I deliberately picked that fight with Jordan at the table, knowing you'd be upset and leave. I told Slade to take some of his men and make you think you were going to be robbed, then pretend to hear something and ride away without hurting you. I only wanted to scare you off that land. I had nothing to do with what happened later, when they tried to burn you out. That had to be Jordan's doing. I never wanted you hurt, child. You have to believe me."

Finally Dancy found a match. She removed the glass globe and touched it to the wick, and the room was instantly aglow. She could see Addie's pale, drawn face, her expression wretched and pleading. Sitting down on the side of the bed, she soothed, "It's all right. I didn't get hurt, so we can forget it ever happened. Now I'm going to stay with you till you fall asleep. You've nothing to be afraid of."

"But you have to believe me," Addie cried, pounding on the bed with her fists in frustration. Squeezing her eyes shut, she ground her teeth together and prayed for the right words to make Dancy see she was not crazy. "Oh, why, oh, why, won't you listen? Why won't anyone listen? Why did you even come if you aren't going to help me? Clinton is going to die, and it will be your fault, because you're the only one who can stop them."

Addie stared at her in accusing wonder. "I dreamed you would help me, did you know that? I dreamed Jordan sent me away to one of those places where they put crazy people, and I was so miserable I tried to kill myself, but you came and saved me, and when I saw you here, I thought it was an omen.

"But you won't listen." She began to flail at the mattress once more, tears streaming down her cheeks, her whole body convulsed with frantic sobs. "I even dared think after that day we talked in the cemetery that I was wrong, that if Dooley wanted you to have his place, you should, and I'll help you, but dear God, you've got to help me now. Don't you see it's breaking my heart to know my own son is the leader of that bunch of killers and there's not a damn thing I can do about it? Don't you think it's tearing me apart to know they're out there now, waiting to murder my stepson?"

It was a jolt to hear Addie refer to Clint as her stepson, and Dancy was moved. "It will be all right, Miss Addie." She patted her hand. "You've had another nightmare, that's all."

Addie raised her head from the pillow to glare at her with such vehement fury that Dancy pulled back instinctively.

"It's no dream, I tell you, but I wish it were. My own son, responsible for murder. Dear God, if I could, I'd go and stop them myself, but I'm sick. My stomach feels as if it's on fire, and I know I've got a fever. It's too late to ride into town and head off Clinton now, and I'd never be able to find my way to Honey Mountain in the dark anyway, even if I was able to get on a horse."

Dancy raised an eyebrow. Her dreams were certainly vivid, and it was obvious Addie believed they were real. Gently she said, "Now why would you want to go to Honey Mountain, Miss Addie? That's all the way out at my place."

"Don't you think I know that? I know every square inch of Dooley's land. Through the years I've ridden it, walked it. Again and again. I knew how much he loved it, how it was a part of him, and by being there, I felt he was with me.

"When he died," she continued, "the feeling was even stronger. He was there. I could feel his spirit with me. Don't you see that's why I wanted it? At first it was only because I felt as if it should've been mine, that if it hadn't been for him falling in love with your mother, he would have married me. Then I finally realized if he'd really loved me, the way a man's supposed to love a woman, no one could've stopped him. . . ." Lowering her face to her trembling hands, Addie succumbed to racking sobs.

Dancy waited quietly, unsure of what to say. It was heartbreaking to witness Addie's derangement. She only hoped that when Addie's fever went down, she would think more clearly and realize it could not possibly be so.

Abruptly Addie stopped crying, suddenly

remembering the tragedy about to take place. "It's where they meet." Again she reached to clutch Dancy's arm, eyes wild, frantic. "You should know that. You were spying on them the other night. That's how you knew they were going to attack Molly's folks, and—"

Dancy was on her feet instantly, heart pounding wildly. Hoarsely she demanded, "What did you say?"

Indignant, Addie repeated, "You were spying on them—"

"I know, I know, but how did you know that?" Dancy's head was spinning.

"I heard them talking." Addie bit out each word. "How the hell do you think I found out they were planning to kill Clinton? Jordan is the one who's been giving orders to Slade, like I told you," Addie went on, struggling to sit up. "I was outside his door and heard them talking yesterday morning when Slade came to tell him he'd found out you'd been spying. Jordan said it was time to get rid of Clinton, before you told him what you knew. They planned to get a message to him, telling him you were in trouble out at Honey Mountain, so he'd ride right into a trap.

"So you see?" Addie finished triumphantly, despite her horror, "I'm not crazy. I haven't lost my mind. That's just what Jordan is saying so nobody will believe me."

Dancy admitted, "I didn't either, till you said they knew I was spying, because I was. Only I'm still not convinced Jordan is behind it all. I saw their leader. They call him the Grand Giant of the Province, and he was on horseback. It can't be Jordan. It has to be someone else, Miss Addie, because that man wasn't crippled."

"Which proves she's crazy for even suggesting something so preposterous."

Addie gave a startled cry, and Dancy whipped about to see Jordan rolling himself into the room with sure, vicious strokes of the wheels on his chair.

"I heard noises and thought she was ranting again, then I got closer and heard your voice." His forehead was furrowed with annoyance as he drew closer. "While I'm always pleased to see you, Dancy, I'm curious as to why you're sneaking into my house in the middle of the night."

"My house, you ingrate." Addie found the strength to make her voice strongly castigating. "You may be my son, my flesh and blood, but if you have your brother slain this night, I will turn from you as I foolishly did him.

"Go for help, Dancy." Her nails dug painfully into Dancy's flesh. "I don't know who to tell you to trust, but do something, please. Try to catch up with Clinton and stop him before he walks into their trap."

Jordan was furious to see that Dancy believed her and pressed to convince Dancy otherwise. "She's hopelessly tetched, my dear," he said with feigned distress, then, eyes narrowing angrily, he asked, "Did she talk Gabriel into going to you with this nonsense? If she did, so help me—"

"Stop it, Jordan. Right now." Dancy held up both hands to fend off his lies. "It's no use. She heard what Slade told you about me spying, and it's true. I *was* there. I saw them burning that house, just as I spied on a meeting and saw where they hide their costumes.

"I know everything," she went on coldly, angrily, "except the identity of their leader, but I'll find out, because I'm going out there."

His laugh was meant to be scornful but instead bordered on hysteria. "Don't be ridiculous, Dancy. Can't you see she's crazy? She doesn't know what she's talking about. It's obvious she had a nightmare, and she's feverish, and—"

Dancy cut him off to ask Addie, "Will you be all right? I can go out and wake up Gabriel."

"I'll do that myself," Addie said. "And I'll send him to Nashville to fetch the provost marshal, and soldiers, too. This evil is going to be stopped, in my county anyway, no matter who's behind it." She looked at Jordan in damning accusation.

As Dancy brushed by him, he caught her

wrist, but she shook free, continuing on her way as he shouted after her, "Don't be a fool. She's crazy, I tell you! Come back here, and let's talk about it. It's not like you think, Dancy, I swear. . . ."

But she was on her way, hurrying in the darkness and bumping into a table. A statue toppled to the floor and broke, but Dancy kept on going. Nothing was going to stop her now.

She all but tumbled down the stairs in her haste, rushed out the back door and leaped off the porch to hit the ground running.

Dancy did not see Gabriel move out of the shadows. Every nerve in his body taut with anger, he headed for the barn to saddle up the fastest horse there. He hated leaving Miss Addie at the mercy of Master Jordan, but he knew it was much more important to get on the road to Nashville.

Curiosity getting the best of him, he had decided to follow Miss Dancy and thus heard everything from where he'd lurked in the hall. Master Jordan hadn't seen him as he'd come rolling up, so Gabriel had continued to listen and now knew Miss Addie wanted him to get the provost marshal.

And by God, he was on his way.

* * *

As she rode, Dancy wished she could take the fastest route to Honey Mountain, across McCabe land onto what had once belonged to her father. But she dared not go the same way the Klan traveled and knew Clint would not have gone in that direction, either. No doubt the Klan was leading him into a trap at the old shack, and he would be coming in from Dooley's side. She hoped to follow him, catch up with him before he made it through.

The ride seemed endless, and when at last she reached her place, she had but a brief glimpse of Roscoe's astonished face in the moonlight as she charged right by him and onward toward the ridge.

At the falls, Dancy dismounted and forced herself to move slowly, cautiously, lest she trip and fall into the water. The path around the pool was narrow and precarious, but at last she managed to find the opening into the tunnel, despite the hampering darkness. Crouching, a gun in each hand, she moved stealthily, struggling for balance.

Clawing hands of cool dampness wrapped about her as she pressed her back against the wall of the passageway. Something slithered across her foot, and she froze momentarily. A frog. A snake. Whatever it was, she prayed it would pass, and when it did she crept on cautiously.

Inside, Clint's words taunted. She was her mother's daughter and had been about to make the same mistake her mother had made when she'd run away from Dooley. Maybe theirs had been the sin of adultery, but Dancy believed with all her heart that God would have understood and forgiven. Her mother had been sold to her father, had not married him willingly.

Dancy had witnessed her mother's misery through the years but had never understood the reason for it . . . till now. Fearing the same anguish her mother had suffered, she had refused to surrender her heart, but Clint had stolen it despite her resolve.

And now she could only pray with all her might that she got to him in time to save his life, for without him her own life was meaningless.

Every so often, she would pause, straining for any sound indicating Clint was somewhere in front of her. All she heard was the rushing water, mere inches below. Several times she stumbled and nearly fell as she fought to maintain her balance without dropping her weapons. When at last she sensed she was almost to the other side, her pulse began to hammer even harder. If he had come this way, he was already out, which meant chances were slim she could prevent his walking into the ambush. Maybe they already had him. Maybe, she thought, a choking sob escaping her lips, he was already dead.

"Dancy, what the hell—"

Clint grabbed her, crushing her into his arms so hard that the breath was squeezed from her. Gasping first in terror, then in relief, Dancy gulped in great swallows of air before she was able to cry, "Thank God! I was afraid I hadn't got here in time."

"And I was afraid you'd come and gone." He laughed uneasily. "Now what's this all about. Why—"

"Hush and listen." She remembered to keep her voice down as she pressed shaking fingertips against his lips. In a rush, she told him everything.

Clint listened, rage building like floodwaters straining against a dam. "Listen to me," he said when she had finished. His hands firm on her shoulders, he held her so close she could feel the warmth of his breath on her face. "I want you to turn around and get out of here."

"No, I'm staying. You need me—"

He gave her such a vicious shake, her head bobbed to and fro. Through clenched teeth he warned, "Don't argue with me. Turn around and get out of here now. Jordan is their leader. He has to be, and you can bet once you left he was right behind you—"

"Wrong." Jordan laughed at the same time that

he pulled the trigger, blasting into the night and sending a bullet into Clint's leg.

Clint dropped his gun, and went down in a painful grunt, helplessly aware that Dancy was being torn from his arms, her own weapons falling out of her hands.

Jordan cackled as he watched Clint clutching his bleeding leg. "I was never behind, you fool. I took the short way, and I've been waiting for you. I knew about the secret passage through the mountain, because I wasn't always the obedient sissy you took me for. I followed you lots of times, back when we were children, and you were Daddy's favorite. . . ." His voice rose shrilly.

Slade Hawkins, dressed in his red robe and hood, had pressed his arm against Dancy's throat, choking off her screams as she struggled to breathe, clawing frantically at his hold. She saw two others in white Klan garb as they stepped from the brush after hastily lighting torches.

Dancy was torn with panic, struggling futilely to free herself and get to Clint, all the while washed with horror to realize Jordan was standing there. *Standing. He could walk.*

Jordan saw her astonishment and chuckled. "Yes, isn't it wonderful?" he confirmed cheerily. "Those stupid doctors didn't know they were dealing with a man who wouldn't give up. I worked my legs every day, no matter how much it hurt, but by the time I'd taught myself to walk again, I knew it was to my advantage to let it be my little secret."

He went on to divulge how by then he had organized the local Klan. And as long as everyone believed him confined to a wheelchair, he'd not be suspected of having any part in their activities.

"By the way, allow me to introduce my two Night Hawks," Jordan continued with a flourish, all the while keeping his gun trained on Clint. "You probably already know their names—Buck Sweeney and Emmett Peabody."

Buck and Emmett gave loud gasps of protest as Slade yelped, "Shut up, damn it! Maybe she don't know who they are."

"Oh, it doesn't matter. She's never going to tell, are you, my darling?"

He grinned at her in the torchlight, and Dancy was sickened to think how he looked like a demon from hell.

"Wives don't talk about their husband's friends or their business, do they?" He reached to pinch her cheek, but she jerked her head back, stomach heaving with revulsion and disgust.

"Oh, you'll change your mind later. . . ."

"Stop it, Jordan," Slade said then. "There's only one way to take care of this mess, and you know it."

For the first time, Jordan saw Slade had drawn his gun. Uneasily he reminded him, "I said I'd take care of this, that I want Clint to know why—"

Buck yelled, "That don't matter. You take care of him. We'll take care of her."

"No." Jordan began to shake his head, slowly at first, then faster, breath coming in sharp, jagged heaves as it dawned on him what they were about to do. In a hysterical torrent he cried, "No, you can't kill her! She'll never say a word about any of this, I swear! When he's gone, she'll realize she has no one, and she'll marry me, and I'll see to it she keeps her mouth shut. If I have to beat her, torture her, whatever it takes, she'll never talk, I promise. Just let her go, please—"

Slade told him grimly, "We can't take any chances. Not with her. Not with your mother. As soon as this is over, I'm going back to the house and take care of her, too.

"The Klan is bigger than you realize, Jordan," he went on proudly. "It's outgrown you. We're going to keep things like they were before the war, and people like you have either got to accept it, go along with it, or get trampled along the way."

Buck chimed in, "There's nothing you can do, Jordan. It's how it's gotta be—"

"No!" Jordan screamed. Taking them by surprise, he lunged to tear Dancy from Slade's arms and fling her to the ground. At the same instant, he grappled for Slade's gun.

Despite the white-hot pain ripping through his leg, Clint seized the chance he had been waiting for and dove for his gun where it had fallen. He grabbed it, brought it up, and fired at Emmett, killing him instantly.

At that precise instant, Slade was able to land a blow to Jordan's head that sent him reeling into the bushes.

Clint felt the zing of a bullet creasing the side of his head as he again pulled the trigger and hit Buck square in his forehead. But Buck tumbled on top of him, knocking him backward. That gave Slade the break he needed to rush forward and twist Clint's gun away to tower over him.

"Now, who wants to die first?" He swung to point it at Dancy, who had found one of her guns and was bringing it up to fire.

Jordan saw and shrieked, "No!" as he threw himself at Slade and took the bullet intended for Dancy. As he slumped to the ground, Slade was a clear target.

Dancy pulled the trigger and blew him away.

Epilogue

They stood on the steps of the church and watched as the last of the wedding guests rode away.

"I still can't get over how many people came," Dancy marveled, clinging tightly to Clint's arm, wanting never to let him go.

It took his breath away to look at her, so beautiful in her white silk gown. "I think Addie had a lot to do with it."

Beside them, Addie swelled with pride as she said airily, "Of course I did. As I've always said, those folks know which side their bread's buttered on, and I spread the word it's time to forgive and forget. The war's over. Time to get on with living. You young folks are a part of this community, and they'd better start treating you with respect."

Dancy and Clint exchanged warm glances.

They had made their peace with Addie, which only enhanced the happiest day of their lives.

Gabriel moved to assist Addie as she started down the steps, but she shook him off, annoyed. "I don't need your help. Doc Casper says I'm doing fine, but if everybody keeps treating me like an invalid, I might as well crawl in Jordan's wheelchair, and—" Her voice caught as she swallowed against painful memories.

Dancy touched her shoulder. "It's all right, Addie. No matter what he did, you loved him, and in his own way he loved you, too."

"No, not really." Addie lifted her chin and gazed mournfully toward the fresh grave in the McCabe plot. "I've thought about it a lot and come to realize I made him resent me by clinging to him like I did. I guess I just thought he was all I had and was afraid I'd lose him."

"He saved my life," Dancy said quietly. "That bullet was meant for me."

"I know. Maybe he redeemed himself at the end. I like to think so." Addie took a deep breath and mustered a genuine smile for the newlyweds. "So, you're going to honeymoon in that wretched little cabin."

"It's where it all began," Clint said with a twinkle in his brown eyes. "Can't think of a better place."

"Well, I guess I best be getting home." She

waved her parasol at Gabriel to bring the carriage. She started to walk away, then hesitated. Suddenly her life seemed as empty as the mansion awaiting her. "You all come and see me when you got time," she murmured. "You're always welcome."

She didn't see the way Clint and Dancy grinned at each other before Clint ventured, "If it's all right with you, we were thinking about more than a visit."

Slowly Addie turned, pulse quickening. "You don't mean—"

"We can't let her live in that big house all alone, now can we, Dancy?"

"That's right," Dancy chimed in, eyes shining.

The corners of Addie's mouth twitched as she fought to keep from smiling. "Well, maybe it would be nice to have somebody around in case I do get sick, but . . ." She tapped Clint's chest with the tip of her parasol. "You'd both better remember it's my house. I'll not have either one of you trying to take over."

"Yes, ma'am," Clint said obediently, and Dancy nodded.

"I'll not be pushed around," Addie warned, turning away as Gabriel drove up. "Remember that now."

Clint helped her into the carriage. "Yes, ma'am. We know our place all right."

"Get on home," she grumbled to Gabriel loudly.

"I reckon I've got my work cut out for me making room for those two. Should've known when I made peace with that boy, he'd want to move right in, take over. . . ."

Gabriel was so happy he was shaking. "Yes'm, I knowed it, too, but don't worry. I'll help out, and we'll get things ready, trouble though it'll be."

Addie leaned back against the leather seat, looking once more toward the cemetery as they passed. The sight of the raw mound of dirt wrenched her heart. But as her gaze moved to Dooley's grave, she felt a strange sense of peace.

At last she had let the hatred go and could get on with her life. She lifted the parasol and threw it as hard as she could into the brush.

Somehow she knew she wouldn't need it any longer.

When they reached the cabin, Dancy paused at the steps to pick a bouquet of daisies from the patch blooming there. "These have been my favorite flowers ever since the day Uncle Dooley told me how you can always seem to find them blooming somewhere.

"Other flowers have seasons, like a daffodil in the spring, or a rose in summer, but you can always find a daisy. He said"—she straightened and turned to stand on tiptoe and brush her lips against his—"that daisies are a forever flower.

"But did you have to pretend to be Uncle Dooley?" She suddenly felt the need to admonish him. She had wanted to bring it up before, but the time never seemed right, and she'd kept telling herself it was best just to forget. Now, however, with the daisies inspiring thoughts of Dooley, she was driven to ask.

"All right. I'll admit it," Clint said sheepishly. "I know it was a silly thing to do, but at the time, I was desperate to get you out of the danger I knew was bound to come and dared hope you might be scared of ghosts."

"But to do it twice? Really, Clint, I . . ." She fell silent, seeing his confusion.

"What are you talking about?" he demanded.

Uneasily she recounted, "The night I went to Addie's, you tried to scare me again, but what I couldn't figure out was how you knew she was so sick. And it was just a blessing she'd overheard Slade and Jordan plotting to ambush you, or I'd never have got there to warn you. . . . Clint," she cried, "what is it? Why are you looking like that?"

He gripped her shoulders. "Where did you see something?"

She pointed to the tree at the foot of the ridge.

Hand in hand, they walked to the spot.

Dancy saw it first and, with a choked cry, knelt and picked it up.

"A daisy," she breathed in wonder. "It wasn't growing here. It was just lying here, as though somebody left it."

"A wedding present from Dooley," Clint said quietly.

Dancy swayed in stunned disbelief. "Uncle Dooley once told me that when you believe something with your heart, it's so. And I believe I saw him that night, Clint."

He drew her into his arms. "I'm not sure what you saw, Dancy, and it really doesn't matter. There's only one thing important to me in this world—our love for each other."

"Like the daisies," she whispered as his lips claimed hers, "forever."

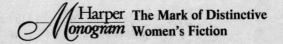

COMING NEXT MONTH

THE MIST AND THE MAGIC by Susan Wiggs

A spellbinding romance set in 17th century Ireland. On a cliff high above the sea, John Wesley Hawkins meets Caitlin MacBride. With true Irish whimsey, Caitlin has just grasped a white and blush-colored rose and wished for her true love. Hawkins walks into her life, but danger and adventure lie ahead before these magnificent lovers can find a happy ending.

SILENA by Terri Herrington

A powerful romance set in Nebraska in the late 1800s. Silena Rivers is on a quest to discover her true identity, with the help of handsome Wild West showman Sam Hawkins. But along the way, they find that love is the only thing that really matters.

THE ANXIOUS HEART by Denise Robertson

An enchanting contemporary novel set in London about a courageous and feisty young woman who pulls herself out of a low-income tenement building to discover the amazing world outside.

THE MAGIC TOUCH by Christina Hamlett

Beth Hudson's husband, Edward, was a magician obsessed with the occult. He had always promised her that he would be able to communicate with her from beyond the grave; and two years after his death, his prophecy seems to be coming true. With the help of Lt. Jack Brassfield, Beth reopens the investigation of her husband's death and gets more than she bargains for.

AMAZING GRACE by Janet Quin-Harkin

An engaging romance set in Australia just after World War I. Grace Pritchard, a beautiful young Englishwoman, is forced to choose between two men . . . or face a difficult future alone in the male-dominated and untamed Australian outback.

EMBRACE THE DAY by Susan Wiggs

A Susan Wiggs classic. An enthralling and romantic family saga of spirited Genevieve Elliot and handsome Roarke Adair, who set out for the blue-green blaze of Kentucky to stake their claim on love.

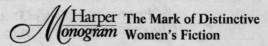 Harper **The Mark of Distinctive**
Monogram **Women's Fiction**

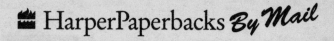

YESTERDAY'S SHADOWS
by Marianne Willman

Bettany Howard was a young orphan traveling west searching for the father who left her years ago. Wolf Star was a Cheyenne brave who longed to know who abandoned him—a white child with a jeweled talisman. Fate decreed they'd meet and try to seize the passion promised. 0-06-104044-4

MIDNIGHT ROSE by Patricia Hagan

From the rolling plantations of Richmond to the underground slave movement of Philadelphia, Erin Sterling and Ryan Youngblood would pursue their wild, breathless passion and finally surrender to the promise of a bold and unexpected love. 0-06-104023-1

WINTER TAPESTRY
by Kathy Lynn Emerson

Cordell vows to revenge the murder of her father. Roger Allington is honor bound to protect his friend's daughter but has no liking for her reckless ways. Yet his heart tells him he must pursue this beauty through a maze of plots to win her love and ignite their smoldering passion. 0-06-100220-8

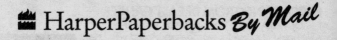
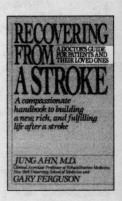
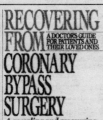